To Sue

THE

SHADOW SHAPER

My vy good fred
Lots g love and a
good red
    Rosemry Hamer.

ROSEMARY HAMER

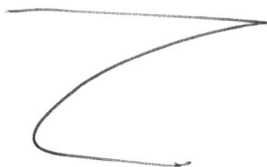

ISBN: 9781980879114

PROLOGUE

Krakow 1955

Marika Petrova delicately extracted the gun from behind the picture of her mother, and moving silently towards the door of the kitchen, finger poised on the trigger, sprang forward and threw open the door. There he was calmly buttering bread.

'My God Alex, you frightened me half to death, disappearing for months without a word, then having the gall to just stand there making sandwiches. Where on earth have you been? I could have easily shot you.'

Unphased Alex continued to stand there smiling his disarming smile butter knife poised. 'But you wouldn't have my dear. You're far too careful for that; after all I trained you myself. Shall I make you a sandwich? I'm starving. I never seem to get enough to eat these days. Perhaps they like us lean and hungry, it adds to our mystique, what do you think?'

Marika irritated by his sanguine approach, threw down the gun in disgust.

'Careful, my dear, a loaded gun is no match for your temper.'

Marika flounced off into the tiny back room. She never knew

where she was with him. At times, he could be so sincere and real, at other times unreadable and terribly upper class. Why were these British men so cold and unfeeling? Of course they were all brought up by nannies and shipped off to public school at an early age, whereas her countrymen had to fight for survival. Unfortunately it was Alex she loved, though she would never dare tell him. She could lose him if she was too honest. He had never mentioned the word 'love' in all these years. She was never sure of him however close they became. Even if he was making use of her she was too cowardly to find out, especially now.

Pulling herself together, she re-entered the kitchen saying, 'Am sorry, Sasha darling – it was the shock. There's something important I must tell you. I've been waiting a long time,' she grimaced, 'though it might not be a welcome surprise.'

Alex pulled her close, kissing her gently, 'Let me get you a brandy first, and then I have a surprise for you too.'

Carefully turning his back to Marika and pouring out the brandy, Alex picked up the gun she'd carelessly discarded on the dresser and turning round brandy in one hand gun in the other, shot her straight between her beautiful luminous stunned eyes. Looking down at her body he shook his head, saying, 'A betrayal too far, my darling Marika One double agent per family is all that's allowed.' He downed the brandy, and was about to leave when he heard a shrill cry.

2

Holding the gun tightly, he crept along the landing stopping to listen for further sounds. Reaching the bedroom he shoved the door open, and was flabbergasted at the sight that confronted him. A baby lay in the middle of the double bed, murmuring to itself and rolling about. This was obviously 'the surprise' that Marika had hinted at.

Checking there was no one else in the room, Alex inched towards the bed. It was as if the baby heard him, and rolled over on its side to look straight at him. It was a little girl, beautifully dressed in some sort of pink romper suit, her name embroidered on the pocket. Still holding the gun, Alex bent forward to read what it said. It looked like 'Eleanor'- surely not, his mother's name! No, Marika wouldn't have picked an English name for her baby, and he'd certainly never told her his mother's name. Looking closer, Alex could see it was spelt in the Polish way as 'Eleonora'.

Was it a coincidence? Was this child his? Counting backwards he'd been in London for over eight months. Why hadn't they told him? Or perhaps they didn't know. Could Marika have kept it secret all that time? There were a lot of unanswered questions, but he hadn't got time for them. Of course he could kill the baby that would tidy everything up. He tried putting the gun to the child's tiny temple, but she chuckled and pulled the barrel into her mouth. He gently drew it out of her tight grasp; it was no good he couldn't do it.

Taking a step back he considered his options; what if the

3

child was his? In his line of work, this might be the only child he would ever have. Of course he could leave her to be found, but that might be a while. This was hardly the most salubrious part of the city. No, he'd have to take her, but take her where.... a local orphanage? He couldn't afford to be seen especially with a baby. There was nothing for it, but it would have to be England. He suddenly had a thought; there was his brother of course. Why not his brother, he and his wife were childless after all?

Alex looked at his watch. They would still be up at this hour. He dug deep in his pocket, and pulled out the Russian phone. Whether it would work was debatable. It had its moments however this time he got through in one try.

Robert's gruff voice answered. Alex didn't allow him his usual moans and complaints, but launched straight into conversation:

'I have a package I want you and Marjorie to take care of.'

'........yes, it's extremely valuable.'

'.......criminal, certainly not.'

'......drugs, hardly.'

'Now no more questions. Remember who shells out for you both when your businesses fail. How much was owed when your last enterprise went bust? You might as well call me your banker, the way you go through money.'

'.........the package? You'll see soon enough.'

'.........how long? ......As long as it bloody well takes.'

'.........dangerous .... of course not.'

'........yes, it will cause some inconvenience, but I'm paying and making the arrangements.'

Alex hung up, tired of his brother's gripes and grievances. Once their father had decamped and succumbed to a stroke, the family estate had fallen into the hands of debtors. His younger brother lived from hand to mouth speculating and failing. What a disaster of a family we are, he thought. That stupid brother of mine doesn't even know what I do for a living, nor has the nous to ask as long as the money keeps rolling in.

Anyway he must get going and not be discovered with Marika's body. He gingerly picked up the baby who immediately cuddled into his chest, wrapping her tightly in an embroidered shawl, and looking down into her trusting grey, blue almond shaped eyes that echoed his own, said, 'Well Eleanor, it's up to you now. You are destined to be the keeper of the family secrets, whether you know them or not. Let's hope you do better than us. He jiggled her almost tenderly in his arms, whispering, 'Ready to start your new life, my dear?'

INNOCENCE AND INITIATION

1

London 1975

'Take the Tube to Liverpool Street and cross Appold St and carry on to Sun Street. You'll see the office midway. Ask for Mr Caruthers. Good Luck!' And that's all the instructions she ever received. There was no discussion over what type of company it could be or what they were looking for, just the name, bald directions and an inauspicious 'Good Luck' as an afterthought.

Eleanor wished she knew more, but she was out of the door of the secretarial agency before she had time to think. Well beggars couldn't be too choosy. Eating her last egg that morning had brought that home to her only too clearly. Whatever the job was – if they offered it to her, she would take it, and make the best of it.

The journey to Liverpool Street took forever, though there was hardly anyone on the train. It was too early in the season for tourists. Anyway, they would hardly be going to Liverpool St, surely they would all be travelling the other way. Goodness was she losing it – all these idiotic thoughts jostling with one another, and filling her mind with complete nonsense. It must be nerves.

Why hadn't she thought to wear her best suit – but no – there was still that tomato stain on the skirt where she had bitten into a sandwich and a squirt of tomato sauce had shot onto the beautiful cream linen. Still it would have been much too thin for today; there was a nip in the air. This purple mini and long jacket should do, at least it accentuated the grey blue in her eyes. Celia, her so-called landlady, had been kind enough to bequeath it to her in one of her more generous spirited moments.

Celia had condescendingly agreed to rent her the spare room to supplement her income. However she had made it abundantly clear to Eleanor that she was there under sufferance. This meant Eleanor getting up at the crack of dawn to use the bathroom, often rubbing the ice off the inside of the window with her threadbare dressing gown. Celia only allowed a lit fire in the drawing room in the winter, and a three bar electric fire in the summer.

Every morning Eleanor was forced to skitter quickly and noiselessly into the kitchen to boil her one egg, and rush back with it to her room, so as not to interrupt Celia's languid promenade through the flat. It was no good feeling sorry for herself, as the flat was ideally located in the heart of London just off Great Portland Street. Celia was old, certainly by Eleanor's standards, and had some fancy job as a P.A to a firm of publishers in Bedford Square, sauntering to her office by ten every day.

This particular morning Celia was away at a Book Fair, so Eleanor took her time luxuriating in a long bubble bath followed by a leisurely breakfast. It was lovely to be free to wander about the flat, and indulge in three bars of the electric fire. Eleanor was usually never allowed into the drawing room or the sitting room as she called it. If there were guests she might be summoned so that they could all snigger at her West Country accent or marvel at her C&A clothes.

The guests were the usual bunch of writers and journalists, thinking themselves a superior breed, sneering at the world and their contemporaries. Eleanor would join them nervously, trying to feel relaxed, attempting to juggle a glass of wine and a plate of tiny hors d'oeuvres (or horses'arses as she wanted to call them), and fearful that any minute she would spill the lot on the Persian carpet. They were always eating some sort of little black egg things that Celia's man friend smuggled in from Moscow in the diplomatic bag. But for Eleanor they were so salty she had to drink glass after glass of water to quench her terrible thirst.

Celia's special friend was a bit of an upper class twit who worked in the Foreign Office. Sometimes he would pretend to be kind to Eleanor and say, 'Come and sit next to me, and tell me what you've been up to in this great big wicked city.' In the beginning Eleanor would be pleased to have some attention, but later understood it was a malicious game. He delighted in using her confidences against her, shouting out, 'Hey everyone – do you know what our little Eleanor has been up to this week? She made friends with a bag lady in Regents' Park. I do hope for your sake, Celia, she doesn't

8

start bringing home tramps.' They would roar with laughter. Celia would glower at her and with a dismissive flick of her head make it clear that Eleanor should retire from the fray immediately.

Eleanor hated being treated like this but what could she do? The humiliations were like the type her father used to dole out. It was no use dwelling on all that – perhaps this interview might lead to a new exciting job. Then she might be able to afford somewhere to live on her own.

Following the directions and early as usual, Eleanor took her time studying her surroundings. Liverpool Street was full of city gents with furled umbrellas. It was hard to believe they still wore bowlers. They looked like caricatures from the comics.

Eleanor wondered if there was time for a coffee but she had barely enough cash for the Tube home, let alone a drink. Did she need a toilet? Not yet, she could wait till she found the company. No doubt she would have time to tidy herself up before the interview.

Sun Street materialised sooner than expected, and wandering past all the other offices, Eleanor speculated as to what these new employers would be like. It was probably only a temp job but the agency hadn't said. In fact they'd said nothing about the job, only where it was and that the firm was called Sentry Inc. What was Inc? Was that short for International, perhaps she would travel? Eleanor could visualise herself boarding a plane with stewardesses taking her boarding pass and her briefcase, and sitting in First Class with a glass of champagne. Wouldn't that be one in the eye for Celia!

Eventually Eleanor found the address. It looked unprepossessing with just a small sign in black lettering stating Sentry Inc. There were no windows on the street, just a mahogany door set back in the wall with a bell – certainly no smart reception. Eleanor didn't much like the look of the offices, but decided she might as well go through with it.

Tentatively, she pushed the bell. It boomed, reverberating loudly through the building like a fire alarm. The shock made her jump; perhaps she'd pressed the wrong bell. No, it was the only one there. Possibly this was some sort of warehouse where the bell had to be heard far away.

Nobody came. Eleanor paced from foot to foot. She began to question whether she'd come to the wrong place or on the wrong day. What should she do now? She was tempted to make a run for it, but that could cause trouble with the agency. Perhaps she should ring them but she only had her underground fare. Rummaging through her pockets and her bag, all Eleanor could find was a half chewed mint and a ripped up ticket not a penny to be seen.

While she was considering what to do, the mahogany door inched open and a gruff voice enquired, 'Can I help you?'

Eleanor was disconcerted, but gathering her wits, said meekly, 'I'm from the Atlantic Secretarial Agency to see Mr Caruthers.'

'Wait,' the voice commanded. The door closed. After a long interval Eleanor was beginning to think she'd imagined the door opening. Finally it opened again, and the anonymous voice said as if they were still continuing their earlier conversation, 'Well come on in then. He's ready for you now,' in a tone that made it sound as if Eleanor was the one who'd been keeping him waiting.

Eleanor inched forward, moving into a dark passage way that led through to a gate. The gate opened out onto a courtyard, and beyond to a big grey stone house. She could quite see why they needed such a loud bell. Who would have thought there was all this behind that insignificant door? As they mounted the steps to the house, Eleanor began to settle down; perhaps this was a respectable international company after all.

There was certainly a sense of style about the place. Her guide was officious and mute, pointing to another door just inside the foyer. He gestured a knocking movement to her and disappeared. Eleanor obeyed, striking the door hard with her clenched fist. It was all very odd; she was beginning to feel irritable and resentful. Why was she being treated like some sort of unwelcome intruder?

There was a curt, 'Come', and she had no further time to

take umbrage.

Pushing the door open, Eleanor was confronted with a tall portly gentleman with jet black brilliantined hair, in some sort of lightly striped double breasted suit that looked expensive. His aftershave had a piquant almost spicy smell about it. He seemed to fill the room with his presence, making her feel insignificant.

'Miss Duridge Smith, I presume. I'm Caruthers. Take a seat. I expect the agency briefed you about the job.'

Eleanor couldn't make up her mind whether to offer him her hand or not and quickly dropped it to her side. She cleared her throat swallowing hard, and sitting as upright as she could said, 'I prefer plain Miss Smith thank you, and no, the agency only gave me your address and how to get here.'

The portly gentleman nodded, stroking his chin thoughtfully and staring long and hard at her, his flinty eyes probing in a calculating manner, 'Probably for the best, after all we don't know yet if you'll suit.'

The statement rankled; Eleanor could feel her irritation quickly turning to fury. She had no idea what the job was yet and who were they to judge her suitability? Determined to be more assertive, she spoke up sharply, 'What is the job? What would be expected of me, sir?'

Her terseness seemed to provide Mr Caruthers with some form of secret amusement. His mouth quivered just the tiniest bit at the edges.

Without preamble, Mr Caruthers proceeded to launch into a long glib and seemingly practiced explanation, 'We are worldwide importers and exporters. Our actual warehouses are elsewhere. We employ a number of subcontractors. Your duties would be to answer the telephone, handle a small switchboard, take down orders and relay them to the appropriate personnel, and of course filing, let's not forget filing. There would be typing of letters and reports and some shorthand required,' he paused, 'I take it your speeds are up to date.'

Eleanor nodded, 'The agency put me through all the required tests, and I passed every one. I was trained at Pitman's,' she added proudly.

'That's fine then – perhaps we can move on to the next stage. We like to give candidates our own battery of tests. This takes a few days. In the meantime we'll cover all your expenses for travel, food etc, and give you a small stipend to keep you going.'

Eleanor was bemused, why did she need to sit tests if all she had to do was answer the telephone and take a few letters? Nevertheless the sound of expenses and a stipend was enticing. Perhaps she could even afford a chop for supper. Anyway what did it matter about some silly old tests, she had nothing else to do and nowhere else to go. The last thing she wanted to do was to alienate the temp agency.

Finding her voice eventually and modulating her tone, she enquired meekly, 'What sort of tests are they, and what if I fail, sir?'

'Oh they're not exams;' Mr Caruthers passed them off airily, 'you can't pass or fail. They're more about personality and aptitudes. We also like to check your background and family,' adding, 'as we have a range of clients who expect the highest level of security from us.'

Eleanor winced inwardly. Personality – at barely twenty, she hardly knew if she had one yet and what kind of aptitudes? She'd been good at drawing at school, but what use would that be here? Background and family, that was tricky too. The last she'd seen of her parents was them setting off for Bermuda prospecting for yet another dubious business. At least they were far enough away, but who on earth would vouch for their characters. 'My parents -- my parents, sir,' she stammered bleakly, '---- out of the country ----- not coming back any time soon, will that matter?'

'No, not at all,' Mr Caruthers suddenly grinned, as if he was aware of some private joke, 'I'm sure we can find the information we need.'

He seemed to find her situation faintly entertaining, though for the life of her Eleanor couldn't see why. Registering her frown, he attempted to reassure her, 'Don't worry your pretty little head; everything will turn out for the best.'

But what best? Eleanor wondered, and on second thoughts didn't much like 'the pretty little head'. Suddenly it dawned on her that the firm might be involved in some form of drug smuggling, or even 'the white slave trade'. It was only yesterday she'd been reading one of her James Bonds about that sort of thing. What if their clients were wealthy Arabs who would whisk her off to work in some nightclub abroad? London was rife with foreigners at the moment. Perhaps she should leave now before she was in any danger.

Mr Caruthers appeared able to decipher the anxious thoughts flitting across her face. He patted her arm and said, 'Everything is above board here. We are a most reputable company. If you are right for us, we certainly won't be using you for any criminal purposes.'

Eleanor gasped. How could he know what she was thinking was she that transparent? She didn't know what to make of the man. One moment he was offhand, casual and disinterested, and the next benevolent and charming, and yet there was something slightly sinister and threatening about him.

Standing up, he gestured to her that it was time to leave. However suddenly pausing, and using her first name in a more informal way he said, 'Well Eleanor, we'll see you tomorrow – nine sharp, to start the testing.'

Eleanor couldn't wait to leave. She shot out the door like a frightened rabbit, but half way down the front steps his voice summoned her back,   'Not so fast, young Eleanor, don't be in such a rush. I still have to give you your expenses.'

Feeling wary but needing the money, Eleanor slowly remounted the steps. Mr Caruthers was standing at the top. He beckoned her back inside. Stopping at a desk, he drew out a cash box and a sheet of paper.

'Let's see,' he said, 'there'll be travel, food and of course all the inconvenience. Shall we make it a round 100 that should see you through? What do you think?' and not waiting for a reply began to count out crisp twenty pound notes.

Eleanor's eyes nearly popped out of her head. Had he really meant one hundred pounds? That amount would last her months.

'Just sign here,' he said in a blasé manner as if he was used to handling that sort of money on a daily basis, which she supposed he was.

Eleanor's palms were sweating as he counted the notes into her hand. Then taking her clammy paw notes pressed tightly to her palm, he shook it firmly saying, 'It was good to meet you Eleanor, make sure you're on time tomorrow.' Was there a touch of intimidation in the way he said that? Eleanor wasn't sure. She would have liked to have taken the money and run, but there could be some sort of reprisal, and ultimately she was too cowardly.

Making her way back to Liverpool Street, Eleanor was still clutching the notes in her hand, reluctant to let them go. It was wonderful to have money. She felt like going on a mad shopping spree but that was hardly sensible. If she wasn't taken on by the company, she would need the money. The big debate in her head was should she put it in the bank? However there was still that £30 overdraft lurking in its depths, ready to swallow up all this delicious cash. No, she would be level-headed, buy something nice to eat on the way home and perhaps go to afternoon pictures, and secrete the rest of it under the loose floor board in her room. No one would find it there.

…

No sooner had she left than Mr Caruthers picked up the telephone and dialled an outside line, 'Yes I've seen her. She seems a sweet pliable girl. There may be some steel there; it's too early to tell. Of course sir, I'll keep you informed, it goes without saying.' He glanced down at the black file lying open in front of him and frowned momentarily, closing it and attaching a clip which proclaimed, 'Eyes only' and 'Ongoing'. He sighed heavily and locked the file securely in his desk drawer.

2

Turning up at Sentry Inc the next morning the glow of the money had worn off. All Eleanor was left with were a lot of worries. During the night she had wondered what she'd let herself in for. She tried to console herself, wishing she didn't feel as if she was going to her own execution. Back at the dreaded door bell, Eleanor decided to gird her loins and make a brave entrance.

This time the door from the street was opened promptly, and not by the morose guide of yesterday or even the overwhelming Mr Caruthers, but by a smart pretty girl in her late twenties who said cheerfully, 'Hullo, I'm Claire, you must be Eleanor, we're expecting you. Please come with me.' Eleanor immediately relaxed. Claire appeared normal and friendly; this was definitely an auspicious start.

In the big house, they climbed the stairs to the first floor. 'Do you need to freshen up before you start?'Claire asked. Eleanor was nonplussed; did that mean a visit to the toilet or what? Attempting to appear sophisticated, she politely declined, 'I'm fine, honestly,' trying to ignore the queasy stirrings in her stomach.

The room they entered was laid out like a classroom. There were desks, comfortable chairs and some sort of charts on the wall.

Claire said, 'I'll get you started, and then come back in two hours, and see how you're getting on.'

Two hours, Eleanor thought with a sinking heart. That's a lot of tests. What if I don't do well? However the scary Mr Caruthers did say there was no pass or fail. I do need this job though Eleanor deliberated, but if I'm here I can't be out looking for anything else. For a split second she'd forgotten the precious hundred pounds that she still had in her possession, well what was left of it. That cache of gold under the floor boards could help her manage till something else came along.

Claire provided her with pencils, scrap paper, a rubber and a bell to summon help and left. Eleanor was faced with a whole series of papers – first, one about different situations with multiple choice answers. Then one on spatial ability whatever that was, followed by basic Maths and English, colour choices, and finally one on risk taking. Eleanor couldn't see the point of any of them. What were they to do with the job of a receptionist or a typist? There were no clerical, typing, or even shorthand tests.

Two hours was soon over, and Claire returned grinning broadly, 'How did you get on? You've finished everything. That's fine. You can go home now. We'll see you same time tomorrow.' She collected up all the papers, and breezed out the door.

Eleanor was left to find her own way back to the courtyard. There was not a soul about. Pushing her way through the outer door, she breathed a sigh of relief. Perhaps tomorrow they'd tell her she wasn't right for them. But then what about the money – would they expect her to pay it back? She was annoyed with herself, having never had the sense to ask. She'd spent some of it seeing, 'The way we were'.... at Leicester Square. What a film – she hadn't been able to stop crying at the end, when Barbra Streisand spots Robert Redford across the road with his wife. It was such a sad finish; she wished there'd been someone to share it with. Celia of course, would have been far too superior to deign to come to anything like that, preferring 'live theatre or opera at the Garden.'

The following day, Eleanor was back at Sentry half hoping for bad news about the tests, but the imposing figure of Mr Caruthers strode into the classroom, saying, 'Well done Miss Smith, Eleanor – you've done satisfactorily on all the tests. Your Maths leaves a little to be desired, but that's of no account.'

Eleanor couldn't fathom that. Wouldn't she be expected to be good at figures if she was to write up orders? However she felt too inhibited to make any comment. Mr Caruthers continued, 'We are pleased to offer you the job Eleanor, on a trial basis to start with. That means a probationary period of three months. There will be a lot more training in the long term you understand.' He didn't seem to be looking for any form of acknowledgement from her, just taking it for granted that she was pleased.

Eleanor though thrilled to be offered the job, wasn't sure this was the right one. All she felt able to do was nod.

He continued, 'Take the rest of the week off, and start fresh on Monday at nine. Claire will show you the ropes. You'll soon get the hang of it. Welcome to Sentry, my dear. '

He bolted out of the room, as if he was rushing off to something urgent. Right on cue, Claire followed in behind, beaming from ear to ear, 'I'm so glad you're starting. I thought you were a good fit from the first. It will be nice to have another female in the office. Come on I'll show you out.' She stood on the steps waving Eleanor goodbye, and saying, 'See you Monday.' On the Tube home, Eleanor speculated what she was a 'good fit' for? It was all a mystery. She hoped in her heart of hearts she wasn't doing the wrong thing.

But it was marvellous to be able to announce to Celia, that she had a job in the City with a firm of importers/ exporters. Celia's eyes widened, 'How much will you be earning?' she demanded. Eleanor felt stupid. She'd never bothered to ask about salary or even holidays. 'Enough', she said blithely as if it was a completely private matter. Surprisingly Celia seemed unduly interested: asking exactly what they did; where they were located; what would Eleanor be doing; who her boss was, and what was he like? This seemed so out of character for Celia, who usually paid no interest in anything not remotely related to her, that it made Eleanor think how little she knew about Sentry or the job. Maintaining an air of nonchalance she bypassed the questions with a vague offhandedness.

To allay her own growing unease, Eleanor decided to ring the company and find out more details, but no matter how hard she searched there was no entry for Sentry Inc in the phone book. Perhaps they were ex-directory but why would that be if they were a commercial business? A visit to the main library did little to help, as there was no mention of them in the reference books either.

It was no good worrying unnecessarily, being she had their cash she might just as well enjoy the rest of the week, and see what happened on Monday. Ever since Eleanor had lived London she'd never had the time or the money to indulge herself. Money allowed freedom and choices. Maybe she would have a Berni set meal, or visit C&A to look at clothes for the office, or take a trip on the Thames, or maybe do it all. Eleanor hugged herself with delight. It was hard to believe that she could have such a wonderful time in London on her own. At last it made sense. The move to London however painful, had allowed her to be her own person at last - a grown up with no one to answer to.

Monday morning came round all too quickly. During the weekend Eleanor had shelved any further disturbing thoughts, but now no doubt all would be revealed. Anyway, she could always leave if she didn't like it.

Sitting next to Claire on the first day, and taking her courage in her hands, Eleanor asked shyly, 'I didn't think to ask what my salary would be, or my holiday entitlement?'

Reassuringly Claire replied, 'Don't worry; you'll be getting a contract with everything outlined in it. The terms are generous, and as for your salary, they'll be starting you on a trainee basis at £50, with luncheon vouchers and expenses as and when.'

Eleanor gasped, 'Is that a week or a month?'

'A week, silly, you'd never survive on that for a month in London, would you?'

Eleanor thought but I did, and existed on much less. Grinning like an idiot she imagined what she would do with all that money.

Claire was still talking, 'Of course, once you're more experienced your salary will double I expect, depending on where they think you fit.'

There it was again 'fitting in'. What on earth was expected of her? What would her fit be? Perhaps it was best to make every effort to 'fit in', whatever it took. Eleanor began to daydream. With that sort of money she could move out of Celia's and find her own place. Perhaps privacy and freedom were in sight at last, something she had never experienced.

The rest of her first day seemed to be taken up with sorting out folders in the file room, some with the word 'Confidential' in big red letters, and some in black files with codes plastered on the front.

23

Claire pointed to them, 'On no account, open those black files or touch the black cabinet they're for 'Eyes only'. I have the key and I am responsible for signing them in or out.'

'What does 'Eyes only' mean?' Eleanor asked.

'It means people have to have the right level of Security clearance, and be very senior indeed to have access to them,' Claire replied in a serious voice.

Eleanor was still trying to get to grips with this, when a cheeky voice shouted round the corner of the file room, 'What do you girls get up to in there? Come out, and let's be seeing you. I could do with some pretty young thing to rest me eyes on.'

Claire rolled her eyes, 'It's only Paddy over from Belfast. He's always like that, the charm of the devil. Keep your distance; he can be lethal especially with green innocent girls like yourself.'

Eleanor was mortified to be described like that. She wasn't that innocent or that green. A few months in London must have knocked off some of the corners by now. Who on earth was this Paddy? Was he one of the clients? She was dying to take a peek at him, and lagged behind Claire to try and squint through the hinge of the open door.

Before she knew it she was spotted, and a big hairy hand came out grabbing her shoulder and pulling her into the light. 'There now I knew I could smell the blood of a new recruit,' he said triumphantly, looking her up and down appraisingly, ''tis a fine specimen we have here, Claire.'

Claire came forward from the back office, saying, 'Leave her alone she's far young for you.' Paddy, six foot four in his socks with a build to match, had dark hair highlighting green eyes gleaming with mischief. Although smart in a three piece suit, he had the swagger and brashness of a pirate rather than a businessman.

'D'ya not have a tongue of your own?' he demanded looking intently into Eleanor's startled face.

'Of course,' she stuttered, 'I don't think you should talk to me like that.'

'And why would that be, Chile?' he said pretending to be threatening, but smirking at the same time.

'It's not very professional is it,' Eleanor murmured.

'Ay, if it's professional you're wanting what about this then?' and before she could utter a sound he tossed her over his shoulder, and started to move towards the entrance with Eleanor whimpering in alarm.

'The joke's over now Paddy. Put the poor girl down,' Claire said sternly, 'pull yourself together, I expect Mr C is waiting for a report from you. He won't be pleased if you're messing about with the staff. Be off with you, you great big lug,' she added affectionately.

Setting Eleanor down delicately as if she was made of bone china, he patted her down gently, hanging his head penitently, saying, 'It's just a bit of fun – never meant you any harm m'acushla, just letting off steam,' and hurried off in the direction of the boss's office.

3

It was weeks before anything remotely exciting happened at Sentry. Every day ticked by with monotonous regularity. Eleanor had come to believe that she had landed a sinecure. Loving the money she found herself lulled into a false sense of security. So far there'd been a new wavy hairstyle and a trendy winter coat in shocking pink from Selfridges that her mother would never have approved of. At long last Eleanor was beginning to make plans for herself. Once she passed her probationary period, there would be no holding her back.

Every day, all she did was juggle switchboard calls from a 'Mr Watson' or a 'Mr Jones' or a 'Miss Simpson'. Each seemed to ring at a set time of the day, and ask to be put through to Mr Caruthers or Mr C as they called him. Their voices were polite but non-committal. There was no cheerful 'Hi, it's me again' or 'How are you today?' It was strained and formal. Eleanor supposed they were agents working for another company yet they never mentioned the name of any firms.

Eventually Eleanor plucked up the courage to ask Claire about them. Her response was curt and she shrugged saying, 'They're reps working for our branches out in the sticks. They report in daily.' She seemed reluctant to add anything more, and buried her head in her shorthand notes. Later that day it was as if Claire had thought better of her attitude, when she suggested she and Eleanor treat themselves to a late lunch on the firm.

'Are you sure?' Eleanor queried, 'Are we supposed to do things like that?'

Claire pursed her lips quirkily, murmuring cheekily, 'There's perks and then there's them there perks,' whatever that meant!

Arriving at one of the smart new wine bars just opened in the City, Claire enquired, 'What will you have to drink?' Eleanor, still trying to find her feet in relation to alcohol consumption after a tea total upbringing, opted for lemonade, 'We've still got to work this afternoon.' Claire laughed, 'Oh poo to that. Have a port and lemon. Study the menu while I shoot off to the little girls' room.'

Eleanor considered the menu. Her mouth watered at the mention of 'steak and chips', with desserts of 'bread and butter pudding', and 'sherry trifle' – all homemade. A waitress appeared at her elbow, pad poised expectantly. Eleanor said, 'I'm waiting for someone. Do you think you could give us a minute?' 'No worries,' the waitress said cheerfully, 'will I get you a drink while you're waiting?'

Eleanor didn't know what to do and looked round the bar. There was no sign of Claire. Where was she? Surely it didn't take that long to go to the Ladies, was she ill? The waitress was still there, so trying to show how urbane she could be, Eleanor ordered two ports and lemon. The drinks duly arrived but Claire didn't. Alarmed by now, Eleanor stood up and checked the room. There on the further side of the bar well away from public view, was her colleague talking earnestly and intensely to a suited and booted City gent in his fifties.

What a cheek Eleanor thought, to use me to have a rendezvous with some man. Determined not to be ignored Eleanor waved across the room. The gent saw her signal, and murmured in Claire's ear. Claire looked irritated but concluding her business made her way back hurriedly, brimming with smiles and apologies, 'Am so sorry, bumped into an old friend. Can you forgive me? Do hope you've ordered something nice.'

Eleanor immediately felt ashamed, and the meal carried on in a lively fashion. Laughing their way back to work arm in arm, Claire said vehemently, 'I do hope you like working at Sentry. You are doing ever so well you know, even if no one tells you.'

Eleanor wondered why Claire had gone out of her way to praise her like that. So far all Eleanor had done was man reception and the switchboard, make tea, do some filing, and type the odd letter; nothing demanding or taxing. But then again perhaps she shouldn't look a 'gift horse' in the mouth, if that's all that was required.

It was peculiar though that despite the Sentry office appearing very busy there weren't many staff, certainly not on the ground floor. Apart from her domain at the switchboard and reception, there was the filing room with a room to the side that she and Claire shared, and Mr Caruthers office - his sanctum sanctorum. The grouchy porter type man responsible for the operation of the front door occupied a cubby hole near the front door. However at the back of the building there were ranges of clerical people on different floors who never communicated with her, and who used a separate switchboard. Interestingly there was a back entrance to the building, as people would appear as if from nowhere.

One lunch time Eleanor decided to investigate. Wolfing down her sandwich she stepped out into the glare of the midday sun and sauntered casually down the street as if she was heading towards Bishopsgate. Wondering to herself why she was being so sneaky, Eleanor concluded that her gut was telling her there was some sort of mystery. Of course, it could just be her imagination particularly as she'd just seen, 'The Spy who came in from the Cold'.

Turning left into Appold Street Eleanor was aware she was moving too quickly. Slowing down she spotted Earl St, running parallel to her building. Maybe there was a mahogany door that side as well. Studying one building after another, Eleanor thought this was going to be a lot harder then she had envisaged. Deciding to cut her losses she headed down Crown Place and back to work. It was then she saw it. On the corner building and barely noticeable, was a very tiny scribble in some sort of red pen which said 'Sentry'. There was no door, just some form of push button next to the scribble. What was hard to understand was why the back of the building didn't match the front. The main building where she worked must go a lot further back and sideways. Eleanor was intrigued but she would be late back if she didn't hurry.

Towards home time Claire said to her, 'I wondered if you'd mind staying late tonight. We may have unexpected visitors, and I've arranged to meet my mother.' Eleanor was happy to oblige.

Life at the flat had become difficult. Celia was entertaining night after night, and all Eleanor could do was make her meal and retire to her room. She was no longer asked to participate. No doubt her novelty value had long worn off. But it was tiring as their racket went on till the early hours. Sleep was out of the question until they all left.

Eleanor hunted through the Standard for accommodation but everything was too expensive and so far out of Central London. She could ask Claire for advice however Clare was always busy, and more often than not quite aloof.

By six thirty that evening the office was deserted, Eleanor and Mr C being the only people left downstairs. He came through to reception, frowning at seeing her, 'Still here Eleanor, at this time. You should have gone home hours ago?'

Eleanor explained, trying to make light of the situation, but he continued to stand there glowering and mumbling, 'This is not at all appropriate; I will have to have words with young Claire tomorrow. I don't know what she was thinking of.'

Eleanor couldn't see what the problem was but all Mr C would say was, 'Get orf home now and I'll await any visitors,' adding ominously, 'isn't your probationary period up this week?'

Eleanor's heart sank. Were they going to get rid of her? Please not now, just when she was starting to build up some savings. He stared right through her as if he was delving into her very soul, and then his expression softened, 'Don't look so miserable, young Eleanor; I'm sure there won't be a problem with it. I'll speak to you at the end of the week, orf home with you now. I've things to do.'

Eleanor took him at his word and rushed out. Flustered and not thinking she turned right into Crown Square, then noticing her mistake turned the corner into Earl Street. As she did so, it suddenly dawned on her she could see straight into the back of Sentry. The wall had disappeared, and there was a garage with cars parked in bays. As she stood there bemused, a Jaguar with blackened windows pulled into the building and without warning the wall descended.

Obviously these were the late night visitors, but why did Mr C not want her to see them or them to see her? Eleanor inspected the so-called wall, touching it cautiously. It seemed bricklike and solid enough again, hardly like a fake one.

Back home and with the flat to herself for once, Eleanor munched her way through bacon and eggs and reviewed her day. There was obviously something going on at that firm – but what? She just hoped it wasn't anything criminal.

As the week progressed, Eleanor became more and more apprehensive about the end of her probationary period. She had conflicting feelings about Sentry. On the one hand she felt suspicious of the goings on there, and yet on the other hand she wanted to stay because of the money and the sense of being settled. In the middle of her cogitations, Claire shouted from the office, 'Mr C is free now, Eleanor, he wants to see you pronto.' Eleanor quickly tidied her hair, straightened her skirt and knocked on Mr Caruthers's door.

'Come in my dear,' he said, obviously in one of his more avuncular moods, 'tell me all you've been doing.'

Eleanor started off with panache but soon ran out of steam, her confidence rapidly draining away. Mr C's only reaction was to pyramid his hands, and say bluntly and directly, 'One thing we have noticed about you my dear Eleanor is that you are very observant and curious. Of course that can be a good thing – but there is the saying 'curiosity killed the cat', and too much of anything that is not focused in the right direction can be dangerous.' He stopped abruptly.

Eleanor's white face showed how shaken she was. She had certainly not been expecting this.

'However,' he continued, ignoring her loss of composure, 'we do like your attitude to work in particular your reliability and punctuality. We shall of course wish you to stay on. Once you are more experienced, there will be extra duties and training. Putting that to one side, let's talk money; (he smiled affably) your salary will be doubled now you have completed the first three months. This could help you find a flat of your own, and we are willing to advance you the deposit you might need for a retainer.'

Eleanor was floored. First, a veiled threat; then the fact that she'd passed her probation and they were pleased with her; then a salary increase, and finally the offer of a loan for a deposit. What should she do? She ought to voice her reservations about the nature of Sentry's work but how?

She started, 'I am concerned, sir...' But Mr Caruthers held up a hand to silence her, 'Say no more, young Eleanor. I have a good idea what your fears may be but be assured there is nothing illegal going on here. You will learn all about us in due time. Be patient and you will find out everything you need to. However this isn't the right time, and I've to go out.' With that he headed off leaving Eleanor dazed.

On her return to the office, Claire looked up from her work and asked, 'Everything go alright?' Eleanor still attempting to digest the turn of events, couldn't summon up the energy to speak, so just smiled and got on with her work.

4

A month later Eleanor thought it's all coming together at last. My job is settled even if I'm still not sure about the firm, I'm in a new flat (thanks to Mr C's advance) and I've made a new friend. I feel I'm home at last.

The new flat, though it hardly merited the name 'flat' was located in a mews just behind Baker St. Eleanor had to climb up an outside spiral metal staircase to a set of rooms over a garage, rooms which once would have housed the chauffeur to one of the big houses behind. Her entrance was through a tiny kitchen, to a square of landing which led to her bedroom, part of which had been made over into a shower room, but the pièce de resistance was a smallish lounge with doors to a Juliet balcony. The only downside was the toilet perched at the top of the stairs outside the kitchen door but Eleanor didn't care a jot. This was her first home, and she was going to enjoy doing it up.

It was extraordinary how it had come about. Claire always immersed in her work had stopped to chat one day, remarking that a friend of hers was looking for someone to lease her flat whilst she was abroad. Before she could take it in, Eleanor had been hustled round to see the flat, with Claire extolling its virtues almost as if she was acting as her friend's estate agent. Eleanor barely listened; she had already fallen in love with the flat.

'But I could never afford it Claire, particularly in this area. I do so want it now I've seen it,' Eleanor muttered glumly.

'Don't worry,' Claire assured her, 'I'm sure we can do a deal. Leave it with me; I'll sort it out for you.'

Eleanor was overwhelmed, 'Thank you, thank you so much. I can see myself living here. Do find out if I can redecorate. I can pay for that myself.'

Eleanor was so keyed up she barely thought about anything else for the next few days, and couldn't wait to find out if it was even possible. A week went by and then Claire said casually, 'By the way Eleanor, the flat's yours as from today. You can move in straight away. My friend is leaving the furniture. You can decorate however you want. She'll be away indefinitely, and may not come back. Of course there'll be a deposit, but Sentry will sort that out for you, and dock it from your monthly pay.'

It was all too easy. Claire had even worked out that Eleanor could afford the rent. Eleanor could hardly believe it was true. However on her way to the flat that night armed with the keys, she began to wonder if it had been made much too easy. There were little suspicions crawling round her head despite her efforts to ignore them. Why was Sentry doing all this for her? It wasn't as if her job was that important, anyone could do it. She was paid well in fact more than well, and now she had a flat in W1 thanks to them. Thinking back over the last four months, Eleanor tried hard to find some justification for her suspicions. Sure there were various odd visitors coming and going – even late in the evening. But it was an international company; clients might well be flying in from all over the world at different times. What else? Mr C was a man of variable moods but then so were a lot of bosses. Claire whom Eleanor had initially thought of as a friend was also quite erratic in her behaviour, sometimes distant, and sometimes warm and friendly. Any other people she saw round the office barely acknowledged her. Was there really anything concrete to back up her qualms, or was this just the way people acted in business? With nothing definite to go on, Eleanor decided to put it all to one side and enjoy the flat instead.

The good thing about the flat was that she had a lovely neighbour who had gone out of her way to offer friendship. Barbara lived in one of the larger cottages in Durweston Mews. She arrived on Eleanor's doorstep on her very first day, bringing coffee and cakes and all sorts of goodies. She worked in the City as a PA to stockbrokers Rankin and Reeves in Moorgate, and from then on commuted to work with Eleanor most days. Though she was in her mid thirties, older and more mature than Eleanor, she was easy to talk to and confide in. Eleanor supposed Barbara had a private income as some days she would say, 'I'm not going in to work for a few days, Eleanor. I thought I'd nip down and see some friends on the South coast, or I'm taking the week to go over to the Cannes Festival, expect me when you see me.'

Eleanor wondered if Barbara would eventually get bored

with their friendship, as Eleanor's life was far more mundane just work and the flat. But on the contrary, it was as if Barbara had decided to take Eleanor in hand. They would go shopping in Knightsbridge and Kensington, where Eleanor could only gawp at the prices and the fashions. Before she knew it she was being transformed into a smart attractive young lady. She protested to Barbara, 'But really Barbara, I can't afford to dress like this. Most of my month's money has gone on that outfit you persuaded me to buy. When will I ever wear a cocktail dress and one that elaborate?'

'Eleanor I have a treat for you, and somewhere you can wear that gorgeous dress. I'm having a drinks party on Saturday and you are No. 1 guest on my list. It'll give you a chance to meet more people instead of spending your night hidden away in the flat or at the cinema.'

On the following Saturday afternoon, Eleanor did her best to sort out her hair and makeup but had no real idea where to start. An hour before the party she turned up at Barbara's door in floods of tears. Barbara took one look and ushered her into the bedroom; an exquisite room furnished in silver grey with wide expanses of mirrored wardrobes. She sat Eleanor down and scrubbed everything off, brushed her hair, put it in Carmen rollers and then set about making up her face. It was done in a trice.

'You don't need a lot of makeup on that youthful complexion. Make the most of that skin and take care of it.

Now the dress,' and she drew it on over Eleanor's head, carefully avoiding the rollers. 'Give them twenty minutes and then we'll brush them out. You'll look and feel wonderful, darling.'

The evening was a blur. There were so many guests: titled people; people from the arts; business men; glamorous starlets, and everyone who was anyone. They crammed into Barbara's living room, spilling over into the walled garden beyond. It was a beautiful night and the drinks were flowing. Eleanor was introduced to so many of the guests that her head began to swim. Once she thought she even spotted Claire, but no, it was someone who looked like her.

Eventually Eleanor found herself a chair in a hidden corner. But there was no escaping Barbara who took charge saying, 'We'll have none of that. Come, I've found just the right person for you to talk to. Donald lives in the West Country now. You'll have a lot in common.'

Donald was the oldest person in the room and he was sitting in a corner too. Eleanor took one look at his kindly lined face and liked him immediately. He said gently, 'Come and keep me company over here away from all the noise and razzamatazz, and tell me all about yourself.' He was just what Eleanor needed. The whole evening had been overwhelming, and she had completely lost any vestige of confidence she'd had at the beginning of the night.

Donald was in his seventies. He explained he was well and

truly retired and living in Cornwall. Being Barbara's godfather, he'd come up to London to take her out to dinner, 'Not to come to this over packed, over loud rumbustious party but,' he said ruefully, 'that's what comes of being such an elderly godfather I suppose. I was really a friend of Barbara's grandfather you see.'

Eleanor talked to him as she had never talked before. It was as if she had been waiting all her life to find someone she could relate to. Before they knew it they were the last ones in the room. Barbara was washing up and chatting in the kitchen, and there were one or two stragglers loath to depart. Donald got up and reached for his coat saying, 'Well Eleanor, it's past one. I must retire to my club, and you need your beauty sleep. We're friends now so we must keep in touch, what do you think?' Eleanor agreed, and they discussed meeting up before he left for Cornwall. It was wonderful to find a kindred spirit. At last she had two friends. Thanking Barbara enthusiastically, Eleanor practically danced her way up the spiral staircase to home and bed.

…

In the next weeks Eleanor felt as if her life had turned full circle. There was so much to do and enjoy in London, a busy social whirl, the like of which she'd never experienced.

Donald decided to extend his stay in the capital and at weekends he and Eleanor would visit the museums and

41

galleries. He was a fount of knowledge and Eleanor lapped it up. She felt guilty that she might be depriving Barbara of his company, but he and Barbara reassured her that was not the case. Occasionally Barbara accompanied them, but mainly it was just the two of them.

Taking tea at the Ritz on one of their weekend days out after Eleanor had ooed and aahed at the decor, the cakes and the diminutive sandwiches, she decided to confide in Donald about Sentry.

'Everything seems so normal on the outside and on a daily basis. Yet my instinct tells me there is something going on, but I can't quite put my finger on it.'

Donald sipped his tea thoughtfully, placing his cup carefully back on its saucer and meticulously folding his damask napkin, as if he was playing for time, 'What makes you think there is anything untoward?'

'I sense a kind of atmosphere though I feel silly voicing it now.'

'I don't think you're at all silly Eleanor, better to express these thoughts rather than let them build up. You are an imaginative, insightful person, and probably need a job that stimulates and develops you. You say your day to day job is fairly uninspiring; perhaps you are attempting to make it more enigmatic and mysterious than it really is. What do you think?'

'Yes, that's it, Donald, that must be it. I think that's what I'm doing,' Eleanor said eagerly. 'I hadn't thought of it quite like that. You're so sensible.'

'It comes with the years, my dear,' Donald replied with a touch of irony.

When they next arranged to meet, it was at his club in Pall Mall. Eleanor had never been inside a gentleman's club before and was overawed by the dark wood panelling and leather interior. A member of staff in stiff collar and tails enquired whether she needed help, and she shyly asked for Donald McIntosh. 'Oh Sir Donald you mean, of course, one of our oldest and most valued members. Come this way. I do believe he's in the Library.'

As Eleanor hovered nervously on the threshold, he nodded across the room to Donald who had his back to them, and was deep in conversation with a tall younger man with blonde hair and a rather aristocratic nose who seemed familiar. Eleanor ventured across the carpet, and was instantly noticed by the younger man who murmured something to Donald. Donald spun round in alarm, hurrying across to meet Eleanor. He left the other man mid sentence, but the blonde man melted into the background, one minute he was there the next gone. Feeling embarrassed and gauche, Eleanor said, 'I'm so sorry. Am I interrupting your conversation? Should I have waited somewhere else? '

'Of course not, that gentleman and I are finished now; let's have dinner. Where shall we go? Somewhere special I think tonight?'

Eleanor apologised for not knowing he was a 'Sir', but Donald shrugged, 'Think nothing of it my dear, just one of those cardboard cutout medals the Queen gives for long service and stickability. I'm just Donald to my friends and that includes you,' he remarked patting her arm affectionately.

Eleanor asked what his job had been but Donald made light of his career, passing it off as 'a dull job in the Civil Service.' Arm in arm, they set off to spend a last evening together.

Before Donald departed for Cornwall, Eleanor said, 'I've been so fortunate to have met you; I do wish you'd been my grandfather, what times we could have had.'

The old man stood still for a moment, a tear in his eye, 'My dear, it's been a pleasure meeting you, a real treat for me. What about pretending I'm your grandfather. Then we can write to one another. You can keep me up to date with all your adventures.' Eleanor nodded. The thought of him being a stand-in grandfather gave her a sense of security. They agreed to write weekly, and Eleanor thought, 'At last I have some family - someone interested in **me**.'

LOYALTY AND LIES

5

Returning to work after Donald had left was a letdown. Eleanor felt deflated and sorry for herself. But there was no time to indulge her misery as she was summoned to Mr C's sanctum.

'Eleanor, take a seat, we think it's time we extended you somewhat. It's a shame to see such a lively talent as yours going to waste,' he announced.

Eleanor had no idea what he was referring to. What talents did she have? Certainly nothing she was immediately aware of. It was almost as if Mr C had been listening in to her and Donald's conversation the previous week.

Mr Caruthers continued, 'We would like you to start running a few errands for us around London, what do you think? '

Eleanor was only too willing. Life in the office was so dreary. This sounded more interesting. It would be fun to get to know London better.

She nodded vigorously, 'Definitely, sir.'

Mr C laughed saying, 'Hold hard young Eleanor, it's not going to be that thrilling. It might even be boring. Claire will give you your instructions and some maps so you don't get lost. We'll give you a kitty for expenses as you might need taxis or meals out.'

Eleanor went home early that afternoon buzzing with pleasure. She was dying to tell someone about her new role. Catching sight of Barbara's mini in the mews must mean she was home. Eleanor knocked on her door but there was no answer. What a disappointment! She knocked again. Still silence. She was about to leave when the bedroom window opened and Barbara stuck her head out, 'Oh Eleanor, this isn't a good time. Can I pop round, and see you later?'

Turning back to the room, she seemed to be answering someone's question. Eleanor heard the phrase 'Of course, don't worry she'll be fine,' and saw Barbara put her finger to her lips, as if she was telling the other person to be quiet. Swivelling back to Eleanor she smiled reassuringly, repeating, 'See you later,' as she closed the window.

Relaxing in her flat and drinking tea, Eleanor speculated as to who Barbara could be entertaining in her bedroom in the middle of the afternoon. Honestly it was none of her business. Maybe a boyfriend though as far as she knew Barbara hadn't got a boyfriend.

 This is stupid Eleanor thought, being prudish and narrow minded considering all the things her parents' friends used to get up to. Barbara, being older, probably had all sorts of relationships Eleanor wasn't aware of. So why did she feel hurt? Perhaps she'd invested too much in their friendship, expecting Barbara to be as open as she was herself. It won't do, Eleanor thought, I need friends of my own age.

…

Catching the fleeting disappointment on Eleanor's face, Barbara moved away from the window muttering half to herself and half to the man lying sprawled on her bed, 'I think I've let her down. She's started to look on me as a friend and a confidante, as she has no one else to talk to. We're used to popping in and out one another's places. But it's getting more problematic with my other work. I've hardly any privacy. Why they wanted me to live practically on top of her I don't know.'

Back came the laconic reply, 'That's the point isn't it - far too dangerous to leave her run free. Don't worry she'll probably soon find friends of her own though of course any new friends would have to be vetted. Stop being a mother hen. Come back to bed, I haven't long. You can catch up with her later.'

…

When Barbara eventually came round, Eleanor decided to be grown up, not ask questions and not be stand offish either but keep some distance between them. This turned out to be harder than she thought as Barbara was particularly friendly and cheerful, bringing along a couple of bottles of wine and some delicious canapés from Harrods. Before she knew it or could stop herself, Eleanor was pouring out her heart, all about work and her new role. But at no point did Barbara confide in her or mention that afternoon.

Barbara began retailing stories about old Mr Rankin, her boss's father who would come and sit for hours in the office in a corner next to the filing cabinets. 'He's like the Aged P in Great Expectations, and he does the same thing, reading snippets from the newspaper. It's off putting for us and for clients but no one has the heart to get rid of him.'

Eleanor said, 'I'd love to see your office and meet the Aged P. Perhaps I could meet you there one day and we could go for lunch.'

Barbara froze. She shook herself briskly, saying, 'I've had far too much wine. I think I'm running off at the mouth. You must be tired. We've both got to get up in the morning.'

Eleanor persisted, 'What about next week. I could meet you at Rankins, and we could find somewhere to eat in Moorgate.   Whenever's convenient for you? I'm not that busy at the moment, and I've more freedom now.'

Barbara said tersely, 'It's difficult, Eleanor. You wouldn't be able to come in to the office because of security. Only clients with appointments are allowed. Leave it with me. I'll ring you next week.'

The weeks went by but though Eleanor saw a lot of Barbara at home and when they travelled to work, there was no further mention of lunch or meeting up at Barbara's office. Eleanor was distracted herself as she was being sent out on more and more deliveries. There was often a chance for lunch or a snack wherever she was, and she was encouraged to take taxis if it was a distance or if there was something heavy to carry. But Eleanor loved taking the bus, getting to know the routes and bus nos. There was a generous kitty but she hardly spent any of it and every week meticulously wrote up her expense sheet.

Claire said to her teasingly one day, 'You can take some time out you know when you're working. Have a look at the shops or walk in the park. Enjoy some space, honestly Mr C won't mind. He is pleased with your diligence, so you can have some leeway.'

Eleanor decided to take them at their word, and the next day when she was sent on a delivery to Victoria hopped on the no. 19 bus, to go window shopping in Oxford St. Sitting on the top deck, Eleanor gazed down at the passersby laden with shopping bags. It was near Bond St that Eleanor suddenly thought she sighted Barbara. But it was a very different Barbara, nothing like her usual smart sophisticated self. The woman was wearing a dull brown duffel coat, and looked older and shabbier with short gray hair rather than Barbara's usual shoulder length ash blonde curls. Yet the brisk walk was Barbara all over. Surely it couldn't be her mother? But hadn't Barbara said her mother died when she was young? Maybe it was a doppelganger? What a laugh to have a double. Eleanor couldn't wait to tell her.

On the Friday night, Eleanor and Barbara were sitting on Barbara's patio enjoying the last of the sunshine, and drinking white wine to toast the weekend, when Eleanor mentioned the person she'd seen, thinking what a joke it would be. Barbara was not amused, saying adamantly, 'You must have been mistaken, Eleanor. I just have one of those faces. After all you said she was much older.' Taking a moment to compose herself, she attempted a lighter tone, 'It must have been my doppelganger. Don't we all have one somewhere in the world?' adding as an afterthought, 'Tuesday, yes of course, I went to Brighton with one of the partners to see an elderly client. I could hardly have been in Oxford St.'

That's odd Eleanor thought I never mentioned the day or Oxford Street, funny that. Not knowing what to make of it Eleanor decided to say nothing further, and they went on to discuss their weekend plans. Barbara had seen an exhibition on modern art at the Tate she wanted to see, and suggested Eleanor come. But for once Eleanor resisted saying she had a lot to do in the flat. After a few more drinks they went their separate ways.

Eleanor spent Saturday flat cleaning and thinking. She needed to go out more and socialise, or as Donald rightly said her imagination would start working overtime. But how to do that - perhaps an evening class, maybe she could improve on her languages. She had a smattering of French and Spanish from school, so that was a start. As it was already September, it might be too late for her to enroll but that afternoon determined to follow her plan, she found City Lit in Covent Garden. There were no openings in French, and was talked into attending a Spanish Intermediate course. The level was probably too advanced but Eleanor was assured that the teacher would assess everyone's ability and work at the classes' pace.

Eleanor resolved not to tell anyone. Since she'd been in London people had tried to sort her out, and make her over. It was time to be independent and self sufficient.

The first Thursday evening at the college, Eleanor's nervousness nearly overcame her. Taking deep breaths, she finally found the right room. Being twenty minutes early gave her a chance to settle down and find a seat near the back. Eventually all types and ages of people flocked in and the course began. The tutor was in full flow with, 'I will just go round the room, and you can tell me what level of Spanish you have,' when Eleanor noticed a slight dark young man shyly trying to slide into the seat next to her. He said in a whisper, 'Have I missed much?'

'No,' she whispered, 'it's just getting started.' The teacher worked her way round everyone then read out a list of names saying she was going to suggest that the students on the list would be better taking a step back, and joining Beginners Spanish the following night.

However for this evening everyone should try to talk Spanish in pairs, and find out as much as they could about the person sitting next to them.

Eleanor was annoyed to find herself on the Beginners List, but deciding to make the best of it turned to the dark young man, and asked, 'Cual es su nombre?' He answered, 'Mi nombre es Georges Duval lo que es suyo.'

'Mi nombre es Eleanor Smith,' Eleanor replied. After a shaky beginning they began to find out more about one another. Georges had an English mother and French father, both now dead, and lived in Islington with his French grandmother. Eleanor was dying to know if he was on the list for Beginners but her Spanish was not that advanced. Undercover of the noise she asked in English, 'Have you been moved back to Beginners?'

'Yes, unfortunately,' Georges shrugged, 'and you?'

Eleanor nodded, 'Will you go tomorrow?'

'Of course,' he said smiling at her with his beautiful deep brown eyes and long lashes, 'particularly if you're there. We can both soldier on together. Shall we discuss it over coffee, and you can tell me all about yourself?'

He didn't seem anywhere near as shy as Eleanor had first thought. She began to wonder if he was actually flirting with her but was too inexperienced to know.

On the Friday morning at the office, Claire remarked, 'You seem unusually cheerful. What's happening in your life now you've got your flat sorted?'

Eleanor grinned, and said, 'Nothing much really, just the usual,' without any further comment. Perhaps she was growing up at last.

All through the day, she hummed little tunes to herself looking forward to the evening. At five thirty on the dot, Eleanor was out of the office, racing home to change and eat. She wondered if she was being foolish, maybe Georges would have changed his mind. But no, as she shot up Keeley Street towards City Lit., he was loitering outside. He smiled disarmingly at her saying, 'I thought I'd wait for you here. We can beard the Spanish dragon together,' and with that he took her books adding them to his, gently holding her hand as they went inside.

6

That same evening leaving Eleanor at Covent Garden Tube, Georges made his way to Leicester Square changing Tubes several times and whistling as he went. At one stop he visited the Gents, reappearing in a capacious brown overcoat and tweed hat, and carrying a battered briefcase rather than his former book bag. Adopting a limp, he walked stiffly and upright with a cane. At Leicester Square, he made his way to the Odeon Cinema, bought a single ticket for 'The Eagle has Landed', and taking his seat in the back row of the deserted cinema proceeded to take off his coat. This was carefully packed away in his briefcase with the foldable cane, and he quietly left through the exit door dressed in a plain sports jacket, jeans and carrying a large sports holdall.

Choosing a dingy dark bar down a side street, Georges collected a beer from the bar, and moved towards a back table in clear sight of the door. After an hour of carefully nursing his drink and studying The Evening Standard, a tall slim fair man in his fifties arrived and sat at the next table.

Georges carefully folded his paper to the Accommodation section, underlining various 'Flats to Let.' None of them seemed to appeal to him, and throwing the paper to one side in disgust, shouldered the heavy sports bag again and left throwing some money on the table. The other man finished his whisky and soda, reached across for the discarded paper and nonchalantly rifled through the pages. He stopped at the sports section, and checking the odds on a particular horse enquired from the barman where the nearest betting shop was. The barman gave complicated directions pointing vaguely before shuffling off to serve a paying customer.

The fair man taking his time strolled in the direction given, and then doubled back. He stood for a moment or two lighting a cigarette and puffing away before vanishing through a blue doorway. Inside the building he stood listening and waiting before making his way up to the first floor, his hand thrust into his inside pocket. Slowly he edged open the first door on the landing.

Georges sat at a table opposite the door, 'At last,' he said, 'there's being careful, and then there's being too careful.'

'I don't think so; it's not your risk. You're merely a young pup in this game,' was the grim reply. 'What is this place - surely not one of the safe houses? You might have stretched to something more upmarket by now I would have thought.'

'I know. It's purely temporary. They'll probably find somewhere better for us next time.'

'I hope there won't be a next time. This is far too dangerous for me. In future, you can either deal with me by telephone or through Vasily unless it's urgent of course.'

Georges nodded: 'Whatever suits you. What should I call you? They didn't give me a name.'

'Anubis will do fine. Let's make a start.'

Georges trying to relieve the situation said, 'These codenames, wherever do they get them? Isn't Anubis an Egyptian god?'

'A golden jackal,' his companion commented, 'based on my once golden hair, I imagine; a god who ushers souls into the afterlife. It is certainly an apt description of some of my earlier work,' he added dryly, 'now can we move on to your report. I've little time for chitchat. I don't like time wasters.'

Georges winced, 'Sorry. This isn't my usual line of work but they had no one else. I have made preliminary contact with the target.'

Anubis frowned, 'Am not sure I want to hear her described like that?'

Georges sat back for a moment, 'Perhaps we could refer to her as 'Butterfly'; she does seem to be breaking out of her chrysalis.'

'As long as she doesn't fly away altogether,' Anubis remarked sarcastically, 'I suppose it will do.'

Georges continued, 'How far would you want me to go? She seems lonely and impressionable.'

'As far as it takes to win her confidence and keep her under wraps for the duration, do you understand what I'm saying?'

Georges nodded, 'I guess so. I'll do my best on the charm front and develop a relationship. I think however there may be more to Butterfly than you realise. What if she becomes suspicious?'

'Then it's up to you to control her and the situation,' Anubis said authoritatively, 'I hope your cover story with the travel agency is authentic enough. I've important work to do, and will be out of the country for the next months so can't be nursemaiding you. Talk to Vasily if there are problems and guard your cover well. I take it no one at Sentry knows about you?'

'No, I have a strong impression that Butterfly wants to keep her private life private. She seems unsure about Sentry and was evasive about talking about them and their work.'

Anubis scowled, 'Look here Georges, or whatever your real name is, impressions are no good to me in this game only facts. These are delicate circumstances, and require the fine skills of a balancing act. I hope you're up to it. Maybe you'll find out for yourself what my code name implies. I haven't built my career so far on lightweights like you, and I don't intend to start now.'

Georges bristled with indignation, 'I'm no lightweight or they wouldn't have given me the job. I'll manage Butterfly. She'll be eating out of my hand before we know it.'

'Let's hope so. As I said your head's on the block, and I'll be there to make sure it parts company with your body if necessary whoever you work for,' Anubis stated harshly as he left.

Georges continued to sit at the table, hoping and praying he could live up to his show of bravado.

7

1976

Eleanor was enjoying life. Evening classes were going well, and she was seeing Georges on a regular basis, either going to the cinema or out for a meal. Barbara was still a friend, and they would visit for coffee, but Eleanor no longer chose to confide in her particularly not about Georges. She was writing every week to Donald but again referred to Georges as a 'friend'. These were early days in their friendship, and Eleanor didn't want to expose their budding relationship to all and sundry.

Work itself was taking an interesting turn. Mr C seemed to be treating her more favourably than previously. Claire's attitude was more inclusive than usual, inviting Eleanor for meals and to events. Eleanor concluded it was because she'd been there eighteen months, and they'd got to know and trust her. Perhaps she herself was more grown up, and not as naive as when she'd started.

It was one of the days when Claire was on holiday that Eleanor was asked for a special file from the black cabinet in the filing room. Eleanor didn't know what to do when Mr C rang through. He had forgotten Claire was on holiday and bellowed down the intercom, 'Claire, bring me the Lenard file from the black cabinet immediately.'

Eleanor knew where Claire kept the key, and thought to herself he won't be happy if I make excuses. Without a second's thought Eleanor took the key, scribbled the name in the entry book, and entered the file room. The cabinet was double padlocked but easy enough to open. Eleanor felt as if she was handling an unexploded bomb. Gingerly thumbing through 'L', she spotted a familiar name 'Leighton, Barbara' with the address 'Rose Cottage, Durweston Mews, London W1.' Surely it couldn't be her Barbara?

There was no time to delay as Mr. C was blasting on the intercom again, 'Where's that file, girl? Have you gone to sleep out there?'Eleanor found the offending file, quickly locked the cabinet and taking to her heels sped through to his office. He was on the phone and grabbed the file out of her hand without looking at her.

Eleanor went back to her desk and started thinking. Why would there be a file on Barbara? She worked for stockbrokers, and Sentry Inc. were importers and exporters. What was the connection? Why would there be a personal file when most of the files were company files, and why in the black cabinet? The questions went on and on until by the end of the day Eleanor had developed a terrible headache. She collected the black file from Mr C's desk when he was at lunch replaced it in the cabinet and signed it back in. But her curiosity was starting to get the better of her.

Deciding to leave work early and reassess everything the next day, the first person she bumped into in the middle of the mews was Barbara of all people.

'Eleanor, you look very pale, are you alright?' she asked, sounding concerned.

'I seem to have developed a terrible headache and need to lie down.'

'I daresay it's the weather, it so muggy today,' Barbara said sympathetically, 'let me know if there's anything I can do. I'm at home this evening,' she said reassuringly disappearing into Rose Cottage.

Eleanor only wished there was something Barbara could do for her but if Barbara was mixed up in something questionable, she could hardly be trusted. Eleanor badly needed someone to talk to. Georges came to mind, but they didn't know one another that well as yet. Eleanor could hardly ring, and tell him that she wanted to snoop through secure files.

Tossing and turning all night reinforced Eleanor's determination to find out what was in Barbara's file. Maybe it was nothing but though she felt a strong loyalty to her friend, she was itching to know. She'd always been like this. When her parents went off on yet another of their fruitless excursions dumping her on so-called friends, Eleanor would amuse herself by nosing through their drawers, reading personal correspondence, and pretending she was a private detective. She had no idea why she did it, maybe some sort of voyeurism or because her own life was so empty she had to fill the void with other peoples' secrets.

Arriving at the office early next morning fate was on Eleanor's side. Mr C was on his way out as she came in, wishing her a hurried 'good morning' as he left. The ground floor was deserted. Eleanor messed about finishing off bits of work as the morning progressed. By early afternoon and checking Mr C's diary to make sure he wouldn't be back for some time, she planned her strategy. She mustn't get caught.

Picking up her large handbag Eleanor moved stealthily to the file room, shut the door, opened drawer H to M, quickly pulled out Barbara's file and slipped into her bag. Her heart was beating in her throat but she was on a high. Sprinting into the Ladies Eleanor sat in a stall, and opened the file. The first pages were about Barbara's education, schooling, and various addresses where she'd lived. However further in, Eleanor's attention was caught by her own name and a whole lot of blacked out pages. There seemed to be reports referring to codename 'Babybird', and its movements. The more she read the more Eleanor realised that 'Babybird' was her. Surely not, why would anyone be interested in her comings and goings?

In the midst of her deliberation there was a shout from outside, 'Ahoy, anyone here, anyone? Where's all me ladies on such a lovely afternoon? Is there no one to welcome the poor auld traveller returning home?'

With a start, Eleanor realised it was Paddy. He certainly turned up at the most inopportune moments. Shoving the file into her bag and zipping it tightly, Eleanor emerged from the Ladies with a forced smile.

'Oh that's more like it – my little Nell, ready to give me the greeting I deserve,' and he swung her round, bag and all.

'What are you doing here, Paddy? You're not expected. Mr C is out.'

'Right on my little cherub, I just happened to be passing through London, and thought I would drop in on my old muckers for afternoon tea. Any biscuits or cakes around, little one?'

Eleanor tried to calm down and laugh, but it was an effort. She mustered up some enthusiasm saying, 'I'm sure I can find something to tempt your appetite. I'll put the kettle on.'

'Now you're talking, though you be the one tempting me appetite,' his eyes sparkling with humour, 'but cake will do.'

He perched on the side of her desk saying, 'Tell me your news. How do you like the big bad city so far? Have they turned you into one of them Londoners yet – all posh, unsmiling and looking into the far distance?' Taking a good long look at her he said, 'No, I can see they haven't yet. You've still got that lovely innocence about you,' and in a more serious tone whispered, 'don't whatever you do become one of us. We've got some very bad habits, even dangerous ones.'

Eleanor wondered what he meant. He was a strange one. Sometimes she could hear nothing but his Irish lilt yet at other times he would drop into other accents and slang. You never could tell with him. She carefully brewed the tea, keeping a watching eye on her bag stashed behind the desk, and hoping he wasn't intending to stay. Eleanor was desperate to get back to the file – her mind was abuzz with queries. Why oh why would she be of interest to anyone, and why would Barbara be watching and reporting on her? Barbara was her friend, wasn't she? All these thoughts tumbled through her head, whilst she kept smiling and making conversation but it was hard to control her face.

After a long telling silence, Paddy enquired, 'What's up with you mavourneen this afternoon? There's something on your mind. Tell your uncle Paddy, and I'll make it right.'

'There's nothing, Paddy. I'm just feeling a little under the weather, and need a holiday.'

'Now you're talking,' Paddy said shooting off on a tangent, 'and where would your highness like to go, somewhere in the tropics maybe or somewhere exotic?'

Eleanor giggled continuing to play the game, 'What about Australia?'

'Oh no,' he pooh poohed, 'they're all savages and colonials over there - what about somewhere in the Far East with beautiful women, curries to die for, and elephants?'

'Elephants, definitely elephants, there must be elephants,' Eleanor said keen to distract him.

'Why elephants?' said a voice, 'I doubt you ever saw many in the West Country Miss Eleanor, except at a zoo,' and Mr C's large frame and girth filled the doorway. Eleanor's stomach turned to water. She felt her guilt showing. But Mr C for once in a genial mood, addressed Paddy directly, 'What are you doing here you old scoundrel bothering my staff? I thought you had other fish to fry.'

Paddy was tense for a moment as if the clown mask had suddenly slipped, 'Boss, I came for a word – have you a moment?'

'Of course. Eleanor, you can go home now,' and without a further word, they disappeared into the inner sanctum leaving Eleanor abandoned and wondering what to do next.

There was nothing for it but to take the bag and the errant file home and bring it back tomorrow, but that was when Claire was returning from holiday. Eleanor was panic stricken. She needed to keep a cool head. Back at the flat she locked all the doors and windows and sat in the dark with just a lamp, feeling that at any moment the police might arrive and arrest her. There was nothing very exciting in the rest of the file, though the reports were definitely about her: her move from the West Country to London; sharing a flat with Celia; her interview and tests at Sentry; the move to the mews; her correspondence with Donald though nothing about Georges. What did it all mean? Why was Sentry interested in her? How did Barbara fit in? Maybe her so-called friend was some sort of secret agent.

Without warning there was a ring at the door followed by loud knocking. Flustered, Eleanor raced round the flat brandishing the file as if it was red hot. Rushing into the bedroom she forced it under the mattress with one almighty thrust, and breathlessly ran to throw open the flat door to be confronted with the figure of Barbara waving a bottle of wine. By now Eleanor was totally speechless, only to be further confounded by Barbara exclaiming, 'Oh what a shame, I thought we could share this but I can see you're going out.'

Eleanor took a second or two to figure out that she hadn't taken her coat off since arriving home, and taking advantage of the situation she said, 'Sorry Barbara. You're right. I'm on my way and late as it is.' Giving no further explanation she grabbed her bag, and took off down the mews as if she was possessed. At the corner Eleanor looked round briefly to see a nonplussed Barbara still standing at the top of the staircase.

Eleanor ran all the way to Carnaby Street looking for the smallest dingiest cafe she could find. She sat there shaking. It felt as if she was in the middle of a conspiracy, and one she couldn't make head or tail of.   She also had the sticky problem of getting the file back into the black cabinet without being seen.   After hours of soul searching, an exhausted Eleanor headed for home and bed deciding to sort things out the following day.

The next morning at work Claire was in a high old mood, showing off her holiday snaps, and giving Eleanor a beautiful, expensive turquoise scarf. It was hard to envisage all these people being involved in a wicked plot against her - surely not Claire?

As the morning wore on there was little opportunity to return the file. It sat broodingly in her bag. Towards lunchtime Claire still in the holiday spirit, suggested an oyster and champagne lunch. Eleanor was all for it and as they ambled down Moorgate, Eleanor clapped her hand to her head saying, 'What an idiot I left my bag in the office.' Before Claire had time to say anything Eleanor was off and careering back full pelt. Grabbing the offending bag Eleanor took a quick recce of the office, slipped into the file room with the key, and carefully shutting the door behind her replaced the file. Catching up with Claire outside the oyster bar, she could barely get her breath; she was panting and wheezing so hard.

'Honestly Eleanor, you needn't have raced off like that. It's my treat. You didn't need your bag.'

'Oh it wasn't that. I remembered I had some important papers about my flat insurance in my bag, and didn't want to leave them unattended,' Eleanor said blithely, smiling and beaming away, relieved to be shot of the wretched file at last.

FRIENDSHIP AND FANTASY

8

Weeks later Eleanor was mulling things over when Mr C called her into his room. Standing in front of his heavily carved oak desk as he continued writing notes in his florid looped script, Eleanor had time to think. She attempted to weigh up everything she had learnt so far. On the plus side, she was paid well and liked working at Sentry. On the minus side there was her friendship with Barbara. It was never going to be the same if they were using Barbara to spy on her. But then so what, her life wasn't that exciting. Clearly there was nothing to report. She and Barbara being neighbours meant they would still visit, but from now on Eleanor intended keeping herself to herself. After a few minutes Eleanor cleared her throat and sighed audibly, Mr C looked up frowning drawing his heavy eyebrows together in a straight line.

'Well young Eleanor, and what have you been up to lately, I wonder?'

Eleanor's heart sank. Could he know about the file or was he doing his usual trick and trying to throw her off guard?

He stared at her. Eleanor daringly returned his gaze eyeball to eyeball, hoping she wasn't showing any signs of guilt. In the ensuing silence he seemed to relax giving a snort of laughter.

'You seem to be progressing, perhaps not so young Eleanor any more. I see a measure of defiance bordering on insolence; just don't let it go too far. Anyway I've an important job for you. Do you think you're up to it?'

Eleanor relieved to be off the hook said eagerly, 'Absolutely, I'm ready for anything.'

'I'll remind you of that later,' he countered narrowing his eyes in a calculating fashion. 'This job is not too taxing. I want you to go to Gatwick and meet one of our people coming in from Berlin. Claire will give you the flight details. You are to take this lady for a drink in the bar. She will give you a package. Be friendly to her. She is a charming lady who has had a tough time. Come straight back afterwards. Any questions?'

Eleanor had lots, but noting the expression on his face decided it wiser not to push her luck, and with that he waved her out of the room.

Clare wrote down the details for her and armed with a wad of money for taxis and trains, Eleanor set off for the airport. This was a bit of an adventure, and a change from trekking round offices in London. She wondered why she'd been sent. Obviously they trusted her; either that or she was still the dogsbody. But she'd never been asked to meet anyone in person before or even take them for a drink. What did people from Berlin drink? Was it schnapps?

70

Once the train pulled into Gatwick it dawned on Eleanor that she'd never been to an airport before. There was so much happening and so many people. Eventually she found the Arrivals Board. The plane had just landed. Not sure where to stand Eleanor asked one of the ground staff who pointed to the correct Gate. Eleanor wriggled her way to the front of the crowd holding up her prepared sign, 'Frau Schmidt, Willkommen', whilst attempting to look blasé.

After a wait, a slight blonde lady approached. She was pushing a laden trolley and nodded at Eleanor, 'Guten Tag, ist ein long journey from Berlin.'

'But not so far as America,' Eleanor stammered with the reply she'd been told to give, 'can I help you with your trolley? Would you like a drink?' she nodded across to the bar.

'Danke, would be nice.'

Together they wended their way through the crowds to the deserted bar. Eleanor parked the trolley at the nearest seat but her companion said, 'Nein, I think over there - private,' and moved towards a red leather banquette in one of the darker corners.

'What would you like?' Eleanor asked nervously, hoping the lady wouldn't ask for anything complicated.

'A double whisky mit soda, no ice danke,' Frau Schmidt answered wearily. She looked as if she was about to fall asleep at any moment and as Eleanor made her way to the bar, Frau Schmidt rested her head on the table. Eleanor thought I hope she isn't ill or so tired I can't wake her. What will I do? Perhaps the drink would revive her.

Arriving back with the whisky and a bitter lemon for herself, Eleanor clanked the tray down loudly. Frau Schmidt looked up rubbing her eyes, 'Es tut mir so leid liebchen, I nod off.' She took the drink, knocking it back in one go.

'Would you like another?' Eleanor enquired reluctantly. She didn't want a drunk on her hands; after all she was only the courier.

'Nein liebchen, I recover myself now. Was ist your name? You seem sehr jung for all this?'

Eleanor told her name but wondered what the lady meant by 'for all this?' Concerned about the effect of the alcohol Eleanor offered to find food but Frau Schmidt declined saying, 'Nein, I've no time. I transit. Mein flight leaves in der hour. I need tell you things.'

'I don't understand,' Eleanor said, 'my instructions are to collect a package from you and take it back to the office, nothing more.'

'But that liebchen is point,' Frau Schmidt said in a whisper with her hand over her mouth, 'I not retrieve Paket.' Meine legende was how you say,' as she puffed out her cheeks and blew with her lips, 'disappeared.'

Eleanor struggled to understand the bits of German, intermingled with broken English and miming gestures. What on earth was it all about? What was she going to take back to the office? She'd better try and pull herself and this lady together, and find out the facts.

But Frau Schmidt by now had completely run out of steam, and was drooping and crying softly to herself saying, 'Es ist meine Schuld, meine Schuld.'

Eleanor fast running out of patience and sympathy, shook her arm, 'Madam I can't understand you, please speak English.'

But Frau Schmidt was now shivering and moaning, and mumbled, 'Meinen Flug, meinen Flug', and before Eleanor could stop her she was up and running pushing her trolley at top speed towards the Departure Gate. Eleanor, completely taken aback, rushed after her. In the background the tannoy was blaring out the next flight to Belfast. Trying hard to hold on to Frau Schmidt, Eleanor grabbed the back of her raincoat but Frau Schmidt was too quick, slipping out of it, leaving Eleanor clutching an empty coat. Feeling irritated and frustrated Eleanor was about to leave, when she saw Frau Schmidt come to a halt on the other side of the barrier. She was waving furiously at Eleanor and shouting, 'Maulwurf, tell them, Maulwurf', and then she was gone.

Eleanor, still holding the raincoat, wandered disconsolately towards the train and back to London. What was going on and what was that 'maul----something?' Who was Frau Schmidt? What did she have to do with Sentry? What was she going to tell Mr C? It was peculiar. The woman's manner was bizarre and where had she shot off to? Eleanor hated returning empty handed. There was the raincoat of course. How embarrassing and infantile trying to tussle with Frau Schmidt and her coat, hardly professional. On the train Eleanor tried to sort out the sequence of events and decide how to present them to Mr C, so that she didn't look completely stupid.

At Victoria it had started to rain and with a long queue for taxis; Eleanor put on the blue raincoat rather than get wet. It was too short and too tight for her, but she could leave it open. Fed up, she dug her hands deep into the pockets and felt something in the lining. There was a small hard object between the outer layer of the coat and the pocket.

Once in a taxi on the way back to Sun St, Eleanor took off the coat and extracting nail scissors from her bag worked on the inner seam. Carefully undoing some of the stitching she was able to extract the object. It was only a coin. On one side it said 1 Deutsche Mark and on the other Deutsche Demokratische Republik. It had probably fallen through the lining. It was of no account. She might just as well hang on to it as a souvenir of her day at the airport and dropped it in her purse. 1 mark wouldn't be worth much.

At Sentry, before she even had time to take the raincoat off Eleanor was ushered into Mr C's office, 'Well,' he said, tapping his pen impatiently on the desk, 'where is it then, and why have you been so long? I hope you didn't stop to do shopping or you'll be in trouble.'

Totally forgetting her prepared story, Eleanor began talking rapidly explaining the missing package, Frau Schmidt's strange conduct, and how she had tried to stop the woman rushing off to catch the plane. Hearing the panic in her voice, Mr C said more kindly, 'Take a deep breath. Calm down and sit down. Tell me everything in detail from the very beginning.'

Making no comment throughout except for the odd question to jog her memory he sat for some time doing his usual pyramiding of hands, saying eventually, 'Give me that word she was shouting at you again. Did you write it down?'

'No, I can remember it, but didn't understand it. It sounded like 'malver' (Eleanor spelt it out) or something like that but the lady mixed her English with German. It was difficult to know which language she was speaking in.'

'And did anything else happen or it that it?' Mr C persisted.

'No, nothing that I can think of,' Eleanor said as she gave him the raincoat.

'You did well young Eleanor, under difficult circumstances. I'm pleased with you. You kept your head. Orf home now – you deserve an early finish.'

Eleanor didn't know whether she did deserve it or not, she'd hardly done anything. It wasn't until she got home that she remembered the German coin. She supposed it didn't matter, it was nothing. No one would mind her keeping it.

9

A few weeks later Eleanor had cause to remember the coin. Trying to force her overfull purse shut, the errant German coin shot out and rolled under the table. Eleanor ignored it and left, already late for work.

Later that week, expecting Georges round for a meal, Eleanor decided to give the flat a cleanup and hoovering vigorously under the table collided with something hard. Impatient and wanting to get the job done quickly, she kept pushing and pushing until she heard a distinct click. Oh damn, she thought I think I've broken the Hoover, and bending down caught sight of the German coin now completely split in half. Reaching for it Eleanor could see the two halves fitted together with a hollow middle. There was a minute piece of black plastic stuck to one half. Easing the plastic off and studying it Eleanor couldn't see anything even through a magnifying glass. It was flimsy film of some description.

The problem was what to do with it. The clock had already struck seven. Georges would be arriving any minute and Eleanor hadn't even made the salad. There was no dressing so there was nothing for it but to run down to the corner shop. Georges was always punctual. She had no time now to think about the coin or the film. Hiding it in the bottom drawer of her jewellery box was the best option. Racing back from the shop Eleanor bumped into Georges on his way up the mews, armed with flowers, wine and his usual charming self. He kissed her lightly on the cheek remarking, 'You seem flustered tonight, cherie. Can I do anything to help? I'm a dab hand at salads,' noticing the dressing in her hand. At the flat, Eleanor set him up with everything and went to check on the pasta.

She was of two minds whether to tell him about the coin or not? He was a level headed businessman with his own travel agency after all. On the other hand what would he think about her pocketing the coin in the first place? She decided to tell him everything after the meal, but as they ate kept changing her mind. What if this was something secret and confidential relating to Sentry? However if they were truly only import/exporters what could they be doing that was hush-hush unless of course it was some sort of industrial espionage? But wasn't that when firms were developing or researching a new product; Sentry wasn't producing anything. All the letters, telexes and telephone calls Eleanor handled related to suppliers, buyers, transport and distribution and all sorts of dull things like that.

Georges seemed to sense she had something on her mind. 'Ma cherie Eleanor, why don't you tell me what's worrying you maybe I can help. Is it work or the flat?'

Eleanor gave a hefty sigh and decided to 'bite the bullet', relating everything about her day at the airport and the mystery coin. Georges listened attentively wincing at her attempts at German.

After she finished, he laughed saying, 'It sounds like one of your James Bond novels. Unbelievable!'

'Oh, but it's true Georges, of course it is,' Eleanor protested, 'would I make up something so elaborate? Anyway I have the coin to prove it,' and with that she rushed off to her bedroom, returning and waving the coin triumphantly in her hand, 'see for yourself,' and thrust it at him.

'But where's the film?' he asked studying the two halves of the deutschmark carefully.

'I must have dropped it,' Eleanor said, sprinting back to the jewellery box. But there was no sign of it.

'Come on Georges, we'll have to look for it. Perhaps it's stuck to the carpet.' They both crawled on their hands and knees up, down and back to the bedroom but nothing.

'It can't have vanished not just like that,' Eleanor complained. Ever the optimist she said, 'It's probably not that important. It'll turn up, I expect. You do believe me, don't you?'

'Of course I do, it's just a pity we don't have the film. Do you want to run through again what that lady said to you, and that word?'

Frustrated, Eleanor attempted to recall Frau Schmidt's conversation and spell out her last word. She tried different versions and spellings of the word but Georges didn't seem to recognise any of them, despite his fluent German. Taking possession of the coin he said, 'I'll take this into work tomorrow, and see if anyone has come across anything like it,' and with a hasty kiss on her cheek he rushed off.

Eleanor began to wish she hadn't confided in him. Their whole evening had been ruined; even his attitude to her had changed. He had become quite a different person, interrogating her like that and making her relate the story again. What with that and his hasty departure with her coin, she was beginning to have reservations about Georges.

The following day being Saturday, Eleanor decided to undertake some research herself at the local library. Studying a German dictionary Eleanor looked at every possible combination of letters for that troublesome word finally opting for 'maulwurf', as a possibility, which translated into English as 'mole'. But what did it mean? She decided to keep her findings to herself, and as she was meeting Georges for lunch made her way to his office.

Worldwide Travel was on the second floor of a building in Lower Regent Street, and organised trips for exclusive corporate clients. When Eleanor opened the door there were three people in the outer office busy on telephones. One of them nodded, smiled and gestured to Georges' office. Eleanor knocked lightly on the door and went in. Georges was sitting with his back to her hunched over the telephone talking animatedly in some guttural language that sounded faintly Russian or Slavic. Eleanor sat quietly by the door and waited. He was nothing like the shy student she'd originally met, talking confidently as if giving orders to someone. But then she supposed most people acted differently at work maybe even she herself did. Becoming aware of someone in the room, Georges spun round in his chair raising scowling eyebrows at seeing her. Momentarily there was something faintly sinister in his expression, but in a split second his face changed. His usual friendly smile returned and Eleanor felt reassured.

'Have you been here long?' he asked 'You should have let me know.'

'No, not long, you seemed busy. What language were you speaking? It sounded a lot like Russian.'

'Da,' he laughed, 'yes, I get by in a few languages but only the basics.'

Eleanor quickly retorted, 'That didn't appear to be very basic, more like a conversation.'

Georges narrowed his eyes in an unpleasant manner, stood up and throwing his coat over his shoulders said, 'Let's think about food instead. I'm starving. There's a lovely little Spanish cafe in Soho I thought we could try. We can eat tapas and practice our Spanish, what do you think?'

Eleanor was all for it, but registered he had cleverly changed the subject. Over lunch she brought up the subject of the coin but got nowhere. All he would say was that he'd sent it off to someone who might know more about it. Eleanor was not pleased. Irritably she said, 'You might have asked me. It's my coin, and I would like it back.'

Georges folded his arms looking across at her thoughtfully, 'But Eleanor it's not your property. By rights it belongs to Sentry if Frau Schmidt worked for them. You should have handed it in with her coat, don't you think?'

Eleanor made a face, 'It can hardly matter now. It's a bit late for me to own up. Just let me have it back, will you?' and had to accept his reassurance that he would.

After lunch they went their separate ways, Eleanor to shop and Georges to return to work.

....

Back at Worldwide Georges locked the door, pulled out one of the drawers in the filing cabinet, took out a green painted telephone and dialled a long number. There was a slight delay then a voice the other end enquired, 'Have you got the film?'

'No,' Georges replied.

'Did Sentry get there before us?' the voice asked.

'Not as far as I know, unless of course they or she know more than we think. They may be bugging her flat. We shall have to be more vigilant from now on,' Georges added.

There was a pause. The voice at the other end said darkly, 'You mean you will have to be more vigilant. Anubis will not be happy,' and rang off.

Georges sat rigidly holding the phone. Eventually he slammed it down. Damn and blast, why was everything so complicated? The job had looked straightforward. Butterfly had seemed so naive and ingenuous at the beginning, how on earth was he to continue?

10

During the following months Eleanor and Georges saw more and more of one another. The closer they became, the harder it was for Georges to keep track of his cover story. He had conveniently managed to sidetrack Eleanor from asking anything further about the coin or the film, but at times she would ask penetrating questions about his family and his background. His apparent evasiveness only provoking her into probing further. Eventually admitting defeat he rang Vasily.

Vasily not keen to be seen at the travel agency, arranged a meeting at Paddington Station. Georges was often meeting clients there so arriving early it was easy for him to blend with the crowd. Ever watchful he made his way to the nearest gents, coming out dressed in a British Rail uniform and made his way to the staff canteen. Within the hour Vasily arrived also attired in uniform, and they sat companionably for some time not speaking.

Georges said at last: 'Butterfly is becoming more and more curious, constantly asking questions about my family, my living arrangements and my background. I think as her parents aren't around, she's looking for a substitute family. Any ideas as to what I can do?'

Vasily shrugged laconically, 'It was bound to happen, Georges. Building intimate relationships have their problems. We can take care of anything you need in the way of background. Just let me know where and when, and I'll make sure it's in place.'

Georges didn't have a clue where to start. His lack of experience was beginning to tell, and he felt out of his depth. Finally reassured after talking it through with Vasily, arrangements were made and they departed separately.

Meeting Eleanor that night, Georges casually mentioned that his grandmother was keen to meet her, and had invited them both to lunch the following Saturday. Eleanor was beside herself with delight.

Perhaps this was a turning point in a rather static relationship. Now was a chance to find out more about Georges and get to know him better. Eleanor was not sure what sort of relationship they had. Yes, there was kissing but it was more brotherly than anything else though how could she judge, never having had an actual boyfriend before.

The following Saturday they arrived at the house in Thornhill Square; Eleanor in her best outfit, and Georges in a smart suit. It was an imposing Georgian house with tall gates surrounded by trees.

Georges pressed the bell and laughed, 'I know I've a key but my grandmother likes to greet her guests at the front door. She's rather formal and old fashioned that way.'

Eleanor, feeling her nerves rising said, 'I do hope she likes me.'

'Of course she'll like you, who couldn't love you,' Georges replied impatiently.

Eleanor thought did I hear that correctly? Did he say 'love' or was it a throwaway comment?

She was still pondering over this when the door opened. A white haired lady standing ramrod straight greeted them, 'At last, Georges, where've you been? I thought you were going to get here earlier, and this is your Eleanor. Do come in my dear, I don't know what this dratted boy gets up to half the time,' and without further ado she ushered them into a long elegant drawing room suffused with light.

'Sit down, my dears. Tell me all, I'm agog for news and gossip. I lead such a secluded life. Growing old and outliving your friends is hard,' she chitchatted away as if she'd known Eleanor all her life.

Eleanor was enchanted. On first appearances, Georges' grandmother was a soignée, sophisticated lady but her informal manner was totally at odds with her looks. She was in her seventies about the same age as Donald, but rushed around like a person half her age mixing cocktails and constantly talking.

Georges sat back grinning, 'There's no holding Mamie back when she has guests. She has twice my energy. She's led a very exciting life. Do you know that when she was younger than you she was a courier for the resistance in France?'

'Oh pouf,' Annette said, 'that was the dark ages. This poor child doesn't want to hear about a war that happened long before she was born.'

'But Madame Duval, I would love to hear about it. My family never talked about the war. It wasn't until I met Donald, you remember Georges, my neighbour's godfather that I heard anything at all.'

'Do call me Annette my dear not Madame Duval, it makes me sound so old,' and without thinking added acidly, 'I'm sure Donald had little knowledge of the real war sitting in some ivory tower in Whitehall,' and on she went prattling relentlessly.

Eleanor attempting to stem the flow said sharply and loudly, 'I had no idea you knew Sir Donald, Annette?'

The question stopped Annette in her tracks, in fact everything stopped.

Georges threw his grandmother a look that made her lower lip tremble.

Playing for time and taking a cigarette from a silver box, Annette attempted to light it with shaking hands saying, 'No, of course I don't know any such person. It was just a turn of phrase to dismiss all those silly Englishmen sitting out the war in London. You must forgive me Eleanor, even after all these years my English lets me down.'

But Eleanor quick to smile and reassure her noticed how pale Annette had suddenly become, and how unexpectedly agitated.

Georges stood up, taking charge and asking roughly, 'Lunch Mamie? What are we having for lunch,' and then attempting to smooth things over said with his usual suaveness, 'or am I taking my two beautiful girls out?'

'Of course not,' his grandmother replied. She appeared to make a rapid recovery from her earlier distress, and led them into the dining room. The table was laid with a pristine white cloth, silver place settings and beautiful fresh flowers.

Annette sat at the head of the table ringing a small silver bell until a maid appeared. 'I don't have help every day,' Annette confided, 'but today is very special as Georges has never brought anyone home before.'

They feasted on a light consommé, fresh grilled sardines, and a lamb cassoulet with plenty of French wine. Eleanor felt as if she was floating on air, maybe this was love after all.

Throughout the meal Eleanor tried to find out more about Georges, curious to know what he was like as a young boy and where he grew up, yet the conversation always seemed to revert back to her.

It was as if she was being grilled, first of all about her job, then her background and family. Eleanor was not inclined to talk about her fractured childhood or her work at Sentry with its strange undercurrents. In order to divert Annette she talked about London, her flat and Barbara. Georges played little part in the conversation concentrating on his food and seemingly completely disinterested. However he livened up at the mention of her neighbour in the mews.

'It's surprising,' he said, 'I've never bumped into Barbara when I've been round to your flat.'

'She has a demanding job,' Eleanor said, by way of an excuse, 'and I think she has a boyfriend. She certainly has a busy social life. I did see a lot of her when I moved in but not so much these days.'

Georges not to be put off continued, 'Who did you say she worked for? Wasn't it some firm in the City?'

Determined not to be drawn further into this particular conversation, Eleanor said firmly, 'Honestly Georges, you seem inordinately interested in Barbara's comings and goings. I know next to nothing about her life. She's only a neighbour and an acquaintance at that.'

As they retired to the drawing room for coffee and sweetmeats, Eleanor was feeling more than a little merry and said to her hostess, 'This has been the most wonderful day of my life. Thank you so much. I have felt so welcome.'

Annette looking at her tenderly and almost regretfully, murmured, 'I do hope life works out well for you, ma petite. Things are not always as they seem however much we would like them to be. Take care who you trust. Depend on your own judgment and good sense always. '

Eleanor looked puzzled, was this a warning?

But Georges had had enough and frowning angrily said, 'I think it's time to go, Eleanor. Mamie needs her rest. Her mind is starting to wander. She's had far too much excitement for today, haven't you?' he added, tapping his grandmother's hand before kissing her on both cheeks.

As they made their way down the path, Eleanor turned to wave noticing the distinct look of sadness or perhaps anguish on the older woman's face before she shut the door.

At the gates Eleanor linked arms with Georges, saying, 'Is your grandmother ill?'

'Of course not, what makes you think that?'

'I don't know she seemed upset at times.'

'There's nothing, absolutely nothing wrong with her. She's old and probably more than a little bit senile,' Georges said in a rough peremptory tone. Eleanor winced. What was wrong with Georges today?

Before they reached the corner and the Tube, Georges pulled a face, 'I don't know where my brain is today. I've completely forgotten to tell Mamie something important. Wait here a sec., and I'll run back. I won't be long.'

At the house Georges inserted his key into the lock, and crept back into the drawing room. The old lady was slumped in a chair.

She sat up with a start, 'I thought you'd both gone.'

'We had,' he said harshly, 'but Annette, you're a liability. I thought Vasily had briefed you. This is a sensitive operation. You allowed yourself to run off at the mouth without any thought. Remember, we work for people who will have no compunction in keeping that mouth of yours permanently shut. I only have to give the word.' He turned on his heel leaving her dazed and terrified.

Returning to the patiently waiting Eleanor, Georges hummed quietly to himself.

'You seem to have got something off your chest. You certainly look much happier now,' Eleanor remarked cheerily.

'I am,' Georges replied, 'most definitely.'

CROSSING THE LINE

11

The following Monday at work, Eleanor's peaceful existence was shattered. One minute she was feeling smug and satisfied with her life, the next it was in ruins. She was at her desk when Claire rang through from the switchboard saying there was an urgent call from overseas. Not having an inkling who it could be, Eleanor spoke into the mouthpiece. An anonymous voice announced, 'I am just connecting you with the Governor of Bermuda, Sir Peter Ramsbotham.' It must be about her parents. They had hardly been in touch since they'd left, merely a postcard to say they'd arrived.

An authoritative voice came on the line, 'Am I speaking to Miss Eleanor Duridge Smith?' Eleanor acknowledged her name. The voice continued, 'I am sorry to have to tell you that your parents, Mr and Mrs. Robert Duridge Smith, have been involved in a terrible accident and unfortunately didn't survive.'

Eleanor's mind went blank. What did he mean, 'Are you saying they're dead?'

'I'm afraid so,' came the reply, 'their car hit a tree and spiralled out of control over the side of a steep embankment into a ravine and caught fire.' There was a second and then the voice continued as if the person on the other end had swallowed hard, 'There was nothing, absolutely nothing anyone could do to save them.'

Eleanor was in shock and carefully replaced the receiver with trembling hands. She'd never been close to her parents, in fact she'd barely known them, but this was a terrible way to go. Her thoughts moved to the past. Why had they always treated her badly? As soon as Eleanor was eighteen her father had told her she was no longer their responsibility, and would have to fend for herself. He had sunk the last of his savings into a tourist venture in Bermuda, and he and her mother had vanished overnight. Eleanor had been packed off to an elderly relative in London to attend Pitman's, and then family friends had stepped in to find her a room in Celia's flat.

Eleanor was not sure whether she was upset at losing her parents or just shocked by their sudden death. She had no idea what to do next, having not asked about any funeral arrangements or bringing the bodies back to the UK. Who could she turn to? There was Georges of course, though his moods could be unpredictable and she was hesitant to bother him at work.

There was Mr C, but some instinct made her wary of approaching him about something so personal. Who else was there? Barbara was no longer a close confidante, and as for Donald, he was too far away and probably too old to be of any practical support. Eleanor was aware of how much she'd changed in the last year, and how secretive she had become, but maybe she needed to be guarded and cautious about her private life.

Ringing through to the main office, Eleanor explained she wasn't feeling well and needed to go home. Claire asked no questions and was sympathetic offering to get her a cab back to the mews. Eleanor accepted, deciding to do a detour via Georges' office. Luckily he was in and for once glad to see her, listening intently to her news and providing tea, tissues and kindness.

'Don't worry cherie, I shall handle everything for you. Take yourself home, and relax. I'll ring you later.'

Eleanor felt relieved, never being entirely sure about Georges and his reactions, however this time he had come up trumps.

...

As soon as she left Georges pulled out the green telephone and spoke quietly into the receiver, 'I thought we were only observing them from afar. What happened? .... Robert was probably driving too fast. You always said he was a madman on the road. Oh I see..... maybe he did spot our car. It can't be helped. I will need someone to sort it out with the British Embassy there. We can't have her upset, panicking and flying out there or even mentioning it to anyone at Sentry. It has to be handled. Of course, I'll leave it to you. Let me know the details, and I'll relay them back to her.'

...

Later that evening Georges went round to the flat. Eleanor looked bleary eyed but more in control.

'How did you get on?' she asked.

'It's all in hand,' he said, 'you've nothing to worry about. Your parents will be cremated. Their ashes either sent to you or scattered in Bermuda near where they live, whichever you wish.'

Eleanor thought for a moment and said, 'Probably scattering their ashes there would be better. My parents never stayed in one place. My father was always talking about the old estate where he and his brother grew up but it's long gone, sold off to pay his father's gambling debts.'

Georges sat up suddenly, 'Did you say there was a brother? Do you know where he is, couldn't he have helped?'

'No,' said Eleanor shaking her head, 'I don't know anything about him; he was five years older than Robert, my father, and disappeared abroad never to be seen again.' Georges nodded knowingly.

'What about a will?' Georges asked, 'Are they likely to have left you any money or property do you think?'

'Probably not,' said Eleanor, 'they were always broke. My father used up all his savings going to Bermuda and they never owned property.'

Thoughtfully she said, 'How will I pay for their cremations.

I haven't enough savings?'

'Don't worry about that,' Georges said, 'any possessions they have will be sold and the shortfall will be covered by the British Embassy.'

'It sounds straightforward Georges, and yet it's the utter waste. I never got to know them. There was little affection between us, and now they're dead in their early fifties. It wasn't much of a life.'

Trying to cheer her up Georges said, 'Forget about them, Eleanor. You have your own life ahead of you. Anyway I have something in mind which might help. I've been asked to a posh travel dinner at Claridges next week and wondered if you'd come as my guest.'

'I don't know, Georges. It seems a bit soon to be going out enjoying myself.'

'Of course it's not; it will do you the world of good. Take a few days off, and go shopping. Buy a little black dress as a concession if that would make you feel better.'

Eleanor decided to sleep on it but kept replaying the circumstances of her parents' death. Georges was probably right, she needed something to distract herself or she would go mad. Ringing work the next day she explained there'd been a family death but didn't elaborate, and was given a week's compassionate leave.

Setting off for Fenwicks in Bond Street, a store Barbara had introduced her to; Eleanor began to feel that perhaps it wasn't all doom and gloom. Finding the right little black dress was no easy matter. The assistant did her best but Eleanor's pragmatic mood had changed to one of despondency. Eventually they both settled on one 'that would do', and Eleanor was on her way out of the shop when she spotted a sparkling display of earrings and necklaces.

It reminded her of a time when she was a child. Her parents were so poor Eleanor was always dressed in hand me downs. As she was left to her own devices on a regular basis, she would wander round shops surreptitiously pilfering a trinket or two to take home. With no excitement or treats to break the monotony of her young life, this was the only way to lighten her existence. Of course it was wrong but neither of her parents ever discovered her cache of jewels. They were her personal treasures and travelled with her everywhere. But it was no good remembering; her world was different now and all the better for it.

Daydreaming and stepping out into Oxford Street, Eleanor suddenly felt a firm hand on her shoulder. An authoritative voice said, 'Excuse me madam, you need to come with me.'

'But why?' Eleanor stammered.

'I think you know. Come along quietly. Don't make a scene.' A strong arm propelled her through to the back of the store and practically manhandled her into the staff lift.

Eleanor found herself in the manager's office being ordered to empty out her bag and coat pockets, and to her dismay a beautiful filigree necklace covered in semi precious stones dropped onto the desk.

'And what do you have to say for yourself?' the manager demanded, 'There's no receipt or packaging. In fact the floor walker saw you slip it into your bag. We take this type of crime seriously at Fenwicks. It's our policy to charge shoplifters.'

Eleanor was dazed and didn't know what to say. Of course she had been reminiscing about her old days of petty pilfering but nothing on this scale, and she had no recollection of taking the necklace. Eleanor tried to explain about her recent bereavement but the manager was having none of it. He dialled the police before she'd ended her first sentence. Would crying help? But no, she couldn't shed a tear. In fact she was in such a strange state that by the time the police came, Eleanor went off with them passively not caring whether she lived or died.

The young policewoman concerned about how pale she was, kept asking, 'Is there anyone I can call for you, my dear?' After repeating the question a few times she finally got through to Eleanor, who mentioned Georges. A call was put through to his office. The policewoman explained to him what had happened, and suggested he come straight away as his girlfriend might be ill. He said he would come immediately but as the hours rolled by and Eleanor sat shivering on her own in one of the interview rooms; it looked as if he wasn't coming.

…

At Worldwide Travel, Georges was in a panic. He rang Vasily who was nowhere to be found, and had to speak to the Rezedent who said frostily, 'I regret I have no knowledge of this. You are on your own. Make sure the police have no cause to contact us,' and cut the connection.

There was nothing for it but to contact Anubis himself. Georges felt the sweat running down his back; his hands were shaking as he rang the number.

'Yes?' said a peremptory voice. Georges explained stuttering through the explanation.

'What a mess. It's never a good idea using amateurs,' the voice remarked, 'I suppose I'll have to close the operation down if Vasily isn't around.'

'What about Butterfly, I can't leave her stranded in a police station?' Georges protested.

'Leave her. She'll survive I'm sure. I daresay she'll contact Sentry if she has any sense.'

'And me, and the other staff here, what should I do?'

'I'll send people round to sort out your grandmother and the Agency staff. You'd do well to disappear sharpish, Georges, or I might just think about sending them round for you as well.'

And that was that.

12

At the police station Eleanor was interviewed by two officers who could get nothing from her. By now she was on the verge of collapse. They asked her if there was anyone else they could contact. What about her employer? Eleanor summoned up all her strength to refer them to Sentry.

The police surgeon had been called and he diagnosed delayed shock, maintaining she couldn't be questioned further. He prescribed a sedative and by the time Mr Caruthers turned up, Eleanor was dopey and slurring her words.

Mr Caruthers took command of the situation in his usual inimitable way. All charges were dropped and the whole thing was explained away as a misunderstanding. It was as if he had some secret power or influence that made everyone fall into line with his wishes. Before she knew it she'd been whisked away to her flat wrapped securely in a blanket, deposited on her bed, and her shoes removed.

Mr C's last words rang in her ears as she fell asleep, 'Now young Eleanor, what have you got yourself into? Forget all about it, we'll take care of you. Things will look different in the morning.'

Waking in the early hours, Eleanor was dimly aware of someone in the room. Claire looked up from her book noticing Eleanor's restlessness, 'Go back to sleep, dear. I'm here. You're safe.'

The sound of the radio and a boiling kettle woke Eleanor next morning. Claire was making breakfast, 'Good timing, Eleanor, I was about to wake you. What do you feel like eating? I see you haven't a lot in, but I can always nip to the shop.'

'Just toast please, Claire. I'm sorry you've had to stay. I'm in a mess.'

Claire dismissed it airily, 'Don't think twice about it; it's all in a day's work. We all make mistakes and get in messes at times. But I'll have to get off soon and go into the office. Will you be alright?'

'Of course,' Eleanor said forcefully, 'I'll be back at work tomorrow.'

'Oh no, you won't, a few days rest is what you need. I'm sure Mr C will be round to see you. He's concerned about you, and feels responsible that we haven't been taking care of you.'

And there it was again, hadn't Mr C said something similar about 'them all taking care of her'. Why should she be their responsibility?

Eleanor would have preferred to avoid Mr C after yesterday's debacle. Might she get the sack and if she did, what would she do and where would she live? She would never be able to afford to continue living here.

Mid afternoon Mr Caruthers arrived armed with a large bouquet of flowers, magazines and of all things a bottle of brandy.

'Now young Eleanor, I don't want to get you into bad habits, but I think a tot of brandy is required. There's the girl, make some tea, we'll spike it up a bit and you can tell me everything.'

Over tea Eleanor explained about her parents' deaths, Georges' involvement, the trip to Fenwicks and the shoplifting incident. Mr C encouraged when she stuttered or stopped, and waited till she was finished.

He said quietly, 'I didn't realise Eleanor you had a boyfriend. You certainly kept that to yourself. Who is he, and why didn't he turn up to help?'

This was exactly what Eleanor wanted to know too, yet why had Mr C zeroed in on her boyfriend and skimmed over her parents' deaths? As Eleanor had no explanation for Georges' non appearance at the police station, Mr C moved on to the subject of her parents' funerals. He offered to make the arrangements, just as she and Georges had discussed earlier in the week.

When Eleanor hesitantly asked if she still had a job now that she had a police record, Mr Caruthers snorted. Appraising her, he said, 'There'll be no further involvement with the store or the police. All that has been dealt with just like that,'

(He pursed his thick lips, and blew into the air as if he was blowing away a pretend dandelion clock), 'and as for you my dear, we would never get rid of you. You're one of us. We look after our own.'

Eleanor had no idea what he meant; inscrutable as ever it was as if he knew more about her than she knew herself. He got up to go assuring her, 'Your job will be waiting, my dear. Take a week off. Isn't there a neighbour who could keep an eye on you? I'm sure Claire will pop over as well to do any shopping you want.'

He was out of the door with his usual speed, his heavy frame clanking down the staircase before Eleanor could express her gratitude or protest she didn't want help or anyone coming round. It was all a bit too cosy like being wrapped in cotton wool. She certainly didn't want to be watched by Claire or Barbara. No, she was going to pull herself together, get in some groceries and find out what had happened to Georges.

Her first thought was to ring him at his office. Surprisingly he had never given her his home number in the twelve months they had been together. However there was only a continuous engaged tone. Eleanor rang the operator only to be told the number had been disconnected. That was weird; maybe Worldwide Travel had changed their number. There was nothing for it, but to take a trip to his premises.

Livening up in the fresh air, Eleanor walked down Regent

Street stopping to look at the amazing toys in Hamleys' window and beginning to feel more like her old self. At Georges' office, there were no lights, no people, no telephones and no sign on the door. Perhaps she'd mistaken the floor as she'd only been there a couple of times. But there was no sign of Worldwide Travel on any other floor. It was as if they had completely vanished into thin air. Could they have moved but Georges would have told her, wouldn't he?

Eleanor retired to a cafe and sat drinking coffee. What about the college course? Of course, neither of them had been attending classes recently. Georges saying he was too busy and Eleanor because of her parents' deaths. There was of course his grandmother's house; would she still be able to find it?

Studying the tube map, Eleanor walked down to Piccadilly Circus to pick up the line to Caledonian Road; Thornhill Square being a short walk from there. On the journey, Eleanor kept making excuses for Georges. His grandmother could have been taken seriously ill or even died, but why close the business? He could have gone bankrupt but not overnight surely? All the possibilities were sending her mad, just when she needed to keep her wits about her.

Checking her A-Z Eleanor found the Square and spotted the house with its big gates and Georgian exterior. Determined to get an explanation she marched up to the front door, rapped loudly on the knocker and rang the doorbell. Minutes went by but there was no sign of life. Determined to find someone Eleanor scouted round the back, remembering there were French windows in the drawing room leading to the garden. But peering in through the windows all she could see was an empty room – with not a stick of furniture. Hesitantly she tried the handles hoping against hope there wasn't a burglar alarm. Incredibly the doors weren't locked and she stepped inside.

Frantically running from room to room, Eleanor could find nothing and no one – not a scrap of paper or a shred of material. Could it be she was in the wrong house? And yet the layout was familiar. Here was where they sat down to that beautiful luncheon, and here in the drawing room she and Annette had chatted. Had there been something peculiar about that conversation? But what was it? She'd had far too much to drink, and her recollections of that day were very fuzzy.

Wandering upstairs Eleanor studied every room as if trying to magic up furniture that wasn't there. Then at last in one of the rooms a charred paper in the grate caught her attention. She picked it up. It was only a series of strange letters which meant nothing to her. Pocketing it, she left through the front door. It was certainly the right house, so where had Georges and his lovely grandmother gone? It was as if they'd been a figment of her imagination.

What a mystery. Eleanor wished she could make sense of it but there was one thing about it, she had no intention of telling anyone at work. She felt a bit of a fool having been so emotionally involved with Georges, and then finding she'd been discarded. It was if she'd meant nothing to him. This was how her parents had treated her, someone of no significance in their lives.

13

Late 1976

Life had been so eventful that Eleanor had quite forgotten that Donald was returning for a visit. She couldn't remember when he would be at his club, but no doubt he would contact her. She felt she'd lived a lifetime in the last week and a half, and was doing her best to avoid Claire and Barbara when they visited with provisions and offers of help, making excuses that she was tired and needed rest. The situation with Georges' and his grandmother's disappearance was so weird that Eleanor felt she needed time to herself to puzzle it all out.

There had been no further visits from Mr C. Although he'd been understanding Eleanor didn't want to remain the object of his scrutiny. He saw more than she wished him to know. A notification had arrived to inform her of her parents' cremations. Their ashes were to be scattered on the island as she'd instructed. It was as if they'd never existed. Utterly depressed by the letter and the state of her life Eleanor would have liked to retire to bed, pull the covers over her head and stay there forever blotting everything out.

Loud rapping on her kitchen door brought her back to the real world and wrapping her dressing gown tightly round her, she peered through the window. Donald stood there, bent over and breathless pleading, 'Eleanor, do let me in. It's freezing out here. I think I've done myself a mischief on your stairs. These old bones aren't what they used to be.'

Eleanor opened the door, and threw herself into his arms sobbing.

'Hey there my dear, it can't be as bad as all that.' Moving her back to the sitting room, Donald sat her down holding both her hands, 'What on earth has been going on? Last time you wrote you sounded so happy and settled.'

Crying uncontrollably and pouring out the story of the last weeks, Eleanor felt Donald was the nearest thing to family she had. Donald, a patient man, produced a snowy white handkerchief and attempted to dry her eyes.

Squinting through red puffy eyes, Eleanor asked, 'Are you shocked by the shop lifting? I'm so ashamed.'

'Of course not, I'm unshockable at my age. You seem to have suffered far too many ordeals for one so young. It's no wonder you're in a state. Tell me what I can do to help?'

'There's nothing to be done. My parents' affairs are sorted, and I have no idea where Georges or his grandmother are,' Eleanor said.

'Why don't you tell me about Georges and I'll see if we can piece the mystery together?'

Eleanor described going to Georges' office, then to Thornhill Square and the house.

'It was brave of you,' Donald remarked frowning, 'but foolhardy.'

109

'Whatever do you mean?' asked Eleanor, 'Georges and Annette are hardly criminals. They're both normal, charming people.'

'Did you find any signs at all that there had been someone living there recently?'

'No,' Eleanor said wearily, too tired to think and then remembered, 'there was a tiny scrap of paper in the grate with strange letters on it.'

Rummaging round the sideboard she found the scrap and passed it to him.

Donald peered at the letters, 'Yes, they look like some form of Cyrillic letters.'

'Georges spoke some sort of Slavonic language. I heard him in his office one day.'

'Could it have been Russian, do you think?' Donald asked thoughtfully.

'Maybe,' Eleanor said, 'but what does it matter? That scrap is probably a piece of some business papers he burned.' Impatiently she said, 'All I want to know is why they vanished? It's a puzzle and one I can't get to grips with.'

Donald looked at her shrewdly, 'I don't think we're going to be able to solve your mystery that easily, my dear. I'll make enquiries at my old firm, will that help?'

Eleanor said sharply, 'I thought you worked for the Civil Service not a firm?'

'You're quite right my dear, it was a term of speech. I did work for the Government – but of course I've been out of it a long time. I will see what I can do. In the meantime get dressed and I'll take you to lunch. Maybe that will take your mind off things.

A few days of entertainment and good company brightened Eleanor up considerably, though at the back of her mind she was still puzzling over the Georges' conundrum. It was as if there was something ominous waiting to happen. Could this be a legacy from her childhood; her father was always up to something nasty? But Donald was another matter; with him she could relax and enjoy herself.

Their days together sped by until it was time for Donald to return home and Eleanor to return to work. Several times Eleanor asked Donald if he had uncovered any information about Georges, but he was non committal. Eventually Eleanor became more forceful, and Donald had to admit he had nothing for her but strongly suggested she talk to Mr C. Eleanor was not keen, saying bluntly, 'I know he's been good to me. I'm grateful to him for rescuing me from the police but he makes me feel on edge. In fact, he frightens me sometimes, and I'm reluctant to tell him anything.'

Donald nodded, 'Trusting people can be hard and knowing which people to trust is even harder, but you can count on

111

me as long as I'm physically able,' he laughed jokingly and left it at that.

Eleanor resigned herself to going back to Sentry dreading her first day back. She needn't have worried; she was greeted with open arms. It was as if she'd returned after an illness, rather than been caught shoplifting. There was a bouquet of flowers on her desk, and a Welcome Card from staff that she'd never seen or heard of. Claire constantly fussed round her, giving her coffee and making small talk.

Mr C surfaced from his lair to check on her, saying, 'Now ease yourself back in slowly, young Eleanor. Take an early mark today to get you back in the swing of things.' His efforts at trying to act like one of the staff encouraged him to lapse into what he thought was the current vernacular but it hardly fitted his formal persona.

Eleanor acquiesced, glad to leave early and escape the creepiness; it was all a bit much. She wondered if it would be wiser to look for another job but she was in a difficult position. Was she prepared to take a massive drop in salary? A flat share or a bedsit was not an attractive proposition after her lovely flat.

14

Months went by and as autumn came round, Eleanor joined yet another evening class at City Lit. This time there was no Georges, and as it was a drama class it had more of a social feel. They were soon putting on one act plays and Eleanor was relishing pretending to be someone rather than herself. Work plodded on. She was doing her best to keep to herself, be grateful for the generous salary and the easy demands on her time, when she was called in to see Mr C. The great man hadn't been much in evidence since her shoplifting fiasco to Eleanor's enormous relief.

This time on entering his room she was surprised to be asked to sit down, 'Well Eleanor, I don't seem to have had much sight of you lately. You seem to be keeping a low profile,' he said, stroking his chin meditatively, 'perhaps that's sensible. I daresay you have recovered from that nasty incident by now?' He looked at her enquiringly.

Eleanor kept her mouth shut. She noticed he'd stopped calling her 'young Eleanor'. Was that a good sign or not?

'I've got a job for you. I think a pleasant one maybe a bit of a distraction. I have to attend a party at the British Embassy unfortunately Claire is unable to accompany me, so I wondered if this might be something you would enjoy. What do you think?'

Eleanor was thrilled to be asked answering instantly, 'I would love to go.' Barely able to contain herself, she said,

'But what do I have to do and what should I wear?'

'There's nothing for you to do but be your charming self. I will do any talking about Sentry if needed. These occasions are deadly dull but the food and drink is often pretty decent. Claire will fill you in and I'll send a car for you. That's all,' and there it was again the offhand dismissal, but Eleanor didn't care. This could be fun.

Claire explained evening dress would be required, and Eleanor reviewing her wardrobe found nothing suitable except the cursed little black dress she'd bought for Georges' dinner, and the cocktail number that Barbara had persuaded her to buy last year. Eleanor considered shopping but her anxieties shot through the roof. She couldn't face all that again and understanding her dilemma Claire said reassuringly, 'I have the very dress for you. What if I bring it to the flat tomorrow night and see if it fits you?'

The following evening, Claire arrived round with a beautiful sea green taffeta evening gown with an elaborately beaded bodice. Eleanor adored it, but trying it on thought it looks brand new and very expensive. She pranced about the flat, checking herself this way and that in a small hand mirror, 'Honestly Claire, I can't wear this. It looks as if you've never worn it. What if I spill something on it; it would cost a fortune to dry clean.'

Claire shrugged, 'It suits you wonderfully. It was bought for me but you're right I've never worn it, not my style, too

114

youthful. But it brings out the colour in your eyes. I'm sure you'll be careful with it. If the worst comes to the worst we'll have it cleaned. Now are your ready for the evening? Do you have a bag, shoes?'

Eleanor assured her that she had the accessories needed and barely slept that night. All through the week she fingered the dress, marvelling at the intricate work and the beautiful material. She half wondered what would be expected of her at this party. What if there were titled people there – how do you address a duke or a lord? She hoped Mr C would be nearby and not leave her to her own devices.

On the night, Eleanor left work early rushing home to bath and dress. She carefully pinned her should length blonde hair into the type of French pleat that Barbara had taught her, made up her face and then gently eased on the dress. She felt a million dollars. Adding bits of jewellery, bag, shoes, and fake fur wrap and checking herself in the mirror Eleanor felt transformed into a princess; it was like being Princess Grace on her wedding day.

The door bell shrilled urgently breaking her dream, and gingerly she manoeuvred her way down the staircase. Before her was a gleaming limousine complete with chauffeur who opened the door and helped her in. Easing back in the soft leather seat, Eleanor wondered where Mr C was. She hadn't thought to ask; perhaps he was meeting her there.

Once they'd pulled into the gates of the Embassy, the

chauffeur helped her out of the car and Mr C came down the steps to meet her. 'Well Eleanor, you certainly scrub up well,' he beamed and offered his arm. Eleanor was hesitant about taking it – but had no choice. What was there about this man that made her uncomfortable? He had been nothing but kind to her.

They were offered drinks by the butler, and then moved down the receiving line to meet the Ambassador and his wife. Eleanor wondered if she should curtsey but no, that was just for royalty. She bobbed her head instead. The Ambassador's wife greeted her warmly remarking to Mr C, 'Jonah, what a delightful protégée, I didn't think the Service recruited them so young.' Her husband gave her a nudge and glared at her mumbling, 'Careful dear, there are ears everywhere.'

Eleanor couldn't get over Mr C being called Jonah. What an unusual name. The only Jonah she'd heard of was Jonah and the Whale from the Bible. Wasn't he unlucky or something? But the Ambassador's wife remark was disconcerting. What Service was she referring to?

All through the evening, Eleanor was introduced to crowds of people - ministers, ambassadors, princes, industrialists, businessmen and diplomats. It was a revelation for a girl from the country. Much of the conversation was over her head but she smiled and answered questions when addressed, with her face becoming stiff from all the smiling. Eventually Mr C looking down at her said, 'I think you need

116

a break. There's a charming young Swedish diplomat I'd like you to meet.'

Eleanor was not at all sure and muttered, 'Does he speak English?'

'Oh he has perfect English my dear; he was educated in this country.'

They wove their way through the crowds towards a tall blonde young man with film star looks, 'Erik, I would like you to meet Eleanor who works for me. Eleanor, meet Erik Andersson from Stockholm. Erik works for the Swedish Embassy in London. I'm sure you two will find plenty to talk about,' and with that brief introduction Mr C evaporated into the crowd.

Eleanor grinned apologetically at the young man, who bowed gravely over her hand, 'Don't look so anxious, Eleanor; I was dying to meet you the moment you came into the room. You're like a breath of Spring in that dress - such a change from all those matronly ladies in their dark dresses.' Offering his arm he said, 'Shall we go into supper? Meeting all these people must have given you an appetite.'

Eleanor realised she was ravenous. She hadn't any food since leaving home and been on her feet for two hours. They moved into the dining room, sitting at a small table away from the main traffic. Erik said, 'They have a wonderful buffet here. Shall I go and get you a plate?'

117

Eleanor could barely speak, her feet in these heels were killing her, but being waited on by this striking young man was definitely a novelty. He returned with plates laden with food and a bottle of champagne, saying, 'I didn't know what you liked so I've brought a bit of everything.' He uncorked the champagne with panache pouring them both glasses as they launched into the food without a word.

Feeling revived and refreshed, Eleanor said, 'I hear you were educated in England. How did that come about?'

'My parents were in government service and travelled a lot. They sent me to boarding school here when I was quite young, and I was only able to go home for the holidays.'

Eleanor continued to ask endless questions about Sweden and Stockholm, and the pair soon found they were getting on well. Although Erik asked a lot of questions in return, Eleanor avoided talking about Sentry, her parents or her background.

Towards the end of the evening he said, 'I would like to see you again, Eleanor. Perhaps you could show me some of the London I haven't seen so far.'

Eleanor, only too happy to agree, gave him her home number. By then she could see Mr C waiting at the door gesturing to her and said, 'I must go, it was lovely to meet you Erik,' adding artlessly, 'I do hope I see you again.'

Erik stood up and escorted her to Mr C – bowing over her

hand and looking deeply into her startled eyes.

In the car Mr C said, 'I see you got on well with Erik. I think he may be taken with you.'

Eleanor demurred, 'He was just being kind as this was all new to me, and I was out of my depth.'

'I think you underestimate your charms, my dear Eleanor,' was Mr C's response as he dropped her at the flat.

15

The next week was a letdown after returning to work and giving back the dress. Claire was avid for details, suggesting Eleanor hold on to the dress in case she went to other events. But Eleanor was adamant. She'd decided when something was not her property it would be returned to its rightful owner. Honesty was the best policy for her in the future.

Erik wasted no time in ringing and suggesting they go out to dinner. Eleanor was reluctant; she didn't want a rerun of Georges. However Erik was determined to wear her down, sending roses to the office, chocolates and even bottles of champagne. Surprisingly enough no one remarked on any of this or made jokes at her expense – it was as if it was expected. Paddy on one of his odd visits said ominously, 'Someone's keen on you me darlin,' and with a more sombre look, 'and if you can't be good, be careful, very, very careful indeed.'

Dinner with Erik was entertaining. He was good company, a man of the world. Eleanor felt childlike and unsophisticated beside him. They found they both enjoyed flea markets, antiques and art, and every weekend Eleanor was walked round the smaller more obscure galleries in London. It was as if the educational path Donald had started her on was to be continued by Erik. Eleanor's social life with Georges had revolved around eating out, the cinema and theatre. Now she was introduced to music, opera and paintings and she lapped it up. Aware of how limited her schooling had been,

Eleanor hung on Erik's every word and he was flattered.

He said teasingly, 'One of these days you must come up and see **my** etchings. I think you're ready for the rest of your education, what do you think?' But Eleanor just grinned as if she didn't know what he meant. Her relationship with Georges had been bordering on the platonic with the odd kiss thrown in, and she wasn't sure she wanted anything more as yet.

After a month or so Mr C asked to see her, casually he asked, 'How are you getting on with Erik? Are you still seeing him?'

Eleanor didn't want to tell him. Was it really any of his business? But thinking better of it she replied, 'Yes, we do see one another. Is that a problem?'

'No, of course not, I'm pleased you have someone to spend time with. Keep enjoying yourself the way you are.'

…

Once Eleanor had left the room, Mr C made a call, 'Caruthers here. Yes, we have the target in our sights. The cultivation is progressing. No, she knows nothing of it. I'm not sure how far we should let it run with her. We didn't have anyone else available at that short notice. We do need someone more experienced but for now the target is hooked...... Yes, I do understand the urgency. These things take time. Of course sir, I'll be in touch.'

As the weeks went by Eleanor started to enjoy Erik's attentions more. Georges had been lovely but changeable and moody. Erik was all sunshine, smiles and charm, in fact, oodles of charm. He was always complimenting her on her clothes and her looks, and she began to take more trouble with her appearance. There were new outfits and new hairstyles; even Claire was disconcerted. She raised her eyebrows almost to her hairline one day when Eleanor came to work in a shimmering gold silk blouse, her hair in a chignon, saying, 'Eleanor, I don't think that's quite suitable for the office. You look as if you're going to a party or the theatre.'

Eleanor was unconcerned and said, 'I'm being taken to lunch at the Savoy, and I won't have time to change first,' and bent her head over her work. She and Claire had an uneven relationship – sometimes it was sweetness and light all giggling and laughing, and at other times disinterest and frostiness. Eleanor would have liked her as a friend, but closeness was impossible.

On this particular day Eleanor's mind was absorbed with Erik. Idly she wondered what it would be like to live in Sweden. How would she cope with the language? Before she could stop herself, she was doodling 'Mrs. Eleanor Andersson' on her blotter. How juvenile this was when she barely knew Erik, she ripped the sheet off, scrunched it up and threw it in the waste bin.

At lunch Erik said, 'You still haven't been to my flat. It's just down the road from here, please do come and see it for yourself, darling,' he leered. Embarrassed, Eleanor laughed it off. She wasn't ready to be alone with Erik. It seemed crazy to have considered being married to him earlier, and now be hesitant about going to his flat. He noticed her confusion, and said soothingly, 'I'm only joking. There's plenty of time for us to get to know one another better.' Patting her hand, he continued, 'I must get back to work and so must you. We'll meet at the weekend, shall we? I'll ring you at the end of the week.'

Eleanor was relieved. What sort of relationship did she want? It was difficult to know. Who could she discuss it with? There was Barbara but Eleanor had avoided her since the shoplifting incident. The girls at the drama group were older and they would probably laugh at her. She could hardly write and ask Donald's advice. That only left Claire, and that was out of the question. It was curious to be in the heart of the metropolis surrounded by people and still be isolated and alone. If only she was less gauche.

A week later any decision about whether or not to visit Erik's flat was taken out of her hands. Summoned to Mr C's inner sanctum, he said, 'Eleanor, I wonder if you would do me the greatest of favours and deliver this package,' he pointed to a large well wrapped parcel tied with string and tape.

Eleanor was only too willing to agree. She owed Mr C a lot. If she could do something for him in return at least it would make her feel less obligated.

'Where do you want me to take it?'

'To that young man you've been seeing, Erik Andersson. It's to go to his flat in Covent Garden. I wouldn't ask, but it's by way of being a gift from an important friend in Sweden who asked us to hand deliver it. It's very valuable.'

Eleanor bit her lip and said, 'Wouldn't it be better to deliver it to the Swedish Embassy. Erik will be working. I'm not sure I should be responsible for something valuable?'

'As it happens,' Mr C said authoritatively, 'Erik is at home today. He's unwell. This will be a welcome surprise for him; it's something he will really like.'

Eleanor, not able to find further excuses, reassured herself that it being mid morning there should be no problem visiting Erik's flat. After all it was business.

A taxi was arranged and clutching the bulky parcel Eleanor arrived at Erik's building. The doorman doffed his cap to her stating 'Mr Andersson is in residence', and called the lift for her. On the third floor Eleanor looked for Flat 6, feeling in her gut this was a bad idea. What would Erik think of her turning up unannounced?

She needn't have worried. Erik opened the door resplendent in a wine coloured brocade dressing gown and beamed with pleasure at seeing her, 'Oh, you've come to minister to the sick, how wonderful. Come in, come in, my darling, and you've brought me an early Christmas present.'

Eleanor attempted to explain about the package but he was too heated and over excited to take in what she said. He tore into the parcel, ripping the paper to shreds, and exposing a rather stark, modern painting which he examined hungrily, breathless with enthusiasm, ' I can't believe, I can't believe it, you've found me a genuine Axel Kargel. What an amazing girl you are! However did you know?' Without giving Eleanor a chance to speak he grabbed hold of her, raining kisses on her like a man possessed, 'My darling, my darling, you don't know how I've longed for this moment. We can finally be together and with this amazing painting. It's too much.'

Erik was holding her so tightly and kissing her with such fervour that Eleanor was suffocating, unable to breathe. She struggled weakly against his strength but he seemed to have summoned up an astonishing amount of vigour for a sick man.

Finally Eleanor drawing on all her might shoved him off her with one massive push. He appeared to lose balance momentarily, rocking backwards and forwards and then as if in slow motion began to topple and fall, his hands grabbing at the empty air, his eyes beseeching her for help. There was a loud crack.

The glass coffee table he'd fallen on exploded like a gunshot, slices and splinters of glass shooting high in the air.

Eleanor was frozen to the spot - too stunned to move. The crashing went on and on and then stopped. Erik was left exposed drowning in a sea of debris, a shard of glass embedded deep in his throat. Eleanor finally came to her senses and bent over him. Without thinking she reacted - pulling hard on the shard. Out it came, followed by a volcanic geyser of blood that shot straight in her face. Desperate to staunch the blood, Eleanor grabbed a nearby tablecloth but it was too late; there was nothing to be done. Erik's earlier excited feverish eyes were blank, his body lifeless. He was gone.

Eleanor felt sick. What on earth had happened? How had she killed him? All she'd done was push him away. What was she going to do now? Who could help her this time? It would have to be the police and probably prison. She wanted to run and hide. Maybe that's what she should do - disappear altogether but where? The only place she'd ever felt safe was her old convent school in Dorset. It was the one place she'd been happy as a child. There was no school there now of course – but surely the nuns would take her in. She had a right to sanctuary.

But what about Sentry and Mr C, they knew she was here. The doorman had seen her too. Not aware that she was crying and on the verge of hysteria Eleanor wiped away her tears thinking, 'I must be practical'. Stepping over Erik's body to make her way to his bathroom, Eleanor thought she was going to vomit. But the sight of herself in the bathroom mirror was even more of a shock. A blood soaked ashen face looked back at her through wild staring eyes. Doing her best to clean herself and her blood spattered clothes up Eleanor decided to ring the office, say she was unwell and was going straight home.

At Sentry, a stranger answered the phone so it was easy to tell a convincing lie and be believed. Eleanor now had to get out of the building without bumping into the doorman. There must be a back exit. Letting herself out of the flat and avoiding looking at the body, Eleanor made for the stairs. She ran down as fast as she could go, ending up in the underground car park and the exit. It was risky to go back to the flat for a change of clothes. She had no choice she would have to go as she was and hope the nuns took pity on her.

Sitting on the tube to Waterloo Eleanor could see people staring at her, her stained coat and bedraggled appearance. They probably thought she was a 'druggie' or a 'down and out'. How have I ended up like this, she thought, when everything was beginning to sort itself out?

SANCTUARY AND SECLUSION

16

Dorset, December 1976

Later that day after a four hour train ride from London Eleanor arrived at the convent. She had used her last few pounds on the ticket to Weymouth, and trudged the last five miles in the freezing rain. Her thin coat was more suited to the London climate. The newly bought stilettos pinched and rubbed her heels. Her fair hair was lank and dripping and the remnants of her original makeup had run down her cheeks in black streaks, combining with the tears she had shed on the journey. She had no idea of the welcome she could expect or if she would be admitted.

Pulling on the bell, Eleanor could hear the sound of running feet and one of the nuns peered through the grille. A lever was pushed and the door swung open. 'Come in,' was the greeting – and Eleanor obeyed gratefully, dripping her way into the dark interior. What should she say about what she had done or why she was there? Before she could conjure up a reasonable explanation she was ushered along an even darker and gloomier passageway to an oak door.

A formidable rather stern-faced woman in a white wimple and habit stood behind a carved mahogany desk smiling stiffly, 'I am the Mother Superior. Come in my dear, travellers are welcome. We ask no questions here.'

Eleanor was grateful for that. The last thing she wanted to do was talk about the morning's events. Sighing heavily it was as if a great sense of relief overwhelmed her. This could be a bolthole.

'Please sit down,' the nun invited. Shivering and stammering through chattering teeth Eleanor said, 'I'm Eleanor ....I need.......place to stay........ safe, hidden, secret. I went to school here...... all I could think of,' and tailed off.

Mother Superior laughed raucously showing a set of perfect white teeth, 'We are certainly a place of safety, and possibly could be described as hidden and secret. Stay as long as you need.'

'What should I call you,' Eleanor breathed indistinctly.

'Oh Mother, will do. Everyone calls me that. We don't have titles as you may remember. Would you like to see your room? It will be mealtime soon. You must be hungry. The supper bell will summon you.'

Eleanor was shown into a small sparse room with a plain trestle bed under the window, one chair, a crucifix on the wall and a no nonsense wardrobe. The only luxuries if you could call them that were a multicoloured knitted rug by the bed, a small bedside cabinet and a lamp. However the one and only window faced west filling the room with late afternoon light, and permitting Eleanor a view of the garden. The little nun who accompanied her hardly spoke, gesturing to the wardrobe where various sets of clothes were hanging, and departed saying she would be back when the bell rang.

Peeling off her drenched coat, shoes, and stockings, and sitting on the hard mattress, a bemused Eleanor tried to gather her thoughts - of all places to end up in a convent, but there had been nowhere else to go. Feebly she rifled through the clothes, finding a white shirt and pinafore dress. None of the shoes fitted but at the back of the cupboard Eleanor found lace up boots in her size. What did it matter what she wore? Her life was over.

At supper the nuns greeted her warmly as if she had been expected. They gathered round a large refectory table with Mother at the head, tenderly placing Eleanor in their midst – ensuring she was served with homemade bread and vegetable soup. Eleanor was struck dumb, barely nodding or acknowledging their efforts.   The morning's scene kept replaying in her mind; the sound of the cracking glass; the image of the dagger in his throat and the blood, all that blood.   Barely able to swallow Eleanor could feel the glass stabbing her own throat, making her choke on every mouthful.

After a while the nuns let her be, and began talking amongst themselves about their day's work. They introduced themselves explaining what they did. 'I'm Sister Theresa; I work in the garden. I'm Sister Mary Agnes; I make the jams and chutneys from our own vegetables. We sell some of the produce and store the rest for winter. I'm Sister Ursula; I bake the bread and do the cooking.' They made little jokes against themselves whilst the others roared with laughter. Reluctantly Eleanor began to unwind and attempt a smile, though her face felt stiff and unwieldy. Mother Superior intervened at last saying, 'Now everyone back to work. Eleanor needs rest.'

Returning to her room Eleanor felt she'd done the right thing by coming here, though nothing seemed the same as when she was here as a schoolgirl. None of the nuns were familiar. That in itself was unusual as nuns generally stayed in the same convent until they died. The layout of the place was different as well. Too exhausted to think, Eleanor lay on the bed and slept.

The following days passed in a dream. The peaceful routine of the convent lulled Eleanor into a kind of soporific trance. The nuns carried out their duties interspersed with prayers in the chapel, and there was silence with little communication. The afternoons allowed a period of talking and conversation, but even this was carried out in muted voices.

Eleanor was never asked to participate in the work but would hesitantly offer saying, 'Please let me collect the eggs today, I'm used to hens,' or 'Do let me make the pastry; I was told I have cool hands.' The nuns would willingly step back smiling and allowing her more and more participation. They never praised her efforts but neither did they criticise or reprimand her. Helping out meant Eleanor had less time to remember the outside world, and it became a blessing. There was a lot of preparation for Christmas and Eleanor was able to keep herself busy.

At first Eleanor found it difficult to differentiate between the nuns. Their dark habits blended together as a group with their arms and legs constantly in motion. Eventually she started to recognise individual personalities.

Mary Agnes was one of her favourites. She was about Eleanor's age and had an air of serenity about her that never faltered. Her smile was contagious. When she laughed it sounded like tinkling bells. Drawn to Eleanor she would choose to sit next to her in the Recreation period, working away on some religious tapestry. She never asked Eleanor direct questions but managed to elicit all sorts of information from her, by remarking on Eleanor's state of mind: 'Eleanor, you seem a little upset today.' Eleanor acknowledged this, unwillingly admitting, 'I don't know. I can't stop thinking about what I've done, and what will happen to me.'

Mary Agnes kept her head down seeming to concentrate on her work, and Eleanor found herself continuing, 'Since I've been here, I wonder sometimes if I believe in God, even if there is such a person. If there is, will he forgive me?'

Mary Agnes looked up sighing, 'Eleanor, no one can make you believe in God. You have to decide for yourself. If we regret what we've done, and many of us here certainly do,' she said almost forcibly, 'forgiveness will follow. Everyone deserves redemption and a second chance, maybe more than one. I know I do, considering my past,' she added biting her lip hard.

Eleanor was taken aback to hear the nun express herself with such passion and so personally. Maybe there was a tiny glimmer of hope for her too. After all you could always trust a nun, couldn't you?

17

Early 1977

Christmas at the convent had been celebrated with great simplicity but with such love and devotion, Eleanor wished she could stay forever. However after weeks of robotic oblivion Eleanor's fears and anxieties started breaking through. Night after night she dreamed about Erik as if she was talking to him, and trying to hold on to him but he was slipping further and further away, his body dissolving piece by piece until he vanished, leaving her holding his throbbing heart in her bloodied hands.

One night sweating her way through the nightmare and waking abruptly in the early hours of the morning, Eleanor decided to go in search of hot milk. Feeling quite at home in the convent kitchen no one would question her. But when she went to open her bedroom door it wouldn't budge.

Pulling hard on the handle it appeared to be locked, in fact she was locked in. Panic rushed over her, and Eleanor began banging on the door hysterically shouting, 'Someone. Help, help I'm locked in. Let me out, let me out. I need to get out. I can't take anymore.'

It was as if the shock and distress of Erik's death had finally surfaced and she'd lost control. There was the sound of running; a key turning in the lock and Eleanor all but fell into the arms of Mother Superior. Surprisingly Mother wasn't dressed in her usual habit or even a dressing gown, but wearing a dark tracksuit, her hair bound back under some sort of covering. She was distinctly fractious saying in a harsh voice, 'What's all this fuss about? You'll wake the whole convent.' However noting Eleanor's terrified face, she changing tack saying gently, 'My child let me take you along to my room. You'll be comfortable there. We can't have you wandering the corridors at night. Perhaps a whiskey might be in order, what do you think?'

Eleanor allowed herself to be supported along the corridor, though at a rapid pace and was soon seated on Mother Superior's overstuffed ancient sofa with a glass in her hand. 'Drink up and stay there, Eleanor. Don't move on any account. I have business to see to. I'll be back shortly,' Mother commanded as she rushed off down the corridor.

Eleanor knocked back the drink. Her nightmare began to recede. Revived Eleanor felt some stirrings of curiosity. There'd been no explanation as to why she'd been locked in her bedroom. Mother was hardly behaving in character. Why was she dressed like that and racing around during the Great Silence?

Having no intention of sitting meekly till Mother's return, Eleanor crept to the oak door and inched it open. What she saw astounded her. Reverend Mother, Sister Mary Agnes and Sister Ursula were half dragging a very dishevelled man down the corridor. He was either drugged or drunk and they were heaving him around like a sack of potatoes. This couldn't be anything to do with their charity work not in the middle of the night. There'd never been any men in the convent since Eleanor's arrival not even a priest.

Not knowing what to make of it, Eleanor decided to follow them. The corridor was dark enough only lit by the odd wall light. Eleanor grabbed the habit hanging behind the door and threw it round her. The trio were making such slow progress she had to lag behind. Eventually they moved into the chapel but unfortunately it was flooded with moonlight so Eleanor was forced to take refuge in the back pews. She could still see them clearly.

They were moving purposefully toward the back of the altar. There was a grinding noise and after a moment or two, obviously having deposited their burden, the three of them moved rapidly back up the aisle. Eleanor had to take to her heels arriving breathlessly back at Mother's room, throwing off the habit and trying to compose herself.

The first thing Mother did was apologise, 'Dear Eleanor, am sorry to have left you for so long. We sometimes have dirty work to do at night hence my clothes. How are you feeling?' Eleanor described her nightmare and subsequent panic at being locked in. Mother dismissed it all saying 'It's only to be expected.' It was as if somehow she was familiar with Eleanor's history and her recent trauma. Giving a glib explanation of how Eleanor's door had been locked by mistake, Mother assured Eleanor it wouldn't happen again.

There was no further allusion to the night's work but she

136

insisted on escorting Eleanor back to bed, telling her to sleep as late as she liked.

…

Georges came round with a start, having no idea where he was. It was if he'd been walled up. He was lying on a concrete floor, walls pressing in on him on every side with only a thin sliver of light showing along the edge of the floor. Alarmed he tried to stand up, lurching against the nearest wall. Touching the back of his head, he felt blood dripping down his face and on to his arm. Pushing at the walls in the direction of the light, he tried to see if anything moved but there was nothing. Utterly depleted, he was forced to lie back down and hope someone would come soon.

The last thing he remembered was boarding the boat train for Calais. After that it was a blank. Assuming he'd be safer in France than London, he'd packed his belongings and fled. No one knew where he was going not even Vasily, so who had tracked him down and how? Hoping against hope he wouldn't be subjected to torture; Georges closed his eyes, visualising his home in Provence, the cypresses, the orchards, and the sun beating down on him.

The sound of grating metal on brick shocked him back into the present. Part of one of the walls slid open. Georges shielding his eyes against the brightness of the light, tried to make out the figure standing there.

A harsh voice said quietly, 'It's Anubis, Georges. The others will be here soon. I thought I'd come ahead. It's a shame you let yourself be caught. I did warn you about consequences. So it's finale time for you mon cher, I'm afraid. We can't have you talking, can we? Who knows what you'd tell them?'

Georges cowered back into the corner and shut his eyes waiting for the bullet.

Anubis laughed hollowly as if he'd read his mind, 'Oh no Georges, not in here, a bullet would ricochet and who knows where it would end up? No, I think an injection will do the trick,' and before Georges could make a sound, a needle was thrust deep into his thigh.

'It'll take no time at all,' Anubis consoled him as he slipped out quietly.

Georges was dead in seconds.

18

Since the night time incident Eleanor no longer felt safe at the convent. She knew she must get away. Not sure whether she was wanted by the police, and fearful of being recognised she determined to be resourceful.

Taking Sister Mary Agnes into her confidence Eleanor said, 'I feel so much better today; I would like to go into Weymouth if anyone is going. The sea air will do me good.'

Mary Agnes looked doubtful, 'I'm not sure what Mother Superior would say; perhaps we should ask permission.'

Eleanor retaliated, 'I'm not a prisoner here, am I? Nor am I a nun. I have the freedom to do what I like.'

Mary Agnes smiled ruefully, 'None of us are free to do as we like, Eleanor. We all have to answer to someone but I will arrange for you to go in with Sister Ursula when she does the weekly shop. Will that satisfy you?'

Eleanor was triumphant. At last she could find out about Erik's death, and if there were any repercussions for her. Sister Ursula was a large, heavy boned woman who looked as if she should be driving a tractor instead of a minivan. Any conversation Eleanor attempted on the journey was greeted with sullen responses. When they reached Weymouth and parked, Ursula said grumpily, 'You can help me with the shopping Eleanor, and if we have time we can take a walk on the promenade.'

But Eleanor was having none of it, 'No thanks. I've errands to run. I'll see you back here in two hours,' and before Ursula could respond, she hurried off down the street. Spotting the library Eleanor carefully hid her face in her scarf. She needn't have worried about being seen; it was empty except for an old man snuffling and snorting away in a corner. Picking out the nationals and the London papers Eleanor scanned them carefully. But there was nothing. Not so much as a short paragraph about Erik's death. Perplexed and to gain some peace of mind Eleanor knew she must contact the Swedish Embassy as a last resort, but how? She had no money and could hardly ask Ursula or borrow some from passersby. There was one telephone at the convent but it was in Mother Superior's room.

Joining Sister Ursula again for their return to the convent the nun was even more morose, 'Where've you been?' she demanded.

'Oh here and there,' Eleanor responded noncommittally.

'Mother will want to know,' Ursula said threateningly.

'Well, it's for me to know, and for her to find out,' Eleanor quipped defiantly.

Her attitude to the convent and the nuns had changed drastically. There was no way Eleanor was going to allow herself to be bullied by Mother or Sister Ursula. Whatever they were up to that night was certainly not nuns' work and

Eleanor's respect for them had rapidly diminished.

Astonishingly back at the convent, Mother made no comment on seeing Eleanor alight from the van. She merely acknowledged them both and continued about her business, betraying her displeasure by a slight tightening of the lips.

During the rest of the day Eleanor was on tenterhooks, waiting for an opportunity to use the telephone. Once afternoon tea break was over and the nuns started moving to Vespers, Eleanor grabbed her chance. She sneaked into Mother Superior's office and shut the door. Lifting the receiver she called the operator. There was a minute or two's delay and a voice asked what number she required, Eleanor practically whispered, 'The Swedish Embassy.' When the Embassy switchboard answered, Eleanor asked for Erik Andersson. There was a palpable pause and a woman's voice said, 'I'm sorry Mr Andersson is on extended leave. Please, who is calling?'

Eleanor slammed down the phone in alarm. He couldn't be alive could he? He was certainly dead when she left him. Someone must have checked his flat. What was going on?

The telephone rang. Eleanor still standing right beside it nearly jumped out of her skin. What if one of the nuns heard it and came running? Vespers must be almost over. Should she answer it, and pretend she was just passing the room? Picking up the receiver she held her hand over her mouth, and said a muffled 'Hullo'. The other end said, 'Who am I talking to? Is that you, Mother? We need an update urgently on our mutual friend.' Eleanor said nothing and hung up.

She was a bag of nerves now and glad to get back to the shelter of her room. Who was 'the mutual friend' they were talking about? Could it be the man from that night, and if so where was he? To think she'd come to the convent for sanctuary and there were all these unsettling things happening.

Perhaps they weren't real nuns at all despite carrying out their rituals of prayers and Mass. Thinking of Mass; Eleanor had never seen a priest officiating or even taking confession. That evening Eleanor was glad to get to bed at eight thirty after the Night Prayer.

Unusually Mary Agnes tapped on her door to enquire whether she was alright, 'You must have had an exhausting time in Weymouth Eleanor. I must say you do look rather strained. Is there anything I can get for you?'

'No Mary Agnes, I'm absolutely fine. It was probably more tiring than I thought going out for the first time. I just need an early night,' and Eleanor shut the door firmly.

19

Mother Superior had kept her temper in check until after Eleanor had retired to bed, and then incensed with rage confronted both Mary Agnes and Ursula, 'I don't know how you allowed her to go outside the convent without telling me,' and turning the full force of her wrath on Ursula, 'and of all things losing her in Weymouth. Goodness knows what she got up to. Having a dead agent on our hands is enough of a problem let alone anything else. I don't know what I'm going to tell London. Heads will certainly roll over this fiasco. Now get to your duties and watch her for all your worth. I'll have to ring the office.'

Once connected to Sentry, Mother Superior was in no mood to mince words, 'Now look here Mr C, things are in one almighty mess here. We need one of your people to clean up as soon as. It's not convenient having that girl here. She was passive enough to start with but she's beginning to notice things, and she managed to disappear for two hours on her own in Weymouth. Yes, I know **he** wanted her to stay longer, but that's not possible now. She'll have to go, the sooner the better.'

…

In the next weeks, life in the convent went on as before though Eleanor did start to discern a certain coolness towards her. The friendliness and openness had gone. It was as if she was tolerated rather than welcomed. Even Mary

Agnes avoided her during Recreation, making excuses and saying she had no time to talk as there was too much to do.

Eleanor kept thinking about how to leave. Where could she go especially with no money? The only people she knew were tied to Sentry. She'd stopped writing to Donald since the incident and though she knew he would help his relationship with Barbara made it impossible. If only Georges was around, what an odd boyfriend he'd turned out to be vanishing like that. Her relationships hadn't been promising so far, either with her parents, friends or boyfriends. Was she destined to spend life on her own?

It was no good feeling miserable Eleanor decided. There was nothing for it but she must take matters into her own hands. Whatever the convent was doing she must find out before she left. Up till now she'd kept her head in the sand disregarding even the mysterious goings on in London. She'd wanted to pretend everything was normal despite running away at the first opportunity. It was time to confront her fears. Later tonight when everyone had gone to bed she would investigate the chapel and search for the mystery man.

However her resolve came too late. That afternoon Mother Superior summoned Eleanor.

'I've been thinking my dear about your situation; I think it would be a good idea if you talked to someone outside the convent, someone you could confide in, a counsellor. To that end I've called upon one of our visiting clerics, a lovely priest called Father Patrick. He'll be arriving later this afternoon. I'm sure he can be of help to you.'

Eleanor shook her head, 'I don't see how he can help. You know I'm not a Catholic. I'm not interested in Confession.'

'I know that my dear, and that's why I think a friendly chat will not go amiss,' Mother said in an uncompromising voice, 'I will give you both the use of my room when he arrives. You may go now and have lunch. I will let you know when you are required.' Mother's manner made it clear there was nothing more to be said. Eleanor was hardly bothered about chatting to some ancient priest. She was more interested in anticipating her night time adventure.

At teatime Eleanor got the call to return to Reverend Mother's office. She tapped gently on the door and went in. To her complete astonishment she was grabbed in a great bear hug, lifted off her feet and swung round. Never Paddy – surely not him! But there he was, large as life, dressed in a cassock and collar, 'Well well mavourneen, surprised to see me, and looking like this.'

Eleanor choked hysterically, her breathing becoming louder and more laboured. Paddy slapped her hard on the back pushing her down in the nearest chair and pouring her a glass of water, 'Sure an all it's a bit of a panic attack, and me with no paper bag to hand. Hold your whist, darling, 'tis the shock. Have a drink. Breathe slowly. I'll see if the old besom

145

has a touch of the hard stuff anywhere's about.'

Eleanor still couldn't recover, getting whiter and whiter in the face. Paddy pushed her head between her knees. Tracking down the whiskey, he held a glass to her trembling mouth. 'There, there,' he soothed, 'everything will be alright little Eleanor, you'll see. Take a little more. You'll be feeling fine and dandy before you know it.'

Eleanor pushed the glass away, coughing furiously, but her colour was returning, and Paddy studied her carefully as he relaxed his grip and settled her back in the chair.

'Well and all, I didn't think seeing me would give you such an upset, me darlin. I am a thoughtless monster.'

Eleanor managed to stammer out, 'But how is it you're here Paddy? I don't understand. You're not a real priest are you?'

'O course not, me darlin – just a bit of disguise for old Paddy. Nothing is as it seems, take my word for it. There's no need to worry your sweet self. I've come to rescue you, and take you back.'

'Back where?' Eleanor queried.

'Back to your family at Sentry of course. You didn't think we'd forget you, did you? Don't we always look out for you? Mr C sent me down especially to collect you and sort out some business.'

'But how did you know I was here, and-----,'Eleanor

146

hesitated leaving a long pause, 'and what about what I've done?'

'You mean Erik; don't worry your pretty head, that's all done and dusted. It was an accident after all, wasn't it? It certainly looked like one. His body's been dispatched back to Sweden. Everything's been taken care of.'

Her head in her hands Eleanor said, 'But surely I'm wanted by the police. I don't understand. There was no sign of his death in the papers. I even telephoned his Embassy; they said he was on extended leave.'

Paddy chortled in a macabre way, 'Well he is certainly that alright, very much extended. Don't get yourself in a state; Mr C will explain everything to you when we get back to London. I just have to see to my other business first and we'll be off.'

Eleanor roused herself briskly, 'Now look here, Paddy, I'm not at all sure I want to go back to London with you and what is your other business here? Is it something to do with that man I saw dragged in here the other night? What goes on in this place? It's not a real convent is it?'

'Hush there child, you've seen a touch too much for my liking. That man's in absolutely no danger from me. You could say he's having a little holiday with us now,' Paddy laughed wryly. As for the convent, do you not see the nuns at their prayers and devotions; sure we wouldn't want to

147

upset their routine would we? We at Sentry add a little flavour to the place, using it as a rest home for some of our unhappier clients. And as for you not coming back with me,' he smiled broadly and ruefully, twinkling his eyes as if to soften the harshness of his next words, 'let's face it acushla, you have nowhere to go, no money, no friends, what choices do you have?' and throwing the door open so it vibrated on its hinges, he rushed off down the corridor in his usual bombastic manner.

Eleanor sat there pensively. Finally getting up and moving, it was if she'd been through some great ordeal. Her limbs were stiff and heavy, literally weighing her down. Trudging disconsolately back to her room she felt like an old lady.

There was no option but to return to London. Certainly there was no chance of running away again if Sentry was always watching her. If that was the case and they had known all along where she was, why had they left her to stew here? Who was Sentry? Eleanor wished she'd never heard of them. She felt like a fly caught in a web.

The return journey was smooth enough with Paddy alternating between singing Irish songs and telling questionable jokes, trying to make Eleanor unwind. He tugged at his dog collar and threw it forcefully out of the window mumbling, 'That's that old thing for now.'

All Eleanor could think about were the last stilted goodbyes at the convent. Mother Superior had said, 'My dear, you've

148

been a breath of fresh air here. We wish you well, God Bless,' in such an insincere fashion that Eleanor had wanted to throw up. She was never going to thank them for their hospitality when it was all clearly a front. None of the other nuns bothered to turn up not even Sister Mary Agnes, who probably wasn't any sort of friend at all.

Insulating herself from Paddy's jollity Eleanor shrank into herself and wondered what fate awaited her in London. Would this be another new start, and what would Mr Caruthers say to her this time?

Back in London it was almost the start of yet another Christmas. The streets were bustling with shoppers. The decorations were up, and store windows were full of farfetched fantasies of Father Christmas, sleighs and fake snow. Eleanor couldn't believe she'd been away so long or had it been that long? The days in the convent had merged into one another and with all the praying, the routines and chapel, it was difficult to tell day from night.

Eleanor had missed London; it was the centre of the universe as far as she was concerned. There was always an air of excitement about the city as if it was waiting for something to happen. However this time there was no tingle of anticipation of pleasures to come, all she felt was a tremor of fear running down her spine and a sick feeling. Paddy looked across at her as he wended his way through the busy streets, saying, 'Don't worry, me little darlin, all will be fine. I'll get you back to your cosy flat. Your salary's been going into your bank account on a regular basis. Go out and buy yourself something nice, and settle back in as if you've never been away.'

Eleanor was relieved to be home. She'd had visions of torture chambers or being locked in a padded cell, starved and interrogated, but Paddy dropped her off in the mews with a laconic, 'See you later mauvoureen,' and without waiting to see if she'd found her key, drove off like a bat out of hell.

Eleanor climbed the staircase and opened her door. Everything was the same though it looked as if it had been cleaned recently. All the surfaces sparkled and it was wonderfully tidy. On the table was a vase with a huge display of winter flowers and a card. Eleanor bent to read it. It said plainly in big black intimidating letters, 'Welcome back from all at Sentry.'

CONVINCING AND CLASSIFIED

20

London, late 1977

Settling back into the flat again, days went by and Eleanor heard and saw no one. Restocking her fridge with food, she kept looking out for Barbara and even went as far as to knock on the cottage. But there was no sign of her; it was as if the place was deserted. Sentry hadn't made any contact either and Eleanor was beginning to wonder if she should get in touch with them herself. Her life was bleak yet she was beginning to relax back into old routines. It was lonely though.

Thinking about Donald, Eleanor decided to write to him. There was no way of getting hold of him except through his mailbox address. He must think she had forgotten him altogether. On one of the days before Christmas not knowing what to do with herself, Eleanor went to the cinema to try and escape her anxieties. On her return she noticed a large black limousine in the mews. Perhaps Sentry had come for her at last.

Approaching the mews Eleanor saw the car door open, and to her amazement out stepped Donald spruce and sprightly as ever, beaming all over his face. Eleanor was overcome with emotion, and rushed straight at him.

'Hold hard my dear; I'm not as young as I was. You knocked

what little breath I still have right out of me. But you're pleased to see me?'

'Oh I am, I am,' Eleanor cried, 'you've no idea how much. Come in out of the cold. I need your advice, I'm in trouble again.'

Comfortably ensconced in the sitting room and revived with hot chocolate, Eleanor blurted out her story. Her feelings had been bottled up for so long; they threatened to explode. Donald, his kind, lined face creased with concern and biting hard on his lip, patted her hand at every gulp until she was able to carry on. As Eleanor described Erik's death and the blood, she thought she was going to faint but Donald offering his ever present pristine white handkerchief said, 'Have a good blow. Take a moment. We've all the time in the world. You've been through a traumatic experience and haven't dealt with it properly.'

Eleanor nodded, determined to soldier on. At no point did it cross her mind that Donald might not be the right person to confide in. Recounting the events at the convent, Eleanor finally became aware of Donald's reaction. He was sitting still as a statue, his pale face growing whiter. She wondered what had affected him so much but she ploughed on coming to an abrupt stop. With no more to say Eleanor waited for a response, but the silence was deafening. When there was nothing forthcoming she asked, 'What do you think? '

Donald pursed his lips, 'It's a lot to take in. You've thrown me a curve, my dear. I think a stronger drink is in order. Do you have any spirits?'

Eleanor nodded and brought out a bottle Georges had brought back from one of his trips. They sat nursing their drinks; eventually Donald asked cautiously, 'Has anyone been round to see you from Sentry?'

'No,' said Eleanor, 'not a soul considering they seemed to know where I was all along, and took their time sending someone to bring me back.' She was beginning to gain some equilibrium. Unburdening herself of her guilt had given her some relief.

'I'm sure they have your best interests at heart. They would never want anything to happen to you.'

'But how would you know Donald? Who is Sentry? I have always had my suspicions about them, and even more so now.'

Donald looked stricken and taking a heavy swig of his drink, reluctantly began to talk as if he was half reminiscing, 'A long time ago I had dealings with a similar type of organisation. It wasn't called Sentry in those days but they did the same thing. They were then, and still are concerned with covert matters of national security. It was all top secret, hush-hush, very cloak-and-dagger, if you know what I mean.' He smiled to himself, lost in past memories, 'Back then I knew your father well. He and I worked in tandem.

He was much younger than me of course, and we eventually went our separate ways.'

Eleanor was stunned, 'Are you trying to tell me Donald, that my father and you were some sort of spies? I can't believe that of my father. He was always such a disaster area.'

Donald blinked hard, and looking flustered and panicky mumbled, 'You have to forgive me Eleanor, I'm an old man, and very forgetful. My memory plays tricks on me these days. No, of course, it couldn't have been your father. I must have been mistaken. It was quite another young man I was thinking of although it was a similar set up to Sentry.'

Getting to his feet Donald began to pace the room, 'I hope my dear you don't mind listening to an old man's advice. I think you should contact Sentry. Talk to your boss. Everything will become clearer then.'

He was suddenly anxious to leave, holding his hands out to Eleanor and kissing her on both cheeks, 'I wish I could offer you more, but I think Sentry will always be there for you. They're like a family you know,' and with that he threw his coat over his arm and left.

Once he'd gone Eleanor was confused and had no idea what was going on. Donald had given her nothing concrete. He'd not mentioned Barbara or asked about her, and certainly not suggested anyone else who could help. It was all very well describing Sentry as a family – but what sort of family? After all the Mafia looked on themselves as a family and that wasn't much of a recommendation.

Eleanor felt as if her last form of consolation had been stripped away. She'd depended on Donald since the very first time they'd met. Yet he'd let her down. Could she even trust him? He seemed to know about Sentry's work. Was he tied up with them in some way? It was like being abandoned all over again. She was completely on her own again as she'd always been? It was going to be another lonely Christmas, and what would happen in the New Year?

…

Returning to his car, Donald pressed the intercom button saying to his driver: 'Johns, get me a line to Sentry,' and sat back unsteadily, taking deep breaths to calm himself.

When the connection rang, he picked up the receiver,
'—went well – I don't know about that. I may have made a bad situation worse. I think Jonah, you should handle this yourself. In many ways Eleanor is naive and very young --- yet there is something of her father about her---- his sharp enquiring mind, picks up every detail ---- isn't easily fobbed off. Don't underestimate her. I hate feeling I've let her down, and deceived her; I'm too old for this mularkey.'

'...........Yes I'm leaving for Cornwall tomorrow. I've done all I can. Don't involve me in this any further.'

155

21

New Year 1978

Following Donald's departure and despite the fact that she might never see him again, Eleanor slept better though she was none the wiser as to what to do. The decision was taken out of her hands, when Sentry in the person of Mr Caruthers made contact. It was a brief phone call requesting her to come in and see him that afternoon at her convenience. Of course there was no 'convenience' about it as she had nothing else to do, and he certainly knew that. However Eleanor responded politely quietly determined to find out exactly what was going on.

That afternoon Eleanor presented herself back at Sentry. Escorted into the main reception it was as if she was twenty all over again and coming for her first interview at Sentry. The roller coaster of the last few years had been obliterated. There was no sign of Claire or anyone she knew just the presence of a rather superior looking girl sitting on the front desk polishing her nails. She glanced at Eleanor in a bored languid fashion as if everything was too much trouble, and staring her up and down waved her hand towards Mr C's room saying, 'Oh it's you. He's expecting you. Go straight in.'

Eleanor couldn't believe it had all become so casual. She would have been carpeted for treating visitors like that when she'd started. Making her way to Mr C's room Eleanor knocked softly. He obviously couldn't have heard her so shuffling her feet and straightening her jacket, she tried with more intent. An irritated 'Enter' answered her second attempt and Eleanor slipped into the room. Nothing had changed there at least. Mr C as usual was deeply absorbed in mountains of files. There was a significant silence and then he noticed her. His face changed but as usual Eleanor couldn't read his expression. To her surprise he stood up, walked round the desk and hugged her as if she was a long lost relative, 'At last young Eleanor, what a sight for sore eyes. You look well, and if I may say quite grown up. Come and sit here in the more comfy chairs and we'll have tea.'

He leant over the intercom and buzzed reception, 'Virginia, bring in tea and biscuits .... Yes, of course, straight away, what else have you to do?' He turned back to Eleanor, 'I don't know Eleanor, since you've been gone, I've been saddled with the most inept and lazy assistants. Did you notice that girl when you came in? Her mother was some sort of debutante back in the fifties and pulled strings higher up to wangle a job for her daughter? I ask you what is the world coming to.'

Eleanor thought how uncharacteristic of Mr C to descend into such a gossipy mode. In all the time she had been there he would never have dreamt of discussing the staff with her. In fact, she had never even been asked to sit down in his office let alone take tea. Was this some sort of ploy to relax her? It was not the treatment she'd been expecting.

Virginia arrived without knocking and proceeded to pour

tea into the bone china cups with Mr C tut-tutting in the background, 'That's all, Virginia, you may go.' He dismissed her peremptorily in his usual curt manner advancing on Virginia as she backed out of the room, and snarling directly into her startled face '..... and make sure we're not disturbed by anyone.' Eleanor almost felt sorry for her. At last Mr C was back to his normal self. This was more like it.

They sat drinking tea in quiet contemplation until finally Mr C broke the silence with, 'I suppose by now, Eleanor, you've some idea what we're about. I daresay Paddy filled you in or maybe Donald?' He looked at her questioningly raising his eyebrows.

'Not really, Paddy said nothing and Donald well, he explained the firm has something to do with national security, and mentioned working with my father years ago.'

Mr C frowned, 'I think he was mistaken. Your father Robert, (and for some reason emphasised the words '**your father Robert**') had nothing to do with us.'

'That's what Donald said eventually,' Eleanor interjected. Why were they suddenly wrangling over her father when there was a far bigger elephant in the room?'

Mr C continued: 'Sentry is as you know, primarily an import and export business. This is a front for our main work which is to protect national security (adding pompously), to keep the people of this country safe in their beds.'

158

'Does that mean you work for the government?' Eleanor asked warily.

'Certainly an arm of the government,' Mr C answered silkily and smoothly as if this was all rather mundane. 'This is top secret, of course. I have to remind you of the Official Secrets Act which you signed when you first started here.'

Eleanor couldn't remember signing any such paper, 'I don't recall doing that or you explaining any such papers. When I was recruited I thought I was coming for a straightforward office job, and you didn't tell me any different.' By now Eleanor was losing her cool and working herself into a state, 'What you are in effect is a bunch of spies, however you wrap it up. I'm not sure I want to be involved.'

'But you are involved, whether you like it or not.'

The temperature in the room dropped as Mr C in a far more ruthless tone spelled it out, 'Don't forget Erik, Eleanor. You've caused us a lot of trouble. Granted it's been sorted out now but not without serious political implications. There have been major repercussions for us as part of the Service. However,' he smiled ruefully, 'we're your family, and we stick by our own. That is of course, if you still want us to?'

Eleanor's barely controlled anger erupted, 'But what about the business with the convent - leaving me to stew there..... People constantly watching me since I've been in London....... All the so-called friends I trusted, Barbara,

Donald, Sister Agnes and what about Georges?'

Reverting to far more conciliatory manner Mr C replied, 'Those people were and are your friends. They all tried to help you in their own way. Everything was done for your own good, I can assure you. I can't speak about Georges. I know nothing of him. He certainly isn't one of ours,' adding thoughtfully and almost inaudibly, 'of course, he could be one of theirs.'

Deflated Eleanor hardly listened. Everyone she knew or had known as a friend could never be trusted. They all worked for Sentry in one way or another. Perhaps she should leave all this behind and begin again but how and where, and what about Erik? What if the authorities, the government turned nasty? Where could she run to this time? There were no more options. There hadn't been many to start with certainly not in this country, if Sentry could track her down that easily.

It was as if Mr C was suddenly aware of her state of dejection, and changing tack he said consolingly, 'It's not all bad young Eleanor. We see great potential in you. You could be an asset to our little family. Will you give us another chance?' adding pragmatically, 'You've really nowhere else to go now, have you? Start back next Monday and I might be able to find something interesting for you to do- something challenging. What do you think?'

Eleanor was too bemused to think clearly. Before she knew it she found herself manoeuvred out the front door, and back onto Sun Street. Preoccupied, not knowing what to do, where to go or who to turn to, Eleanor could see she was trapped. Would she ever get away from this so-called self-appointed 'family'? How ironic, to think she'd longed for a proper family and this was what she'd ended up with. Dismally she headed home, praying for a miracle that would wipe out the past three years and give her back a completely blank slate.

...

Once Eleanor had left a perturbed Mr C, picked up the telephone, dialled a number, replaced the receiver and when it rang again answered, 'Are we secure? Good. Things are moving along here. We've got her back. She seems fine maybe a bit shaken up but in one piece. I had a job convincing her to stay but it looks as if she will ... it was touch and go.... but she has no alternative particularly after the Erik incident. That old fool Donald mentioned you, and then blustered his way out of it..... I don't know...... she's smart perhaps smarter than we realised and growing up fast. We can't protect her forever....... we'll do what we can to train her.'

TRUTH AND TRADECRAFT

22

Later 1978

A reluctant Eleanor returned to the Sentry fold as ordered early in 1978. Nothing was mentioned about her time away. It was as if she'd always been there. Claire eased her back into the routines as usual, and before Eleanor knew it she'd replaced the recalcitrant Virginia and they were ambling along as previously. Months went by and Eleanor carried on as before, but it was as if she was waiting for something to happen.

…

'Honestly Mr C, I don't see why I should get lumbered with your novice. What am I some sort of wet nurse?' Paul Kerris hunched himself over the phone whilst focusing binoculars on the block of flats opposite.

'Of course we're busy, there's only Mike and I here. Charlie's gone off sick. We're already a man down and things are about to happen. What we need are experienced men, someone to cover us and another to help out with the mobile. What I don't need is some stupid young pup. Well be it on your own head,' and he slammed the phone down.

Turning to Mike, Paul said, 'They've only dumped some green trainee on us, probably a relative of someone. They know quite well this is a delicate surveillance, and the shit will certainly hit the fan if we don't handle it right. There could even be questions in Parliament.'

'We could do with some help though, Paul. Maybe they won't be too bad. Am sure we can knock them into shape.'

Mike always the balanced one attempted to pour oil on troubled waters. They made a good team, Paul, the innovative one and risk taker, and Mike the plodder, coping with the daily grind, keeping notes and making sure that every contingency was covered. They'd been partners now for the last five years since being recruited together in '57.

Those were the years for spies - Burgess, Maclean, Philby, and the Portland Spy Ring. He and Paul had learnt their trade from the ground up but Paul was a different animal in those days, ambitious, sharp as a tack, good company and charming. Nowhere near as hard as he'd become as promotion after promotion passed him by. There weren't many people in the Service who could cope with him, even Mike at times found his intransigence bordering on callousness. It was as if twenty years of professionalism had eaten away at his basic humanity.

Paul paced about the scruffy enclosed space they were working in, 'What worries me Mike, is we've nothing concrete on the Right Honourable John Curtis M.P, and we've been here for weeks. Do you think the Intel is right? We know that's the mistress's flat - Elena Novotna, father

163

Czech, mother British, here on a student visa but other than the Honourable, she has no visitors.'

'What about Jack, what's he found out?' Mike queried.

'Not much really, Elena goes to a daily dance class at ten near the Angel and meets a girlfriend for lunch some days. We've checked out the girlfriend, there's nothing there. In the afternoons she wanders round the West End - no 'brushes' , no contacts, no letter drops nothing, does a minimum of grocery shopping at Harrods and comes back to make Curtis' meal in the evening. They stay in most evenings. I daresay he doesn't want to bump into anyone he knows. If there's a handler we're certainly not seeing it.'

'What about his wife?

'She's dumped in the constituency with the kids, doing good works and rarely venturing to town.'

'What have we got on Curtis, anything reportable?'

'No, just a load of rubbish he spouts in bed about boring meetings and who he's cultivating in the Party. Nothing about his job, though it's early days I suppose. He's a careful man, gets his driver to drop him and his red boxes off at his rooms in Westminster, and makes his way here by tube and bus. The trouble is we can't let Madame Elena work on him too much or it may be too late. The silly fool may finally tell her something he shouldn't. He's vulnerable enough already and we certainly don't want the Press catching on. There have been enough scandals over the last few years.'

...

After months of slipping back into the old ways, Mr C summoned Eleanor, 'We think it's time to spread your wings and show us what you're made of. One of the jobs we do in our line of work is keeping surveillance on questionable people or situations. We've such a team operating in North London at the moment. They are short handed and I want you to go there and make yourself useful, take notes, make tea, run errands. Do whatever they need. Is that clear? Claire will fill you in.' His demeanor showed he was going to have no truck with any discussion.

Eleanor scowled was this how it was going to be from now on? She supposed she would have to put up with it. However there was the tiniest ripple of anticipation. This job might prove more interesting than answering phones all day or collating bills and paperwork.

...

Making her way to Islington Eleanor wondered what the team was like, and what were they doing. She'd been told to go to Halton Road and find no. 40 in a block of flats. Neither of the two lifts was working and climbing the concrete stairs Eleanor felt uneasy. At no. 40 she tapped lightly on the door. It opened a sliver, and a threatening voice said, 'What do you want? You're at the wrong flat, get lost,' and slammed the door viciously in her face.

Eleanor tears welling up, swallowed, and resolutely tried again.

This time the door opened wider and before she knew it she was being dragged inside. Her throat grabbed by an extraordinarily handsome man with dark curly hair and the bluest of eyes, 'Tell me who you are and what you want?' he demanded roughly.

Eleanor made a gagging noise pawing at the hands on her throat, once released she started to cough violently, and through the coughs gasped, 'Mr C---- Mr C sent me.'

To her amazement the man started laughing uncontrollably, shouting up to his colleague, 'Hey Mike, you won't believe what they've sent us as a trainee - a puny little blonde waif, barely out of nappies. What the hell is the Service coming to, I ask you?'

He took hold of Eleanor by the scruff of her neck and prodded her up the stairs to their lookout and shoving her towards Mike said, 'See what I mean. I wasn't joking about wet nursing. They've obviously taken me at my word.'

Mike always the gentleman, came over, took her hand and led her to one of the many broken down chairs in the tiny room, 'Sit there my dear, it's not your fault. We were hoping for a more seasoned professional. Take no notice of Paul, his bark's worse than his bite. He'll calm down in a minute.'

'I bloody won't,' said Paul, 'what on earth are we supposed to do with her. She looks frightened to death and I've hardly touched her. We'll have to send her back. There's nothing for it.'

'I can speak for myself if you'll let me,' Eleanor retorted between clenched teeth, 'once I get my breath.'

'Oh, the tiger cub has claws, has she?' Paul remarked, 'very well tell us what you're here for?'

'To run errands, make tea or help with notes, I suppose,' answered Eleanor, 'I'm not sure I want to be here either but it was an order so what could I do?'

'OK,' said Paul, 'just sit there and be quiet. Don't open your mouth whatever you do. We'll pretend you're not here for today and I'll sort it out with Mr C later.'

Eleanor was dying to know who they were watching and what it was all about but kept silent.

Eventually it grew dark and they were packing up, when Mike suddenly noticed her sitting in the corner.

'My God Paul, we forgot all about her. You poor child, you've had nothing to eat or drink all day. I'm so sorry. What were we thinking of? The night shift will be here soon. We'll take you for something to eat.'

'Oh no, we're not,' Paul said adamantly, 'you go off home whatever your name is. Don't come back tomorrow, d'ya hear.'

Eleanor nodded miserably. Stiff, aching and starving she set off for home. She never wanted to see either of them again. If this was surveillance it certainly wasn't exciting or dangerous just deadly dull.

…

Paul could barely wait till she'd left before he rang the office, 'What on earth were you thinking to send this little bit of a girl. Talk about 'wet behind the ears', she's barely out of her mother's womb.'

Listening to the other end he said, 'Good grief Mr C, you mean that little runt actually killed a potential asset.'

……. 'Eh----- an accident, well that's quite different. Mind you she doesn't look as though she could blow a breath of wind let alone topple a man.'

…..'Well I suppose if I must I must. I still can't see what we can use her for though. She'll be more of a liability. We've enough problems of our own at the moment.'

….'Very well, send her back tomorrow then. Tell her to be here at seven sharp and wearing something old and not noticeable and to check she's not followed.'

…..'You mean I've got to do that as well. What do you think we are some sort of training school? Mike, Jack and I are pushed as it is.'

....'Very well, but be it on your own head if this op. goes tits up. I'm not carrying the can.'

23

At the office the following day Eleanor couldn't believe that she was being sent back to Islington. Despite her protestations she was dispatched wearing a grungy old mackintosh they'd dug up from stores and arrived back at no. 40 just after nine. Mike greeted her with open arms and set her to writing up the previous day's notes. Paul hadn't arrived and Mike explained, 'He's checking things out with Jack and last night's team. Finally he made an appearance but barely acknowledged her just reiterating yesterday's message, 'Keep out of our way. Don't ask questions.'

The week went by painfully slowly with Paul complaining they were getting nowhere and Mike being his usual long suffering self. Sensing their levels of frustration Eleanor finally plucked up the courage to say something. She'd been hearing about Elena's daily schedule all week and muttered to Mike one morning out of Paul's earshot, 'The dance class - isn't there likely to be something happening there?'

Mike said quietly, 'We've checked it out but access to the changing rooms or the class is difficult. Sentry hasn't got a female agent they can spare. The class is all women who've been attending for some time so it would be difficult to penetrate.'

'What about me? I could do it,' Eleanor whispered timidly, 'no one would suspect me?'

'What are you two gabbling about?' Paul barked across the

room, 'I thought I told you whoever you are to keep your mouth well and truly shut.'

'Look here, Paul,' Mike said with some force, 'Eleanor has come up with a suggestion that might be worth looking at.'

Hearing it Paul snorted, practically blowing a gasket, 'You must be kidding - a child with no experience, scared of her own shadow and you want to put her in the front line. She'd blow her cover in the first five minutes and then where would we be?'

Livid, her eyes flashing, Eleanor let rip, 'You're obviously not doing very well. I'm no child with what I've been through in the last few months. If you give me a chance, I'm sure I can be useful.'

By now Eleanor had developed such a fierce hatred for Paul that she wished she could get a knife, and stab him through the heart. He might be the best looking man she'd ever seen but he was a pig, and stabbing was entirely too good for him. Each day she'd come up with a new fantasy as to how she could torture him causing him maximum pain.

Paul threw back his chair and walked purposefully towards her. Eleanor hoped he wasn't going to hit her, instead he gazed at her in a thoughtfully, 'Well my little fledgling, there's something stirring in that delicate frame. Stand up and let's take a look at you.' Eleanor did what she was told; trying not to feel ill at ease and doing her best to return his

171

stare steadfastly though it took every ounce of effort.

Instead of addressing her, Paul turned to Mike, 'She might do. She hardly looks like one of us so no one is likely to be suspicious. We'll have to make do with her and see if we can knock her into shape.'

Eleanor was not thrilled about 'the knocking into shape' bit but gritted her teeth, willing to go along with it. Anything was better than sitting in the corner for another week. There was the tiniest feeling of satisfaction in having won a small battle over Paul However it was no good being too smug about her victory as no doubt he would soon put her in her place.

Paul was already planning ahead, 'She'll need a good cover story. We'll have to come up with something fast if we're going to get her into the class by next week.' and turning to Eleanor he said, 'We'd better know something about you. What's your name and your background?'

Eleanor thought swiftly, there was no way she was going to tell him about her family and rackety upbringing so said plainly and baldly, 'I'm Eleanor Smith. I was sent by a temp. agency to do secretarial work at Sentry. I handle the switchboard, do typing, filing, deliver and pick up packages, and whatever other jobs are needed.'

Paul chortled, 'Can you believe it, Mike. We're using secretaries now for undercover work. Anyway I suppose that will do. Better to keep your own name and story, it will be more straightforward that way. We'll find you somewhere local to work part-time, some place accessible to the Dance Centre. Now can you dance at all?'

Eleanor not to be outdone or out fazed said, 'I did tap and ballet when I was young and can pick up new steps quickly.'

'That's something I suppose,' Paul said. 'You better go straight home now. We don't want you seen hanging around here.' He reached into his pocket and took out a wad of notes, 'Find a shop in the West End and buy some dance gear. Don't forget the receipts. Then go straight home. When Mike and I have finished making the arrangements, I'll come over to your place and brief you.'

He quickly scribbled down her address, and ushered Eleanor out through a back entrance hailing a taxi for her. This was more like it thought Eleanor – this was exactly what undercover work should be like – she all but said to the cabdriver 'Follow that car' but restrained herself. She was starting to feel the thrill of it all; it was going to be exciting.

Wandering round Selfridges, Eleanor bought everything from tap shoes and dance shoes to leotards, legwarmers and head bands. She was dying to see how she looked, and could hardly wait to get dressed up back at the flat, cavorting round the living room to the sound of 'Stayin' Alive.'   A knock at the kitchen door stopped her in her tracks and throwing on a dressing gown, Eleanor carefully peered out

173

of the window. Paul stood on the steps, impatient as ever, drumming his fingers on the metal balustrade. As he strode into the living room, studying Eleanor, he said sardonically, 'I think you can manage without the headband and the legwarmers. Shall we get down to business?'

During her absence, he and Mike had worked with Sentry to set up a part-time job for her at a solicitors' near the Angel. Eleanor was to work three afternoons a week, and be free every morning to attend the dance class. All she had to do was enroll at the class, observe Elena's movements and report back to Paul, who would make contact with her at the solicitors.

Eleanor thought for a moment, and then summoned up the courage to remark, 'Won't they think it funny that I only work part-time. How could I be expected to keep myself in London?'

Paul frowned, 'Now listen to me Eleanor, and listen well, I don't want you getting chatty with anyone in the class especially Elena, do you understand me?'

Eleanor determined to make her point said, 'But what you don't understand, Paul, is that women are more talkative then men, and if most of them have been there a while they'll want to know all about anyone new.'

She could see he was none too happy with her expressing an opinion. However scratching his head, he was forced to agree, 'If asked then, you can say you've come into a small inheritance from your parents who've recently died, and you're living on that whilst you find a more permanent job. Does that suit you?'

Eleanor agreed, at least it was close to the truth. She wondered if Mr C had told him about her parents. If not it was surprising that he'd picked on that particular back story?

Sitting there still chewing on her cheek, Paul studied her and said, 'Well spit it out, what other little gems have you thought of that we haven't?'Eleanor grinned. He sounded almost human then.

'What if they ask me where I live? That's something they're bound to want to know, anybody would.'

Paul, back in professional mode, said, 'We've thought of that. We have a safe house in Islington we rarely use. That can be your address. Anything else?'

Eleanor shook her head. He was obviously keen to go but at the last minute he said severely, 'This isn't a game or some sort of dress-up Eleanor, this is serious. Don't let your guard down at any time and relax. Do not and I mean do not for any reason go beyond your brief. You are there to observe and report, do you understand?'

'Yes, Paul,' Eleanor answered in a subdued manner. She wished he'd not found her running round the flat wearing all the dance gear. No wonder he found it irritating dealing with a 'chit of a girl' as he'd called her. From now on, she must start acting more like a professional.

24

The following Monday at exactly half past nine Eleanor presented herself at the City Dance Studio. She enrolled for six weeks and filled in her Islington address. The receptionist showed her round, fixed her up with a locker and told her the class would start promptly at ten. Eleanor changed and hung around the changing room hoping to spot Elena from the photograph she'd been given. There was a rush at quarter to ten and a big group of women piled in. It was no good trying to pick Elena out of the crowd, so Eleanor made her way to the studio and pretended to do warm up exercises while keeping an eye on the door.

The instructor, busy at the front sorting out music, eventually noticed her and came over saying pleasantly, 'Welcome to the class.' She enquired whether Eleanor had any dance experience and explained, 'We've been going for quite a few weeks now. A lot of the girls are very experienced. Don't let that put you off. I'm sure you'll catch up. I'll partner you with someone who's been here some time. Watch her and learn the ropes as we go along.'

Eleanor was hoping the partner might be Elena but no such luck, it was a very friendly girl called Helen with red curly hair and a bright smile who chatted away. Eleanor found it hard to concentrate on the steps, and look for Elena in the midst of all the flailing moving bodies at the same time. She was forced to be standoffish with Helen, giving terse answers to her onslaught of questions until the poor girl

177

gave up. The instructor moved round the room constantly, making it difficult for Eleanor to observe from her position near the front of the class. She decided that tomorrow she would arrive later and slip in at the back of the room.

The class broke for a brief interval, and Eleanor had a chance to walk round the room. Finally she caught sight of Elena leaning against a wall, drinking water and chatting to the person next to her. It was too obvious to join them, so Eleanor continued walking trying to think of a different approach for the following day. After the class finished Helen made one more effort to engage her in conversation but Eleanor said she had to rush off to work.

That afternoon, she was busy typing at Daventry and Proctor Solicitors when Paul came into the outer office dressed as a motorcycle messenger, asking for Mr Barnaby the solicitor Eleanor was working for. Once in her office he carefully shut the door and asked, 'How did it go?' Eleanor outlined her tactics for the next morning. But Paul was not impressed and said roughly, 'On no account make contact with her, do you hear. You are only there to watch, nothing more. I will check back at the end of the week. Ring me on this number if there is anything unusual to report,' and tossing her a scrap of paper he left.

Eleanor was annoyed; Paul could have at least acknowledged her efforts. If he wasn't checking back till the end of the week, he could hardly have much faith in her. Despite her ambivalent feelings about him Eleanor was determined to make headway and prove herself to him. Why she wanted to impress him she didn't know, but there was a part of her that wanted him grovelling at her feet.

In the next few days arriving late at the dance class proved to be a useful ploy. Eleanor was able to slide in at the back of the room and watch Elena easily. When the break came, Eleanor retired to the same wall she'd seen Elena lean against on previous occasions. Seeing her on her own, Elena came over to her, and asked her in a friendly manner, 'How do you like the class?' Eleanor explained she was a novice but loved to dance and was hoping to improve.

Any further conversation was cut short as the instructor began again and the music started up, but at last Eleanor felt she was making progress. Of course she wasn't following Paul's instructions but as he wasn't there she had to think for herself.

Eleanor noticed that though Elena was outwardly sociable she didn't have any close friends in the class, so why had Elena had chosen to talk to her? Maybe she felt sorry for her, as Eleanor was clearly much younger than anyone else and on her own.

Towards the end of the week, Eleanor made sure she was the last to leave as she tried to sort out the straps on one of her shoes. Everyone had gone and there was only herself, Elena and the instructor in the room. They seemed unaware of her presence. A telling glance passed between Elena and the instructor and Eleanor saw Elena nod imperceptibly. After a minute or two, they became aware of Eleanor's presence at the back of the room, and Elena enquired sharply, 'Are you having a problem?'

'It's my shoe; I think one of the straps has come loose. I was trying to see if I could fix it myself,' Eleanor said in a helpless voice.

They both came over and inspected the errant shoe. 'It needs a cobbler,' Elena remarked, 'there's a good man near me who'll fix it in no time. Come back with me if you've the time and you can have a coffee at my place while you wait.'

Eleanor was beside herself with delight and then had second thoughts. What about Paul and Mike? They'd be watching the flat, and Paul would go mad, but what an opportunity to get into Elena's flat. Eleanor had to take it.

Accepting gratefully she said, 'That's so kind of you. I do have time before work. I'll just get my things.'

On their way out Elena said, 'I don't even know your name. I'm Elena.'

'And I'm Eleanor,' and they burst out laughing at the similarity.

Elena said, 'You remind me of my baby sister. She has your exact colouring and build.'

'Is your sister with you in London?'

'No, she lives with my father in Prague. I rarely see her,' Elena said sadly.

They left Eleanor's shoe at the menders and walked amicably on to Elena's flat. Eleanor was conscious of the eyes observing them from across the road. She felt like giving a naughty wave but curbed the devilish impulse.

If she could have heard the conversation from no. 40, she'd have been more perturbed. The air was blue, when Mike focusing the camera pointed out the two of them.

Paul was furious, 'I told her - I told her to observe, nothing more. That's what comes of using amateurs. That wretched girl I'd like to wring her neck. What the bloody hell does she think she's doing?'

Mike said quietly and urgently, 'This could be dangerous. Do you think Elena has sussed her out?'

'Who knows? We can't do anything at the moment, but wait, watch and hope she comes out in one piece.'

Sweating it out their eyes glued to the lens, an hour went by and then along came Eleanor walking nonchalantly down the road as if she had all the time in the world.

Paul said, 'I'll have to pull her out. It's no good if she doesn't follow orders.'

'Hold hard,' said Mike, 'sure she used her own initiative but you don't know the circumstances.'

Still contemplating what to do with the wayward Eleanor, Paul's phone rang.

'I need a delivery pronto,' was all Eleanor said and put the phone down before Paul had a chance to say anything.

Mike took one look at Paul's face, 'I think Jack or I should go and see her. You might not be able to control yourself and we don't want a shouting match.'

'Very well,' Paul said tightly, 'but unless this is something worthwhile, I'm sending her back to the office and that's an end to it.'

Mike arrived at Daventry and Proctor's in the messenger garb, and was shown into Eleanor's room. The relief on her face was tangible. She heaved a big sigh, 'Thank goodness for you, Mike. I know I'm in hot water but honestly the chance to get to know Elena better just happened. I did look round her flat when she was changing but found nothing. However there was something going on between her and the dance instructor. I don't know what but it was definitely something. A look and a nod passed between them, that's all.'

Mike was thoughtful, 'You did well but following orders is crucial in this business unless you're experienced. Had you thought of what might have happened to you if Elena had become suspicious?'

Eleanor chewed on her cheek sheepishly, 'You're right. I

didn't know what to do when she asked me back. I was so excited to be able to do something useful for a change that I didn't think,' and attempting to distract him by changing the subject asked, 'what about the instructor though? Could she be Elena's contact?'

'Maybe,' Mike said cautiously, 'we'll look into her. Leave that to us.'

'But what shall I do about the classes? Won't it look odd if I stop going?'

'You'll have to keep going.' Mike said, 'I'll square it with Paul. But you need to ease back on any friendship with Elena. If she invites you back to the flat again, say you've taken on more work and aren't as free as you were. Play it cool.'

Over the next weeks, Eleanor continued the classes but though she was chatty with Elena, left as soon as class finished. There were no more invites and Eleanor was relieved.

She'd heard neither sight nor sound of Paul until one evening he arrived at her flat unexpectedly. Studying his face as she sipped her coffee she wondered what sort of mood he was in, but relaxed back in her chair when he smiled at her. 'It's over,' he pronounced. 'No more dance classes or part-time jobs for you. You can go back to Sentry full time.'

'What do you mean? What's happened?' Eleanor asked feeling oddly disappointed.

'You actually did alright despite not doing what you were told. It turned out the instructor was passing messages to Elena from her handler. We tracked the handler back to the Russians, and the Right Honourable John Curtis M.P will have to quietly resign from the government 'due to family reasons' and move back to the country to his ever loving wife. Elena is being deported, and our team will move on to the next op.'

Eleanor made a face. Paul laughed at her expression, 'Do you think you're a fully fledged undercover agent now? Heaven help us! You've done one little job for us reasonably so back you go to the safe world of clerical work.'

Eleanor was disconcerted. This was a very different Paul, jovial, laid back and enjoying himself at her expense. Eleanor began to see how charming he could be as he stayed chatting and teasing her the rest of the evening. She found herself offering to make a meal. To her amazement he accepted, and they sat down to eat pasta with wine and cheese.

Suddenly noticing how late it was, Paul stood up apologising, 'Sorry, I stayed far too long. You need sleep at your age. It's been a real change; I haven't chilled out like this in a long time.'

His nervous energy returning he sprang out of the kitchen

door tossing her a throwaway remark, 'We might even use you again who knows.'

Eleanor was over the moon, maybe her undercover career wasn't over. This evening had certainly made her change her opinion of Paul.

SECRECY AND SURVEILLANCE

25

1978

Back at Sentry Eleanor carried on as normal. It was hard after her venture into another world. Feeling restless and bored she tried to talk to Claire. Perhaps Claire might understand as there was a definite air of mystery about her sometimes. Eleanor was dying to confide in someone. Mr C came and went, barely noticing her as if she'd suddenly faded into the background again. Finally Eleanor cracked, saying to Claire, 'I really would like to talk to you about what I've been doing.'

Claire pursed her lips, 'I'm not sure that's a good idea. I'm not party to all of Sentry's activities. If I do notice anything I keep it to myself. It's wiser that way.' She turned away as if that was the end of the matter, and then thinking better of it remarked, 'Maybe it would be a good idea for you to get everything off your chest - better me than an outsider. What about if I call round to your place this evening?'

Eleanor agreed with enthusiasm. She felt as if she was going to burst. Recently it had been like being on a Ferris wheel, one minute up in the air and the next on the ground.

…

Later that day Claire disappeared into Mr C's office to

explain her dilemma, 'I don't want to break protocol but Eleanor seems to be close to the edge. I'm concerned if she doesn't find a confidante soon she might lose control and do something silly.'

Mr C nodded, 'Yes, we forget she's young and been through an awful lot. We are monitoring her flat so be careful what you say. Paul suddenly seems to be taking an undue interest in her. I'm not at all sure that's what we want. Warn her off. She's too vulnerable and fragile for his antics.'

…

That evening after Eleanor had served a light supper and recounted all the exploits of the last weeks, Claire brought up the subject of Paul.

'Eleanor, Paul's a very experienced officer and knows what he's doing, but he has a lethal charm when he's in the mood and is an out and out maverick. He has a reputation with women, and I do mean 'women' in the plural. He uses them and discards them and it's probably not a good idea for you to see too much of him.'

Eleanor knew she was being warned of. Not wanting to take it too personally she said, 'I barely know him,' adding defensively, 'he's called round a couple of times to brief me. The last time he stayed for a meal but that's all. I really hated him when I first met him,' carefully omitting to mention that her feelings had changed.

However hard she tried Eleanor was never at ease with Claire. She was enigmatic; warm and friendly one moment and cool and glacial the next. Someone at work had nicknamed her 'the ice queen', so Eleanor couldn't be the only one to find her impenetrable.

At the end of the evening Claire said, 'You can always talk to me, Eleanor; I can be a safe haven for you when things get tough.' Eleanor wondered why she'd said 'when' and not 'if'. Was her life going to become more difficult? What did Claire know that she didn't?

…

The next morning playing the tape back, Mr C frowned. He would venture a bet that Eleanor was never going to listen to the warning about Paul. Perhaps it was time Paul met the Chief. He would certainly put him right if anyone could and perhaps the Chief could find Paul a job to keep him busy elsewhere. He picked up the telephone and called Paul, 'Look, Paul, the Chief wants to meet you.......... Yes, it's unusual but he's in the country just now......what about? I really don't know.... maybe something to do with your last op...... Very well, I'll arrange it.'

…

Alpha was annoyed. Setting up meetings between flights was a terrible inconvenience. If Mr C hadn't said it was urgent, he would have completely blown it off. Who on earth was Paul Kerris anyway - some lowly officer working in the trenches? What was he supposed to do with him? Why couldn't Mr C handle something at this level?

Settling in a secluded area of the cafeteria, Alpha sipped his black coffee and skimmed the Standard. He spotted Paul as soon as he entered. Why did they all look the same, these Sentry officers? Had they all been to the same tailor, though Paul looking much younger than his 43 years and well over six foot with his dark hair and blue eyes, stood out more than most. He had an arrogant bearing and walked towards the bar with a confident stride.

Alpha began to warm to him – there was a definite look of himself ten or fifteen years ago. Perhaps this young man might prove useful after all. Alpha watched him order a beer, and make his way towards the window where he sat staring into his glass. There was an element of tension in his posture. Alpha wondered if perhaps he was not as self assured as he appeared.

Waiting a good half an hour Alpha moved to leave, and then as if by accident passed close to Paul's table. As he did so a look of recognition crossed his face, 'Well I'll be, isn't it Johnnie Richards. I haven't seen you since.... Since, now when was it?'

Paul looked up, similarly surprised, 'My goodness Charles Leighton, gosh it must be ten years or more since we were at Cowes. Do you still sail? Sit down for a minute if you have time, and we can catch up.'

Alpha sat down and studied Paul, 'It's certainly been a lot of years. You haven't changed at all.' He lowered his voice and said, 'Good to meet you, Paul, I've have heard great things about you. I'm surprised you're not further up the ranking order with all your experience.'

Paul momentarily let down his guard. An expression of pleasure crossed his face, 'Honoured to meet you too sir,' he mumbled, 'your reputation precedes you.' adding bitterly, 'You're right, I don't seem to have done very well in the promotion stakes. I don't think my face fits in the Service – not the right schools or background you see.'

Alpha looked round the cafe checking there was no one in their vicinity, and murmured, 'I might be able to do something about your future prospects. We'll have to see. Now we've got all the introductions out of the way perhaps we can get down to business. I'm limited for time. I need to brief you on your next assignment.'

Taken aback Paul said quietly, 'But I usually get briefed by Mr C, sir.'

'I know,' Alpha replied, 'but this is something I want you to do for me personally. I have cleared it with the office. You will be reporting directly to me orally, nothing in writing. I don't want any of this going through Sentry; you'll be on your own with this, do you understand?' Paul nodded, and wondered what was coming.

With no further explanations and keeping his voice soft, Alpha launched into the briefing, 'There's an East German couple taken up residence in North London. I want you to put them under surveillance. The husband's real name is Lukas Schmidt. He came here a few years ago via Sweden and married Freya Lindbergh (we don't know how or when she entered the country). They have anglicised their names to Lucas and Freda Lindberg. He professes to be an interior designer working from home, and she is a translator in Central London. Not only have they entered this country illegally but we suspect they are part of a Russian cell.

I want to you to set up an operation in a neighbouring house as a married couple team. This could be a long job, and you need to find a partner who can work with you and maintain that level of cover.'

Paul bit his lip, 'This could be tricky. We don't have many available females, and how do I get one released without informing the office.'

'Well, that's up to you,' Alpha said snappily, 'I don't want an officer whose hand I have to hold. I understood you were a bit of a self starter and an opportunist, and looking to move up. If that's not the case, please let me know before we go any further. It's up to you to sort out the details, your cover story etc. I will make arrangements for the house and money to be made available to you, and if you need them,

191

extra support. This has to be underway within the next few weeks. Ring me on this number if you want to set up a meet or you encounter any problems. I am always available, but I don't want to be bothered by trivia. You are an experienced officer so this should be child's play.'

Paul was infuriated at being spoken to in this way but kept calm, merely asking, 'Roughly how long is this op. to go on for, sir?'

Alpha shrugged, 'As long as it takes to get some hard info. on these people. As you know these things take time, but don't take your eye off the ball. Find someone reliable to act as your wife. Anyway I have to get going,' and raising his voice several pitches said loudly (in his Charles Leighton role), 'Good seeing you, old man, we must get together with our better halves for dinner one of these days, and maybe set up some sailing dates.' He shook Paul by the hand and departed.

Paul didn't know what to think. He decided to return to the office and sound out Mr C. Obviously he couldn't tell him details, but he might be able to get more insight as to what this was all about. Why was he being asked to do this undercover op. without the office's say so? Where could he find someone to pose as his wife at this short notice?

Making his way through Sentry's reception, Paul noticed Eleanor flitting about. Hearing footsteps she turned, giving a start when she saw him but caught herself and smiled

192

hesitantly. Paul used to having this effect on women, usually barely gave it a second's thought unless it was worth his while. But taking a good look at her, he thought what about Eleanor? She's only some sort of gofer here. There's certainly something about her, and she did use her initiative on that last op. She's malleable enough, young enough to be trained, and of course easy on the eye. He blasted her with the full beam of his charm until Eleanor looked ready to faint, and the pile of files she was carrying teetered. Paul skillfully caught them before they ended up on the floor, 'Eleanor, you do look lovely today. Is that a new dress? That greenish colour really brings out your eyes.' As she stood not knowing how to respond, mouth agape, he rescued her by asking, 'Mr C is he in? – I need a minute?'

Eleanor managed a mute response and Paul marched straight past her into Mr C's office, banging the door shut.

…

Mr C was not in the least willing to allow Eleanor to become part of this mission, 'Honestly Paul, she's a complete rookie in this business. Yes, I know she coped with the last job but it wasn't that demanding. You can't expect her to play the part of a wife for goodness knows how long. She's barely a grown woman let alone wife material. Give her a few years then maybe but not now. Anyway she probably wouldn't be willing. It's a big ask.'

They argued amicably about who else was available until Mr

193

C capitulated begrudgingly, 'Put it to her but be it on your own head. I'm glad this is nothing to do with me. It'll be up to you and the Chief to sort out any messes or repercussions. I wouldn't have thought the Chief would have sanctioned anything like this, particularly with Eleanor however this is your show.'

Paul neglected to tell him the Chief had absolutely no knowledge of this turn of events.

Eleanor was summoned from the outer office. She was amazed when the proposal was put to her, and so overwhelmed she had to sit down. Mr C raised his eyebrows at Paul as if to say, see how young she is. At first, they were both in agreement that it would be too much for her, but Eleanor was having none of it, 'Of course, I'll do it, there's no question. Perhaps Claire could keep an eye on my flat,' she said, overcome with the thought of such an adventure.

'You would have to do what you're told,' Paul said sternly, 'we want none of your school girl tactics like last time.'

Eleanor agreed trying to hide her air of delight. This would be some mission with this gorgeous man. She started romanticising in her head about their life together as if they were really going to be married.

Mr C took one look at her, and shook his head, 'Look at her Paul, she's hardly tough enough for this. She's an inexperienced girl with her head in the clouds. Leave it with me. I'll see if I can find you a more mature woman.'

But Paul demurred, 'I haven't the time. She'll have to do. The Chief wants this set up in the next weeks. I've lots of preparation,' and glancing across at Eleanor, 'as well as sorting her out. Keep her here for the meantime,' dismissing her as if she was a package, 'and I'll pick her up next week, and take it from there.'

26

Eleanor couldn't wait for the op. to start. She was dying to ask questions but there was no sign of Paul all week. True to his word he arrived at the office late one afternoon just as she was packing up. He waved away all her greetings and said, 'We'll go to your flat. I'll take the next few days briefing you and getting our cover story sorted.'

They were to be married couple Ralph and Linda Whitman moving into No.46, The Limes Avenue N11 the following week. Their targets, Lucas and Freda Lindberg had been living opposite at no. 53 for some time. Paul had arranged the furniture removal and set up the services. To Eleanor's great delight there was to be a dog – a Jack Russell called Max.

'I can't abide dogs,' Paul admitted, 'but it's the easiest way for us to explore the area, and keep an eye on the targets' comings and goings. No one gives a dog walker a second glance.'

Eleanor had to spend the rest of the week memorising and learning her cover story. Paul said, 'I'll be back on Wednesday to test you and check your wardrobe. We'll have to buy you suitable clothes.'

On the Wednesday night they sat down to go through what she'd learnt. Paul said, 'It'll be easier to do this in a natural conversational way. You need to live and breathe your identity or you'll trip up.'

Paul began, 'Hullo, I live a few doors away. I see you've just moved in. I'm Vera; my husband's Fred. He works for the council. What's your name?'

'I'm Linda Whitman,' Eleanor said, 'my husband and I moved in last week. Ralph is self employed and works from home. He helps people sort out their finances.'

'Already too much information,' Paul said, 'just answer with the minimum. There's no need to give your full name or say much about your husband. You don't want to encourage friendships; after all we're doing a job.'

He moved on, still as 'Vera', 'Where did you move from?'

Eleanor answered, 'We moved from the other side of London?'

'Whereabouts, I know London well?'

'East London. I'm sorry, I have to rush. My husband will be wanting his meal.'

'Better,' Paul said, 'if anyone is too nosy, cut them off and make some excuse. Shall we move onto the marriage?'

'Have you been married long, Linda?'

'Just five years.'

'Any children?'

'No, but my husband had two sons from his first marriage.

Oops,' Eleanor said, hand to her mouth, 'I shouldn't have added that, should I?'

'No, but you're doing OK,' Paul said reassuringly, 'the more you practice the better it will get. It needs to be like a second skin. You can't afford to forget. Relax enough to talk to people but tell them nothing. Smile a lot and get them to confide in you instead.'

On they plodded till the early hours of the morning, when Paul could see Eleanor was drooping and hardly able to keep her eyes open.

'We'll finish there. Have a lie in tomorrow, and I'll bring Max round so that you two can get acquainted. I've picked out some clothes for your new persona and I'll bring them as well.'

Eleanor wondered how he knew what size she was but was too exhausted to ask.

Paul's parting words were, 'Believe you are Linda. You may have to be her for some time. You will need to be resourceful if people ask you something unusual. If you make something up, be sure it can't be checked. Be vague.'

By the time she was ready for bed, Eleanor's brain actually hurt. She dreamt all night long about rows and rows of faceless women called Linda and was shattered when she woke up. This wasn't going to be as straightforward as she'd thought. She wandered round the flat trying to think herself into the part of Linda, a younger woman married to an older divorced man. This must be how actors feel, trying to get into character. Maybe Paul was right and clothes would make the difference.

He arrived later in the day with a suitcase, and Max in tow. Eleanor fell in love with Max and him with her. They sat together on the sofa looking at one another adoringly as Paul unpacked the contents of the suitcase. He said briskly, 'Now don't get attached to him. He goes back to the kennels at the end of the op. He's only on loan.'

Eleanor had never had so much as a gerbil when she was young, and was delighted to have a pet at last. Whatever Paul said she was determined to keep Max. After the job was finished no one would want either of them and she could do what she liked. Keeping her thoughts to herself, she surveyed the clothes. Paul certainly had good taste but they were clothes designed for a much older woman than her. Goodness there was even underwear; she blushed at the thought of it. Paul caught the blush, 'Don't worry I didn't buy everything myself, I had help from a very lovely woman friend.' He laughed ironically as if this was a private joke, 'Go and try everything on. I'll wait here and read the paper.'

Eleanor was eager to oblige. New clothes were still a novelty to her, and she paraded round in a trouser suit, a cocktail dress, halter tops, denim jeans, flares and even platform sandals. Posing and preening, she finally got a smile out of Paul.

He said, 'Well you look the part of a beautiful fashionable young wife. We just need to get that hair of yours sorted and we're ready.'

Eleanor realised afterwards that Paul had actually called her 'beautiful.' But there was no hold in him now. He dispatched her to a beauty salon where they cut her hair into a wedge, coloured it into a deep golden blonde, and gave her lessons on makeup to define her almond shaped eyes.

Eleanor practically danced up Bond Street, and then thought she must start acting like the mature Linda Whitman not the young Eleanor. She was dying for Paul to see her new look but when she saw him he barely gave her a passing glance, saying, 'Monday morning is lift off. The house is ready. I'll collect you from the flat at eight on the dot. Be ready with your case, and anything else you need as I'll have no time to wait.' He waved an indifferent goodbye and raced off.

Eleanor had all weekend to get everything together. In all the months since she'd returned to London, she'd never seen sight nor sound of Barbara, and took it for granted that Barbara had outlived her usefulness for Sentry and been moved on. But on the Sunday, there was a knock at the door and there she was. She did a double take at Eleanor's new image, apologising profusely for not having been around for so long, 'I've been abroad on assignment for my company. There was no time to tell you before I went. You look absolutely amazing. What's been happening?' Pushing her way in, she plonked herself down on the sofa as if she was planning to stay not giving Eleanor a chance to object.

Eleanor saw this as a chance to practice her new skills. Using monosyllabic answers to the cascade of questions was an effective stratagem and Barbara soon departed. Eleanor had wanted to ask about Donald but thought better of it. Still fond of him, despite his letting her down, it was far better to keep quiet now she knew they were all watching her. But there was Monday to look forward to and a new life – even if it was a borrowed one, and she was going to make the most of it.

…

Back at her cottage Barbara rang Mr C: 'It was embarrassing to see Eleanor after all this time. She gave nothing away and was very tight-lipped. She is certainly a different girl from the one I first met. The new hairstyle, clothes, have made her look far more grown up and sophisticated...... No, I have no idea what she and Paul are up to. Isn't he reporting to you?........ Oh, the Chief, I understand..... What about the bugs in the flat, you think Paul swept it?......No, she didn't ask about Donald. The poor man has had enough of these complicated games, and wants to be left alone to enjoy his old age......I'm sorry I can't see what else I can do. I think I've outlasted my usefulness when it comes to Eleanor.'

ACTIVATION

27

Late 1978

On the Monday Eleanor was up at the crack of dawn, applying makeup as she's been taught, and wearing one of the new outfits. She'd added a radio and books to her suitcase but everything else was left at the flat. She scrawled a quick letter to Claire who was holding the key, left a cheque for the most urgent bills, and found herself ready and waiting with an hour to go. She was keyed up but did her best to keep calm. Hearing the honk of a horn, she locked the door and pushed the keys through the letterbox. Paul had stressed there must be nothing of her old life in her possession, keys, photos, bills etc. He had gone through her handbag thoroughly and packed away anything valuable.

He was impatiently checking his watch as Eleanor climbed into the Chevette. He pulled out as soon as she'd thrown her bag in the back and said, 'The removals will be there dead on nine. I've got the keys so we need to be there before them.'

On their arrival at The Limes Paul took charge of pointing out where the furniture should go. With nothing to do Eleanor wandered round her new home. It was a Thirties house with one bigger bedroom, one medium, a box room, a bathroom, and downstairs, a tiny kitchenette, a dining room and a living room. There was an excuse for a garden with a shed and a small scrappy lawn. Generally it was all a bit shabby but Eleanor was elated. This was her first house and she floated through the rooms imagining what she would do with the decor. It was only when Paul called up the stairs, 'Linda, where in heavens name are you?' that she came to with a jolt. Of course this was all pretend and not children's type of pretend either.

Once the furniture was sorted, Paul set off to collect Max, and Eleanor sat in the dining room drinking tea admiring the cornices and high ceilings. Still in a daze, she heard a knock at the door. Thinking Paul had forgotten his key, she rushed to the door. A grey haired elderly lady stood there holding a tray of tea and cake. Eleanor was flustered but recalling her lessons smiled and invited the lady in, who introduced herself as Doris, and said, 'I know what it's like moving. I live next door. I've have brought some tea. I don't know if you're anything like me but I can never find the kettle.'

Eleanor showed her into the dining room saying, 'This is kind of you. I was having a cup of tea but your cake looks delicious. I'm Linda. Let me pour you a cup.'

Just then she heard the click of the front door and Paul arrived back with the over excited Max, who made a rush for her. Paul was not at all fazed by their visitor, 'Hullo, this is a nice surprise,' and directing the full volume of his charm on Doris, said, 'I'm Ralph, this is Max,' and proceeded to launch into all the traffic problems he'd had driving to the kennels.

Before Doris could get her breath, she found herself ushered out the front door with assurances that they would return the crockery later.

Paul made a face, 'This isn't a good start, having someone like that as a neighbour.'

Eleanor said, 'But she seems nice enough and didn't ask many questions.'

'That isn't the point,' Paul said, 'it looks as if she's retired. That means she'll be home all the time, and interested in our comings and goings. Anyway we'll manage, I suppose. You might as well unpack. I'll wash up these cups. It would be better if I take the tray back. I can be friendly and non committal so maybe she'll get the message. When I get back we'll go out for a meal and do some shopping.'

Eleanor hovered wondering what to do about the bedroom situation. Gathering herself together she asked, 'Which bedroom should I use?'

'The biggest of course - in the front,' said Paul, 'we'll sort out the sleeping arrangements later. We are a married couple, so people will expect us to sleep in the same room.' He went off to the kitchen leaving Eleanor struggling to hump her heavy suitcase up the stairs - so much for married life, she thought crossly.

Sitting in the local pub after having a late lunch, Paul said quietly, 'We need to get down to business a.s.a.p. I'll start a routine of going out jogging in the early morning with Max, and timetable the Lindbergs' daily movements. You'll take Max out mid morning and do the same. I'm setting up all the listening equipment in the box room, and we'll use the front bedroom for the surveillance station.' He looked across at Eleanor, 'I hope you're taking all this in?'

Eleanor mind's was elsewhere, racing ahead thinking about living day to day with Paul. Besides her parents and their dubious friends, she'd never lived with anyone. What would it be like living with a man and particularly this very attractive man?

But Paul had no time for daydreams. He was a man of action focused on the job in hand. In the next hours they completed the grocery shopping and were back in no. 46. Leaving Eleanor to unpack the food, he headed for the bedrooms. She could hear him moving stuff about and hammering. Some hours later he came down and asked, 'Can you cook, Linda? Anything - pasta will do.'

Eleanor assured him she could cook but only a limited number of dishes. It was strange getting used to her new name. It made her feel unlike herself.

Paul noticing her confusion said, 'We must maintain the cover even between ourselves. Get used to calling me Ralph or if you forget, 'darling' or 'dear' - something affectionate will do. Anyway about the cooking, I'm a dab hand so we won't starve.' He patted her shoulder reassuringly, 'You'll get used to everything. Honestly, it'll be second nature by the end of the week.'

They began the routine next day. Eleanor's concerns about the bedrooms had been dispelled. Paul had set up a bed in the second bedroom but there were to be no lights in use there. The main bedroom lights would go out promptly at eleven, and she and Paul would be on duty in shifts with the infra red camera in use at night. No. 53 had been bugged before she and Paul had arrived, and the box room was to be the listening post.

At first Eleanor found the regime arduous, and frequently dozed off during the night shifts, but as the weeks wore on she became more and more used to their split shifts. Paul made little or no conversation. In the first weeks he tended to bark orders at her or give her instructions in a patient tone as if she was a child. However they soon fell into a more equable arrangement, and he began to lighten up and make the odd joke at her expense. Eleanor took it all in good part, aware of how much was riding on this job for him. Paul was obviously keen to impress the Chief so she did her best to accept his moods with equanimity.

Max was the one who made the difference. He was a lively soul who united them. They would take it in turns to teach him tricks which he responded to with enormous enthusiasm.

Before they knew it, three weeks had gone by and Paul had

started to get edgy.

He complained, 'Nothing is happening. I am beginning to wonder if there is anything worth finding out about this couple. Perhaps the Chief is wrong. The Lindbergs never have visitors. Their conversation in the house is unremarkable. There must be something I'm missing. I have two mobile people following and photographing them but there's nothing so far. I think I need to search their house but it's going to be tricky as Lucas seems to spend a lot of time there.'

Eleanor thought for a moment, 'What about my getting friendly with Freda. I know you're not keen on my being active, but it would be a start wouldn't it and better than nothing?'

Paul studied her, 'I don't think you're experienced enough. How could it be done without raising any suspicions?'

Eleanor said, 'Well, let's think about what they do every day. Freda leaves the house at eight and catches a Tube into Central London. She eats lunch at her desk and leaves at four, shopping en route sometimes at the corner shop, and arriving home about five thirty. In the meantime Lucas makes telephone calls to clients, goes on odd visits in the Sierra, and sits working at his drawing board. Once Freda arrives back they cook dinner together, chat about their day, watch television and are in bed by ten thirty. Doesn't that seem strange to you?'

'What do you mean, surely most people lead pretty dreary lives don't they?'

'But not that dreary,' Eleanor persisted, 'most people have hobbies, interests, go to the cinema, the theatre, the pub, a restaurant, have people round or even have a day out, but they've done nothing like that or go out as a couple.'

'You're right,' Paul said, 'most people do have some sort of outlet even if it's just a pet or jogging. We certainly never see them together and they don't go anywhere. It appears as if they need to make sure there is always one of them in the house.'

'So maybe there is something in the house,' Eleanor said, 'perhaps they're 'sleepers', waiting for instructions.'

For once Paul looked at her with respect and completely forgetting her pretend name, said without thinking, 'At last Eleanor, even if all your information comes from films you are beginning to behave like someone on surveillance.'

She laughed, 'You mean Linda, don't you. Who is Eleanor? Not some old flame surely,' she added jokingly. He raised a hand to her mockingly and joined in the merriment. It was as if they were finally coming together as equal partners.

28

Uncertain what to do next, Paul got summoned to a meeting. He was careful not to tell Eleanor as she had suddenly become fixated on solving their current situation. She was listening into the Lindbergs morning and night as well as keeping watch, and could barely tear herself away to sleep.

Paul had seen this behaviour before with rookies; moving from the tedium of surveillance to obsessively entering into the watched peoples' lives. This was the same as officers who 'went native.'

Leaving Eleanor to her own devices and taking Max, Paul dressed in a tracksuit made his way past Arnos Park to Broomfield Park. He let Max off the lead. The little dog took off like a bullet. It was a quiet time of the morning, and Paul stopped off at a bench and in a random fashion picked up a newspaper that had been left there. Leafing through the pages, he spotted the sign and calling to Max who returned reluctantly, they sauntered on to the band stand. Here there was another chalk mark. Paul moved to the further side of the stand where he wasn't in view. He let Max off the lead and lent against the balustrade smoking a cigarette. The Chief passed carrying a sports bag and mouthed, 'This is too public. Meet me at the sports pavilion near the running track.'

There was no one at the track. The Chief emerged from the pavilion wearing a tracksuit and the pair of them jogged in silence with Max running alongside. Gesturing to the pavilion, the Chief disappeared inside leaving them to follow. Paul tied Max up outside and went in. The Chief, back in his everyday clothes, asked hurriedly: 'Any progress?' Paul explained that they had come up with nothing so far, questioning whether the Lindbergs were even Russian agents.

Alpha waved away his worries, 'Take it from me they are. We know what we're doing. You will have to be more direct. Make some sort of contact with them or check out their house. I don't care how you do it; I want it done and fast now. There's no time to lose.'

Paul queried the urgency but received short shrift. Alpha said, 'I'm disappointed in you, Paul. From everything I'd heard, I thought you were the man for the job, ambitious and wanting to go places, and I'm the right man to help you do that if you do your part. Meet me here in two weeks time and let's hope you've uncovered something by then.' He grabbed his sports bag and stalked off.

 Paul hated being reprimanded like an errant schoolboy. The last few weeks had been stressful enough living cheek by jowl with Eleanor. He'd never got used to working with women, although Eleanor hardly qualified as a woman. Working with men was straightforward. You could be direct with them even shout at them without hurting their feelings, then go down the pub and put everything right with a drink. In Paul's experience women were ornamental and entertaining, someone to have fun with and seduce. This nurturing, mentoring role he'd been forced into didn't come naturally. Granted Eleanor was now doing the job competently but he could hardly discuss his concerns with her as he would a man. There was nothing for it but he'd have to take action to get the Chief what he wanted.

Back at the house Eleanor honed in on something of interest from the previous night's tapes. Lucas had been booking tickets for the forthcoming visit of the Bolshoi Ballet. This was unusual. Perhaps they were intending to meet some contact there. She was dying to tell Paul but he'd been out all morning.

He was grouchy when he returned, but once she'd filled him in, he visibly relaxed and appeared impressed, 'Well done, El (he'd started calling her this diminutive as it seemed to cover both her names).Perhaps we'd better go to the ballet as well although this would be a perfect time to search the house. I just wish I could get more help from the Chief. There's very little support forthcoming. Maybe you'll have to go to the ballet while I search the house. I can get you a seat near the Lindbergs and you can keep them under observation. It might look strange though if you go on your own. I'll ask Claire to go with you. I needn't tell her why.'

Eleanor was indignant, 'But I thought you weren't supposed to involve anyone from the office. I'm sure I can manage on my own. If you buy two tickets there'll be an empty seat, and then if I get asked I can say my husband got held up at the last minute, what do you think?'

'That could work but whatever you do, don't make contact with the targets. It would look too much of a coincidence if they learned we lived opposite.'

The night of the ballet, Paul arranged for a car to take Eleanor to Covent Garden, and pick her up afterwards. Dressing the part Eleanor set off beautifully made up, dressed in a midnight blue calf length tulle dress sprinkled with tiny stars, and a darker blue velvet cloak that she'd bought that morning. Paul hardly registered her departure; he was preoccupied with monitoring the occupants of no. 53.

The Lindbergs left the house shortly after Eleanor. Giving them a good half an hour, Paul dressed head to toe in black surreptitiously made his way through their gate to the backdoor. Using skeleton keys he entered, carefully checking for telltale booby traps. Moving through the house soundlessly, he leafed through books and papers with gloved hands until he got to the study. Their safe was easy to open, possibly too easy, and there was nothing of interest except their false passports and money.

At first glance there was nothing significant. The contents of the house reflected the couples' dull lives - no photos, no pictures, nothing personal. It was then Paul noticed something about the main bedroom. Peering out of the window, he saw that the outside corner of the house didn't tally with the inside corner wall behind the bed and knocking on it he heard the hollow sound of a false wall. Pressing all the fixtures on the wall to open it, Paul was about to give up when he noticed the carpet. For such a pristine house the carpet was unduly wrinkled and creased - perhaps the bed had been moved. After a lot of feeling around under the springs, he located a lever and pulled it. The bed and wall slid back to expose a narrow space with a desk, a shelf and a stool.

The shelf housed a suitcase radio and headphones, and various papers. Paul sat down and studied the papers. Most were in Russian which he photographed, but amongst them was a slim book of English poetry, possibly a code book, but why in English? There was nothing for it but he'd have to examine every page.

Running a letter opener over the pages, he eventually found a microdot used as a full stop. Using tweezers he removed it but there was no reader. Undecided as to what to do, Paul took the dot and placed it carefully between pages of his diary. Looking round he wondered if he could replace it with something similar to avoid suspicion. At the back of the shelf were rolls of blank microfilm and he delicately fashioned a replacement.

Consulting his watch, far more time had elapsed than he'd realised. The ballet would be about to finish. Replacing everything in the room down to the exact wrinkles in the carpet, and double checking everywhere he'd been Paul slipped quietly out the back door and continued down the street on the same side, ready to double back and make for no. 46.

Idly he wondered how Eleanor was getting on, hoping against hope that she wouldn't draw attention to herself. That was highly unlikely considering the way she'd looked tonight. He'd pretended not to notice when she left the house but she'd looked stunning.

Much to his horror he'd begun to think about her a lot. She was occupying his thoughts more each day. There was no doubt; Eleanor had a certain appeal once she got over her diffidence. Surprising strength and resilience inhabited that delicate frame. He'd certainly overlooked those characteristics previously. On occasion she showed signs of ingenuity that were astonishing. He just hoped she'd kept that side of her under control tonight. Having made so much progress himself during the evening he didn't want his efforts sabotaged by a novice. At last he had something for the Chief.

...

Eleanor was enjoying herself at Covent Garden, gazing at the theatre and the beautifully dressed people. The ballet hadn't begun and the orchestra was tuning up. Seated in the stalls she was only a row behind the Lindbergs who were busy studying their programme. They were whispering between themselves, and pointing to a name. Eleanor only wished she could see better and leaning across to the couple

214

next to her, asked to borrow their opera glasses. Still not able to see the name they were so interested in, she worked out how far down the page they were pointing and compared it with her own. There were two possible names Anna Petrova and Anton Nikolayev – both in the corps de ballet.

However at that moment, the conductor raised his baton and the orchestra began to play so there was no further chance to watch the Lindbergs. Eleanor sat back to enjoy Covent Garden and her very first ballet. Donald had taken her to a great many places in the capital and so had Erik, but neither had been keen on ballet. This was a real treat.

During the interval the Lindbergs made a move and Eleanor followed. They headed for the bar and pre-ordered interval drinks. Eleanor had not been that prepared, and attempting to look less conspicuous took out her compact and with her back to them redid her lipstick, observing them in the mirror.

The Lindbergs stood apart from the crowd and finished their drinks. Mrs. Lindberg, Freda, made for the Ladies Room leaving Mr Lindberg, Lucas, finishing his cigarette. Eleanor was hesitant about following Freda. Thinking about Paul's instructions she didn't want to look obvious but decided to follow her anyway. She needn't have worried there was a queue. Freda Lindberg was merely retouching her makeup and washing her hands. Eleanor slumped down at the back of the queue, and as Freda left, Eleanor did too keeping a safe distance between them. They all returned to their seats, and Eleanor began to doubt whether the Lindbergs were there to contact anyone at all.

Once the ballet finished with all its encores, the Lindbergs got up and instead of making for the main exit speedily disappeared backstage. Eleanor was in a quandary. How could she follow them without being seen? Then her chance came. A whole gaggle of ballet students laughing, talking, and carrying flowers were making for the same door and Eleanor smiling merrily mixed in with them. They hardly noticed, linking arms with her and saying; 'Another ballet fan, I suppose?' and she beamed in agreement.

The leader of the group said, 'They'll never allow us to meet any of the ballerinas. You know what the Russians are like with security. But it might be worth a try. What do you think?' she said addressing Eleanor.

Eleanor grinned and said, 'Let's overwhelm them. They won't know what's hit them,' and in unison they forged through the doors. The officials were there blocking the way but the group practically ran them over and raced towards the main dressing room where the prima ballerina was presiding. She laughed seeing all these young people proffering autograph books and presenting her with bunches of violets but the Russian manager was not amused, calling to the Security men to escort them out.

Eleanor looked round for the Lindbergs. There was no sign of them. Escaping the main crowd she crept down the corridor, catching sight of them talking to one of the ballerinas and giving her a folded paper which she slipped down her cleavage. Chatting away the three of them started back up the passage. Eleanor ducked and hid behind an open door as they passed but was able to pick up one or two words of their conversation. They mentioned 'Someone they recognised in London.' This surely couldn't refer to her and Paul could it? After all they'd never even met the Lindbergs since they'd moved in.

Eleanor had to get out of there quickly. Cultivating a helpless face she allowed herself to be accosted by one of the burly Russian security men, tearfully saying, 'I've lost my escort, what can I do?' He put an arm round her in a fatherly fashion, saying, 'I take you to entrance. No worry, any man wait for lovely girl like you. I stay with you till he come.' Eleanor felt trapped but seeing the crowds awaiting the ballerinas, she waved animatedly as if she'd spotted her companion and said, 'There he is. You've been so kind.' The man shrugged, 'Is nothing,' and turned away.

Eleanor sped round to the front of the theatre and to the waiting car, desperate to get home and update Paul.

29

Once home and revived with a large brandy and soda, Eleanor and Paul exchanged stories.

Eleanor was elated, 'We've made progress.'

Paul reprimanded her, 'You took too many risks. When will you learn? This job is all about caution, and planned and calculated risks.'

'But what about opportunities,' Eleanor responded boldly, 'surely if the opportunity presents itself, you have to take advantage of it?'

'I think you're getting tipsy. You're not used to strong drink. You better get off to bed.'

Eleanor annoyed to be treated like a child said, 'Well I think I deserve another drink after all my hard work,' and before he could stop her she'd downed a second glass. This time he pulled the bottle away from her and corked it, 'You've definitely had enough now,' he said, and throwing her over his shoulder took her upstairs and dumped her unceremoniously on the double bed, dress and all. He did however take off her shoes and pull the covers over her, as she murmured, 'Don't I get a kiss good night?'

'I hardly think so in your state,' but he leant over her and kissed her gently on the brow.

'That's no good,' she mumbled sleepily, 'that's for babies.'

'But that's all you're getting for now,' Paul said, amused by her attitude, 'you'll have a mammoth hangover in the morning and it serves you right.'

He went downstairs and poured himself another drink. Should he contact the Chief? It was two o'clock in the morning but this couldn't wait. He dialled the scrambler number. A grumpy voice demanded, 'Who the hell is waking me up at this time?' Paul explained, and they arranged a rendezvous for later on that morning. 'Now get some sleep,' growled the voice, 'and let me get some too.' Paul lay back in the chair and mulled over everything. He felt uneasy but didn't know why.

Meeting the Chief the next day he still couldn't shake off the feeling of foreboding despite the good news. They went through the meeting ritual as before, with Paul tying Max to a post outside the sports pavilion. It was a long time before the Chief appeared.

Apologising Alpha said, 'It was tricky getting away at short notice. I've only a minute or two. What have you found out?'

Paul outlined everything concisely including Eleanor's part never mentioning her by name, and produced the microdot wrapped in a piece of tissue. Alpha pocketed it carefully showing no sign of emotion. Paul mentioned the English poetry book, 'I wonder why they used an English book as a hiding place?' he muttered.

Alpha said carelessly, 'I daresay they thought it would look less suspicious if they left it casually behind on a table or bench.'

'I suppose so,' Paul replied. He could see the Chief was eager to be off and asked, 'What's our next move? Should we carry on? Perhaps follow them and try and locate their handler, or are you going to lift them for interrogation?'

'No, none of that at this stage,' Alpha said firmly, 'leave everything to me. You and the girl sit tight and I'll be in touch. You've both done well, better than I expected.'

Irritated and frustrated, Paul returned to no 46 with Max. If there was anything he hated it was sitting and waiting. Surveillance of course was all about waiting but at least there was some activity involved. Hanging around with no plan in view was unendurable especially with Eleanor. In fact where was the wretched girl? There was no sign of her in the bedroom. Then he heard retching sounds in the bathroom. Poor girl, he supposed he better do something for her.

She arrived in the kitchen just as he boiled the kettle, looking pale and listless, her hair tangled and plastered to her forehead. Paul couldn't help but feel sorry for her and said, 'Here's some Alka Seltzer and hot water. Drink it down there's a good girl.' He wrapped ice cubes in a cloth and popped them on her head, 'Hold on to that, you'll feel better soon. A good fry up will put you right; I'll nip out for eggs and bacon and be back in a jiff.'

Eleanor shuddered and protested weakly, 'No, please, no – just dry toast. I think I'm dying.'

Paul grinned, 'No such luck, it's just one almighty hangover. You'll improve shortly and we'll go out for a walk and some fresh air.'

Eleanor suddenly remembered last night and her behaviour, and felt the heat of embarrassment rising up her body. What must Paul think of her, all that asking to be kissed, how unprofessional. Trying to distract herself she asked, 'Have you seen the Chief? What did he say?'

Paul was noncommittal, 'Yes I've seen him. We have to sit it out until he contacts me again.'

'But,' Eleanor said feebly, 'was he pleased with us?'

'Satisfied we'd done our job,' said Paul, 'you don't get thanks and pats on the back in this line of work. You either succeed or you don't. Of course sometimes failure means curtains,' he added ominously.

Eleanor sensed there was something else on Paul's mind. He was obviously not happy, but was hardly going to confide in her. He encouraged her to get dressed and with Max on the lead they set off for Arnos Park. It was a lovely spring day and Eleanor began to feel her spirits lift, and her stomach realign itself. She danced along with the little dog and Paul

221

felt his spirits lift seeing them together. She really was a pretty little thing, he thought, perhaps this waiting might be enjoyable after all.

…

Things were not going well for Anubis. Ever since the incident with Georges, he had begun to feel that his tightly meshed life was unravelling. Keeping his life in separate compartments was alright until they started overflowing into one another. Vasily wasn't helping. He was either out of the country at Moscow Central or tied up with other agents. At long last Anubis tracked him down and arranged a meet, 'It better be secure. We have a lot to discuss.'

Close to midnight, Anubis made his way down to old warehouses at St Katherine's Dock. He stood around in the darkest part of the docks smoking. It was an age before Vasily approached. They were such a pain these old guard. They had all been taught to 'dry-clean' themselves every four hours to shake off counter surveillance. Honestly he was the one who was in constant danger not Vasily.

They found a dark corner to talk in. Vasily wasn't in a good frame of mind either and complained vociferously, 'This is a terrible place to find. Surely you could have found somewhere more central. There's nowhere decent to eat or get a drink.'

'Don't worry about that now; we're hardly here for fine

dining,' Anubis said roughly, 'I'm more concerned with Lucas and Freda. My contact has searched their house. He's come up with a microdot with intelligence about Moscow Central and a list of our assets in this country. I think the Lindbergs are about ready to make their move over to the British. We're going to have to act faster. What Intel do you have?'

Vasily pursed his lips, 'Not much. They did contact one of our people at the Bolshoi but it was about money. They said they needed ready cash as it was so complicated to open a bank account here.'

'That's piffle,' Anubis retorted, 'anyone can open one. They've got false passports for goodness sake. They're trying to milk the system before they defect. I have a bad feeling about them. I'm not entirely sure that Lucas wasn't one of the assets, I used in Krakow. The girl overheard some mention of 'recognising someone in London'. This is getting too close for my liking.'

Vasily shrugged, 'They'll have to be disposed of then I suppose. I'd prefer it, if you could expedite matters. The Residenza knows nothing about our arrangements here as per your instructions - only Central knows.'

Anubis nodded, 'My man on the ground is ready. It will have to look like a burglary gone wrong. In fact, I might just be able to use this to our advantage. My chap's an effective operative and I think he could be turned. They think highly of him at Sentry. This might provide me with the ideal chance.'

'Fair enough,' Vasily said, 'we could do with more assets particularly if he has the potential to move up the Service. I'll leave that to you. I'm sure you'll make a wonderful mentor,' he chortled sardonically, 'particularly with all your years of experience of turning people.'

Anubis not impressed with the sarcasm, narrowed his eyes dangerously, saying, 'Don't ever, ever, take me for granted, Vasily, or you may live to regret it.'

Vasily swallowed uneasily, he had seen the consequences of Anubis' displeasure at firsthand, and it hadn't been a pretty sight. He said softly, in a conciliating manner, 'Of course Sasha I would never take you for granted, please forgive my schoolboy humour it gets away from me sometimes.'

'Don't call me Sasha, that name's gone long ago as you well know.'

Vasily slumped, it seemed he could do nothing right. Anubis had never been easy to work with and had become more demanding as he got older. However Moscow would not be happy with him if he antagonised their golden goose.

'Shall we get back to the matter in hand?' he asked timidly, 'the only thing I'm concerned about is anything incriminating at the house. The last thing I need is to have any blame laid at our door.'

Anubis said, 'There'll be no worries there. I intend to make sure the job is done to my satisfaction.'

'Well then,' Vasily said, 'there's just the matter of firepower - that I can get you, no problem.'

Anubis shook his head, 'No need, I have my own private armoury.'

Vasily's eyes widened but he said nothing further. It was best to keep his mouth shut.

They signalled agreement and evaporated into the darkness.

30

Paul and Eleanor decided to take a day's holiday. It was a late Indian summer and they thought they might as well make the most of it. After the walk in the park they'd agreed to take a break.

There was no point in keeping further surveillance on the house opposite now the Chief was in the know, and there was nothing else to do. Paul had dismantled all the equipment and packed it away and Eleanor had sorted out her belongings.

The sun was shining, the air warm and balmy and with Max raring to go, they set off for Brighton. Walking along the promenade they both felt young and carefree. Paul bought them both ice creams and they sat on the sand watching children building sandcastles, mothers paddling and dogs scampering about.

After a while they lay back and started talking about themselves. Paul was in an easy, confiding mood, 'I didn't do much of this when I was young. We rarely went to the coast. Living in Gloucestershire, it was always a bit of a trek. Of course it wasn't that long after the war so petrol was on ration. What about you, where did you grow up?'

'Oh everywhere, but mainly in the West Country; my parents were always on the move. My father would have thought it a waste of time and money to sit on a beach. We lived in different places and in temporary homes: caravans;

an old army Nissan hut, and once even in the back of his old pickup.'

Paul grinned, 'How on earth did you do that?'

'Father rigged up a tarpaulin over the top and tied it to the back bumper. It was like a tent with the three of us in sleeping bags on a blow up mattress. It was alright until one night there was a mini hurricane and we had to hang on to the edges of the tarp. for dear life. It was always like that I'm afraid until I came to London.'

'It sounds grim,' Paul remarked, 'I certainly couldn't complain about my childhood. My parents weren't well off but they did everything they could for my sister and me. Unfortunately they died during the war; my father in the RAF and my mother in a bombing raid. We went to live with our grandmother in Gloucester but she was too old to look after us properly and I ended up bringing up my sister, Maureen, who was barely four at the time.'

'I would have loved a sister,' Eleanor said, 'where's your sister now?'

'She still lives in my grandmother's old house and takes in lodgers. She contracted polio during the Fifties, has never been strong and works at home as a graphic artist. I'm very fond of her; she's a kind, sweet soul and I stay with her occasionally when I have leave.'

'Does she know what you do?' Eleanor asked.

227

'No, not really though I think she might suspect. She never asks. I joined the Service straight from university, and was based in London. We lead separate lives. I maintain my business consultant cover for anyone who asks, and that accounts for my comings and goings.' Paul yawned, 'Enough about me. This heat will send me to sleep soon. Much as I would love to stay longer I think we should get back.' He surveyed the beach, 'Sometimes it's good to remember that there's a normal world out there.'

Eleanor detected a note of regret in Paul's words. She would have loved to know more about him, but was hesitant to break up this shared intimacy. It was as if Paul had come closer to trusting her today. Being dependent on him as she was had made Eleanor feel close to him, closer than she'd ever felt to anyone before.

Did Paul sense her growing feelings she wondered, however even if he did he would probably ignore them. There was a hard shell about him that was difficult to penetrate. His training and job had turned him into a self contained man wary of personal attachments. But Eleanor was not going to give up easily; perhaps she could change him if they spent enough time together.

Standing up, brushing himself down and calling Max, Paul was suddenly all business. Nevertheless he looked down at Eleanor affectionately pulling her to her feet, 'Come along lazybones, time for home. The Chief may be in touch.'

On their way back to the station he took hold of her arm as if they were a couple, continuing to chat to her as if they were. Eleanor was over the moon, perhaps he felt something for her after all, but she was too inexperienced to know how to exploit the situation.

On their return there was a message from the Chief wanting a meet later that night. Eleanor cooked a meal from her limited menu and they settled down to eat with a bottle of wine. It was so domestic that Eleanor kept envisaging a future like this.

As Paul was leaving he suggested Eleanor go to bed, 'I don't know what time I'll be back. Don't wait up for me.' Without thinking, he kissed on the cheek as he left. Eleanor went up to bed in a buoyant mood.

Arriving at the meeting, Paul could see the Chief was in a temper. 'Where've you been all day? I've been ringing and ringing and leaving messages. You've no business abandoning your post.'

Paul tried to explain about the need for a day off but was cut short. 'Who gave you permission to go cavorting to the coast with the girl? What do you think we're running here some sort of holiday camp? This is a very delicate and urgent operation. I want it finalised by tomorrow night, do you understand?'

Paul kept quiet. Weeks ago when the Chief had briefed him

it had sounded as if this would be a long running op. so why was it unexpectedly being cut short? Clearly this was not a good time to ask.

The Chief continued, 'As far as I understand it the Lindbergs will be elsewhere tomorrow night. I want you to go in and clear the house of all intelligence. We – yes I mean me (as Paul looked bemused) – shall have about two hours. I will be going with you and acting as lookout. I know that's not usual, but I need to keep this op. top secret and involve as few people as possible.'

He held up his hand as Paul went to open his mouth, 'No questions. This is entirely above your pay grade. You have proved yourself reliable and competent so far. All you need to know is that I trust you. Be ready outside no. 53 at eleven o'clock sharp tomorrow night, wear suitable clothes and bring a weapon. That's all. I'll see you then,' and he walked off.

Paul was stumped. Why would he need a gun if all they were doing was clearing the house? Where would the Lindbergs be? He and Eleanor had closely monitored the couple and knew once they were home they never left. How could the Chief know they wouldn't be there? Unless of course they were being picked up for interrogation but then why wouldn't Mr C send Sentry people to clear the house?

It was unsettling, giving Paul a bad feeling. Paul wished he had someone to talk to. He couldn't speak to Mr C or any chances of promotion would fly out the door. He didn't know anyone more senior than the Chief, and it had been made clear to him that he was not at that level of clearance. What could he do?

By the time he got home Eleanor was in bed. There was no question of unburdening himself to an inexperienced girl with no security clearance. Pouring himself a whiskey, he lit a cigar and sat down to think. He was a good officer even if he did have a tendency to bend the rules. There was nothing for it; he would have to do what he was told despite his misgivings.

31

The next morning Paul felt no better about the forthcoming venture but tried to put on a good face for Eleanor.

Eleanor was buzzing about making breakfast, feeding Max, and finally asked, 'What did the Chief want last night? What's our next move?'

Paul said, 'Nothing that involves you, El. I wonder if you wouldn't be better off going home now. Your part in is finished, and I've got to return Max to the kennels.'

Eleanor could barely conceal her disappointment, 'But is it all over? Has it been successful? And can't I keep Max?' she pressed.

Paul sighed, 'I'm as much in the dark as you. They only feed me things bit by bit on a 'Need to Know' basis. And a definite no, you can't keep the dog. I've one more job to do later tonight but that's as much as I can tell you. Why don't you go off home? You must be dying to get back to your flat and see what's happening.'

But Eleanor was adamant, 'No, I want to stay till the bitter end and then we can leave tomorrow as planned. If this is to be my last op. and I have to return to the office again, I'm seeing it through. What about you? What will you do afterwards?'

'Wait for orders, I suppose,' Paul said, 'though I'm owed a

lot of leave. I might take off and see my sister. It's been a long time.'

At eleven that night Paul disappeared and came back dressed in his usual black clothing, 'I shouldn't be long. I've to collect everything from across the road then it will be finished.'

'But surely,' Eleanor said, 'the Lindbergs will be there. I know we haven't been watching them this week but they always go to bed at eleven.'

'The Chief assured me they wouldn't be home,' Paul said, carefully adjusting his shoulder holster, 'I think he was trying to imply they've already been picked up. I've to take his word for it,' and without thinking he blurted out, 'I'm not used to this way of working. Everything is so totally unprofessional, and I've no backup if things go wrong.'

Eleanor didn't like the sound of this. She'd never seen Paul so upset; he was always in control. Before she had time to say any encouraging words, he'd slipped out the door.

Eleanor decided to unpack the binoculars, and watch the road. There was no car in the driveway. Perhaps the couple had been taken into custody earlier in the day. She could just make out Paul scanning the road as if he was looking for someone. He stood still for a moment, undecided, shook his head and then made for the back door. Eleanor thought she caught a glimpse of a shadowy figure lurking behind a hedge at the corner of the street but she wasn't sure. At this time of night, it was difficult to pick out anything in the dark even with the odd street lamp.

She stepped back from the window aware she'd been holding her breath. Everything was quiet. There was nothing to see. On the point of getting ready for bed, Eleanor took one last look. A light came on across the road and was that the faintest sound of a scream? Eleanor stopped in her tracks. The light went out as quickly as it had come on but a Ford Sierra was slowly pulling into the Lindberg's drive, and Lucas Lindberg got out. Unconcernedly he sauntered towards his front door.

Eleanor pulled on her shoes, racing full pelt down the stairs and across the road just as the hall lights came on. Moving soundlessly to the back of the house, she tried the backdoor. The handle turned. Sneaking through the kitchen she heard the sounds of a fight going on upstairs. Panic stricken Eleanor ran up the stairs two at a time. Lucas and Paul were tussling on the ground, whilst a shocked and scared Freda sitting bound and gagged in a chair looked on.

Eleanor stood motionless, stunned and helpless. It was like watching a film, none of it seemed real. Finally recovering her senses she spotted the gun they were scrabbling over. It had shot out of Paul's holster and lay on the floor. Whilst they struggled to reach it Eleanor saw her chance, dragging it towards her with her foot and taking hold of it in her shaking hand. At the same instant they both registered her holding the gun, and Lucas made one almighty leap for it. Hardly aware of what she was doing but intent on saving Paul, Eleanor pulled the trigger. The blast knocked Lucas backwards. He lay prone on the carpet, a star shaped hole in his forehead. Freda slumped in a faint and Paul aghast at the speed of events, seized the gun from Eleanor's limp hand. Turning off the lights as he went, he pulled her barely resisting towards the door, saying under his breath, 'I must get you out of here.'

He all but dragged her to no. 46. Eleanor her legs now like jelly, felt nothing as he propped her on the settee, pouring brandy down her throat. She was in a rigor of shaking, moaning and rocking back and fore. Paul said sharply, 'El, I have to go back and sort things out.' But she clung tightly to him as if he were her life raft. Taking her on his knee he sat with his arms round her waiting for the shuddering to pass. Once she was calmer he laid her back saying, 'Close your eyes, I won't be long. We have to get out of here then.'

Feeling distinctly wobbly himself, Paul made his way back to no.53. It was in pitch darkness and silent as the grave. Thanks goodness no one in the street appeared to have been wakened by the shot. Making his way upstairs by the light of his torch, he mentally prepared himself for what was to come. He had no idea what he was going to do with the body let alone Freda. Why hadn't the Chief turned up? Why had he told Paul the Lindbergs wouldn't be home?

But when Paul got to the bedroom it was completely empty

– no body on the floor – no Freda tied up. Paul thought he must be going mad. He examined the other two bedrooms, but there was nothing. Not daring to switch on a light, he knelt on the floor to see if there were signs of blood – again nothing. What about the hidey hole and all the papers? Feeling under the bed Paul pushed the lever. It didn't budge. It appeared to be stuck or broken, and without it there was no opening the wall compartment. It was as if the Lindbergs had never existed.

Paul was at a loss. Had the Chief been here already and cleaned up. Surely there wouldn't have been time. He tried to think. Had he been at no. 46 with Eleanor longer than he thought? It was no good contacting the Chief now. He and Eleanor needed to disappear. Peering out the backdoor, Paul could see the Lindbergs' car in the drive which was peculiar, with the keys in the ignition. It would look suspicious if the car was left there for days.

There was nothing for it but to take their car, load Eleanor and her baggage into it, deposit her at her flat, abandon the car somewhere and come back and pick up his own. What a palaver! If the Chief had sent in cleaners, why hadn't they disposed of the car?

Paul drove the Sierra across the road, packed his own car with all the equipment and his baggage and looked in on Eleanor. Her eyes were closed and she and was sleeping heavily. Probably the shock and the drink had knocked her out. It was past two o'clock in the morning and he needed to get going. Carefully picking up Eleanor who barely moved and was snoring loudly, he placed her on the back seat and set off for her flat.

The mews was in complete darkness. Darting up the spiral staircase, he picked the lock and opened the door. The flat was quiet. Ignoring the lights, Paul extracted Eleanor from the car, and made his way back up the stairs breathing heavily under her dead weight.

Making sure she was sleeping on her side, he left and drove off in the direction of Arnos Park. Finding a side street he dumped the Sierra, double checked the inside, unscrewed the number plates and threw them away. Taking to his heels, he jogged through the empty streets back to his own car and drove home. He tried ringing the Chief's number but there was nothing- not even an engaged tone.

Later that morning after barely three hours sleep, Paul made his way back to Eleanor's flat. She was out for the count. He took off his shoes and lay down on the bed beside her. There was nothing to be done at this time.

His mind kept running over the events of last night. Why had the op. gone so wrong, and if the Chief wasn't around, who could he turn to?

Eleanor sighed in her sleep turning towards him. He smiled faintly. She had saved his life last night no doubt about it. He put his arm under her shoulders pulling her to him, and letting her lean her head on his chest. He certainly was fond of her, well as fond as he could ever be of anyone.

…

On the other side of London sitting in a car in the darkness, Anubis said, 'It didn't go as planned. At least Freda and Lucas won't bother us anymore. Thanks for the help with the clean up. Where did you get the men from? They were certainly quick and effective?'

Vasily grimaced, 'It wasn't easy my friend, finding freelance contractors at that time of night. I told you I just wanted to keep it between us, and not involve the Residenzia. Unfortunately the men were in too much of a rush to take the car. I daresay your guy was well trained enough to do something about it. But you owe me one, don't forget.'

Anubis grinned, 'Always comrade, always. Don't get your knickers in a twist; I expected it to be dealt with in your usual efficient manner.' He took a hip flask out of his pocket, 'A toast, my friend, to a job well done.' They both drank long and hard.

Vasily said, 'What's the next step for your couple? They know too much to be let loose in London? What will Sentry think?'

'Don't you worry your pretty little head about Sentry? I've notified them that I need their people indefinitely for a special job of national importance,' Anubis replied, 'As for the couple themselves, I have my own plans for them. They'll soon be out of our hair. In the short term there's a safe house far enough away, and in the long-term, once my protégé rids himself of the girl, I have the very mission for him.'

LIVING THE LEGEND

32

Scotland, 1981

'It's hard to believe we've been here nearly two years,' Eleanor said, 'it's the longest I've been anywhere besides London.'

The London nightmare was like a dream now. The morning after the shooting when she'd woken up in Paul's arms none of it seemed real. The only part that was real was when he kissed her. Before she knew it they were in each other's arms and making love as she called it, though in her heart of hearts she knew Paul would dismiss it as mere comfort sex. For once he appeared troubled and uncertain, as if he'd lost his usual self-assurance. Eleanor wanted to console him and confide in him that this was her first time and how special it had been for her, but though he'd been tender and gentle with her, he got up immediately afterwards threw on his clothes and left without a word. It was as if he'd let himself down in a moment of weakness and wanted to forget all about it.

Eleanor had no idea when or if he was even coming back. She tried to cheer herself up with the fact that at last she was a woman, a bit late perhaps at twenty four, but better late than never. Studying herself in the mirror she said to herself, 'I do look different, my skin is glowing and I look older.' Was it terrible to be so exultant about her change in status when last night she'd taken a man's life? But it had been either Lucas or Paul. What else could she have done at the time? She was always going to save Paul.

Paul returned later, making no comment about the change in their relationship just issuing instructions, 'Pack warm clothes. We're going to Scotland - the Chief's orders. He's cleared it with the office. Apparently we have to lie low and unfortunately,' he remarked scowling, 'that means together. We'll keep the same cover story and he's supplied me with ample funds.'

'But what about last night? Where was the Chief? What happened? Why were the Lindbergs at home? Why did everything go wrong, and what happened to.... the body (Eleanor's voice shook) and to Freda?'

'It's no good bombarding me with questions. We need to go. All I got from the Chief was that he was late getting to the Avenue. By then everyone and everything had been disposed of. His only thought was that the Russians had been on to the Lindbergs all along and beaten us to it.' Paul shrugged his shoulders, 'That's how it goes sometimes; nothing is straightforward in this game. You'll have to get used to it.' He turned his back on her discouraging further conversation.

It had taken them a day and a night to drive to the top of Scotland to the Chief's hideaway in Durness. Paul barely spoke on the journey but Eleanor didn't care. She'd got her wish; there would be time to get to know him now. To the outside world they would still be 'the married couple, Ralph and Linda Whitman,' so she might as well make the most of it. She just wished they could have brought Max. The little dog always softened Paul up more successfully than she could. But perhaps now they were really 'together' things would be different.

Eleanor shuddered when she thought about the night of the shooting - her second killing. Erik's was surely more of an accident, but this one..... was she turning into a killer? She'd never even handled a gun till that night. Paul never mentioned the night at all. He was obviously able to blot it all out more successfully than she could.

The first weeks in Durness had been difficult. Paul was moody and resentful as if the enforced isolation was her fault. Eleanor did her best to make it up to him, struggling with the Aga and trying to cook his favourite meals. All she got in return were blank walls of silence. With only one decent bedroom Paul took it upon himself to sleep on the couch in the lounge, ignoring the blowback from the peaty fire.

Eventually after a number of early morning jogs on the shore near the cottage, he began to unwind suggesting they take a drive round the coast to Cape Wrath. Eleanor was relieved; she had begun to despair of them ever getting back to their former easy relationship.

On the drive he said, 'I suppose I've been a bit of a bastard to you lately. You don't deserve it; after all you've been through. Let's call a truce and try and make the most of our time here, what do you say?'Eleanor was only too willing and things began to improve.

They started going out for meals, visiting pubs and touring the area. Eleanor enjoyed being known as Mrs. Whitman, acting out her status as a married woman with enthusiasm. Her cooking was improving and every night they drank homemade wine from the local craft village. The wine would loosen Paul's tongue and once in a while he would reminisce about his early work in counter intelligence in Berlin. He never went into details but would explain some of the tradecraft. Eleanor lapped it up eagerly. It sounded scary but thrilling. It was hard to believe how young Paul had been when he started in the Service. He'd scarcely been more than her age when she'd arrived in London.

Some nights Paul would say, 'Let's go out and eat tonight.' It became a ritual to sample the fresh fish at the Far North hotel, joining long tables packed with visitors. Paul would be at his most charismatic in company retailing adventures of daring do. Eleanor would ask on the way home, 'Did any of that really happen?'

'Of course not El. It's just my job. I'm an accomplished liar. I should have been a novelist.'

Eleanor was not sure about all this fiction. At times it was hard keeping up with the lies, particularly when Paul included her in his stories. Her father had been one for fantastical tales. But Eleanor and her mother had had to live with the consequences of them when they turned into harsh reality.

Despite Eleanor's qualms, she adored Paul. He had given up the couch and was back sharing the bed. Though he could be loving and passionate towards her, Eleanor knew there was a part of him she would never be able to reach. He could turn his emotions on and off like a tap whereas she was always left wanting more.

They had friends now. Jock from the village would turn up in his ancient tam-o-shanter with armloads of firewood and bags of peat. His hair always reflected the constant changes of Scottish weather. Some days it stood up, other days it stuck out. Eleanor nicknamed him 'the weather vane'. He would plant himself in their kitchen, warming his bottom on the Aga, hands on hips and say, 'Och, I dunna know how you folks stick it out here with just yon sheep for company. Come down the pub tonight. We're having a ceilidh at the hall. You can have a fling, d'ya ken.'

Paul would look dubious but generally gave in to Eleanor's enthusiasm. The village folk were friendly enough without being too curious and there was safety in numbers. Eleanor would pin on her tartan and energetically attempt to follow the dances. Paul seeing her carried away with such high spirits worried that she might forget their cover names.

Occasionally she'd start to say 'P--' then change it to 'Perhaps', but most of the time she addressed him as 'Darling' to cover her slip-ups.

As the year had gone on Paul had become more and more anxious about his job and whether he still had one. He regularly tried to reach the Chief, who was surprisingly elusive. When he finally made contact, Paul complained volubly, 'I can't take much more, Chief. I'm going mad with boredom. There's only so much Scottish scenery a man can take. Aren't there any ops I could be involved in?' But his grumbles fell on deaf ears. The only response was, 'Be patient. Your time will come.'

Eleanor noticing his frustrated expression on his return from one of these calls, kept quiet. Inwardly she was delighted their stay would continue. She'd been toying with the idea of a family but dared not mention any such a thing to Paul.

Amazingly, Eleanor had made a woman friend. The first friend she'd ever had - someone without any ulterior motive or agenda. Morag was twenty years older than her but that hardly mattered. They discussed recipes and gossiped about the village. Morag had always lived in Durness and knew everyone and their families. Normally she never asked Eleanor anything personal, but this one day she said, 'I do wonder at you and Ralph coming to such a remote place to live. You're both young and it isn't as if Ralph came here for work?'

Eleanor said carefully, 'We both wanted a change. My husband's been ill and needed rest and peace.' She left it at that hoping it was enough. But Morag continued, 'I'm sorry to hear that Linda, he looks so well and fit now, will you stay do you think?'

Eleanor repeated the conversation to Paul, who was infuriated, 'I told you not to get too close to these people,' he said, 'you are no good at lying. Your face always gives you away. Keep your distance from that woman.'

Eleanor protested, 'But how? It would look odd. We've become such good friends. I do need someone besides you to talk to. In fact,' she added with a tone of sarcasm, 'you don't mind having sex with me but you're not that keen on talking to me.'

Paul narrowed his eyes, 'You're getting too big for your boots, missy. I can find other entertainment in bed if it doesn't suit you. Never ever take me for granted. I'm not your property or anyone's for that matter, and don't you forget it.'

Eleanor badly wanted to say, 'But what about your country surely you belong to them,' but bit back the retort. She was no match for Paul in a slanging match. Feeling bruised she said, 'Well, what shall we do about Morag? I don't want to offend her; she's been so good to me whilst we've been here.'

'It should be 'you' who does something about Morag not 'we'. Paul said coldly, 'You got yourself into this mess and you should get yourself out.'

Then studying her pinched little face and taking pity on her said, 'I think the best thing is to go touring for a week or two. We can see a bit of Scotland and hopefully that will break the relationship. I suppose a bit of travel will pass the time while I wait for the next job.'

In his usual professional way Paul wouldn't allow Eleanor to even leave a note for Morag. They had to be packed and away the very next day.

'Won't she think it funny us rushing of like this?'

'I left word with Jock, don't worry,' Paul said. He had reverted back to his former impenetrable self, deep in thought most of the time. Eleanor thought this is going to be some holiday if he's in this mood. All her dreams about settling down with him and a family were fading fast.

33

London, late 1981

'It's an honour to meet you at last Sir Alan. Your reputation precedes you. I'm James Petersen. Do you hear anything of Sir Donald these days? I expect he's well and truly retired.'

Coolly Alan contemplated the man shaking his hand. He had all the brash excitability of a typical American. Americans were always over impressed by titles, not realising titles didn't mean a lot in the great scheme of things. They had their uses of course – mainly for getting good seats at the opera or the best table in restaurants.

'Call me Alan please - delighted to meet you, young man.'

Petersen was overcome and gabbled, 'I always thought people in your line of work only got knighted when they retired, like Sir Donald, not when they're still operational?'

Alan shrugged as if a knighthood was a mere trifle, 'I don't know about that. I'm hardly active these days. I simply move a few chess pieces round the board.'

'I think you undervalue yourself and your influence Alan,' Petersen returned.

Alan considered for a moment. The one thing he never did in a game of chess was underestimate his opponent or himself. But he merely nodded, smiling in an avuncular fashion. He'd chosen the Travellers Club on purpose. Its clubbiness and grandeur was bound to impress the CIA man. They sat in wing chaired splendour eyeing one another with uneasy wariness.

Alan marvelled at the fact that the agents were getting younger and younger, or was he just getting too old. Of course he should by rights have been meeting the Director at his level, but heigh–ho maybe this was all he merited these days. This rather well-fed, plump young man sitting opposite, ingenuous in his totally unsuitable lightweight suit, could prove to be a useful ally.

'A drink?' Alan enquired raising an eyebrow to a waiting flunky, 'We should toast our upcoming cooperation, what do you say?'

'That would be most hospitable,' Petersen replied rather formally, 'maybe wild Turkey on the rocks?'

'I'm not sure whether they stock Bourbon here,' Alan said, 'but we'll give it a try.'

The drinks arrived. Alan took a long draught and sat there expectantly waiting for Petersen to begin. It was always tactical to wait for the other side to open.

Petersen nervously cleared his throat a few times, wondering how he'd got himself into this and commenced, 'You know we're up against it with the Russkies. They seem to be infiltrating all sorts of countries these days with their Communist claptrap, in particular Central America.'

Alan winced at the terminology, 'You make them sound like an encroaching disease.'

'I suppose that's what they are,' Petersen declared exuberantly and carrying the metaphor forward said, 'of course, we're doing our best to inoculate against it but a bit of help from your good selves wouldn't go amiss.'

'What exactly can we do?' Alan enquired frostily. He wasn't at all sure he should be committing the Service to America's underhand activities. Not only that but he wasn't at all sure that he liked this young man's cavalier attitude to their business. These Americans all acted as if they were still in the frat house with an entitlement to be leaders of the free world.

Petersen licked his lips, suddenly conscious of talking to a superior, 'As you may or may not know, President Carter has been providing millions of pounds worth of aid to Nicaragua since the Sandinista coup last year, thinking to have them on side. But things aren't going to plan. The Sandinista government has a strong left wing and they're likely to follow Cuba's example. We are worried that the Commies might develop more of a foothold.'

'It sounds a mess,' Alan commented drily, 'I suppose the administration wants to retract now, set up another coup and install a new government. It's a pity you people never seem to know which side to back. I can't see that Her Majesty's government would want to involve themselves in such a fiasco. Central America is hardly on our doorstep and no threat to us.'

Petersen looked disconcerted, 'But Sir Alan (reverting to their earlier formality), we're just looking for a favour. You know we're good for a bit of 'quid pro quo.'

Alan was thoughtful, 'Very well, state your terms. I'll see what I can do however it will have to be on the q.t. I can't have questions asked in high places. This would have to be between you and me personally, do you understand?'

Petersen dabbed at his sweating forehead, 'Of course Sir Alan, I wouldn't have it any other way and whenever you call in the debt I'll be ready.'

They went on to discuss details and order dinner, and finally very much to Petersen's relief they began to talk in a more easy and jovial manner. By the end of the meal Petersen began to feel he'd built the basis of a friendly relationship with Sir Alan; perhaps the old boy could be useful after all. Maybe these stuffy Brits weren't so bad despite their penchant for nursery food - toad in the hole and spotted dick honestly- what was so wrong with a decent rib-eye steak and fries followed by key lime pie?

...

Back in Scotland, Paul and Eleanor were at last enjoying one another's company on their tour. Paul had recovered from his ill humour and was once again his beguiling informative self. Eleanor had come to see that he had a great eye for detail, enjoying trudging round museums and castles and giving her potted histories. She sensed there was still an underlying unease about his job but he hid it well behind smart quips and schoolboy jokes.

They were back on a loving footing. Eleanor wished and hoped it would go on forever. They ventured up to Cape Wrath, over to John O'Groats, down to Inverness, Fort William and eventually to Glasgow. By this time they had been on the road for over a month. They were admiring Mackintosh's work in Glasgow when Paul mumbled, 'I've had a message from the Chief. I'm to meet him here in the city tomorrow. It looks as if it's time for me to go back to work.'

Eleanor was stunned, 'But what about our holiday and what about me?'

Paul said, 'Don't worry; I daresay we can make arrangements for you to fly back to London and return to Sentry. I'll make sure you're alright.'

That night Paul booked a suite at the Grand Central announcing, 'As this may be our last night together we should go out in style.'

Dinner was served in their room with champagne, caviar and oysters. Paul was in a teasing mood, 'I better finish your education with the finer things in life,' as he cajoled her into swallowing oysters whole. Eleanor gagged at the slimy way they slid down her throat but loved the caviar.

'Beluga caviar,' Paul scoffed, 'I don't know how they came by that.'

Their night of lovemaking in the four poster bed, curtained and safe from the outside world, encouraged Eleanor's fantasies about them being together forever. But next morning cold reality set in once Paul left for his meeting, leaving her alone and abandoned again.

Paul sat in Kelvingrove Gallery studying the paintings and thinking about his future. It seemed a long time since he'd worked. It was surprising how used he'd got to doing very little and being with Eleanor. Perhaps he was no good to the Service anymore; maybe he'd lost his edge. After the disaster of Arnos Grove, they probably considered him 'burnt.' What would he do if he was kicked out of the Service - a has-been at forty five with no marketable skills? It was far too late to make a change now.

The Chief materialised, as he usually did as if from nowhere. He sat next to Paul and commented on the painting. After a minute or two, they sauntered off together checking and double-checking on any possible tails. The Chief appeared remarkably composed as if he hadn't a care in the world. Walking through the city, they made for a secluded bench in the park.

Alpha took his time but finally said, 'I think you've been out of the picture long enough, Paul. I've a job for you in the New Year, and cleared everything with Sentry and Mr C. You and the girl can go back to London for Christmas, and then in January I want you to fly to Honduras. We'll be working in partnership with the CIA but you'll be travelling under the auspices of World Relief as one of their support workers. You'll be briefed once you arrive.'

Paul was astounded, 'Honestly Chief, I thought you were coming to tell me I'd been pensioned off after the London debacle.'

Alpha laughed, 'Of course not, you're much too valuable. The London incident was just one of those things and couldn't be helped. However the girl who did the shooting is a problem. I'm afraid you'll have to get rid of her.'

Paul choked, hardly able to breathe, 'What do you mean 'get rid of her'? You mean send her back to Sentry?'

'No, definitely not. She's only some anonymous secretary isn't she, from what you said? I don't want any loose ends. I can't have her wandering round Sentry gossiping about what she's been up to or where she's been. She's to have a little accident - something permanent. If you aren't up to it I'll understand and find someone else to sort it, but I want it done.'

Paul's voice shook as he stammered, 'No, I'll do it, leave it to me. Take it as done.'

Alpha patted him on the shoulder saying, 'Good man. I knew I could rely on you, Paul. I picked a good'un in you. You're to work for me exclusively on this. When this job's done I'll see what I can do about that promotion. Money and air tickets will be sent to you in the New Year. Have a good Christmas!'

As usual he vanished in seconds; leaving Paul sitting staring into space. There was no denying he'd killed people before and with his bare hands, even a woman once. Each time he'd been able to justify it, and at least they'd been strangers. But Eleanor.... he'd grown fond of her. You couldn't call it love. He knew he wasn't capable of love. Any emotions he'd ever had, had become blunted with everything he'd seen and done. But killing Eleanor - how could he bring himself to do it? It would be like murdering Bambi. Of course Eleanor was more resilient and tougher now than she used to be but still............. She'd saved his life in London; he'd never have survived a bullet at such close range. There was no doubt in his mind he owed her, and he always paid his debts. That was that then. He'd have to find a way to save her.

34

Back in London, Mr Caruthers was not a happy man. Seemingly Eleanor and Paul had vanished off the face of the earth. It was all very well the Chief co-opting one of his best men – but what about Eleanor – wasn't he supposed to be responsible for her? He rang the secured number but all he got was an unobtainable signal. It could prove awkward to go over the Chief's head and might cause unforeseen problems. It was probably wiser to leave the status quo as it was for the present.

…

Contrastingly Eleanor was in a state of elation to be spending Christmas in London with Paul. Her eventual return to Sentry was the last thing on her mind. Paul dropped her off at her flat promising to return on Christmas Eve, so they could spend the holiday together. Eleanor was upset that she hadn't been able to say a proper goodbye to Morag but Paul had rushed her back to the cottage in Durness, and they'd been packed and out of the cottage within the hour. Goodness knows what the locals thought.

On the return journey to London Paul was more solicitous than usual. His constant enquiries about her welfare made Eleanor suspicious. Finally she said, 'What's going on Paul – you're never that concerned about me usually?'

He grinned sheepishly, 'Maybe I've started to appreciate you after all this time together, who knows?'

It's more likely Eleanor thought gloomily that he was preparing to dump her, and was suffering from a guilty conscience. Nevertheless if that was the case she decided to make this a special Christmas, especially if it was going to be the last one they would ever spend together. Maybe Paul's cynicism had rubbed off on her. However despite these misgivings, Eleanor flung herself whole heartedly into arrangements for the festivities.

…

In the depths of London Anubis had arranged another rendezvous with Vasily, who was late as usual.

'Punctuality certainly isn't your strong point, Vasily,' Anubis remarked in a less fractious mood than usual, 'I've some good news for you. I think we've established a tiny crack in the CIA's armour.'

'Quickly my friend - the details,' Vasily demanded impatiently.

'Hold hard, comrade. I and only I, am handling the details. All I'll tell you is that I'm doing a job for 'our friends' as a gesture of goodwill, and in return I have a tame asset who will owe me whenever I come calling. He's not high up in the pecking order but I think he will have his uses, and he may even be ripe for turning.'

Vasily sulked - it was well known that Anubis kept his cards close to his chest to make sure he was always the one in control. It made you question who Anubis was really working for. However this American thing was a result, and he supposed he would have to accept Anubis' work methods gracefully. He asked tentatively, 'Will this involve your chap on the ground? Have your resurrected him and the girl?'

Anubis laughed, 'I like your choice of words my friend. We'll turn you into a Christian yet. You're right the two of them are back in the picture. He's ready for his next mission but the girl will soon be out of the frame.'

'But who is this girl? Will she be of danger to us?'

'No, she's just a nobody from their office that my man picked up as a last resort. She's being dispatched as we speak.'

Vasily was still concerned, 'I do hope so. That London op. hardly ended well.'

'Well enough though for you, my dear Vasily. Both your double agents disposed of and their proposed defection to the British curtailed. I don't know what more you want?'

Vasily, cautious by nature, said, 'We should both lie low for a while,' adding in an appeasing tone, 'don't you think?'

'Have no worries on that score, comrade, I won't be seeing you for a while anyway,' Anubis responded smoothly. 'I need to be on hand for this new op. to ensure that everything goes according to plan. Am sure you can manage without me, can't you?' he smirked complacently.

Vasily chose to say nothing further, never equipped to have the last word. Why did every meeting he had with Anubis leave him feeling impotent? With nothing left to say both parties departed.

...

The few days of Christmas went far too quickly for Eleanor. She was overwhelmed when Paul presented her with a beautiful amethyst ring, and pretended to herself that it was an engagement ring though she knew better. They'd had so much fun decorating the flat and a tree; it was the best Christmas Eleanor had ever had.

She would have loved to enjoy it with other people even the people from Sentry but Paul was adamant, they were to be private and tell no one. He insisted on buying all the food from Harrods not allowing her to leave the flat. Eleanor said, 'I don't know why all this secrecy. I only ever saw Barbara in the mews, and her cottage is up for sale. I'm unlikely to bump into Mr C, Claire or even Paddy if I go to the West End during the day. They are hardly going to be on Oxford Street shopping.'

'I know,' Paul said, 'just do this for me,' and clenching his jaw he continued, 'I want it to be just the two of us, and be with you as long as I can. I've bought in everything we might want. There's no need for you to go out.' Eleanor was thrilled to hear Paul talk like this. It was definitely a move in the right direction.

Troubled about Eleanor's safety, Paul was not sure whether the Chief might take it upon himself to ensure his orders had been executed. He had no idea what to do about Eleanor, leaving any decisions about her future till the New Year.

Throughout the few days of Christmas they made the most of the food and wine, spending long hours in bed and lazing about the flat. Paul would tell stories about his Russian Jewish grandmother who had come to Britain to escape the pograms, 'She was a brave soul. Very tough. Her husband and child had been killed, and she arrived in this country with nothing. Later she married my grandfather but rarely spoke about those early days. She was a great believer in 'soldiering on', never allowing my sister and I to feel sorry for ourselves or complain.'

Eleanor could see how Paul's childhood and his training in the Service had shaped this controlled, self reliant man. He rarely mentioned his job these days, but Eleanor was willing to accept whatever part of Paul he could share with her.

As they moved into the New Year, Paul said, 'Now Christmas is over I have something serious to discuss. I shall be flying to Honduras any day now for a new op. working undercover for World Relief. I want you to come with me. It'll be challenging but I'll make sure you're safe. You'll have to do what you're told and toe the line. What do you think?'

Eleanor didn't know what to say. She had reconciled herself to going back to work at Sentry, and never seeing Paul again. This was astounding, not only did he want her to come with him but they were to go to another country. She'd never been abroad. Where on earth was Honduras?

Without a second thought she said, 'I'll come. When do we leave?' and then biting her lip with frustration asked, 'But what about Sentry?'

'Not so fast my dear El, this could be a dangerous mission. I don't know much about it myself, and probably won't till I get there. I'll have to make arrangements in the next few days for your travel and a whole lot of jabs. Don't worry about Sentry; I'm sure they won't miss you. They've probably got far more important things to worry about.'

THE MISSION

35

Honduras, January 1982

In the New Year Mr Caruthers began thinking about Eleanor again. He attempted to talk to the Chief but was only able to raise his voicemail, and left a message asking the Chief to contact him urgently.

Days went by and he heard nothing. The trouble was there were so many covert undertakings in the Service all operating at the same time on various levels that it was difficult to be au fait with everything. Mr C decided he could do no more. He didn't want to risk his job by making waves and jeopardising an op. Paul and Eleanor might well be involved in something above his level of clearance.

...

Once they'd embarked on the flight for Honduras, Eleanor began to question Paul about where they were going and what they would be doing. But he turned his head to the window and closed his eyes. It had been difficult enough to arrange for her to come with him let alone answer her questions.

Exchanging the First Class ticket for two Economies and arranging the jabs and paperwork had been simple enough, but liaising with World Relief had been tricky as they'd only allowed for one Support Worker. They'd been extremely obstructive. The last thing they wanted was an untrained young woman working for them in such a hazardous area. They explained to him that their refugee camp was at Mosquitia right on the borders of Nicaragua, in an area at constant risk of random kidnappings by the Sandinistas. But Paul was adamant and refused to be budged. Finally they gave in and Mr and Mrs. Ralph Whitman were given passage. What choices did he have? If he left Eleanor behind she would be killed and if he took her with him, she was in danger. It was a no win situation. But at that moment on the plane, he couldn't cope with Eleanor and explanations.

After hours of travelling they finally landed at Tegucigalpa. Paul was worried about the Immigration Authorities but needn't have been concerned, because as soon as they disembarked a man in combat fatigues gestured to him. He and Eleanor made their way over. The crewcutted young man gave a desultory salute and said in a strong American drawl, 'Mr and Mrs. Whitman, I've been sent to meet you. Welcome to Honduras. I'm Captain Greenwald attached to the military here. Let's get you through channels and we'll head for your hotel.'

Paul could see Eleanor was wilting with the effects of the journey and the overwhelming humidity. Leaving the plane had been like stepping into a wall of heat after freezing cold London. It dawned on him she'd never been overseas before let alone flown on a plane, but she managed a weak smile as if to say 'I'm alright.' Captain Greenwald chatted inconsequentially as they collected their luggage, 'At least you've come in the dry season –it'll be like this till April. The climate in Tegucigalpa is quite palatable when you get adjusted. Your hotel is on a hill above the main square so it'll be cooler there.'

He asked no questions, neither remarking on their flight nor asking about England, but explained the hotel Maya was about four miles away and apologised for the jeep. 'You'll need to get acclimatised,' he said, 'so we've booked you in for ten days before you go to the camp. Make the most of the hotel as the camp will be very primitive.'

Perking up after the flight, Eleanor asked, 'What is Tegucigalpa like? What's the language?'

The Captain shrugged, 'There isn't that much in Tegu - just the Cathedral in Morazan Plaza and a bunch of colonial type buildings, if you're interested. The people are a mixed bag. Spanish is the main language.'

He appeared disinterested but probably had better things to do than point out the sights. Anyway they were here to work though Eleanor had no idea what they would be doing. Hers and Paul's intimacy in bed didn't extend as far as his work. In fact Paul had buried himself in a blanket on the flight and slept most of the way. It was maddening. Eleanor was exasperated realising how dependent she was on him, particularly now in a foreign country. It wasn't like

Scotland where she could pack up and go back to London.

Mumbling peevishly to Paul, she said, 'I hardly know any Spanish, what about you, darling?' underlining 'the darling' with sarcasm.

He whispered in her ear, 'Linda my sweet, I speak a number of languages, Spanish being one of them. Don't worry; I'll give you some lessons on useful phrases before we move to the camp.'

Greenwald dropped them off in front of the hotel saying, 'I've booked you a suite. It's pretty cheap here. You'll find your US dollars will buy you a lot of lempira if you have to change money though I expect they'll be glad of dollars. Someone will be in touch with you tomorrow.'

Checking into the suite Eleanor collapsed on the king size bed. Paul said, 'You have a rest while I check the lay of the land. I'll bring some local food back with me.'

Eleanor was only too willing, and leaving the unpacking lay down and slept. She had a shock when she woke; five hours had gone by. It was dark and there was no sign of Paul. Beginning to get anxious she wondered what to do. There was no one to contact and she felt totally helpless in a strange country. However an hour later he turned up apologising, 'I thought you needed a good long sleep. I've had a good look round and brought you,' he unpacked a load of brown bags, 'a range of tamales – they've got different fillings: cornmeal, meat, beans, vegetables and chillies. I thought we could have a bit of a picnic. There's beer, it's light like lager, and I brought you a 'licuados' –a milkshake made from fruit.'

Eleanor realised how hungry she was and dug into the food. It wasn't as spicy as she thought. Paul explained restaurants provided hot sauce if you wanted it. They both ate more than they should and flopped on the bed. Paul had had quite a few beers. Eleanor thought this might be the time to get him to tell her more about the mission. But he was dead to the world, falling fast asleep with his arms round her.

Eleanor sometimes felt like his teddy bear or a stuffed doll as their relationship was hardly one of equals. Granted he was twenty years older than her but that was no excuse for him to treat as a child the majority of the time, and his plaything the rest of the time.

There were times when Eleanor wished she'd never got into this relationship. How had it started for heavens' sake? It had been so insidious she'd never noticed it creeping up on her. There'd been the supper at the flat after the surveillance operation, then Arnos Grove which she didn't want to be reminded of, Scotland and now Central America.

Why did she go along with Paul's plans? Hadn't she got a mind of her own? There had been times at Sentry when she'd been just as passive. Why couldn't she assert herself after all she was intelligent and capable? It was if stronger more dominating people overpowered her.

Certainly she was still besotted with Paul but she needed to take a stand, show him what she was made of and how independent she could be - resolving to do that the very next day she fell asleep on his shoulder.

In the morning, Paul had already left by the time Eleanor woke up. Determined to put her new resolve into action, Eleanor made her way down to the main foyer and the restaurant.

Entering the restaurant and feeling unsure but determined to act with confidence, Eleanor smiled broadly at the waitress who beamed back at her. She tried some of the phrases Paul had taught her, 'Mi Espanola es muy limitado.Mi gustaria comer.' The waitress replied by showing her to a table asking, 'Desayuno Maya?' Eleanor thought that might be the word for breakfast and nodded vehemently. Nina the waitress patted her on the arm and held up five fingers, which Eleanor supposed meant five minutes.

In no time Nina was back with a laden tray. There was fresh squeezed juice, dark coffee and a plate full of food. Eleanor could see scrambled egg, cheese, and refried beans. On the side was a tortilla. The fried plantains were new to her, and so were the creamy slices of avocado, but it was delicious. Nina hovered around awaiting Eleanor's response. Eleanor looked up and gave a thumbs up. Nina was delighted offering more of everything. But Eleanor held up her hands in horror, pointing to her stomach and shaking her head.

Leaving the restaurant, Eleanor wondered whether she should venture out or wait for Paul. She decided to start down the hill to the Plaza. Halfway down she spotted him on his way up.

Even from that distance she could see he was scowling, and as he got nearer bawled at her, 'Where do you think you're going? It's not safe for a girl like you out here. You don't even speak the language. What if you got lost? I did tell you to stay at the hotel until I came back, and then we could explore together.'

Eleanor not prepared to be bullied as usual, protested just as loudly, 'You said nothing of the sort. When I woke up this morning, you'd gone. I managed to order breakfast in the restaurant despite my lack of Spanish. I'll thank you not to tell me what to do all the time or you'll make our stay in Honduras unbearable. I am wondering now why I was so keen to come with you.'

Surprisingly, Paul looked shamefaced saying, 'You're right. I'm sorry; I do treat you like a child. I know you've a mind of your own. Let me make it up to you and let's have a good look at Tegucigalpa. I'll even buy you a big lunch that's their main meal of the day, if you can manage anything after one of their breakfasts.

268

Eleanor relented, accepting his apology, and keen to prolong his good mood and change of attitude laughed, 'I don't think I'll be able to eat anything for hours. I'm full to bursting.'

At peace with one another again they sauntered back down the hill hand in hand,

36

The next day Eleanor was hoping to enjoy even more of Tegucigalpa. She'd liked visiting the cathedral, but adored the colour and variety of the market. There were vegetables and fruits she'd never seen before and the people, the Mestizos, a mix of Amerindian and European were intriguing but the poverty was shocking. Gangs of ragged children ran after them pleading for money. It was something she'd never experienced before.

Paul was indifferent saying, 'You'll find this everywhere in Central America. These people are dependent on US handouts, but there's so much corruption the poorest never get a whiff of the dollars. Political factions are fighting it out here, that's why it's dangerous for you to go off on your own. You'd be a prime candidate for kidnapping with your blond hair and looks. They'd take you for an American and good ransom fodder.'

Eleanor didn't know whether to be alarmed or flattered. She could understand now why he'd been so angry when she'd left the hotel yet the Hondurans seemed warm and friendly. But taking the warning to heart, she hoped life at the refugee camp wasn't going to be as restricted.

More sightseeing was out of the question that day as Captain Greenwald returned, accompanied by another man dressed in a white tropical suit, a Panama and reflective sunglasses. Now he, Eleanor thought, does look like a spy – just like

Alec Guinness in 'Our Man in Havana.' He had the strangest name, Conrad Regis, and talked with an odd American accent that was typical of Boston. He mixed this with a transatlantic drawl and archaic English phrases, 'So pleased to meet you, old bean,' he said to Paul when introduced, and bowed and kissed Eleanor's hand, 'Mrs Whitman, a joy. We see so few beautiful white women here. Why don't we adjourn to the bar and I will buy us a few snifters, hey what.' Eleanor giggled wondering if he was a big fan of Jeeves and Wooster. Of course in intelligence work nothing was ever as it seemed.

After a few sociable snifters, Conrad said, 'Time to get down to business Ralph, if I may call you that. The gallant Captain here has volunteered to escort Mrs Whitman on a bit of a tour of the area, haven't you, my dear chap,' he added looking pointedly at Greenwald.

Greenwald rose to the occasion and offering his arm to Eleanor said, 'Please be my guest, Mrs Whitman. We can leave these two to their boring chat. Let's go out and enjoy the heat and the scenery. You'll need a hat and sunglasses though. There's no protection from the elements in my jeep.'

Eleanor shot off to collect them, and whilst she was away Conrad observed, 'I had no idea you were bringing your wife to the party, Ralph. This is hardly going to be a picnic and the conditions at the camp are primitive to say the least. Isn't there a way you can send her back?'

271

Paul shook his head, 'No, I'm afraid not. She has to be part of the package. I have my reasons for her presence, and am not prepared to discuss them.'

Conrad grimaced; it was bad enough that they'd brought a Limey in on this op., now they'd been lumbered with his woman. Maintaining a cool jaunty attitude he remarked, 'It's up to you, old man. She's your problem. Unquestionably I won't be responsible for her safety, I can assure you.'

Eleanor sprinted back towards them, her face alight with anticipation and Greenwald patiently escorted her to the jeep saying you better call me, 'Call me Mason ma'm, as we're going to spend time together.'

Eleanor said, 'In that case, call me Linda not ma'm.'

Mason Greenwald turned to her, 'You hardly look like a Linda. It's far too plain a name for you. You should have an exotic name with those eyes.'

Eleanor was delighted to be complimented. Paul rarely said anything flattering about her looks. She might as well enjoy this man's company.

They sped off towards Comayaguela, Tegus' sister town, another colonial town with stone streets and churches but didn't stop. Mason said, 'Sorry, this is a bit of whistle-stop tour. I have to be back at the base in a few hours.'

They moved on to Parque el Picado, where Mason pointed

out the huge statue of Jesus Christ visible across the city, and on to La Tigra, the cloud forest park. Eleanor spotted multi coloured parrots, humming birds and even some sort of eagle. Her guide explained Honduras was about the same size as Tennessee. Eleanor asked, 'Is that where you come from, Mason?'

'Hell, no,' he said amiably, 'can't you pick the accent. I'm a Brooklyn boy born and raised.' When she wrinkled her forehead questioningly, 'Hey, don't you know that's New York.'

'But I've never been anywhere,' Eleanor said, 'in fact; this is my first trip abroad.'

'Well I'll be damned,' said Mason and not thinking, added, 'in your line of business I would have thought you'd have been most everywhere in the world.' Noticing her pained expression he said quickly, 'Sorry ma'm, I was well out of line there.'

'Forget it,' Eleanor said, 'it's of no account.' Sometimes she wished that had been the case. She hardly thought of herself as a fully fledged spy. She'd only fallen into it by accident. Paul was the Intelligence Officer not her, but she could scarcely confide in this brash young man.

Having chatted away ten to the dozen about the area and the people, Mason fell silent after his comment about her work. He said formally, 'I think, we need to get you back to the hotel, Linda. I'm sorry I don't have time to take you to Copan and the Mayan ruins, maybe some other day.'

Eleanor felt sorry he was embarrassed about overstepping the mark. She thanked him profusely and said how grateful she was for the tour. As he helped her out of the jeep, he saluted her smartly and drove off. She wondered how much he knew about what she and Paul were doing in Honduras; probably a lot more than she did.

Back at the hotel Conrad and Paul had retired to their suite. Conrad, losing his former bonhomie, said quietly and urgently, 'Ralph, I think you are aware of the situation here in Central America. Since the Sandanista coup things in Nicaragua are moving rapidly and Reagan's government doesn't want the Commies getting more of a hold, so they are pouring money into Honduras to fund groups of counter revolutionaries. We need to get money to the leaders.

Your job will be to act as courier and deliver funds to them. The UN refugee camp in Mosquitia is thirty miles from the Coco River. The river is the natural border between the two countries. The camp was set up outside Mocoron for some of the Miskito Indians who'd fled across the border. However things there have got out of hand. There are now thousands of the Miskitos with no one willing to take responsibility for them.'

Paul was unmoved, 'But why me as a courier - a Brit. It's hardly my country's problem plus it sounds a nightmare. Why isn't this down to your people?'

Conrad smiled maliciously, 'You've been lent to us that's why, by the higher ups. It means you'll have a good cover story - a British husband and wife team, working for World Relief coming out to help poor refugees, what more could you ask?

I must say when you arrived I wasn't thrilled you'd brought your wife, but on second thoughts this will work better.' Patting Paul on the back in a matey fashion, 'British – I like it and one who speaks fluent Spanish, though most Miskitos speak English. Who would ever suspect, whereas an American would stand out like a sore thumb? This couldn't be better if I'd planned it myself.'

'But surely there must be Americans working at the camp, why not use them?'

'Sure there are but none of them have your training. Most of them have been there since the camp was set up, and I think would object on ethical grounds.'

Paul was fuming; he'd had no idea till now what was involved. In the past he'd either worked on his own or been in control of a team on an operation - nothing as amateur and ill planned as this. 'Won't the camp think it strange when we turn up?'

'Not at all,' Conrad said, 'there are more and more Miskitos arriving every day. They'll be glad of the help. Anyway they're aware you're coming, don't worry on that score.'

'How long is this arrangement supposed to go on for?' Paul asked roughly.

Conrad mused, 'Honestly, Ralph, I don't know –a few months, certainly up until the wet season in May. After that the roads are impassable and the area becomes swamp, so we don't have long. I'll be your liaison throughout. Don't on any account contact the military base. I'll give you a number and a code where you can reach me. In the next week or so we'll let you and your good lady settle in at the camp, and then I'll be in contact about the arrangements. Is there anything else?'

Paul growled, 'I think there's a lot. That'll do for now. I'm not sure I signed up for this. I'll take it up with the Chief.'

'Fair enough,' Conrad replied, 'but I'll think you'll find that men at the highest level in both London and Washington have set this up. You and I are merely pawns in the game and do what we're told. Enjoy the hotel while you can. Give my regards to the fragrant Linda,' and he left waving an offhand goodbye.

Eleanor returned to the suite, bubbling with news of what she'd seen. She and Paul settled down to a snack of baleadas, and chicharrones and local rum. Studying Paul's face as he ate, Eleanor was hesitant to ask about the briefing; instead they munched and talked about Eleanor's experiences as if they were tourists.

37

Washington, Hilton Hotel, Late January 1982

'Good to meet you again, Sir Alan, How was the flight?' Petersen wiped his sweating palms on the backs of his trousers before putting out a welcoming hand.

'Oh so so, you know. How are you, James? You're looking well, I must say. Langley obviously agrees with you,' Alan took the proffered hand with a bare touch of the fingertips.

This time they were meeting at the Washington Hilton Hotel, Petersen's own turf. 'I would have preferred the Mayflower,' James said, 'but it's being completely refurbished. I've booked a private room to avoid prying eyes. Are you staying at your Embassy?'

'No,' Alan said, 'I prefer somewhere less public.' He clearly wasn't intending to elaborate so Petersen moved swiftly on, 'Can I order food for you? They do an excellent fillet here....or maybe something lighter?'

'Just coffee,' Alan said, 'shall we get on. I'd just like to know how my man in Honduras is doing and what's been happening?'

Petersen replied, 'I've a good man on the spot down there, who's settled them both in.'

Before he could go any further, Alan interrupted, 'What 'them'? There's only my man surely?'

'But he brought his wife, didn't you know?'

'Of course not. That wasn't my arrangement with him.' Alan's lips tightened, 'Is she going on to the refugee camp?'

'That's what I'm told,' Petersen said, 'though your man is none too happy with the assignment now he's been briefed. He says it's too risky and ill planned, and he intends taking it up with you.'

'Don't worry about that. He'll buckle down in due course.' Alan said, 'He's got no choice in the matter, if he wants to further or even keep his career.'

'But what about the girl?' Petersen asked, 'What do you want us to do about her? Should we offer to fly her back to London?'

'No, don't do that,' Alan said, 'leave things as they stand for now. Be it on their own heads if she gets killed or kidnapped. It'll be my chap's responsibility – no one else's. We have other more important things to talk about.'

'What sort of things, Sir Alan?'

'I hear rumours on the circuit that you are mounting a massive counter espionage operation throughout the US.'

Petersen appeared mystified, 'Not that I know of, Sir Alan. I only concern myself with the Central American desk.'

Not deterred for a moment, Alan said, 'I suppose it's the

278

usual story; one arm of the CIA doesn't know what the other is doing. I think I'm in a position to help you with that operation. It would be very useful to me, James, if you could find out the details, and keep me in the picture. As you know our two countries have a 'special relationship', and anything to do with counter espionage lies within my own particular area of expertise. What do you say?'

James Petersen squirmed. It was all very well asking for help from another agency but when and how it was reciprocated was a totally different thing. Perhaps he'd been too quick back in London promising to return favours, what was he to do? Maybe Sir Alan thought he was more influential then he really was. Though on second thoughts perhaps the wily old man did know what he was doing.

James racked his brains. There was one chap he knew from their '73 Intelligence Officer Training - Joel Mitchell. Mitchell was a bright guy seconded to the legendary James Jesus Angleton's Counter Intelligence Team. He could try him; after all they were both Yale men and Phi Beta Kappa.

Looking Sir Alan straight in the eye, Petersen said, 'It might take some doing but I think I can find out what you want, Sir.'

'Good enough, James. I'll take you at your word. Shall we meet here a month from today and you can tell me what you've found out. That should give you give you ample time. A list of suspected agents or double agents would be useful. I'm sure being the capable young man you are, this won't be a problem.'

Petersen winced. He'd hoped not to be pinned down to an actual deadline. There was no doubt Sir Alan was not a person to be messed with. He just hoped his former colleague could deliver.

They agreed a date and time to meet in the following month, and Petersen said he would make all the necessary arrangements. Gullible enough to act out the role of errand boy Petersen rushed off to his next appointment, leaving Sir Alan smiling smugly to himself deliberating on James' potential as an asset. Sometimes it was better to cultivate Indians rather than Chiefs in this business.

…

At the Hotel Maya, Paul was fretting over the mission he'd been landed with. Needing further reassurance, he faxed the Chief on the secure number he'd been given saying,

'Dear Uncle, Not sure about holiday here and move to second resort. Feel whole experience, not satisfactory and unsafe. Prefer to return home a.s.a.p, or meet up for chat, your loving nephew.'

Days went by with no reply. Finally just as Paul and Eleanor were due to depart for the camp, he had his response,

'Dear nephew, Am afraid not possible to meet for a chat at this time. Your holiday arrangements stand or be prepared for

280

exceptionally heavy cancellation charges. Enjoy and complete the next part of your journey. Most affectionate love to Linda,'

and there it was, - Paul was stuck. The fax was loaded with ominous implications, and underlying threats. Obviously Paul's chances of promotion let alone his job were on the line, plus the Chief appeared to be aware of Eleanor's presence in Honduras, aware that Paul had not carried out the orders he'd been given in Glasgow. There was no turning back now; he and Eleanor would have to carry on.

38

Conrad Regis returned to convey the 'Whitmans' to the camp. He roared up in a military jeep on a day when Paul and Eleanor had decided to have a leisurely breakfast and a lazy day. 'Now you're both acclimatised,' he said, 'I thought we'd move you to Mocoron. It's going to come as one almighty shock after the luxury of this hotel but I daresay you'll adapt.'

They drove to the Palmerola military airfield. 'We'll fly from here on the relief plane.' Conrad said, 'It's the devil of a place to get to – right over on the North East coast. Driving there is pretty much a no-no. It takes five hours to Puerto Lempira alone. The road's horrendous and not navigable during the rainy season.'

Eleanor wasn't at all sure she wanted to hear this. What sort of place were they going to? Would it even be habitable? As usual Paul hadn't said anything much about the refugees at the camp only that they were Miskito Indians. She was excited and curious to meet them but extremely nervous about the living conditions. Would there be running water? How would she survive the climate as well as the type of work they would be expected to do? Knowing what a sheltered life she'd led, Eleanor had no idea how adaptable she was. What if she couldn't cope or became ill?

Sitting opposite her on the plane, Conrad seemed to read her thoughts, 'You mustn't worry too much Linda, the Miskitos like the British. Your people were the first rulers here, and that's why they speak English. They weren't keen on the Spanish, who came next, or the current Nicaraguan government. They're a primitive people preferring witchcraft to Western medicine. Conditions will be hard though. The Mocoron camp was hastily put together – a kind of mud settlement dumped on top of swamp and jungle.'

None of it sounded good, and Eleanor still had no idea what Paul's real mission was. Landing on the small muddy field was no joke either; the tiny plane skidded and skittered all over the place until it finally braked to a halt. A bunch of Miskitos followed by Peace Corps volunteers opened the door and helped her out. They unloaded the luggage together with the food, mail and cartons of medicines.

Eleanor looked towards Paul for reassurance but he ignored her, proceeding to busy himself unloading the plane with Conrad and the other workers. Finally they packed everything into a dilapidated truck and with Eleanor ensconced in a jeep, the convoy wended their way down the five kilometres of rock-strewn road to the camp, heading for one of the wooden buildings which served as a store.

Eleanor's first sight of the Mocoron refugee camp - her future home - was row upon row of bamboo huts roofed with leaves and other vegetation. There were one or two sturdier wooden buildings, but everywhere there were people: Miskito children playing in the dirt and mud,

Miskito women nursing babies and elderly Miskitos wrapped in blankets staring into the far distance. Eleanor's heart turned over. She thought whatever happens to me in life or whatever has happened, will never be as bad as what is happening to these poor people torn from their homes and eking out an existence in this terrible place on the edge of nowhere.

One of the Peace Corps volunteers accompanying her, remarked, 'This must be a shock for you, Mrs. Whitman, after Tegucigalpa. I suppose we're used to it. There are Miskitos arriving hourly. We are up to 9000 or more. Sometimes the Contras bring them by truck and dump them. Often, their only possessions are a bunch of dead chickens and pillowcases filled with personal items. All they want is to return to their villages in Nicaragua but there's no chance of that. There's nothing for them to go back to. The Sandanistas have burnt over 30 of their villages.'

Eleanor couldn't speak. Her initial apprehension had worn off. The more she heard, the more she wanted to help these poor abandoned people. Looking round for Paul, she saw he was in deep discussion with one of the World Relief people and Conrad. He was probably finding out what they were to do. After a few minutes he came over and said, 'Conrad has negotiated a reasonable place for us to stay.' He pointed to one of the further wooden shacks saying, 'I'm sorry my dear, it's the best we can do. You'll have a bunk and a roof over your head.'

Eleanor said, 'Honestly Ralph, I'm not that bothered. That's the last thing on my mind. Anywhere will do. Please don't turn anyone out for us. I'm sure you and I can manage in one of the bamboo huts.'

'Nonsense,' Paul said, 'it's all arranged. Come and see for yourself.'

Eleanor meekly followed him and ventured into the hut - on the further wall were two shelf beds with straw mattresses, in the middle a table with rough hewn handmade stools and on the other side cupboards made out of what looked like floorboards nailed together. Paul brought in the luggage and surveyed the room, 'Not what we're used to but it'll serve. What do you think?'

'It's fine, a lot better than where those poor people out there are living. In fact, it's positive luxury.'

Paul gave her a hard look, 'I know you've a soft heart but we, or at least I am here to do a job. Sure we'll do our best to help these people, but that's not the real reason we're here just bear that in mind. Don't get carried away. As soon as my part in this is complete we'll be leaving for England, and that won't be soon enough for me.'

'But Ralph, I don't know why we're here, and what job you have to do? Can't you at least tell me something now?' Eleanor pleaded.

'All in good time. I've to have a quick word with Conrad

before he flies back. Why don't you unpack and go over to the main building,' Paul went to the doorway and pointed towards a large wooden outbuilding, 'and find out what our camp jobs will be.'

Eleanor changed out of her sweat sodden dress, put on a fresh cotton shirt and trousers and made her way to the main building, where the sign 'Office' was emblazoned in large black letters on the wall. Before she had a chance to open the door, it flew open and the volunteer she'd ridden with earlier came rushing out, 'Sorry Mrs. Whitman, can't stop, I'm helping the doctor at the moment. We're inoculating for T.B though the Miskitos aren't keen. See Patsy inside, she'll help you with anything you need.'

Patsy was a tall serious young woman hunched over a desk studying a detailed timetable. She looked up frowning when Eleanor introduced herself and asked, 'Do you have any special skills, Mrs. Whitman?'

'Please call me Linda. I'm afraid not,' Eleanor said, 'but I'm willing to learn and apply myself whatever the job is.'

'Don't worry,' Patsy said, 'being there's so few of us and so many of them, we all have to muck in with everything. We've only the one doctor at the moment, and she's struggling. There are about 100 cases of T.B and at least 300 children, who are severely undernourished, with no running water on site. The water has to be carried from the Mocoron River and boiled. We use the river for everything, drinking, bathing and washing clothes. Could you take over from Ethan (that's the chap who just rushed past you) and help the doc. Ethan would be more use sorting and handing out the new foodstuffs?'

'Of course willingly, just point me in the right direction. What about my husband? He'll be along soon.'

'Don't worry, am sure we can find plenty for him to do. There are supplies to be driven around the camp, water containers to be filled and all manner of other jobs. Don't look so anxious, you'll soon get into the routine if we have one.'

Working with the doctor was a revelation. Dr Elodie Malzac hailing from Martinique was a tonic. She was larger than life, a West Indian in her fifties with beautiful light skin and a smile a mile long, who immediately took Eleanor under her wing, ' My dearest girl, I will show you the ropes. We need every willing hand we can get.'

There was a long queue of Miskito children of all ages waiting to be vaccinated. Neither they nor their mothers looked very happy. Elodie murmured to Eleanor, 'Linda my child, we have to be confidant in handling them. These Indian mothers would rather resort to the witchdoctor. Be on the lookout for children on the verge of malnutrition. Smile and laugh with them. Look as if you know what you're doing.'

Eleanor moved along the queue saying 'Hullo' shyly, and smiling as much as she could. Many of the children reached out to touch her fair hair. When the mothers stopped them, Eleanor said, 'It's alright; see my hair is the same as yours just a different colour.' She held out her hand to the child at the head of the line and said, 'You're first, it's an important place to be,' and then chatted to the little girl as Dr Elodie swabbed and pricked her arm.

'You're a natural,' Elodie remarked, 'do you have children back in the UK?'

'No, but I would like a child. Perhaps when we return to London......,' and didn't elaborate further, suddenly remembering that she wasn't married or even in a 'real' relationship. It was easy to forget she had no claim on Paul or he on her.

Working closely together day after day, she and Elodie soon became real friends. On one occasion Eleanor said, 'I really enjoy working with you, Elodie. Do you think I'd make a good nurse?'

'My dear Linda, I think you could do anything you set your mind to. Perhaps you should think about some type of medical training when you get back to the UK.'

'But I haven't any qualifications; my schooling was spasmodic at best and there wasn't much of it.'

Dr Elodie looked thoughtful momentarily and then said,

288

'You're young. You've plenty of time to get qualifications. The experience here will help. I'd be happy to give you a reference.'

Eleanor was delighted. She'd been feeling like a spare part dragged around in Paul's wake. It was great to be appreciated, and for someone to see some potential in her.

Returning to their hut that evening she spotted Paul struggling with sacks of maize and rice, and ran up to him enthusiastically, 'Let me help, I'll take an end.' Between them they loaded the sacks into the storeroom.

'Have you had anything to eat since breakfast?' Paul asked.

Eleanor shook her head, 'No, there wasn't time. I've been helping at the clinic non-stop.'

'That's no good, you must eat regularly,' he said sounding like a parent, 'the work here is hard and the climate's draining. Make sure you drink boiled water regularly, and take your malaria tablets. I don't want you going down with anything.' Frowning he added, 'Thank goodness we've had all the right jabs. This place is a cesspool for disease. Personally, I can't wait to get out of here.'

Together they made their way to one of the huts that served as the staffers' canteen, gathering up tin plates of black beans and rice. Today there was a little fish, an unusual treat. There was plenty of black tea to wash it all down which Eleanor wasn't thrilled about, but Paul said, 'A hot drink can cool your body down. That's what all those nabobs drank years ago in India.'

After a tough day they were relieved to go to bed early in their separate bunks. Eleanor missed the comfort of Paul's body, but in this heat was too exhausted to think about anything. She wished they'd had the foresight to go for an evening bathe in the river but they'd probably have been too tired.

39

Wildlife usually awakened the camp at the crack of dawn. Eleanor was always eager to be up and about early before the overpowering heat of the hut overwhelmed her. In the last weeks, she'd only caught sight of Paul in the distance during the day and wondered if he was doing his best to avoid her. He was constantly on the go, either helping build stilted huts ready for the rainy season or disappearing into the rain forest to hack down logs. But close to dusk, he would seek her out, and together they would join the rest of the staffers bathing in the Mocoron, returning to eat beans, maize and rice.

This was not the same Paul that Eleanor had got used to in Scotland, and later in London. This was the Paul she'd seen when they first met, tough, preoccupied and taciturn, not an easy person to be around. Eleanor missed the relaxed laid back Paul, and wished the job didn't have this effect on him.

Feeling very alone Eleanor attached herself to Elodie. The other workers didn't seem to mind as it freed them for other duties. Elodie had taken an instant liking to the delicate fair English girl, and went out of her way to teach her basic First Aid. She encouraged Eleanor to make the rounds of the huts looking for imminent signs of illness or malnutrition.

At first, Eleanor felt diffident amongst the Miskitos but they were such a warm, friendly people she soon began to pick up bits and pieces of their language, much of which was interspersed with variations of English and Spanish Creole. There were few able bodied men about. Eleanor learnt the fitter younger men had gone to join the nearby Contra guerrilla groups. The Contras caused problems with the daily supply plane; as if the provisions weren't picked up promptly they disappeared into their camps.

Once Eleanor got to know the Miskitos better, she could see what a mix of nationalities they were: descended from English pirates, Caribbean slaves, Spanish settlers and traders, and Moravian missionaries.

One family in particular welcomed her as if she was an old friend. There was: Guadeloupe the ancient grandmother; Maria the mother; Carlos a boy of ten; Ana a girl of six and Pedro the ever smiling baby. Carlos became Eleanor's special friend and guide. He would lead her round the camp by the hand as if he was in charge and spend hours teaching her bits of their language saying, 'Kum, wol, yumpa,wol,' counting them out on his small hand until Eleanor understood he was saying, 'one, two three, four'.

One evening Paul said, 'I'm going away for a few days. Don't be alarmed. If anyone asks for me, say I've gone with the relief plane to pick up special tools I need. I'll synchronise my leaving with the plane's departure so no one will be any the wiser.'

Eleanor remonstrated with him, 'Please, please tell me where you're going and what you're doing in case anything happens to you, and who I can contact if you don't come back?'

Paul sighed, 'I suppose I'd better put you in the picture. I can't have you getting in a panic, and raising a hue and cry. Remember we aren't 'real' relief workers, we're supposed to be intelligence officers, or at least I am. I think you tend to forget why we're here.'

'But you've never told me,' Eleanor said, 'so how am I supposed to know? I don't find it easy playing a dual role when I'm kept in the dark. You know you can trust me by now or I wouldn't be here.'

'It isn't you, I don't trust,' said Paul, 'but we are in a hostile place. Anything could happen to you or me, kidnapping, murder, you name it. I thought the less you knew the better it would be for you. Perhaps I was wrong; I see you do need to know. The Americans want to overthrow the Sandanista government in Nicaragua. Well, I'm to deliver funds to the counter-revolutionary groups - Nicaraguans who've fled their country along with the Miskitos. There's about 500 Contras, 30 kilometres away on this side of the Coco River.'

'But how on earth will you get there?'

'I'm borrowing one of the camp's trucks. I don't suppose the road is too good, so it will be a slow journey there and back. Time isn't on our side. The rains start the beginning of May, so everything has to be done in these months.'

'How risky is it?' Eleanor asked not sure she really wanted to know. Despite Paul's moods and current indifference, he was still all she cared about. In this isolated place he was her whole life. What would she do if anything happened to him?

He studied her concerned face and chucked her under the chin, 'Honestly El, there's no need to worry. All the action is the other side of the River. I'll be safe enough. I don't intend getting into any gun battles. I'm just a courier; delivering dollars. When I get back we'll take a trip to Tegucigalpa and have a couple of days in the Maya. You could do with a treat after all your hard work.'

'Really Paul, I'm alright. I'm used to the life here and I really like the people though perhaps a couple of days together, just you and I, would be nice.'

'That's settled then,' Paul said pulling her close, 'I must say it would be lovely to get out of these horrible bunk things and cuddle up to you.'

The next few days Eleanor was on tenterhooks. Fearful about Paul and his safety, she was also uneasy about telling lies to the other workers. But she needn't have worried; Paul seemed to have covered his tracks well and she wasn't asked any difficult questions. Elodie did say however, 'Haven't seen that handsome husband of yours for a while. Hope you haven't mislaid him.' But Eleanor laughed, making a joke of it, 'No such luck, he's always around somewhere.'

The clinic was so busy that the days sped by. Suddenly one evening Paul appeared in the doorway of their hut, unshaven and filthy. Eleanor ran and hugged him but he pushed her away, grinning, 'Not now, my dear. I smell rancid. Let me go down to the river and clean up and then we'll talk.'

The trip had not been as easy as Paul had envisaged. The road was in poor condition, and he'd had to drive slowly, carefully picking his way through rocks and debris. Eventually forced to abandon the truck, he'd walked the last three kilometres only too aware of his vulnerability.

The Contras might easily take him for an enemy and shoot him, however once he reached the outskirts of their camp he was picked up by an armed escort. By the time they arrived it was dark and Paul was shown into the tent of their leader, an American educated Contra called Eduardo, who though he provided him with food and rum, wasn't exactly welcoming. Opening the haversack of money and shuffling through the money, Eduardo shrugged, 'This is OK but we need weapons. I no think dollars are going to fight this war. Tell your American friends we need supplies. My men can't fight on empty bellies...., and guns, we need guns. Do not return without them.'

Paul was bedded down for the night and the next day two armed men escorted him to his truck, and he drove carefully back to Mocoron. As far as he was concerned he'd completed his part of the deal. Neither the Chief nor Conrad had said anything about gun running for goodness sake.

Back at the camp with Eleanor so delighted to see him, it was a relief to still be in one piece. Perhaps they could both get out of here now. Of course he'd have to see Conrad, so going back to Tegu for a break would do them both good. Clearing it with the World Relief people, they hardly seemed surprised appearing to expect his spasmodic comings and goings.

Returning to the Maya at Tegu was like falling into a warm feather bed. Paul ordered a massive meal in their room and they ate till they were stuffed. Eleanor said, 'I'm so hungry, and definitely for anything other than rice, beans and black tea.'

Paul was in no rush to contact Conrad and they indulged themselves in a siesta and languid lovemaking. Eleanor stretched herself like the cat that'd had the cream savouring every moment with him, 'Does this mean your job is finished? Are we going home?'

'I don't know. What the Contras want is not what I was brought here to do? I'll have to talk to Conrad but we'll enjoy ourselves for a few days first.'

'Definitely,' Eleanor replied, 'I just want to relax with you and make the most of our time.'

Unfortunately for them, Conrad had heard of their arrival and presented himself at breakfast next morning, 'Well, dear old things, camp life seems to agree with you. You are certainly much thinner but you look fit. I'll have to have a stint there myself,' he said patting his paunch.

'It was hardly a health camp,' Paul said dryly. 'We both worked extremely hard, Linda in particular.'

'Of course, my dears, of course, I was hardly belittling your efforts in that direction. Ralph, I need to talk to you privately, if you don't mind sweet Linda.'

Eleanor was only too happy to leave them to it. Try as she might, she couldn't take to Conrad. He was obsequious one minute and chatty the next but underlying all that smooth talk, Eleanor sensed a threatening and distinctly unpleasant presence.

After she'd gone, Conrad turned to Paul and asked for details. When he heard about the demands for weapons and guns he banged his fist down hard, 'Damn and blast, it was bound to happen I suppose sooner or later. They are building up to a confrontation with the Sandinistas before the weather breaks. What do they want?'

Paul said, 'I've their shopping list here. Everything from grenades, machine guns, mortars etc.' He passed the list to Conrad, together with the list of supplies and medicines they'd asked for.

Conrad said, 'I'm sorry Paul. This is one last job for you. We can fly everything in on the relief plane of course, but you'll have to transport it to their camp somehow.'

Paul shook his head, 'Count me out. I never agreed to anything like this. Their camp is hardly accessible, and that old truck won't cope with the state of the road.'

It was as if Conrad was barely listening to him, 'Don't worry about that. We've got an old armoured ambulance that will be just the job. I'll fly that in with two of my best men. On second thoughts, we might have to fly everything into Puerto Lempira as I want to keep the Mocoron camp out of it.'

'I don't think you're listening to me Conrad. I'm not doing it; give the job to your military men. Linda and I will be out of here as soon as we can get a flight.'

'I'm afraid not, Ralph.' Conrad said in a menacing tone, 'Don't think that I don't know you shouldn't have brought Linda here, and that she's at risk in London. I'm not stupid. **You will** do this last job and then and only then will I sort out your flights and escort you both to the airport, do you understand?'

Paul gritted his teeth. He wasn't in a position to argue. It was decided that after a couple of days rest, whilst Conrad made arrangements, they would return to the camp and await the consignment. Hating being pressured and blackmailed Paul couldn't come up with any way out. There was nothing to do but go through with it. Eleanor's life was on the line. He consoled himself with the thought that this would be his last operation and they'd soon be out of there. What could go wrong?

BETRAYAL AND BREAKING POINT

40

Washington, February 1982

Sir Alan sat waiting in the private room at the Hilton drumming his fingers on the table. Never the most patient man at the best of times he got up and paced the room, wondering whether James Petersen was going to show or if he'd got cold feet.

A minute or two later a breathless James arrived apologising for his lateness, 'The traffic was backed up on Dupont Circle.' He sat down wheezing, sweating and trying to sort out papers from his briefcase. Sir Alan poured him a glass of water and bided his time.

At last, James recovered himself and extracting photocopied lists from his case passed them to Sir Alan, 'I think this is what you want. It wasn't easy getting the list from my colleague. There's a bit of a hullabaloo in his department at the moment. The gossip is that someone in the CIA is passing information to the Russians. I'm sure there's no truth in it. It's never been known in the annals of the Service. But they are mounting covert operations in all departments. Everyone is under scrutiny. I've enclosed a proposed timetable they're working to. How do you think you can help us?'

Sir Alan merely glanced at the list of suspected agents, 'I fly back to London tomorrow but I will mark this of the utmost urgency, and ask my colleagues to liaise with your Counter Intelligence. Possibly we have come across one of two of these names before. Our work does overlap. I am extremely grateful, James. Next time you come to London you must let me put you up at the Savoy as my guest and bring your family too, of course. You are probably in dire need of a holiday.'

'That's most kind and generous of you, Sir Alan. I'm sure my wife would be delighted.'

'Do please call me Alan; after all we're more than colleagues now, friends surely?' Alan patted James's shoulder in a friendly fashion.

'Of course, Alan. Do you want me to keep you updated on the situation in Honduras when you get back to London?'

'No, I don't think there'll be any need for that. My man will be returning to London soon. Keep him as long as you like though if he's useful to you.'

They parted on jovial terms indulging in mutual pleasantries. Sir Alan whistled blithely to himself as he collected his baggage and hailed a taxi for Dulles Airport.

...

In London, Vasily was just about to start his morning

briefing meeting at the Residenzia, when he received an encrypted telex saying,

'Contact positive. Our cousins are eyes on. Persuade your local sleeping friends to take an extended holiday. Will be in touch soonest. Anubis.'

...

Returning to the Mocoron camp from Tegu, Eleanor was greeted warmly by Dr Elodie. As much as she'd enjoyed their time in Tegucigalpa, Eleanor knew she preferred to be kept busy. There was so much satisfaction to be gained by helping at the camp, and she didn't even mind the primitive arrangements. Since they'd been back Paul had reverted to his former aloof manner. She knew he was worried about something Conrad had told him, but as usual he was unwilling to confide in her.

They went about their work for a week or so. Then Paul told her that a message had been passed along from Conrad. This was to be his final job, and after they would fly back to London.

Eleanor didn't know if she was happy about this or not. She had found a friend and mentor in Elodie and become attached to many of the Miskito children, Carlos in particular. This seemed to be the pattern of her life. No sooner had she made friends than she and Paul were off somewhere else.

302

There was no doubt in her mind that she loved Paul, and yet any sort of friendship or intimacy between them was sporadic. He was a loner and always would be. Hardly husband material, certainly not the type of husband she yearned for.

At various times during the next week, Paul disappeared for long periods, and shot off twice back to Tegu. He was more than usually morose and uncommunicative and snapped at her every word. Not being able to stand much more, one night Eleanor practically yelled, 'What on earth is wrong Paul, I mean Ralph? I might be able to help. Anything would be better than your backbiting?'

Paul froze, staring at her angrily, 'It's this last job. Conrad has come up with this crazy idea of using an old Red Cross ambulance. One of his men will act as an orderly, the other as a patient and of all things he wants you in the role of nurse. I've been back and fore, arguing with him about putting you in danger but he won't have it. He says it makes sense. It will look more realistic if we run into trouble.'

'I'll do it,' Eleanor said resolutely, 'if this is to be the last job, let's do it together. I'm OK with it. You were alright last time. We're on the right side of the river and the Contra camp is some way from the river border, so there shouldn't be a problem. Go ahead with the preparations. I'll borrow a nurse's outfit from the clinic and medical paraphernalia like a drip.'

Paul was speechless. He hadn't fully appreciated how much Eleanor had matured since they'd been at the camp. He knew Dr Elodie was giving her more and more responsibility. It was as if for the first time she was an equal rather than a dependant.

'Very well then if you're on board, we can get going sooner than planned. The ambulance will be arriving in Puerto Lempira with the two men Conrad's sending, in a few days. You and I will join them. Don't tell anyone in the camp. You will have to find some excuse as to why you're not available.'

Eleanor was eager to get going. She never thought to ask why it was such a complicated set-up, but had complete faith in Paul. He always knew what he was doing, and he was finally taking her seriously. She was determined not to let him down. It had been different in London. The shooting incident had thrown her off balance and she'd fallen apart, but this time she was ready for anything.

Setting out for Puerto Lempira in the old truck, Eleanor felt their relationship was back on track. It was like the old days of travelling round Scotland though Paul was unusually jumpy. Waiting for the plane to land, Eleanor took hold of his hand and stroked it reassuringly saying, 'Am sure everything will go well, don't worry so much.' Unfortunately Paul had a bad feeling about the whole enterprise and wasn't comforted though he tried to raise a smile of acknowledgement.

The ambulance and the men landed and Eleanor changed into her uniform ready to set up the drip, and bandage one of Conrad's men convincingly. Paul and the other man changed into hospital whites and climbed in the front. They set off immediately and were soon well under way with no sign of anyone or on the rough track. The ambulance bounced along easily on its reinforced tyres and all four of them began to relax. Eleanor chatted happily to her 'patient', Chuck, and they exchanged experiences of Tegu with Eleanor retailing stories of the Mocoron camp.

A few hours went by, and then without warning from nowhere, machine guns started blasting them tearing through the armour plating. Paul did his best to keep the ambulance moving and on the road but they were soon surrounded by jeeps and men armed with Kalashnikovs pushing and banging the sides of the vehicle.

The road sloped steeply down to the valley below as Paul fought to control the steering. The ambulance, barely balancing on its two outer wheels, tilted further and further towards the edge. Finally the weight was too much and it toppled, rolling over and over the embankment and down the hill with the four of them flung all over the place as it went. Immediately the guerrillas were after them, chasing down in their jeeps and shooting blindly.

Before the jeeps could reach the tumbling vehicle, Paul managed to kick open his door and throw himself out as far as he could. His leg was damaged but he crawled on his

305

belly as best he could and as fast as he could into the jungle area at the bottom of the valley, not stopping until he was at some distance from the now stationary ambulance lying defenseless on its back. The guerrillas blasted open the doors, dragging out Chuck and a half conscious Eleanor. Conrad's men, both badly injured, were dispatched with shots to the back of the head but Eleanor was left where she lay. The guerrillas were more intent on taking the ambulance apart to find the weapons. Everything was dragged out and loaded onto the jeeps. Then as an afterthought one of the men picked up Eleanor threw her over his shoulder, and dumped her in one of the jeeps as they made their way back up the hill onto the road and drove off.

Paul couldn't work out what had happened. Who were these men? Were they Sandanistas on a raid, but who had told them about the arms in the ambulance? Why had they been waiting for them on such a deserted road?

What was he going to now, and what about Eleanor?

41

Managua Prison, 1982

Eleanor woke with a sore throbbing head and aching body. Momentarily she thought she was back in the camp, but one look at her surroundings and she saw she was in a cell lying on a stone flagged floor with bars to the window. She tried to stand up but was too dizzy. There was blood trickling down her face and into her eyes. Trying to make her pounding head focus, she remembered the ambulance falling. Had there been gun fire or was she imagining that and where was Paul?

Using the wall for support, Eleanor staggered to an upright position. It was a small cell with just a wooden bench to lie on and a bucket in the corner. In the distance she could hear the sound of boots approaching. Her cell door was thrust open. A large hairy, greasy man in uniform grabbed hold of her by the neck marched her up a corridor to a door and knocked.

A harsh voice must have said to come in as Eleanor was pushed inside and dumped on a chair. Opposite sat a uniformed man with a luxuriant curly moustache painstakingly picking his teeth with a stiletto knife. Booted feet planted firmly on the desk, chair leaning back at an angle, the man studied her thoroughly taking his time to speak.

Eleanor flopped over in the chair, her head hammering,

307

ineffectually trying to wipe away the dried blood caking her eyelashes and blurring her vision.

Eventually the moustachioed man spoke, 'I'm Captain Alvarez of the National Guard. Who are you Madame, and why are you, a foreigner, gun running across our borders?'

Eleanor tried to gather her wits, playing for time by groaning, holding her head, then doubling over and pretending to vomit.

In a shaky voice she said, 'I'm Linda Whitman, English, a nurse working for World Relief and the Red Cross at Macoron. I need urgent medical attention,' and with that effort she slumped forward as if she was going to fall out of the chair.

'All in good time,' the Captain said, 'first we will examine the truth together. If you were working at the Macoron camp what were you doing in that ambulance?'

Eleanor replied wearily, barely able to support her head, 'I was helping out with a wounded man. What's happened to Chuck? Is he alright, is he in hospital?'

The Captain grinned maliciously showing a line of gold teeth, 'Unfortunately my men were somewhat overzealous and terminated both men. Of course there was a driver. We don't know what happened to him. He managed to get away somehow,' he shrugged, '–but no doubt will have died of his wounds by now out in that wilderness. Now tell me who they all were. Were the Americans delivering guns to the Contras?'

Eleanor muttered, 'I know nothing about guns or the Contras. The men were Peace Corps volunteers from the camp; I've no idea of their nationality.'

Alvarez ground his teeth in rage, 'You Brits are as bad as the Yanks. It's all about dollar power. We're in charge now, and what we say goes,' and with that he jumped to his feet letting his chair bang to the floor, and striding over to Eleanor slapped her hard first on one side of her face and then the other. Eleanor collapsed in a heap on the floor. Lighting a cigar Alvarez stubbed it out several times on the backs of her hands and arms, nonchalantly kicking her in the ribs with his booted foot until she was barely conscious.

Bending over her, he shouted loudly in her ear so that she could hear him through the pain, 'I don't like your attitude, little girl; you better find some truth quickly. There's no help for you here.' He shouted to the guard, 'Take her back to her cell. You'll have to carry her; she doesn't look like she could make it on own. Get the doc. to look her over when he's available.' The guard half dragged her and half carried her back to the cell, dumping her unceremoniously on the wooden bench.

Collapsing, Eleanor lapsed into a state of blissful oblivion, dreaming that she and Paul were back in the cottage in Scotland. Through her stupor she became aware of a man in a white coat bending over her, checking her pulse and heart. He tut-tutted to the guard in Spanish, 'This girl has severe concussion, let alone what damage there may be to her internal organs from all those bruises covering her body, perhaps internal bleeding. She must be hospitalised, there's no question about it.'

The guard's face was expressionless, 'It's up to Captain Alvarez. He decides.'

Doctor Morales barely able to conceal his irritation barked, 'Well go and tell him. Inform him if she's some sort of foreign national, English or American, there'll be trouble if she dies on his watch. It might start a war.'

A few minutes later the guard returned saying sheepishly, 'He said it's alright for now. Once she's better she'll have to be returned to our custody.'

An ambulance was ordered from the Lenin Fonseca Hospital. Sitting by the fair young girl in the ambulance and setting up drips, Doctor Morales studied the boot marks on her chest and ribs, and the cigar burns on her hands and arms. This was typical of the National Guard. They were no better than animals with no respect for human life. Most people they imprisoned and tortured disappeared for ever. But this was a young and vulnerable girl – how had she ended up with them? Moaning in her sleep, Eleanor moved trying to ease her badly bruised body. Feeling great sympathy for her, Doctor Morales turned up the sedatives. It was better for her to remain comatose he thought, until the worst of the pain eased. He was determined to look after her, despite the lack of beds at the hospital.

Over the next week the best Doctor Morales could do was find her a trolley in a quiet corridor. He and his team ran tests on Eleanor though she was barely conscious. A week later she was moved into an overcrowded ward, full of pregnant women, who assured Doctor Morales they would watch her.

Eleanor's first view when she finally woke up was of a large Mestizo lady, dressed in a multicoloured full length dress and bandana, sitting by her bed weaving a large basket. Having no idea where she was, Eleanor fretfully tried to twist her heavily bandaged head this way and that.

'There, there,' the woman said patting her hand, 'you in hospital in Managua. You safe. Us, we take good care **you**,' and pulling back the curtain, she revealed a whole crowd of heavily pregnant ladies beaming at her. 'The doctor, he back soon, he busy man. Sleep more, rest.' Eleanor closed her eyes, and thought about Paul, wondering if he was still alive and whether he would come and rescue her?

...

Paul was on the run. He'd managed to construct a splint for his leg using the remnants of his medic uniform as bandages, and sorted out a primitive crutch. At night he

311

slowly worked his way back to the river, lying low during the day. There were guerrillas on both banks of the Coco and Paul had no idea which side any of them were on. The scary thought was that no one except the conniving Conrad knew about the operation, and it was unlikely he would ever come looking for them based on Paul's earlier estimation of him; preferring to write them both off as expendable. Paul kept thinking of Eleanor and what might be happening to her. It was no good worrying. He had to obliterate all thought of her for the duration, and focus on his own survival and reaching the Contras if he was to get out alive.

Days went by with Paul existing on berries and fruit as he worked his way up river to the Contra camp on the other side of the Coco. On the eighth night he spotted a bridge, but crossing it would be tricky though he would have to risk it.

He waited till the early hours of the morning and attempted to limp across keeping low in the shadows, but before he could reach the other side figures immerged from the darkness and surrounded him pushing him to the ground. They tossed him into the back of a truck, crutch and all, and climbed in after him. They were all bearded or unshaven dressed in camouflage gear and carrying machine guns so it was difficult to identify which side they were fighting for. Paul crossed his fingers and hoped he could lie his way out if necessary.

In the next hour they entered a camp and Paul, thanking his lucky stars, recognised it. He had never been so relieved in his life to see Eduardo; however the Contra leader was not pleased to see him. There was no warm welcome forthcoming as Eduardo said uncompromisingly, 'One of my people betray you to Sandanistas. They threaten his family in Managua. We begin again. Conrad send plane for you tomorrow. We patch you up. You return with everything we need, no?'

'No, definitely not,' Paul replied angrily, 'this was to be my last trip. I'm getting out of here for good this time.'

'You send arms back with someone else then,' Eduardo said threateningly, holding his Kalashnikov to Paul's head. 'The rainy season nearly here. We need guns, explosives urgentemente.' He ground his teeth menacingly showing blackened stumps.

Paul grimaced, 'Don't worry on that score. I'll make sure they're sent.' All he wanted was to leave all this behind and get back to normality in London with Eleanor, but Eleanor what was he to do about her? At least she knew nothing about the arms in the ambulance, so the Sandanistas hopefully would let her go. The last ten days had been the end, not knowing whether he was going to live or die. This wasn't the type of spying operation he was used to; it should have been in the hands of the military not a civilian like himself. Anyway he didn't care what threats Conrad made on his return to Tegu, he was on the next flight out of there once they'd rescued Eleanor.

42

Managua, Lenin Fonseca Hospital, late Feb 1982

Dr Morales considered the young girl lying in the bed, her eyes shut. She certainly looked better than when he'd brought her in, even though her white bandaged head emphasised the pallor of her complexion. Sensing someone looking at her, Eleanor's grey blue eyes shot open and seeing him she smiled. He was charmed. There was no way he was going to return her to that awful prison.

'How do you feel, my dear?' he asked quietly.

'Oh much, much better, thank you. The ladies have been so kind, feeding me, plumping my pillows, and sitting with me although we can't speak to one another.'

He laughed softly, 'I knew they would take you under their wing. They are all mothers or mothers to be and like having someone to take care of. But on to more serious things, your tests are back. You luckily only had a mild concussion but you will have to be careful with that head injury until everything heals. Your body is coming along nicely,' he shuddered, 'despite all the kicks and the cigar burns. You had no internal bleeding. But there is other news and I'm not sure how you will feel about it?'

Eleanor pulled herself up on the pillows, 'What sort of news, something bad something long-term?'

'No, nothing like that. You are about four months pregnant.

Despite your treatment by the 'good' Captain Alvarez, your baby is holding on.' He paused not sure of her reaction.

Eleanor was overwhelmed and could hardly believe it. Overjoyed, she couldn't control her tears. If only Paul was here.....what would he think? Babies were probably not part of his life plan.

'My dear,' Dr Morales said, handing her his handkerchief, 'I didn't mean to upset you. This is probably not the best time to be pregnant.'

'No,' Eleanor protested, 'honestly, these are tears of happiness; this is the best thing that could have happened to me. I wish I could tell Paul,' completely forgetting she was supposed to be calling him Ralph. What did it matter now?

'I'm sure you'll see your husband soon, my dear. I'm going to do my best to make sure of that,' Dr Morales said reassuringly. 'Now I don't want you worry but Captain Alvarez has insisted on seeing you this afternoon. I can't stop him but I'm going to give you something to make you sleep, and then he won't have a chance to question you.'

'That's kind,' Eleanor said, her eyes filling with tears again, 'I'm not afraid for myself, but now you've told me I can't lose my baby or go back to prison. What am I going to do?'

'Don't worry, querida, I have contacts in Honduras. Be content, I will help you.'

He left her with all the mothers clucking over her. When she pointed to her rounded belly and made a gesture to say 'just like you' they all patted and hugged her, but when she held her finger to her mouth to indicate 'secret' they nodded wisely and copied her gesture.

Later that afternoon Captain Alvarez arrived, but by then Dr Morales had placed screens round Eleanor's bed and she was dead to the world. Without her knowing he had bandaged both her arms so that she looked more like a mummy, lying there with a drip and an oxygen mask over her face. Alvarez took one look at her and stamped about the ward whilst the expectant mothers shrank down in their beds.

He was infuriated he could do nothing about Eleanor. Sighting Dr Morales, he manhandled him towards the bed of the comatose girl, screaming, 'When is she ready for interrogation? Surely she must have recovered by now. It's been more than two weeks.

Morales calm as ever, shook his head gravely, 'Her concussion was a more serious than we thought. There may even be brain damage, and of course there is internal bleeding which requires an immediate operation. She may never recover completely, and if she does she may not be able to speak.'

Alvarez stalked off muttering, 'I'll be back to check on her, mark my words. You better not be telling me lies.'

316

Later that day Morales returned to Eleanor's bedside, saying, 'I'll have to move things along quicker than I thought if we're to get you out of here. I have a contact at the American Embassy in Tegucigalpa. But I need a plan.' He told her about Alvarez's visit, and his threats to return. 'We are going to give you a mock operation to make it look as if you are much worse than you are. I have members of my staff that I can trust but it will have be at night.'

As much as Eleanor was desperate to get away, she was conscious of how much the doctor and his staff were risking. But what else could she do? Her priority was her baby now. Doctor Morales made light of her concerns and went away to make preparations.

He gathered together his few trusted colleagues and checked whether they were willing, explaining, 'I have an idea how we can do this but I'll fill you all in later. Now I have to make contact with the Americans in Honduras.'

...

In the meantime Paul had been transported back to the military base at Tegu; however his reunion with Conrad was less than cordial. Conrad was insistent Paul return to Mocoron with yet another planeload of arms and two more of his men, 'Look Ralph, this will really be your final job for us. Only you know where the Contra camp is. Don't forget it was agreed by your boss and mine that you would do this.'

But Paul was adamant, 'I've done my last job for you and nearly got killed in the process. There was never any talk about my delivering arms. I'll draw your men a map of the camp and good luck to them. Now what about Eleanor? We have to find some way to get her away from the Sandanistas.'

Shiftily Conrad stared out of the window. Then reverting to his old bonhomie style, 'I don't know quite how to break this to you, old boy. The fragrant Linda didn't make it. We heard on the grapevine. She died from her injuries. I'm sorry,' he muttered insincerely.

Paul was stunned, 'But I saw one of the guerrillas carrying her and throwing her into the back of a jeep. Surely they wouldn't have gone to that much trouble if she was already dead?'

Conrad nervously adjusted his shirt collar, 'It was later, old bean, much later when they got her back to the hospital?'

'Which hospital and how do you know? There must be some way of finding out for sure,' Paul asked frantically.

'I daresay it was some hospital in Managua. I can assure you Ralph old boy, our information is A1. You can hardly jolly along there to collect a body. You'd be thrown straight in the slammer, and I'm afraid we don't have the resources to rescue you. I think that's an end to the matter. Now back to our delivery....'

Trying hard to hold himself together, Paul said unsteadily, 'If what you say is true about Eleanor, I'm definitely not staying any longer. I'll ring the Chief, and get the all clear. You've had enough of our services. It's been a complete fiasco and I've had enough.'

Conrad was fuming. Never a man to be thwarted, he retorted, 'If that's the case you're on your own. Find your own way back to Tegu and Timbuktu for all I care. I wash my hands of you,' and he stalked off in a rage.

Paul tried to work out what to do next. He felt disoriented and unlike himself. It was hard to believe Eleanor was gone. He knew he'd become fond of her but this was like having a dagger plunged deep into his vitals. Perhaps she'd meant more to him than he'd thought.   But it was no good wallowing in his feelings; he needed to get out of here. Perhaps London would help restore his sanity.

Making his way off the base, Paul spotted Captain Greenwald talking to the sentry at the gate and hailed him, 'Could you give me a lift to the Maya, do you think?'

'Of course,' Greenwald said, 'give me a minute. Wait in my jeep over there,' gesturing with his head.'

They drove back to Tegu in silence, Paul wrapt in his own thoughts and Greenwald diplomatic as ever. Paul booked back into the Maya and enquired about the next flight to London. He was told there was one in the morning, and he retired to his room for room service and rest. Glancing in the bathroom mirror, he was shocked at what he saw. His face was thin and gaunt. There were bloody cuts all over his face and neck, where he'd tried to get rid of his beard with Eduardo's cut throat razor. His clothes literally hung on his six foot frame, and his leg though stitched up with one of the Contra's best efforts at needlework was beginning to turn septic.

Ringing Reception he asked for a doctor or some way to obtain antibiotics. They said they would send for a doctor but it might be hours before he could come. Paul didn't mind. He needed sleep and would have to ring the Chief.

The Chief elusive as ever, eventually returned his call. Unperturbed about Paul's report of the drama of the last few weeks, his response was casual, 'You better return to London as you suggest. I'll make arrangements for you to pick up your return ticket at the airport tomorrow. Go home. Take a few weeks off and I'll contact you.............. I have another job lined up for you in the UK this time............ and something more exciting further afield in the future.......... oh yes, the girl Linda.....I see..... Died from her injuries.....Very sad......... There's nothing you could have done, dear boy..... Forget about her....... It's one of the hazards of the job....... Perhaps it's for the best; you really shouldn't have taken her with you. Next time follow orders........ Of course all is forgiven and forgotten..... We have to learn by our mistakes.'

The following morning a low-spirited, depressed Paul

320

boarded the plane for Heathrow. London would be welcome especially the cooler climate. A few weeks of leave could make a difference as the Chief said but it would be hard to forget Eleanor? There was always other female company to distract him but they would never be her. She was a one off, no doubt about it. He would have to throw himself into his work, until the longing for her and the terrible guilt wore off.

43

At the Fonseca hospital, Eleanor was recovering well. Most of her bruises and scars had disappeared. She moved about the ward chatting to the mothers but keeping a low profile when there was staff or visitors.

Every day she thought about Paul and hoped he was safe, and was setting things in motion for her rescue. But as the days wore on her hopes faded and she knew she would have to depend unreservedly on Dr. Morales.

One evening the doctor came to speak to her. He motioned for her to follow him into one of the consulting rooms saying, 'This is not going to be easy for you, querida. We are going to get you out, but Alvarez and his men are watching every move. They even have a spy amongst my own staff now, so we can't afford to delay. The mock operation will be tonight at midnight. It's commonplace for us to only have access to the theatres at night. I'll be giving you a drug that won't harm the baby but will knock you out for hours. While you're unconscious you'll be taken to a boat at Puerto Sandino, and by sea through Golfo de Fonseca to San Lorenzo. There you'll be met and driven the last 46 miles to Toncontin Airport, where your passage home is booked.

Eleanor didn't know what to say. The doctor had gone to so much trouble, 'Will it work?' she asked apprehensively, 'It sounds as if your plan involves a lot of people. I wouldn't want to put anyone's life in danger.'

'But we have no choice and neither do you.' Morales was phlegmatic, 'People in Nicaragua put their lives on the line every day with all these various changes of governments. We are a fatalistic people and accept what will be will be. Our lives are not your responsibility.'

That evening Eleanor was gowned up for her operation and wheeled into theatre. Dr Morales winked at her over his surgical mask, squeezing her hand reassuringly. He started a saline drip and injected her with the ketamine anaesthetic. He murmured that they were now moving her to an adjacent room, and his two assistants wheeled her into a side room. They then brought in the patient who was to be operated on that night.

By the time Captain Alvarez turned up and was shown into the viewing gallery, all he could see was a patient shrouded in surgical greens with the operation well underway.

Dr Morales kept up a running commentary as if he was performing a totally different operation making it as explicit as possible. Twice the Captain had to leave the gallery due to nausea. On the second occasion Morales sent his scrub nurse to see if she could help the Captain with his sickness, whilst he and his assistant switched Eleanor for the patient on the table. Morales piled all the blood stained cloths on top of Eleanor's now lifeless body. He turned on the heart machine until it beeped alarmingly, and the two surgeons made pretence of trying to revive her until they seemingly gave up. Morales shook his head at his colleague and went on to pronounce time of death.

Making his way back to the gallery, Morales informed the Captain, 'I'm afraid we couldn't save her. There was too much internal damage and she bled out. Do you want to come and view the body before she goes to the mortuary?'

Alvarez, pale about the gills, was none too keen but reluctantly said, 'I suppose I must in order to sign the necessary papers. Will there have to be an autopsy? It may not look too good for us if the body goes back to England?' For once he had abandoned his bully boy attitude even appearing somewhat cowed. Morales assured him that everything would be done with the least amount of fuss, and the body disposed of covertly, 'There will be no comeback for anyone Captain, you can be assured of that.'

The two of them walked down to the theatre, where the comatose Eleanor still lay on the operating table, white faced and lips coloured a violent purple by one of Morales' assistants. Alvarez glanced at her briefly then looked away mumbling, 'Such a beautiful young girl, what a waste.' Morales practically bit off his tongue in an effort not to remind Alvarez that she had been destined for prison, and more interrogations and beatings from him.

They left the room to sign the requisite papers. Morales' two trusted assistants carefully placed the limp Eleanor in a body bag equipped with pinholes for breathing, and then transferred her into a partially open casket in the back of the Mortuary van which made its way slowly to the nearby port. With all the paperwork in order, Eleanor's boat was soon en route for San Lorenzo.

The first Eleanor knew of her surroundings was the sound of an engine, the swaying movement of a boat and the lapping of waves. She couldn't work out where she was. Most of her body seemed to be encased in some sort of padded box, her head on a pillow. All she could see was a half open lid above her. It took her a second or two to realise she was in a coffin.

Panic set in. Frantic to get out, she kicked as hard as she could against the bottom of the coffin but there was no give. She had the idea of wriggling out through the top half but that was no use either. The coffin was too deep and her feet couldn't gain any purchase - no wonder Dr. Morales hadn't given her the exact details of her escape or she'd have been horrified.

Patience was what was required, and Eleanor tried to calm herself by singing songs. After considerable time, the boat engines juddered to a stop. There was complete silence. Then Eleanor heard the sound of a door opening and footsteps.

A familiar face, one she hadn't seen in a long time and thought she would never see again, looked down at her. Paddy adjusted his whiskers and his seaman's cap and beamed at her, 'Shocked you have I, mavoureen? You do get yourself into some pickles but here's good ole Paddy to the rescue as per. Let's get you out of there.' He opened the lid and helped her climb out, supporting her weight as she tried to find her balance on her jelly like legs.

Sitting her down, he all but dressed her in the seaman's jersey, jeans and boots he'd brought with him, and carefully tucking her hair into a beanie they made their way down the gangplank. 'How on earth did you know about me,' Eleanor asked getting her second wind and trying to shake out the pins and needles in her arms and legs, 'and how did you find me? Who told you to come?'

'Too many questions m'acushla, no time for answers now, let's just say that the Consul here is an old school friend of Mr C's, and he notified him that you and Paul were doing a job here. As you know Mr C likes to know where you are at all times. He has a particular interest in you.'

Eleanor would have liked to know what interest and why but refrained from asking anything further. For once she was thankful Mr C kept such a close eye on her.

Paddy hurried her towards a black hearse that was parked in the dockyard. It had black velvet curtains running round the windows. 'I'm sorry, little one, to put you through this again but we have to continue the charade. You'll have to crawl into the coffin in the back so that we don't arouse the guard's suspicions. I arrived hours ago with an empty hearse to collect a body, and I have to be seen to be doing

326

just that.' Eleanor was not happy to be entombed yet again but allowed herself to be helped in and the lid shut. 'There are plenty of air holes.' Paddy said, 'It won't be long before I come and get you out.'

The hearse moved off and stopped at the gate. Eleanor could hear voices, and then horrifyingly the back door was thrust open. The guard said, 'I see you have the correct paperwork, senor, but by rights I should check the body.'

Paddy's fluid tones interjected, 'O sir, it's just a puir wee girl in there. She's not a pretty sight... not since the container fell on her. Her family want to gather what's left of her to their bosom in her beloved Ireland,' and Paddy continued to spout more blarney. At last the door was closed with Paddy declaiming loudly, 'A blessing on your house, your lordship,' and Eleanor breathed a sigh of relief. Hopefully they were in the clear now.

Further on down the road the hearse pulled over, and Paddy came and helped Eleanor out and into the seat next to him. 'We're on our way to the airport,' he said reassuringly, 'just forty or so miles to go. I've a passport for you in the name of Linda Whitman and before you know it we'll be back in good old Blighty.'

Eleanor badly wanted to know about Paul, and ventured a question about his whereabouts.

'Sorry, can't help you there, m'acushla. I hear he made it

back to London, but there's been no sign of him since. You'll have to ask Mr C when you get back.'

Toncontin Airport was a welcome sight. Eleanor began to relax and feel confident that she was actually going home. She kept thinking about Dr Morales and his staff, hoping they were safe and not in prison. So many people she didn't know had helped her and she owed them a debt, though there was no way of ever paying it back. Paul was the one who should have rescued her but it was no good thinking about him. The baby and home were what mattered.

As they flew over the White Cliffs Paddy said, 'We've found you a safe house to stay in South London. It will be better than your flat. We can look after you while you recover, (he didn't add that they needed to keep a check on her). Claire will be there to take care of you.'

Eleanor wondered if he knew about the baby, and yet how could he? Only she and Dr. Morales knew. But why couldn't she go back to her flat, and why a safe house? Surely she was no threat to anyone? Of course it would be good to see a familiar face even Clare's. She was beginning to see just how exhausted she was. The strain of the Mocoron camp, then the prison, latterly the hospital and the escape had drained her more then she'd thought, so for the moment it was easier to go along with Sentry's plans.

Paul was like a constant ghostly presence as his baby grew inside her, and she felt distraught that she might never see

328

him again. How would she be able to bring up a baby on her own, and would she want to? Was it too late to have an abortion? How could she even consider something like that when she so badly wanted a family of her own?

…

At the Sentry offices Mr C was sitting staring fixedly at his phone. All in all it had been relatively simple to get Eleanor out of Honduras once the Consul had outlined the operation in Managua. However it wasn't going to be as easy to relay that information to 'Sir'.

Gritting his teeth he rang the dreaded number. It rang and rang and just as he was about to give up, the voice answered. Mr C gave the password. The voice said, 'How is she getting on with you? You haven't been in touch for some time.'

'There have been a lot of ups and downs in her life, sir. To cut a long story short she ended up in a prison and then a hospital in Nicaragua. However we've managed to get her out and she's on her way back as we speak.'

There was a sharp intake of breath the other end, 'Nicaragua, you say. You didn't send her off with young Paul, did you?'

Mr C paused, and stammered, 'Um …. We lost track of her after that op. in London. I did try to contact you sir several times, but couldn't reach you. I'm afraid I took it for granted you'd approved the undertaking they were both involved in.'

There was a telling silence, and the voice continued, 'I see. Keep me informed when she returns. Where she will be living?'

Mr C spoke hurriedly, 'We've arranged a safe house for her in South London sir. I can let you have the address when she's settled.'

'Please do,' the voice responded and rang off.'

…

It was a breezy day in Regents Park as two men sat companionably on one of the park benches, gazing at entwined lovers and dog walkers.

Amicably they discussed the vagaries of the weather and how Arsenal was doing that season until Anubis said, 'Well old friend, I do believe my past is fast catching up with me. It may be time to leave the game for good. What do you think?'

Vasily nodded complacently, 'Possibly, but surely there's a chance for one more throw of the dice. You were making valuable headway with our friends across the pond, and you've found us a useful asset there. It would be a shame to walk away now. Nevertheless I'll give it some thought.
 We still need you. Personally I'd miss our conversations. On

the other hand as we know to our cost in this line of work, it's all about timing. Be extra vigilant, comrade. Take every care.'

'Don't doubt that I will, and always have,' Anubis replied, 'au revoir old friend, till next time.'

44

South London, 1982

Paddy helped Eleanor out of the taxi in Lessar Avenue in front of an old Edwardian house that had seen better days. He guided her round the back to a steep staircase, leading down to the garden flat and unlocked the front door, 'This is the best we can do at short notice. It's one of our more basic safe houses but I'm sure you and Claire can fix it up. Abbeville Road shops are close by. It's a short walk to Clapham South Tube and you have the Common right on your doorstep.'

He sounds like a frustrated estate agent trying to sell a disinterested client a poor prospect, Eleanor thought apathetically. He was obviously doing his best trying to provoke some response from her.

Since Honduras she'd barely uttered a word, and now try as she might she couldn't make her lips move or form a 'thank you.'

 Looking at her, Paddy was suddenly alarmed, 'Bejezus, Eleanor. You're completely wiped out. Don't faint on me, m'acushla! We must pack you off to bed immediately.'

He bustled about making up a bed in one of the bedrooms, and then practically carried her along the corridor, and all but undressed her, laying her gently down between the sheets, pulling a coverlet over her and closing the curtains,

'Sleep now. Don't get up even if you hear us moving about. Claire and I will sort things out and make life here more comfortable.'

Later Eleanor woke to hear muted voices talking and laughing, and pulling on her clothes ventured along the hallway. All the sound was coming from the kitchen. Paddy and Claire were sitting at a big rough table, smoking, and chatting softly. She stood for a moment and studied them. It was hard to believe they were the only friends she had, the only ones to rescue her and be there for her. They looked up at the same time with matching expressions of concern.

Claire leapt to her feet and hugged her close, 'My poor Eleanor, what a time you must have had. Come and sit with us, and I'll heat some soup.' Paddy drew the electric fire closer to her saying, 'Your body will have a lot of adjusting to do after all that heat and humidity. When you feel better, Claire will take you shopping for warmer clothes and a coat. I know we're nearly into April, but it's hardly spring like.'

Eleanor felt comforted. At least they were people she knew. Perhaps they would provide her with a semblance of safety and security again, though at this moment all she felt was fear and confusion. Fretful about the baby she had begun to understand how transitory life could be, here one day and gone the next just like those poor Americans in the ambulance with her. They'd never stood a chance. How lucky she'd been to get away.

333

The next few days, she and Claire settled into the flat. To give Claire her due, she did everything she could to make life as pleasant as possible, never asking awkward questions, allowing Eleanor space to brood, and yet available when Eleanor wanted to relax and chat. They talked little about the office. For Eleanor, it had been a lifetime since she'd worked at Sentry.

Once Eleanor's state of health improved, Claire took her out shopping. Wandering round Harrods, Eleanor said, 'But Claire, I haven't the money to buy clothes here. I only have a few savings in the bank.'

'Don't worry about that,' Claire said, 'it's all taken care of. Sentry has a budget for times like these. All you have to do is decide what you want and I'll settle up.' Eleanor made some tentative choices, and Claire went off to pay for them whilst Eleanor continued to wander around listlessly. Without any warning she found herself becoming hotter and hotter then dizzy, and all of a sudden passed out.

There was instant mayhem. Assistants came running from everywhere, Claire included. They sent for a doctor and managed to move her to the sick room. Eleanor came to a few minutes later to find a panic stricken Claire staring down at her, 'How are you feeling?' You gave me such a fright.'

'I'm absolutely fine.' Eleanor said swinging her legs off the bed. 'It was just so warm in there.'

Claire said firmly, 'I think we should get you checked out properly by a hospital. We can detour to St. Thomas' on the way home.'

'No, honestly Claire, I don't need a hospital, it's because I'm having a baby,' the words slipped out of Eleanor's mouth before she had time to think.

Claire's eyebrows shot into her hairline, 'Yes, of course,' she said nodding, 'I suppose I should have thought of that. Anyway we must get you home. Have you seen a doctor at all?'

Eleanor shook her head, 'No, only in the hospital in Managua. I don't even know how far along I am.'

'You should have told us,' Claire chided, 'it explains your extreme tiredness. I could have been making sure you were getting the right nutrition. I'll make a doctor's appointment for tomorrow.'

Later that week Mr C was to drop in for a debrief. Eleanor dreaded telling him about her condition; but she needn't have worried. He arrived armed with chocolates, flowers, magazines and bucket loads of charm. Claire had already informed him about Eleanor's condition.

The first thing he said was, 'I blame myself for being press ganged by Paul into letting you go with him. I don't know what I was thinking, a girl of your tender years. We are going to do everything in our power to help you now and with the forthcoming event,' he beamed, 'we haven't had a Sentry baby for some time.'

Eleanor retorted sharply, 'My baby will **not** be a Sentry baby. I might work for you though that's questionable now, but any baby I have will be mine and mine alone.'

'Of course, of course,' Mr C said soothingly, 'it was just a manner of speech; I didn't mean anything by it. We'll need to look after you.

 The doctor said you are seven months along though he couldn't be entirely sure due to your state of health. Claire will make sure you eat the right foods, take vitamins and start going to pre-natal classes.'

Smoothly he slipped into his usual interrogative approach asking her to fill him in on what had happened so far, and listened closely to her stumbling account. His questioning went on for some time then glided easily into a gossipy mode, describing what had been happening at the office as if she'd just stepped out momentarily.

Eleanor finally interrupted to ask, 'Is there news of Paul? I'd like him to know about the baby even if he doesn't want to be involved.'

Mr C's mood plummeted from the paternal to the distant, 'No, there's nothing,' he said shortly. 'He's vanished altogether, and I fancy he's gone rogue.' His face closed up completely, and turning to leave remarked, 'Best to forget him, my dear. It will do you no good at all to hanker after a man like that.'

...

Returning to the office, Mr C was wary about passing on this current piece of news. He knew he would have to but was not confident as to how it would be received. He rang, took a deep breath and speaking rapidly into the mouthpiece recounted everything to date.

The voice at the other end was enraged, 'This is a mess. Pregnant! That's all I need. How far along? ......Good grief, that far. Too late for a termination I suppose........ I don't know. You'll have to handle it, Caruthers. Keep the girl under wraps. Warn your people to hold their tongues. I don't know what we'll do with the baby. You'd better look into procedures for adoption. If you're too squeamish, I'll see to it myself.'

Appalled with the direction the conversation was taking, Mr C said nothing wishing himself far away on some deserted island.

The voice continued coldly, 'Of course, it would be easier if she miscarried. I suppose there's no hope of that at this stage. Anyway I have to go. Fax me the address, and keep me updated on her progress.'

Mr C was glad when the phone was slammed down. The man might be his superior but he was a callous monster. He used to consider himself cold and uncaring, but he was nothing like his superior.

...

Later that week Anubis and Vasily met on yet another park bench.

Anubis said, 'My man Paul is working out well. He's on the ground now in the US handling our asset. Nevertheless I have further problems. I have an urgent situation I need help with. It would have to be another contract job, I'm afraid. Do you have suitable people?

Vasily stroked his chin, 'Always comrade, always, am sure I can find someone. Give me the details and I'll arrange it.'

Anubis smiled bleakly, 'This time the op. is delicate, very delicate indeed. Nothing can go wrong. My future is on a knife edge.'

'I understand comrade, I do,' Vasily went as far as patting the other man's arm comfortingly as they departed, a gesture he'd never dared try before, sighing with relief when it was accepted in the way it was meant.'

They might be comrades even friends Vasily thought, but never equals.

...

Eleanor was blooming. All the care and attention Claire

lavished on her was proving effective. Eleanor had put on weight, and the baby and she were flourishing. Her days now were focused on the birth and the coming baby. Her scans were satisfactory and she knew now she was having a boy.

Occasionally she gave Paul a passing thought, imagining where he was and what he was doing, and thought about calling the baby 'Paul'. Her father's name had been Robert, but he was not a man she wanted to remember. She and Clare discussed names at length. But neither of them talked about what would happen after the birth or where she and the baby would live. Eleanor had taken it for granted she would go back to her old flat and after maternity leave, return to Sentry part-time. Her days of working out in the field were over, but she could still be useful there.

Clare had returned to Sentry full-time, and now only came back to the flat in the evenings to cook a meal and sleep. She was gone early each morning, and hours later Eleanor would rouse herself and her lumbering body to cook breakfast, retire to the garden and read a book. The summer was so beautiful that one particular morning she decided to make her way to the shops, and look for wool for the matinee jacket she was trying to knit.

It was a huge effort to climb the steep staircase from the flat and puffing hard by the time she got to the top; Eleanor sat on the little wall at the front. Regaining her second wind and rubbing her aching back, she slowly made her way to the wool shop. They were lovely people, chatting to her about the area and the forthcoming baby. It was nearer lunchtime by the time she wove her way back. Claire did all the shopping these days, so there was always plenty of food in the fridge. Eleanor was looking forward to a large chocolate éclair left over from yesterday. Her cravings were taking over so much she needed the baby to come soon or she'd be the size of a house.

Back at Lessar Avenue, Eleanor turned towards the top of the staircase. At least going down was preferable to going up. It was right at that moment she felt one almighty thrust in the centre of her back and she was falling and falling with no hope of saving herself, balls of baby blue wool uncoiling through the air. There was one almighty crash and she plummeted into darkness.

AMNESIA AND ALIENATION

45

Tonbridge, Kent - Spencer Private Hospital Autumn 1982

At Sentry, Clare and Mr Caruthers were beside themselves. Eleanor had disappeared. There was no sign of her at the flat in Clapham, or in the surrounding area, or at her old flat. Claire was all for blaming herself, 'I'm worried sick. I should have never left her alone. Where can she be? How does a pregnant girl vanish like that and what about the baby? She was so near her time. We've checked every hospital and nursing home in the country. Paddy has scoured London. There's no trace of her. How could she melt into thin air like that?' Looking enquiringly at Mr C, Claire said, 'You don't suppose Paul has anything to do with it?'

'No, he's gone for good or so I've been assured. He absconded immediately after the Nicaragua job, and nothing's been heard of him since. Anyway he's probably more interested in his own future. I can't see him wanting to be lumbered with a girl and baby.'

'What about the police- maybe they could come up with leads?'

'I don't think so, Clare. We're in a better position than they are to find any Intel. I don't want to create a panic situation until we have more facts to work with. I'll get Paddy liaising with our contacts and see if anything stirs. Calm yourself, and go back to your work. Leave it with me.'

Mr C returned to his own work wondering when and how he was going to break the news of Eleanor's disappearance further up the line. 'Sir' would not be thrilled. Who knows how he'd react? For the present it was better to keep this current state of affairs quiet.

...

The harsh white light woke her – it seemed to be coming from both near and far away. There were voices but they were hard to make out. Were they whispering or shouting it was hard to tell? Was that someone touching her? Why couldn't she speak? Her mouth was opening and shutting but there was no sound. A feeling of panic rose in her chest. Any minute now she was going to scream, but it was too late the darkness was closing in.

Hours later there was light again. This time it was gentle and golden. A voice said, 'You're doing fine, dearie. Take a sip of water.' Gratefully she drank; water had never tasted so good. But where was she and not only that who was she? Lying back carefully and painfully, she tried to focus on the owner of the soft voice. A smiling soul in a nurse's uniform waited for her to speak but there was nothing to say.

Becoming aware of her surroundings, her hands automatically began to feel round her body for the source of her pain. Her legs seemed fine; she sucked in her stomach with a breath and exhaled. There were definite echoes of pain there, and some sort of dressing. But the baby, what about the baby? Why had she instantly thought of a baby? Had there been a baby? Touching her chest and neck there was nothing, though her breasts ached. Her head was a different matter – it was totally encased in bandages that covered her face except for her eyes and air holes for her nose and mouth.

'Dearie,' the nurse said urgently, 'leave your face alone. You've had an accident, hurt your head badly and your poor face took the worst of it, but you'll be fine. Plastic surgeons can do miracles these days. You'll be back to your old self in no time.'

Shocked she tried to respond. What old self, and what about the baby? Why did she keep thinking about a baby, not just 'a baby' but 'the baby'? Had she been pregnant? However hard she tried to remember there was no memory. It was no use, her mouth was dry, dark curtains were falling over her eyes, and she was slipping away. Was she ever going to find out?

The next time she woke up, it was in a rush. This time the darkness had been shorter. She could clearly see the ward and other beds. A nurse, noticing her trying to sit up hurried over and propped up her pillows, 'I'm glad you're back, dearie. Remember me. I gave you water last time, perhaps another sip. I'll get you some ice to suck.' She was back in seconds with splinters of ice, 'I'm Molly, dearie – let me help. No, not so fast, don't put too much ice in at once. You'll be able to talk when the dryness eases.' Molly rattled on, babbling nineteen to the dozen. Wanting to play her part, she croaked, 'Thanks,' but with her head throbbing so much she was glad to lie back with Molly's help and close her eyes. 'That's right, dearie,' Molly said, 'a bit of shut eye will do you good. I'll be back later.'

The rattling of a tea trolley woke her next time. A kindly WRVS lady offered a cup of tea. How was it she could recognise the WRVS and yet not know who she was? Night followed day in endless succession until one day she woke, her head easier, the pain dulled and her faculties alert.

When the doctors came on rounds, she cried out, 'Where am I? Who am I? What about my baby?'

The silver haired consultant was astounded to be addressed directly by a patient. 'You are in the Stanley Hospital in Tonbridge. I'm very much afraid my dear, we couldn't save your baby. You had such a bad fall in the accident, the cord broke and we were forced to perform a Caesarean. We delivered the boy but he was stillborn.'

Why was it they felt they must call you 'my dear' in that patronising manner? And why was that all she could think about when she'd just been told her baby had died? Her baby..... Her baby..... Her boy! The screaming started then. It was like drowning and suffocating. She was both in and

344

outside her body at the same time. The pain was visceral, crashing and hammering through her in waves, oblivious to the sedative the consultant administered. The sharp jab of the needle barely touched her consciousness.

They kept her comatose for days and once she woke up, milder drugs kept her feeling numb. When the consultant returned he'd stopped calling her 'my dear', as if he'd suddenly become aware of her as a human being and asked quite genuinely, 'How are you today?'

'Better,' she muttered barely able to dredge up the word. There was only one thought in her clouded drugged brain, 'I want to see my baby.'

The consultant considered her carefully, 'You do understand we couldn't save your baby.'

'Yes, but I'd still like to see him.'

The consultant sighed, 'I'm sorry. You probably haven't realised all this happened more than two months ago, and the baby has been cremated. At the time we didn't know whether you would ever regain consciousness as you were so badly injured. This seemed to be the best course of action.'

Her eyes filled with tears. To think she would never ever see her son, Paul's son - she gave a start, Paul, who was Paul, was he the father? Was she remembering something? She needed answers, and said loudly, 'But who am I? I can't remember my name or anything about myself.'

345

Instead of answering her, the consultant glanced at his watch eager to escape and said, 'It'll come back in time; you'll have to be patient.'

Anxious to avoid any more questions, he turned to address the medical students slowly assembling round him, 'We don't get many cases of global amnesia. This patient has been here nearly ten weeks already. Procedures have been carried out on her face and nose, but there is still a fractured skull exacerbated by a former injury with no sign of returning memory.'

'I'm still here.' she said crossly. 'Please talk to me. When will I get my memory back?'

The consultant annoyed at being interrupted, said curtly, 'My dear, my apologies. We are doing all we can to get you back to full health. We are also making enquiries about anyone who can identify and claim you.' (Sounds like a parcel, she thought tetchily.) 'Until then I'm afraid you'll have to stay with us,' and that said, he hurriedly moved the group on to the next bed.

Speaking up for herself had taken so much energy, she was glad he'd gone. Depleted she sank back into a stupor.

The deadly routine of hospital days gave her time to think. Her thoughts kept returning to her baby boy. How pregnant had she been? If there'd been a baby where was the father? Why wasn't there any family or friends looking for her? Did she live in Tonbridge or nearby?

With no name of her own, the staff at the hospital had taken to calling her Miss X which she hated. Eventually a kinder friendlier doctor said, 'What would you like to be called? Pick a name.' He gave her a book of baby names to choose from.

Leafing through the pages she came across 'Anastasia'. Wasn't that the name of the Russian princess who'd been assassinated and who'd later turned up in America suffering from amnesia?   Hadn't she seen a film about it?   How strange to remember that and yet know nothing about herself. It might as well be 'Anastasia' and carry on the tradition but the staff found the name a mouthful, and had soon shortened it to 'Anna'. It was strange to have a name but no identity to go with it. What was her real name? Would she ever find out?

After several miserable weeks obsessing about who she was, Anna decided to see what she looked like. Most of her bandages had been removed by now so she might even recognise herself.   Extracting a mirror from the reluctant Molly was a challenge but Anna persevered.

In due course, one was produced. It was a shock to see the reflection of a beaten up young woman. A pair of frightened grey/blue almond shaped eyes surrounded by yellowing bruises stared right back at her. But she couldn't stop looking at the fair skin crisscrossed with black stitches extending across swollen cheeks to the jaw line. The nose in some sort of beaklike bandage stood out bright red like congealed blood that made her flinch. 'Oh don't worry about that,' Molly said airily, 'that's just the plaster they use. Your poor nose took a bang. It'll mend straight you'll see when the plaster comes off.' Adding proudly, 'They do a good job here.'

Only the lips were undamaged. Anna touched them tentatively. Her teeth gleamed through her half opened mouth. 'You're alright there,' Molly declared brightly, 'all your teeth are intact. That's a relief dear, isn't it?' But was it though? Not only did she have a name picked out of a baby book, but she didn't even know her own face.

Studying her, the incorrigible Molly was forced to say, 'Enough now, Anna, I'll take the mirror. It's been too much for you. Once the bruising and swelling goes down and the stitches come out, things will look different.' Lamely, Molly remarked, 'I do think you are a good looking young woman under all that and will be again,' and bustled off to inflict her brand of cheerfulness on her next victim.

Later that week, a dark suited officious detective arrived. He carefully drew the curtains round her bed and took out a large notebook.

'Now miss, you say you have no memory at all, no idea of your name or address. We've checked 'Missing Persons' and there's no one matching your description listed. Of course we can take your fingerprints. But they're only useful if you

348

have a criminal record.'

'But what happened to me?' Anna asked desperately, 'All anyone has said so far was that there was some sort of fall?'

'That's correct Miss. You were found sprawled at the bottom of steps in Lessar Avenue in Clapham approximately three months ago. Someone rang for the ambulance but didn't give their name. You had no form of identification not even a handbag, and were dressed in a maternity smock and sandals. There was a big bag of blue wool unravelling round you but nothing else. We didn't know if you lived there or were visiting. We tried the garden flat but couldn't raise anyone, and weren't able to trace who owned it except for a fake shell company which didn't exist.'

It was hard to take in. Why had she been in Clapham? Had someone tried to kill her, and why oh why would she immediately jump to that conclusion? Maybe there was something dreadful in her past.

The detective continued, 'We've been through your clothes. They were expensive yet all the labels had been roughly cut out. Does that ring any sort of bell?'

'No, I've no idea. There's nothing in my head at all. I wish I could remember, remember anything at all........,' her voice trailed off despondently.

The detective shook his head, 'It's a mystery alright. Don't take it to heart, Miss. I 'm sure your memory will come back.

We'll leave it for the present. When your face is healed, we'll photograph you and forward your picture to other police forces throughout the country.'

He got up to leave, patting her hand sympathetically.

Anna wasn't at all sure she wanted her picture on display all over the country. What if there was something sinister in her life, and what if she was in danger? Although she was desperate to find out who she was, there might be things about herself she didn't want to know. A strong sense of foreboding and fear hung over her but fear of what or who?

By now the hospital was packed to the rafters with a serious shortage of beds. Not knowing what to do with Anna, it was decided to pack her off to a nursing home for further treatment and recovery.

The ebullient Mollie was full of it, 'It'll do you no end of good, dearie. A good rest and you'll get your memory back. I know you'll miss your dear old Mollie but it's for the best.' Honestly it was a relief to dispense with Mollie's services. All Anna wanted was peace and quiet, and a chance to try and piece things together.

…

In London, Vasily and Anubis were in one of their usual meeting places. Anubis was far from happy, 'I can't understand how your man botched yet another operation. This is as bad as that one in North London. Surely you weren't using the same subcontractors? All your man had to do was get rid of one heavily pregnant young girl, how hard could that be?'

'She was badly injured in the fall but still alive,' Vasily replied, 'and my chap was about to finish her off when some nosy neighbour appeared. He had to make a run for it and contacted me straight away. I arranged for one of our ambulances to take her off to a private hospital in Kent where I have contacts before the public services could arrive. The neighbour didn't question it seemingly impressed with the speed of the NHS.'

Anubis was not placated, 'So what's happened to her now and how can we contain this?'

'She's suffering from severe amnesia. It was touch and go with the baby but he's doing well now. We were able to handle that part efficiently, and I've hired a private nurse for him. Luckily, our girl hasn't asked to see the baby yet. She's completely traumatised after being told he didn't survive.' Vasily smiled sheepishly, 'I'm told the boy's thriving. Did you want to see him?'

'Most definitely not. Make it your business to terminate him or have him adopted whichever it takes. As for the girl herself we'll move her somewhere else when she's better, maybe a nursing home that's closely guarded where she can be monitored.

Put exit arrangements in place for me in case anything else goes wrong. I am counting on you, Vasily. My trust in you so far with this operation has not proved to be exactly warranted. Make sure the rest of it goes perfectly or I may come after you myself next time.'

Vasily scowled. Dealings with Anubis were getting complicated, and there were always orders, more and more orders. If only Moscow Central would give Anubis a new handler, though of course he himself didn't want to be recalled home he was far too comfortable in the West. His superiors regarded Anubis as a precious asset of infinitely higher value than himself, so there was no point in rocking the boat. He would have to grin and bear it.

They parted with perfunctory nods - Vasily only too keen to return home to his comfortable maisonette in Swiss Cottage.

46

Tonbridge, Kent - Shelburne Private Nursing Home , Spring 1983

The nursing home was set in luscious green woodland. The weathered grey stone building glowed silver in the afternoon sun, as Anna was driven through the entrance. This was the place to rediscover her lost life Anna thought; she could feel it in her bones.

Arriving at Reception, she was greeted with smiles and sympathy and wheeled to a spacious airy room overlooking well manicured lawns and neat pathways. Her attendant, a cheerful Jamaican, showing a row of gleaming white teeth beamed down at her reassuringly saying, 'I'm Matt, I hear you've had a rough time, Miss Anna, but you're doing well for all that.'

Anna barely acknowledged him; an overpowering wave of fatigue was swallowing her up. She knew the attendant meant well but everything was suddenly too much. Aware of her lack of response, Matt said quietly, 'I'll turn down your bed. You can get some rest. Ring the bell at any time and I'll be there in a jiffy. I'll come back later to do your checks, and unpack your case if that's alright.'

Anna protested weakly. She had no idea what was in the case. None of the clothes were hers. They were remnants from a local charity shop that the hospital had thrown together at the last minute. 'Don't worry we'll sort things out,' Matt said authoritatively drawing down the blinds and tiptoeing out.

The next months swung by, barely leaving any impression. Finally her nose plaster was removed. At last she could breathe easily but they were reluctant to show her the finished product, 'It's too swollen and red yet. Leave it a few weeks.' Anna would carefully run her finger down it from the bridge to the tip. It felt the same but then how could she tell when she didn't know what it was like before. They were already sorting out her other scars, taking skin from her thighs and attaching it to her face. 'You'll be a new woman,' they kept saying. But Anna thought she might end up looking like a patchwork quilt. If she was to be a new woman, what was the old one like or 'the other woman' as she called her past self?

Visits from various consultants continued. There were also sessions with a dark, rather sinister, psychiatrist, Dr. Julius Janecek. Anna hated him on sight but was forced to endure the daily torture of him prodding and poking her mind. There were endless tests and word association assessments, which sent her mad with frustration. He would stroke his thin, threadlike moustache and comment, 'That's an interesting connotation, Miss Anna – fancy linking sunshine to fear, I wonder what it means perhaps there's some darkness in your past you don't want to confront.'

'I wonder too,' she thought to herself but there was too much blankness, and too many unanswered questions. It was better living day to day. She had found that was the best way to deal with her pain about the baby, and whoever Paul was. Her physical scars were healing but nothing eased her emotional ones.

By now Anna was expected to make her own way to the sun lounge and sit with the other patients in their enforced prison. Thankfully they were too encased in bandages to make conversation. As Anna became stronger, she found herself a secluded spot in the walled garden hidden from sight by an archway of white roses. Each morning the scent of the flowers intoxicated her and she would doze and day dream. Flashes of memory would zoom into her brain, melting away before they became shape or substance. The hot sun on her face brought back flashes of a hot land and Indians. Honduras came to mind, then Nicaragua, surely not ------. Had she lived in one of those countries?

Now her physical health had improved immeasurably and her scars were healing, it was obvious to Anna and the nursing home that it was time to leave. Where could she go? There was no home or family waiting for her; she had no money, and no recollection of a previous existence. How would she build a new life?

The home's Welfare Officer called her in, 'You're more than ready to leave Anna. You've been with us over a year and we can't do more for you. But you'll need money. We would have helped you out of the Welfare Fund but it seems you have a mysterious benefactor. A bank account was opened for you at the beginning of your time here, in the name of Anastasia Smith. You only need to provide a specimen signature and you'll have free access to it. It's a considerable sum with the interest that's accrued. You can start afresh. Have you any idea where you'd want to go? I can make all the arrangements, and we'll arrange for you to see a counsellor, a psychiatrist, or maybe even a hypnotherapist if that would help? There's no rush, think about everything for the next few days and let me know.'

Anna deliberated for the next week. It was frightening to leave this sheltered community with nowhere to go. Her mind was in chaos, worrying about where she would end up. What about that bank account? Where did it come from? If someone knew about her, why didn't they get in touch?

On one of the days when she was attempting to relax in the garden, she had an idea. What about London? Why there? Maybe she'd lived there once; still it was as good a place as anywhere. That's where she'd go and perhaps find something or someone familiar.

The nursing home was keen to move her on, not wanting the responsibility now she was fit. The Welfare Officer sorted out travel tickets and found Anna the name of a hypnotherapist. Other than that she was on her own.

Packing her bag with her few meagre possessions, Anna thought is this all my life is worth? Two well washed white shirts; cotton pyjamas; a polyester dressing gown that had seen better days; slippers a size too small; two different length skirts; the minimum of worn underwear and a nearly new dark overcoat given to her by a generous nurse. All that with some sensible lace up shoes and a vinyl zip up bag to carry everything in was the sum total of her existence.

Once packed, Anna dressed and checking herself in the mirror tied back her long blonde hair with a scarf. She touched up her poor damaged face with foundation and blusher. Of course it wasn't her face but it looked decent enough even if the features were bland and the blue grey eyes lifeless. Recently she had taken to wearing glasses just plain glass, but something to hide behind, making her feel less vulnerable to the world outside. Was she ready to face that world again especially when she had no idea of her place in it?

...

Elsewhere, Vasily was contemplating the baby. He was a lovely little fellow with beautiful almond shaped eyes holding up his arms and chattering away with noises only familiar to himself. Vasily couldn't resist picking him up, holding him gently to his shoulder and stroking his back. The boy cooed and Vasily was overcome. There was no way he could extinguish this baby's life. Killing people was one thing but a baby----. He would have to be placed with some good people – there was bound to be the right sort of couple at the Residenzia – with perhaps a move to new country as well. He smoothed the boy's wispy blonde hair back from

357

his forehead and whispered, 'Don't worry Alex, moy mal'chik, we'll find you a good home and a safe one however long it takes. Maybe even with me,' he mused as an afterthought. He wondered why he'd inadvertently called him Alex, but the Alex he'd known all those years ago would never have killed a baby, would he?

47

London, 1984

At Sentry Mr Caruthers was considering the best way to break bad news. He called through to Claire, 'Paddy been in touch? Has he come up with anything?'

'Nothing. Paddy's scoured the whole of London. It's been such a long time..... Do you think.....' and her voice broke, 'that Eleanor could be dead?'

'No, of course not. We've had the police checking bodies. There's been no sign of Eleanor. Even if she'd lost her memory we'd have heard something. There's nothing for it, I'll have to let my superior know. He wasn't pleased the last time when I said we'd lost her. I don't know what his reaction will be this time.'

The phone call was made. Mr C could feel himself grovelling as he explained, but the reaction was surprisingly mild, 'I suppose these things happen. Perhaps the girl doesn't want to be found. Call off the search; you've done what you can. We'll say no more about it. Carry on as normal.'

Mr C could hardly believe his ears after all the fuss there'd been about Eleanor from the beginning. Now this - he didn't know what to think, he was mystified. There was no doubt about it his boss was a ruthless bastard. All the years in the Service must have bled him dry of feeling.

...

On the train to London, Anna felt ill at ease and edgy; having been on her own so much at Shelburne it was nerve-racking to be cast adrift amongst the chattering masses. Hospital life had been so structured and timetabled that she was at a loss as to what to do with herself. Sitting on the edge of her seat and clutching her bag tightly to her chest, Anna would have given anything to exchange her plain glasses for dark ones. She didn't want to look at people, and she certainly didn't want them looking at her.

Reaching Victoria, everything was unfamiliar. All the bustling people frightened her. Anna had half imagined that when she arrived in London something might jog her memory but there was nothing; even the signs in the station were alien. Eventually she found Information and a superior, sophisticated girl in uniform took pity on her directing her to Left Luggage.

The Left Luggage man, a cheery soul, took hold of her bag saying, 'It's a nice light one, makes a change. Where are you off to then, ducks?' Anna's nerves finally broke at the sight of his kindly face, tears welling up uncontrollably. He took a one look at her and said, 'You poor soul, don't take on so. Nothing can be as bad as all that. Come round the back and have a sit down. I'll make you a cuppa,' and with that he lifted the flap and Anna slipped through. Joe sat her down in a corner and started brewing up, rattling on as if this was all in a day's work, 'London's such a big place, ducks. It can be a bit much your first time.' Anna's immediate thought was but it's not my first time, then how could she know.

'What d'ya doing here in the Smoke, my love?' he enquired handing her a large china mug full of steaming tea. 'Get that down ya and tell your Uncle Joe all about it.'

Anna's hand could barely wrap itself round the mug, but she sipped it appreciatively and managed to utter, 'I'm looking for a flat to rent ....don't know where to start.'

Joe looked at her up and down speculatively, 'You'll need money for that. If you don't mind my saying you look a trifle fragile, that's if you need a job as well.'

Anna didn't know what to say. She was not going to unburden herself to a complete stranger, yet he might be able to help. Ignoring his comment about her physical condition, she said, 'I have money for a deposit and a couple of months rent. I can take my time finding a job.'

'That's alright then,' Joe said, 'don't go throwing money away on those flat letting agencies.' Rubbing his chin thoughtfully, he said, 'I may be able to put something your way. My sister Muriel caretakes a property at the Angel, there may be a flat going there. Shall I give her a ring?'

'Oh please,' Anna said, 'it's an area I know, ideal for Central London.' She nearly bit off her tongue realising what she'd said. Why had she thought she knew that part of London unless perhaps her memory was coming back?

Joe was too busy on the phone to notice her turmoil. In an instant he'd arranged for Anna to view a vacant flat. 'You mightn't be able to move in straight away, ducks, so I'll hold on to your bag for you, shall I?'

Armed with his directions, Anna set off by tube for the Angel. She had calmed down and begun to feel more optimistic. Maybe things would work out. For the moment she'd decided to take the money, all £50,000 of it, in her stride though it was more than she could ever have dreamed of. At least it could buy her security and peace of mind. Of course there was always the niggling worry about where it had come from, who her benefactor might be, and what they would want in return? But for now she needed to concentrate on finding somewhere safe to live.

The flat was perfect despite Muriel living on the premises, however she was a tidy little widow friendly but not too inquisitive. She took an immediate liking to Anna giving her a key and saying, 'Anyone Joe recommends is alright by me. Have a look round, my dear, and then come down and have a cup of tea with me. I've a batch of newly baked scones just waiting to be eaten.'

No. 10 Richmond Avenue was a Victorian house converted into four furnished flats, the bottom one being Muriel's. Anna was to have the top flat, a bedroom, lounge/diner with kitchenette, and a shower room. A tiny balcony outside had space for a potted plant and a chair. Anna didn't mind being at the top of the house. It would be more private with no chance of anyone one traipsing past her door.

After paying the bond and deposit, Anna enquired when she could move in. Muriel agreed to talk to the landlord, clean the flat and it could be hers within the week. Anna was relieved. Making her way back to Victoria, she spotted a Guest House near the station and booked in for a week. It was reassuring to think she would have a roof over her head and with a considerably lighter heart she returned to Joe and Left Luggage. 'You've done well,' he said beaming away and handing over her bag, 'you'll soon be a Londoner. Don't forget your old Joe. I'm here if you need me.'

During the next months Anna enjoyed her new flat. She opened an account at a nearby bank, drew out money to live on and furnished her home. Taking the Shelburne's advice she contacted the hypnotherapist they'd recommended, a strange Russian lady called Olga who spoke only broken English. So far there'd been five sessions and though Anna felt uncomfortable with Olga, she had to admit her past was beginning to take shape. There were flashbacks now on a daily basis.

Anna would continually ask Olga what she had said when she was under, but the therapist would shrug and say, 'It make no sense........ You not good subject... Not open. All disjointed... Sometime in hot country.... Sometime with man.... Sometime Scotland.....Other time, peoples' names... Mr C, Clare.... No real pattern. I think memory return but slowly. Be patient.' Anna never felt entirely satisfied with these sessions, wondering why the clinic had suggested Olga. She seemed more like a stage hypnotist than a bona fide therapist.

The other odd thing was that every time Eleanor attended Olga's sessions, she had the strangest feeling she was being watched and followed. Strolling home one day, she caught sight of a man she thought might be trailing her. Aware that Anna had noticed him; the man turned up his coat collar, pulled down his hat and moved swiftly past her.

Was this her imagination or was there more to it? She decided to pay more attention in future. There was no doubt in her mind she felt under threat but had no idea from where or why.

…

Anubis was not a happy man. Making contact with Vasily was never easy, and these days he was slippery at best. When they finally got together Anubis confronted him, 'It's months since we spoke. I've been trying to get in touch with you. Where you've been? I need an update on the girl..... and of course, the baby.'

Vasily started to say, 'Look I'm sorry Alex,' but Anubis interrupted angrily, 'I've told you time and again, don't call me that name. That was another life. I'm Anubis now as you well know.'

Vasily continued, 'Apologies, I don't know where my mind

was. I was thinking of another Alex. I'm sorry you weren't able to reach me but I had to return to Central. Everything took longer than I thought.'

Becoming more fraught by the minute Anubis said, 'Well get on with it man, I need to know what's going on.'

'The girl's in London now. We arranged a flat for her near the Angel through a contact at Victoria. She's sees Olga regularly but hasn't regained her memory just patches of it. I've arranged constant surveillance so no slip ups there. No one else knows where she is as far as I know. As regards the baby put your mind at rest. He's been disposed of and is out of harm's way.'

'I suppose that's reassuring;' Anubis said begrudgingly, 'just make sure from now on you're available. I'm still of a mind to make my exit but will hold off for now. Meet me here in a month and we'll reassess,' he growled as he stormed off.

Vasily suddenly had a vision of baby Alex beaming and chuckling up at him, and sighed, if only he was dealing with him instead. But no, he was now safely tucked up at home with his nanny.

48

London, The Angel, 1984

In London Anna was beginning to think she should find herself a job. Her days were aimless and though she was careful with money, it was swiftly disappearing. However the clothes she'd been given by the clinic were so poor she would need to buy herself a new wardrobe, nothing eye catching just something serviceable.

The problem was she had no idea about her taste. It was disconcerting to stand in front of mirrors, try on clothes and not recognise yourself. Hiding behind the oversized glasses and studying herself in yet another store, Anna decided to abandon the glasses. They served no purpose and she was tired of hiding. The scars on her face were barely visible. Studying herself from every angle she noted her features were good: her nose, delicate and retroussé, was it like that before who knew; at least her slightly Slavic looking eyes were her own. She must snap out of this fixation with her face and take a good hard look at herself from head to toe. There was no doubt she had a good figure, though perhaps she was too thin. Her blonde hair was long and in need of cutting. But in general terms she looked reasonable enough to look for employment.

An assistant came hurrying up saying, 'I think I've the perfect dress for you madam', returning with a peacock blue dress hung over her arm. For a moment Anna was entranced and then said firmly, 'No, I don't think so, maybe something

366

in grey if you have it.' The assistant started to say, 'But....,' however taking one look at Anna's forbidding expression showed her a plain grey suit. 'That's fine,' Anna said, 'I'll take it together with the white blouse, grey sweater, and that navy raincoat.' The assistant made a little moue with her mouth but did what she was told.

Anna's next port of call was the hairdresser's, and despite the stylist's pleading had her long hair cut into a short severe bob. Feeling she had dealt with her outer appearance sufficiently, Anna sat down with a coffee to prepare her next move. She needed a job but didn't know what skills she possessed. The hypnotherapy sessions hadn't helped at all lately, and she'd decided to dispense with Olga's services and let her memory takes it own course.

All Anna did these days was read, so a job in a bookshop could be a possibility. Scouring the bookshops on the Charing Cross Road, Anna discovered an old-fashioned emporium down an alleyway. Studying the shelves and perusing the books, Anna studied the owner. He was a spry man probably in his eighties sprinting up and down ladders like someone half his age. She must have caught his attention as he came over, and asked, 'Are you looking for anything in particular?'

'Not really,' Anna replied, 'I'm looking for a job. I love books and thought maybe somewhere like this------?' Her voice petered off into a thready whisper.

John Dawkins cautiously weighed up the attractive young woman in front of him. She was dressed more for business than shop work. 'I don't employ anyone, as there isn't much money in second hand books,' then responding to the desperation in her eyes he hesitated, his heart went out to her and he continued before he could stop himself. 'Of course, there are days when I'm out buying and selling and that means shutting the shop. If you were interested in something part-time I could manage that, would that suit?'

Anna's face lit up immediately, 'When would you like me to start?'

'Hold on, what about references. I do have to put everything through the books.'

Anna's heart sank. What should she do, lie or trust him with the truth? Deciding on the latter course of action, she faltered then with a rush said, 'I know it's hard to believe but I had a bad accident some time ago, and suffer from amnesia. I don't know who I am or anything about myself. If you feel that's too awkward, I'll understand. But please give me a chance; I'm sure I could be a good worker.'

John was taken aback, but seeing her sincerity and unable to resist her pleading said, 'I do believe you. I'll give you a month's trial, cash in hand and we'll work things out from there.'

Anna was overjoyed. It was agreed she would do three days

a week though the days might vary. 'You'll need suitable clothes,' John said apologetically, 'it's very dusty in here and there are ladders to climb and boxes to move. Trousers would be of more use.'

Anna started the following week. John showed her where everything was and departed for an auction. She spent all day dusting and arranging books in subject order, so that when John returned that evening he was pleasantly surprised, 'You don't need to work that hard all the time,' he said, 'enjoy some reading. I don't have a lot of customers at the beginning of the week so relax. You can go home now. I work on as I buy books for special clients, and they usually come in the evening.'

Days merged into months until Anna had been working at the bookshop for six months. She and John had become good friends, and he'd started to discuss her amnesia, 'What about seeing another doctor, Anna my dear, I can find a specialist for you. It must be lonely and frightening not knowing who you are.' It was certainly a solitary existence though occasionally she and John would eat out at a pizza or burger place, but that was the extent of her socialising. In her worst moments Anna would think about the son she'd never know and the old familiar ache would start again.

John, true to his word, found her a consultant in Harley Street, but the tests came back normal. She was told she was suffering from post-traumatic amnesia, and her memory may or may not return. By now Anna had learnt to accept her condition, although there were times she could surprise herself with skills she didn't know she possessed. Finding out she could type was a revelation. John had extended her hours and she had come to love the bookshop, in fact that's all she lived for.

As the months went on, her sleep became more and more disturbed, increasingly broken up with unsettling dreams and nightmares. There was a recurring dream with someone called Eleanor screaming, 'It's me. Can't you hear me? I'm lost. Help me, help me.' In the mornings Anna's head would ache and ache.

The only positive side of these troubled nights was that Anna's memory was slowly unfolding. However it was in the form of disjointed snippets very much like snapshots in a photo album, pictures with no captions or relevance. John would reassure her, 'This is promising, it'll all come together one day. Then you'll know everything,' but Anna was not so sure.

On her days off Anna took to haunting the library as if this was familiar territory. She knew she was searching for clues – something that would give her a tenuous link to her past. Desperately scanning the papers (had she done this sort of thing before?) she looked for any mention of someone like her or anything that might prompt her brain. Working her way through that week's Times, an obituary caught her eye. There was a picture of a middle aged man who looked familiar. The piece underneath was brief:

370

Paul Kerris, 49, of Washington D.C was killed on Wednesday last in a car accident. His body will be interred in the family plot in his native Gloucestershire in a private funeral. Paul is survived by his only living relative, his sister Maureen. No flowers. No donations.

Anna couldn't take her eyes off the picture. He was a good looking man with dark curly hair, and light eyes. Was this the man she'd known and known intimately? Certainly the name 'Paul' came into her head every time she thought of her baby. Could he have been her husband or her lover at some point? Surreptitiously she tore out the piece and hid it in her pocket. This was information she was going to keep to herself. It was not that she didn't trust John but it was too private to share.

49

London, Summer 1987

Anna had been at the shop for well over three years and though the years were passing, she still had no idea how old she was. John had proposed she pick a day to celebrate your birthday and suggested, 'June the 7th, the weather's so lovely at the moment; we'll shut the shop and have a picnic in Regent's Park.'

He bought caviar, strawberries and cream and a cake, toasting her with champagne he said, 'I've something serious to say to you, Anna. I'm not getting any younger,' and as she tried to protest, continued, 'No, it's a fact. I want you to be secure when I'm gone. I'm making you a partner in the shop. When I die I have no living relatives, and I'm leaving the shop to you to do with it as you please. It's not much I know but it'll give you a living.'

Anna was stunned not knowing what to say, and stuttered, 'I'm grateful John, very grateful. You've been good to me like family,' her eyes filled with tears.

'There, there, my dear, I'm fond of you. I'd like you to be happy. I can't bring your memory back. This is the best I can do. Anyway a very happy birthday! How old would you like to be? Not many people get to choose their age,' he teased.

'I think I'll go for 29,' Anna said laughing, 'it's probably close to my age I expect and I need never turn thirty.'

That night high on champagne she dreamt of Eleanor again. Was she Eleanor, or was she a friend or relative? The rest of the night was a blank but awakening early next morning, it was as if a curtain had lifted.

She knew without a shadow of a doubt that she was Eleanor. In a flash her whole life was laid out before her: her transient childhood; her disengaged parents; London; the work at Sentry; Mr Caruthers; Georges and his disappearance; Erik and his accident; the convent; Paul; the shooting; Scotland; the camp; the prison in Managua; the hospital and her escape; her pregnancy; the safe house in London; the fall; the hospital in Kent and the Shelburne. It was all there, the story of her life so far. It even felt like a story, not real at all, more like a novel or a film and a lot to take in.

There was relief in knowing who she was, but horror and disbelief at what she'd been through and what she'd done. Shaking and shocked she needed to talk to John. He would be the one to help her put it all into perspective. Frantic to speak to him, she tried ringing but his line was constantly engaged. There was nothing for it but to go to the shop.

It was her designated day off but John would be pleased to see her. When she arrived at the bookshop it was in complete darkness and yet the outer door was unlocked.

Catching sight of John at the back of the shop Eleanor was about to call out to him, when she noticed he was deep in conversation on the phone. No wonder she hadn't been able to get through earlier. He was probably gossiping with one of his old clients.

Tiptoeing nearer to attract his attention, Eleanor realised that John was chatting away in a language a lot like Russian. It brought her up with a jolt; she was suddenly reminded of Georges speaking in the same way. Why would John be speaking Russian? Of course they kept a lot of Slavic and Russian publications (even copies of Pravda) on the premises that must be it.

Lapsing into English as he finished the conversation, John said, 'Yes of course Eleanor's safe with me, comrade. She's no trouble, no trouble at all, and still has no memory of her past. I don't want any of your goons hanging round watching her. I'm quite capable of doing that myself. She trusts me. I'll keep you abreast of her movements. Haven't I proved reliable in my work for you over the years?'

Eleanor was stunned. What did he mean? Did he work for the Russians? Was he a spy? Had he even known her real name and her background all along? Why had he gone along with the trauma of her amnesia? Was there someone or some people out there who never wanted her to recover her memory, and why? Did she have some secret in her past that she wasn't aware of?

Not prepared to face a confrontation, Eleanor practically ran out of the shop hoping he hadn't seen her. How could he? He'd betrayed her. Her whole being was tied up with him

374

and the shop. She felt broken, and distraught. Whatever could she do? The last three years in London had been a haven. Now there was nothing. She'd been given back her former life but at what cost? There was no one left to depend on.

Needing time to think she sat on a bench in Regent's Park, head in her hands. Yesterday's picnic was a lifetime away. Eleanor (she'd have to come to terms with her real name whether she wanted to or not) sat thinking deeply until it grew dark. At the flat she packed the basics, knowing she would have to disappear and this time for good. There was no Joe at the Luggage Office to appeal to, no Muriel to confide in over tea and cakes, and no John to ask for advice. She was on her own.

The next years would be difficult but if she kept her head she might find a way to survive. Next morning as soon as the clock struck eight Eleanor rang the bookshop, carefully rasping her voice she said, 'I'm sorry John, I must have caught a cold in the park. I'm not feeling well today. Can you manage without me?' He was quick to reassure her, asking whether he should call round later with honey and lemon.

'No thanks, I'll probably be sleeping. I'm sure I'll be fine by tomorrow.' Hanging up Eleanor wondered how she was going to leave the flat carrying a suitcase. She didn't want Muriel asking awkward questions.   Decanting all her belongings into a large carrier seemed the best idea. That way she would look as if she was going to the dry cleaners. It was scary to think how devious she'd become. Perhaps this was how the old Eleanor behaved. Tying her bob into a scarf and adding dark glasses, Eleanor dragged on her overcoat though it was June, and pulled up the collar determined to escape the flat without any questions.

She made straight for the bank, and to the cashier's dismay drew out every penny of the forty thousand that was left, asking for it to be placed in a cash bag. En route to Paddington, she changed out of the coat and into a thin mackintosh and flowery dress, bought a backpack for her clothes and money, pinned her hair up under a summery hat and boarded a train to Cornwall.

'GOING GREY'

50

Cornwall, 1987- 8

Cornwall had been the only place Eleanor could think of as she left London. It was far enough away from the capital to give her some breathing space. On the train she relived her memories of Donald Macintosh. He'd been like a grandfather to her in those early days in London. Of course he'd retired to Cornwall but she had no idea where. What if she should bump into him? Could he be trusted? Last time they'd met in her flat, he'd let slip that he'd worked for a government agency similar to Sentry. Perhaps seeing him was not a wise move.

The question was where in Cornwall to go, but with a long journey ahead of her there was no hurry to make a decision. The train was packed with holidaymakers revelling in the sunshine, and Eleanor curled up in a corner trying to sleep and blot out yesterday. Hours went by and she slept fitfully until a ticket inspector woke her shouting loudly in her ear, 'Tickets please, miss. Penzance is it? You've a few hours yet.'

Deciding she was hungry Eleanor set off for the dining car. It was packed but a family beckoned her over saying their youngest would make room for her. Packed together like sardines they bombarded her with holiday plans, asking her a stream of questions until Eleanor exhausted herself with her own lies. They couldn't believe she had come away on spec. 'We're getting off at St Austell. We've a caravan at Fowey. It's not that big or you could stay with us.'

Eleanor thanked them but was glad to get back to her seat. All their exuberance on top of her recent revelations was too much to take.

Arriving at Penzance, Eleanor found a guest house and planned to take her time looking around and coming to terms with 'Eleanor Smith'. However her well meaning landlady had other ideas. Margaret Restarick was a force to be reckoned with and feeling sorry for her rather forlorn looking guest, had decided to take Eleanor under her wing whether she liked it or not.

As Eleanor sat down to her cooked breakfast one morning, Margaret said, 'I've found you a part-time waitressing job at one of the local cafes.'

Eleanor was none too pleased, 'What make you think I want a job?'

For once Margaret was nonplussed, 'Well, you've been here a few weeks and you're not the usual summer visitor. I thought you might want to stay longer or even permanently. Of course I might be mistaken.'

Eleanor wondered why people were always felt they should try and run her life. The old Eleanor Smith would have gone along with it willingly but what about the new version? However it was no good being contrary, a job could be a good idea. Her savings were diminishing fast and working would help occupy her mind.

The job turned out to be a godsend. The hours were reasonable and Eleanor was able to concentrate on getting fitter. At first it had been hard being called by her real name. However after a few months she began to accept the old Eleanor Smith's life as her own.

She kept herself busy running on the beach and working extra shifts; so that by the end of a day she was too exhausted to do anything but sleep. Her days were lonely and isolated, but this is what she wanted. There were to be no more close friendships or burgeoning relationships. Even Margaret had finally given up making overtures or trying to set Eleanor up on dates.

Nevertheless constant reminders of her past were always there although Eleanor did her best to keep them at bay. But she couldn't get Donald out of her mind. At last she made up her mind to try and find him. A familiar face would be appreciated even if she was still wary. Checking a computer at the local Internet cafe, she was amazed to come across a listing for Donald in a local directory with an address outside Truro. How odd that he wasn't ex-directory, but she supposed now he was retired, he didn't need to keep his whereabouts secret.

It was hard to believe he was still alive. He was in his seventies when she first met him, and must be a very old man by now. She was of two minds whether to ring or just turn up unannounced. Not sure of her welcome she decided to opt for the latter.

Taking a train to Truro on her day off, Eleanor found a taxi to drive her to Porthtowan. His house was outside the village and as they reached the turning for Donald's driveway, the taxi slowed to let out a gleaming black hearse followed by a stream of black cars. This was ominous Eleanor thought wondering if she should continue, but they were already half way down the long drive to the house.

Leaving the taxi to wait, Eleanor knocked on the front door. It was a while before anyone came.

An elderly woman opened the door a crack, 'What do thee want?' she demanded unpleasantly. Eleanor asked for Donald saying she was an old friend of his. The woman's face set, 'Sir Donald be dead,' she announced bluntly, 'Didn't ye pass the hearse a few minutes ago? Ye just left.'

'But how did he die?' Eleanor asked, 'Was he ill?'

Her concern must have touched the old woman because her manner softened and she said, 'Na, nowt like that. He be run down on his own drive one day. Them there scoundrels never stopped. I looks after the place for his goddaughter in London. Anything else ye must apply to 'er.'

Eleanor thought she must be referring to Barbara.

'I'm sorry,' Eleanor said, 'I was very fond of him. He was such a good, kind man.'

'He be that, a real gentl'man,' and the woman lowered her voice in a hushed tone, 'but he be involved in strange secret stuff in London, thee knows.'

'What sort of stuff?' Eleanor asked, 'I know he was high up in the Civil Service, that's all.'

'Oh, it be a lot more than that. There was comings and goings at night. Some say round here that.... (and she whispered) he be a real spy, and I wonders if he be murdered,' and with that she shut the big door firmly leaving Eleanor dumbfounded.

Aghast Eleanor didn't know what to do. Getting back in the taxi, she asked the driver to detour via the local church to see if this was where the hearse was headed. The church was a hive of activity with cars coming and going, and asking the driver to wait again Eleanor decided to take a look.

Positioning herself behind some trees, Eleanor stood quietly. To her surprise a short time later, Mr Caruthers, Claire and Paddy exited one of the black Daimlers and headed for the porch. Before they could enter, they stood back respectfully to allow a distinguished silver haired gentleman with an ebony stick precede them as if he was of particular importance and seniority.

Eleanor remained where she was, hardly able to breathe. A

long period went by, and soon they were all pouring out the main door stopping to shake hands with the vicar and Barbara, who must have arrived earlier with the hearse.

Eleanor felt a terrible sense of loss and also betrayal. Donald had obviously played a much greater role at Sentry than he has been prepared to let on. All of her so-called friends and colleagues were all in it together, using her as a pawn in some convoluted game she didn't yet fully understand. Not knowing who to trust she was terrified, afraid to to let her guard down ever again.

On her way back to Truro, Eleanor began to think back to all those wonderful occasions in London when she and Donald had spent time together visiting the sights and dining at the Ritz. She had a vague recollection of him mentioning working with her father, but then he'd speedily corrected himself saying he'd made a mistake. Surely her father wouldn't have been employed by any of the Intelligence Services. He didn't have it in him. Of course she herself had been lured into working for 'The Service' through Sentry and Paul, and she was scarcely professional.

Although the funeral had rekindled memories of happier days, the circumstances of Donald's death stirred up Eleanor's old feelings of dread and fear of being watched and used. It was time to move on.

51

Devon, Winter 1989

During her time in Penzance, Eleanor had taken driving lessons and bought a brand new blue Citroen. As soon as the next summer season finished, she decided to pack up and move up country.

The people at the cafe said, 'Why not stay. We'll find you other work. You can start back with us next spring?'

Eleanor knew they were being friendly and she'd begun to relax with them, but that would never do. It was tough remaining constantly vigilant. She supposed that's how real spies felt. What a strange life to lead never allowing people to get close to you? Perhaps real spies felt superior, aware of secrets the public were not privy to. But that life wasn't for her in the long-term. Anyway what secrets did she know?

Exeter was the next move. Eleanor rented a cottage outside the city; finding a job here should be easier, and one where she could remain anonymous. However once she'd been taken on as a receptionist in a hotel, the question of her identity reared its ugly head. So far Eleanor had been able to manufacture her references but this time the Personnel Manager said, 'Miss Smith, we'll need your National Insurance number on Monday.'

Eleanor explained, 'I've been living abroad, and need to contact the DHSS.' It was agreed to pay her cash in hand for the first month but then she would have to go on their payroll.

At her wits end and wondering how to acquire an NI number, Eleanor recalled Paul's tales on how to manufacture a new identity. Thinking of Paul made her tearful; she still had the tattered scrap of newspaper mentioning his obituary. She would read the tiny news cutting over and over. It was if it only happened yesterday....... Paul's death...... and their son.... the baby she'd never seen...... the pain was raw and Eleanor couldn't bear to relive it. Yet it was the only thing of substance she clung on to in her isolated existence.

It was no good indulging in grief; she had to focus on the present. Visiting a churchyard near the cottage she spent hours studying the graves. Finally she found what she was looking for – a young woman's grave, another Eleanor, 'Eleanor Ramsay (nee Barton)' born 1950, five years older than Eleanor herself.

She felt guilty about stealing a dead person's name but hers was the greater need. The birth certificate for Eleanor Barton would provide Eleanor with a passport and the much needed N.I number. Her sudden change of surname could be explained away by saying she'd reverted to her maiden name.

Months limped along. Work at the hotel in winter and early spring was deadly dull but Eleanor appreciated the monotony of it. There was a stability and sameness that made her feel safe. She'd stopped looking over her shoulder to check if she was being followed, and begun to be less distrustful of the people she worked with. The only snag was she had time on her hands, time to mull over the past. There were still questions she wanted answering.

As summer approached Eleanor became restless and jittery, her nerves jangled at the thought of hordes of tourists and visitors. There was the outside chance that someone might identify her even with her new face, and she didn't want to risk that. There was nothing for it but she had to go. Giving notice to the hotel and the cottage, Eleanor packed and left with no forwarding address. Moving had become a habit.

For months she drove aimlessly round the countryside, staying at farmhouses, caravan camps and bed and breakfasts. Finally, finding herself within easy reach of Dorset Eleanor decided to check out the old convent. The town of Weymouth was as pretty as ever, and checking into a hotel on the front Eleanor sat on the promenade enjoying the late summer sun.

Autumn was on its way and most of the visitors had moved on. She decided to give herself a new look. Booking into a hairdresser she had them dye her fair hair chestnut, and give her a pixie cut. Leaving her old clothes at a charity shop, she opted for a more casual look and armed with sunglasses and a camera set off for the convent. Since the surgery her face had changed so much she was fairly confidant no one at the convent would know her.

The convent itself was relatively easy to find again, but approaching the building Eleanor felt the first twinges of panic.

Feeling foolish as well as anxious she parked the car and lurked outside taking photos. Should she march straight up and ask what had they up to all those years ago?

Conjuring up a quick cover story she plucked up the courage to knock. There was no answer. After a time she tried the handle, it gave. Once inside it looked like the place had been abandoned long ago. Grass was growing up through the cracks in the paving and old papers and leaves clogged up the corridors. The rooms were empty except for discarded hymnals tossed on the floor.

The chapel itself was in an even more appalling state with half the pews upturned, others broken and rotting. Eleanor had to clamber over everything to get to the altar. Behind the altar, where she'd last seen them dragging that body, was a narrow cupboard space its sliding door hanging off its hinges. She shone her key torch into the space. There was nothing to be seen. Looking closely Eleanor saw the white marble floor was badly stained. She bent down and tentatively touched the stains. It was then she knew it was dried blood. Shivers ran down her spine. She had to get out of there.

Running full pelt through the passages, she fell out the front

386

door and into the sunshine, vomiting in a nearby rose bed. Something horrifying had happened in there, certainly nothing remotely related to nuns or religion. Turning she fled for her car eager to put distance between herself and that place.

Driving back to Weymouth the old emotions started up again, the anxiety, the fear, the feeling of being watched. It was no use she would have to keep moving.

....

1989's end was momentous. November 10th, the Berlin Wall was demolished and December 3rd, Gorbachev announced the end of the Cold War.

In London two old men celebrated with a final drink.

'Well old friend,' Anubis said, 'this is it for us. Who'd have thought we'd ever see this day. But we still have one or two loose ends of mine to tie up, you being one of them?'

'What's the other?' Vasily asked uneasily, 'Oh, of course the girl? She's gone to ground completely. We haven't heard of her for years now. You can forget about her. And me ...... forget about me. I'm ready to be pensioned off. I intend finding myself a new country and a peaceful retirement.'

Anubis nodded, 'And the baby..... He was dispatched satisfactorily?'

'Of course,' Vasily replied crossing his fingers, 'most

satisfactorily. In fact he's gone to a loving home and has a new name.'

'Then there are only the records to think about. I wouldn't want my name falling into the wrong hands?'

'They're taken care of, my friend – everything's been burnt or shredded. But what about you, Alex, (Vasily dared to use the old name again) what will you do now?'

'I'll go back to my role as 'eminence grise' in the Service I expect, and no doubt be rewarded with a peerage. Be assured our secrets will die with us, comrade. Anyway I wish you well and a final goodbye. God speed!'

They shook hands cordially, and walked off in different directions.

Vasily smiled smugly to himself thinking this time you old rogue, I had the last word. Well maybe not 'word' but the last trick (taking a photograph out of his wallet, he stared down at the young child who looked back at him adoringly) and muttered incomprehensibly, 'And wherever I end up I'll cover my tracks well, Anubis. You'll never have a chance to dispose of me. What about that for the last laugh!'

DEAD DOUBLES

52

Cheltenham, Spring 1990

Driven to move again, Eleanor gazed miserably out of the bus window wondering whether she was going to spend the rest of her life travelling. This time she had abandoned her car thinking it too identifiable and opted for public transport. Staring out at the passing houses, she imagined all those lives lived behind anonymous windows: happy families, lovers celebrating anniversaries, and children.........What age would her son be now if he'd lived - eight or nine? She couldn't bear to think of him. The ache was always there at the heart of her emptiness. She'd spent years shutting off her emotions and didn't know whether she even had any. Her memories before the amnesia were a lot like faded photographs. The people and the places were familiar but she couldn't connect to them.

It was strange that the way she lived now mimicked her childhood. Those days had been all about movement too. Fleetingly she thought of her parents. There was little to remember: her father with his endless schemes, and her mother sucked dry in a loveless relationship. He had dragged them along in his wake, dumping Eleanor whenever he could and pretending she didn't exist. There were times when Eleanor would find herself looking in mirrors to prove she was a real person. Regrettably she felt the same now. I don't know who I am anymore, the real me. Just now I'm Eleanor Barton but then who is she?

There'd been so many Eleanors, perhaps too many: the nomadic child, the innocent girl in London, the fake wife prepared to kill for love, the betrayed prisoner, the grieving childless mother, the confused amnesiac and the current Eleanor, fearful and homeless.

But that was the past. She was going to a new place. Everything could be different. Sometimes starting afresh was like being given a second chance though each time it was getting harder to convince herself. Perhaps now she could let down her guard for good, and allow herself to make friends instead of being the onlooker and the listener. But then again..........people were so intent in talking about themselves they rarely asked about her, and of course she had too many secrets.

The elegant Regency houses of the town swept past unnoticed. Eleanor had picked the town with a pin on a map. She'd supposed Cheltenham was as good a place as any. It certainly looked impressive. This might be the place to settle.

The woman across the aisle kept casting sly glances at Eleanor obviously wanting to chat and eventually asked, 'Have you been to Cheltenham before? Are you on holiday?'

'No, to both questions,' Eleanor said firmly but politely, and pointedly turned away from the inquisitive face to continue gazing through the window not keen to encourage further questions.

It was then she saw him. At first Eleanor couldn't believe her eyes. Perhaps she was mistaken. As the bus slowed for a red light, she looked again. It really was him waiting patiently to cross the road as if he hadn't a care in the world. He was older, his black curly hair silvered with grey – but certainly not dead. How could he be alive? The crumpled piece she'd torn out of the Times was here in the back of her purse.

She'd read it and reread it over the years; the obituary, brief and concise, gave nothing away: '*Paul Kerris died in a car accident in America in 1984'.* Perhaps it hadn't been her Paul Kerris. Her hands shaking, she carefully smoothed out the picture again. It was him alright. Her heart missed a beat.

She felt this tremendous surge of longing for him perhaps her feelings weren't dead after all. How could he be alive? What was he doing in Cheltenham? Then she remembered he had a sister in Gloucestershire. Maybe she was wrong, and the man on the crossing was someone who looked like Paul. It had been a long time. But no, she was sure it was him. Hadn't Mr C told her Paul had disappeared, implying he'd gone rogue? Of course, he might have faked his death.

Was Paul looking for her? Did he know she was coming? Who would have told him? Had they tracked her down somehow? What did they want with her, and who were 'they'? Without warning a shiver ran through her. What on earth was she going to do?

Gripping her shaking hands tightly Eleanor tried to think, but her mind was a blank. It was a disaster. Should she ring Sentry, but could they be trusted? Anyway, she wouldn't want them to know where she was. There was nothing for it; she would have to handle this herself.

Her neighbour on the bus must have noticed there was something wrong, observing Eleanor's sudden pallor, and ventured to say, 'We're arriving, dear. This is the bus station. It's right in the centre of town. You'll have no trouble finding your bearings,' and with that she pulled down her bag and started to leave.

Eleanor looked up barely able to speak, 'Thank you.... it was kind of you to let me know.' The woman meant well after all.

Eleanor had booked into the Queens' Hotel temporarily and as she wheeled her suitcase along the Promenade, wondered if she might bump into Paul. Cheltenham wasn't that big a town. However she looked very different to the girl he'd once known.

This time she wasn't going to run, but take a stand and see it through, whatever 'it' was. First of all she would track Paul down and through him perhaps discover who'd been watching and manipulating her all these years, and find out what they wanted. She was determined to show some guts at last, or she would be running and hiding for the rest of her days.

53

Eleanor busied herself settling into Cheltenham, resolving to stay at the hotel until she'd worked out a plan. The weather was warm, and she took to sitting in Montpellier Gardens deliberating. Taking no risks and keeping a low profile she decked herself out in a nondescript anorak and dark glasses, with a book to hand if people attempted conversation. She should really be looking for a job but that could wait.

It was vital to find Paul and learn what he was up to. He may well have retired, and decided to take up residence in the town but spies never retire, do they? Years ago he'd made it clear to Eleanor that spies either get killed or turned and work for the other side. Of course the Cold War was over so there was no 'other side'. Alternatively Paul might still be active and based at GCHQ, but Eleanor couldn't see him holding down any sort of desk job.

After sleepless nights, Eleanor decided to attempt to draw Paul out of the shadows. She sat down and designed an advert,

'URGENT. Anyone knowing the whereabouts of Paul Kerris, last living in America, please reply to the box number below as it will be to that person's advantage,'

and arranged for the ad to appear in the Gloucestershire Echo and the Times over the next months.

How effective this would be she didn't know, but couldn't come up with anything better. A month went by and there was nothing. Just as she was about to give up, a letter postmarked Cheltenham arrived. It said,

'To whomever you are. I have information about Paul Kerris. Meet 1130 a.m this coming Wednesday morning at The Boathouse Cafe, Pittville Park.'

Eleanor smiled. Paul obviously hadn't lost his edge, as he'd worked out the person looking for him was living locally. It was typical of Paul to arrange to meet in a park; the sort of place he used to meet the Chief in the old days.

Eleanor reconnoitered the meeting place the following day. The cafe, newly opened for the season, was hidden away amongst trees on the Park's lower lake shore.

On the Wednesday, Eleanor set out three hours early to discover a good observation position. It was a long wait but it was sunny and warm. Two hours later Eleanor spotted Paul sauntering through the trees. He was following her example, and checking the place out. He scouted the whole area without detecting her, and appearing satisfied retreated to a seat outside the cafe where the waitress brought him coffee and a sandwich.

Eleanor could hardly take her eyes off him; he looked healthy and tanned, much the same as when she'd seen him last in Mosquitia, just greyer and bulkier. Memories of their time together came streaming back, and she was barely able to control her emotions. It was as much as she could do not to run over to him and fling her arms round him. Forcefully she reminded herself how he'd abandoned her to the Sandanistas. For all he knew, she could have died in that Managuan prison.

Paul stayed at the cafe long after the meeting time, but finally shrugging his shoulders and checking his watch paid the bill and set off back to town. It was going to be tricky shadowing him without being seen. With a no-show at the meeting, Paul would be expecting someone to be following.

Eleanor had come prepared. Disguised in a blonde wig and green jumper with a large holdall, she strolled after him towards the entrance. Nearing the gates of the park she hid in the trees, stuffed her hair in a tweed hat, threw on a capacious beige mac and with stick in hand managed to limp across the road some way ahead of him. It was hard going. Paul was clearly wandering round town shopping and disappeared into Marks and Spencer's. Eleanor positioned herself on a seat in sight of both exits. By now she'd discarded the coat and hat in favour of her former disreputable anorak, a back pack and trainers.

Considerable time elapsed and Eleanor panicking, wondered if she'd lost him but eventually he reappeared laden with bags, and sat down on a seat nearby discreetly scanning the street. Eleanor quickly unfolded a map, and studied it thoroughly peering at him from under her lashes. On closer inspection she could see he wasn't the man he used to be. He must be at least fifty five now, she thought. There was no doubt he was still good-looking, but there was an air of discontent about him and a worn, world weariness as if life had disappointed him. An hour went by and Eleanor, concerned about being too obvious, ambled towards the Regent Arcade, pretending to look in a shop window. Studying Paul's reflection, it appeared as if he might be giving up and heading for home.

Following him on the side streets was difficult. It was mid afternoon and there were few people going in his direction. Eleanor dodged in and out of doorways allowing Paul to move further and further ahead. Just when she thought she'd he'd vanished, she caught sight of him in the distance entering an apartment block on Bath Road.

Memorising the place, Eleanor shot back to her hotel and changed her clothes. Leaving a few hours' gap, she returned to the street and casually stopped at the apartments to study the names on the bells. Paul would probably use a name he'd used before or something similar. Running her finger down the column, she found a Peter Keynes, at No.4. This could be him, but she would need to be sure.

Eleanor grew tired and bored with the continuous surveillance. By now she'd found herself a flat near his road and was able to observe him, day and night. She'd invested in a second hand car in case she needed transport. But Paul never ventured far afield and was studious in checking for tails. He didn't seem to have any sort of regular job and led a rather dull life: walking; shopping; karate at a local Sports Centre; drinking at the local pub, with no regular friends or girlfriend. On the surface his life looked unremarkable but Eleanor was convinced he was up to something.

Then one day due to her extreme fatigue, Eleanor lost sight of him. She was unnerved, unsure as to whether he'd spotted her and gone. How would she find him again? But hours and hours later he returned to the flat, bringing with him huge cartons of food and wine as if he was expecting guests. From then on Eleanor was on her mettle.

Early the following Saturday morning a taxi drew up and Paul jumped into it. Eleanor was thrown. She raced for her car and sped after him. It was a job keeping up in the traffic, but with her eyes glued to the taxi's vanishing tail lights she made a wild guess they were making for Staverton Airport.

Slowing down she arrived at the airport just after the taxi pulled up at the Main Terminal. It would be difficult not to be noticed at such a small airport. Choosing to park as far away as possible, Eleanor sidled into the airport. Paul had his back to her and was idly studying the Arrivals Board.

Eleanor departed for the Ladies, wondering how to become less conspicuous. A rather grubby cleaner's overall hung over one of the toilet doors, and seizing her chance Eleanor carefully tugged at it until it fell on the floor. There was no sound from the occupant of the toilet, who appeared to be otherwise engaged.

No one takes any notice of cleaners, Eleanor thought, and this cleaner had obviously been in a rush dumping her mop and bucket outside. Eleanor took possession of the mop and moved closer to her quarry keeping her head down, and watching Paul skim a newspaper as he waited.

Eventually a flight from Jersey was announced and Paul walked towards the Arrivals Gate. He greeted a tall, lean silver haired man with an ebony stick warmly, taking his briefcase from him. The older man gestured towards the Luggage area, indicating more cases. By now Eleanor was avid to find out who the visitor was. There was something familiar about the older man, his hawkish face, unusual eyes and the way he walked.

Both men moved to await the luggage. Eleanor hung about mopping furiously, and trying to listen in to their conversation. 'Well Paul,' the older man said, '---- we're still in business. It's all over with the Russkies of course, but there are rich pickings elsewhere.'

Paul mumbled something about, '... the new technology and the Internet.'

But the older man dismissed his concerns, saying bluntly, '....I'm old school. There's other ways to play the game, and still a few games to be had .... not in my dotage yet.'

After while one case arrived, but apparently there was one

missing. There was a great to-do and the manager of the airport came over to apologise, 'Sir Alan, what can I say. We are so sorry, Sir Alan,' the manager kow-towed, 'if you would like to come to my office, I'll take down the details of where you are staying and send the bag on to you tomorrow, if that's convenient.'

Paul and the older man vanished into the office; Eleanor skulked quietly outside with the mop. She was desperate to find out who the older man was. The two men left the office and made their way to the entrance, with the manager running behind them wringing his hands.

Now's my chance, Eleanor thought, if I'm quick? She hurried into the office. In the centre of the desk was the filled out claim form. Eleanor leaned over to read it and had the shock of her life. The name was Sir Alan Duridge Smith. Eleanor was stunned. That was the name of her mystery uncle, the one she'd never seen? She was so shaken she ran straight into the manager, 'What are you doing, girl? You've no business in there. I don't want my office cleaned, do you understand? Now clear off.'

Eleanor nodded numbly. What was she going to do now? She needed time to collect her wits.

SHADOW MAN

54

Eleanor returned from the airport, mystified by the turn of events. Both men had links to her so there must be something involving her. After a night of sitting up thinking, she knew there was nothing for it but to confront them and find out what this was all about.

She was frightened, but she would never know if she didn't try. It was sending her mad not knowing, and it would be better done sooner rather than later. What if they killed her? Still that might be preferable to the half life she'd been living and was living now.

The element of surprise was what was needed. The following night Eleanor kept watch on the apartment waiting for the lights to go out. At two o'clock in the morning, she rang the door bell.

A groggy voice answered the intercom, 'Who's this? What do you want at this time? – This better not be a prank.......'

'No, it's no prank,' Eleanor said clearly, 'I'm the person looking for Paul Kerris. If you want to know more, let me in.'

There was a pause, and the voice continued in a less sleepy tone, 'Come back tomorrow, or at least later today.'

'No,' Eleanor said, 'it's now or never.'

The door clicked, and Eleanor practically ran up the stairs to Flat 4. The flat door had been left wide open and there was a reception committee.

Paul half dressed and disheveled stood in the living room holding a gun, whilst the older man still in pyjamas reclined in a chair, a look of amusement quivering on his lips.

'You won't need the gun, Paul,' Eleanor said, 'I'm not armed.'

'Who are you?'

'Don't you know me?' Eleanor asked pleased to be the one in the position of power.

'Come nearer the light,' Paul started to say and as Eleanor moved forward he gasped, '..... Eleanor, it can't be...... You're dead....... I don't understand. How did you get away from the Sandinistas.....? ....And why didn't I know?
 (He looked accusingly at the older man). You sound the same but you look so different. I barely recognise you.'

'It was the accident, the fall,' Eleanor said nonchalantly, completely in control, 'I was broken. They couldn't put me back together in quite the same way.'

Hearing the name the older man jolted to attention, 'Eleanor, surely not, 'he murmured to himself, 'there's something....... a look of her......' his voice dwindled away.

'What do you want? Why've you turned up now?' Paul

demanded, waving the gun at her.

'I want the truth after all these years. Surely, I deserve that,' Eleanor said coolly.

The older man nodded, 'I suppose you do at that, my dear Eleanor.'

She turned towards him, 'Why are you here with Paul? Who are you – besides my errant uncle?'

Alan laughed wryly and clapped his hands, 'Well done my dear, well done for tracking me down. I didn't think you had it in you. As to who I am.... there's the rub. I've been known by a number of names but if we are talking truths.....
I'm your father (he shrugged), well as far as I know, anyway.' He twisted his mouth in a sardonic curl, 'Of course your mother Marika could have been cheating on me. She was already betraying me in one way so why not another?'

'Father.......,'stammered Eleanor, '.......but what about Robert and Marjorie?'

'Oh they were merely caretakers, my dear. The life I led hardly equipped me to take on a child, let alone a babe in arms.'

Paul now completely out of his depth, exploded, 'Your daughter! You never breathed a word in all those years when she and I were together, or since I've been working for you.'

'It was never your business my dear Paul, the less you knew about me or Eleanor the better. I've always kept my life in separate compartments, it's safer that way,' Alan quipped.

'But does she (Paul jerked his head towards the silent Eleanor) know what your real work was?'

'Of course not, Paul, my days of Anubis and Alpha are in the past.... and Alex or Sasha are distant memories. I'm just plain Alan now .... an elder of the tribe with my distinguished and respectable career behind me.
There's no Iron Curtain ......no Cold War. I can hardly have betrayed my country can I? After all nowadays the Russians are our friends? We live in a different world. I agree Eleanor was a loose end, but now I've entered my senior years a daughter could be a comfort to me, don't you think?'

Eleanor could hardly believe what she was hearing. It was difficult fitting the pieces together. Was this what it had been all about?......Her father - a double agent?..... So which side had Paul worked for?...... And what about Sentry, and all those people she'd trusted once – Mr C, Claire, Barbara, Paddy, Donald, Georges, the list was endless – which side had they been on?

Paul shook his head hard as if he was trying to come to terms with what he'd just heard. He felt betrayed.
He'd revered the Chief as he'd always called him, agreeing to follow his lead even when it meant betraying the Service. Later he'd become his one and only friend............... and now

404

what.........?

Feeling cornered and desperate he said, 'I'm sorry Chief. She's got to go. You're getting soft in your old age.   You may be able to paper over the cracks with the Service because of your position, but what about me? I wouldn't be so lucky. It would mean years of prison for me.'

Eleanor was shaken. Was this the same Paul she'd loved for so long, the person who could be so charming and tender, so funny and kind. It was as if that side of him had been destroyed completely, leaving only the hard headed survivalist.

Grieving for the old Paul and their relationship, Eleanor scarcely registered what was happening. She was completely oblivious to Paul flexing his arm, gun pointed at her head. In the split second he was about to pull the trigger there was a quiet pop, and Paul dropped to the floor like a stone. Alan indifferently threw away his silencer as if it was of no account, and pocketed the automatic.

Distraught Eleanor cried out, 'How could you? There was no need for that. He would never have gone through with it. He cared for me despite your influence over him.   I loved him......... and never had the chance to tell him about his son.'

She knelt over his prone body. There was no sign of life. Turning him over, blood welled up through his chest and Eleanor bent and kissed his still warm lips. She took the gun from his dead hand and aimed it at her father, 'Now you can tell me everything.'

Alan said dispassionately, 'Of course my dear, why wouldn't I? We shouldn't have secrets. I never knew for sure whether you were my child or not – but I needed to keep you close. Sentry was as good a hiding place as any at the time. You were my weak link. A double agent doesn't need that.

I never expected you to be operational, certainly not with Paul of all people, and then to disappear like that. You've done well to keep under cover all these years, even Vasily couldn't find you and he can track anyone down. It seems as though you might be a chip off the old block, after all.

Now Paul's out of the picture..... (Looking down at the comatose body, Alan gave it a shove with his foot).He'd outlived his usefulness anyway; we can get to know one another. You could prove to be an asset.'

Eleanor was loath to listen to more of this; but she had questions, 'What happened to my mother?'

Her father sighed, and then as if he was reciting a biography said, 'Marika your mother, was born in Lublin.... a Polish mother, Russian father...... brought up in Belarus when her mother died. She was trained and worked undercover for Moscow Central as did I until of course, she decided to be clever and pass information to the Brits.' He pursed his lips,

'Whether she had some half-baked idea of bringing you up in Britain, I don't know. All I know is she betrayed me. There was no question then, other than that she was disposable..... Imagine the gall of it betraying me to my own country, my own Service. She made life very complicated for me until the dust settled.'

'Disposable'- was that what she was too? He'd disposed of her mother, now her lover – what chance did she have?

Alan seemed to read her mind as if they had both come to the same conclusion. He lent across as if to try and take the gun from her, but looking at her face thought better of it. It was perhaps politic to bide his time, and assess the situation. She was his daughter alright, there was no doubt about it, perhaps there was more of him in her than he realised. In a strange way he was proud of her. It was a pity she wasn't younger and more malleable, he could have made something of her.

Eleanor asked accusingly, 'Did you ever care for me, or was it about controlling my life? Are you even capable of love?'

Alan frowned, 'I was fond of your mother. I think she loved me though her love would never have been enough. As for you, I don't know anything about you except what I've heard through other people. I'm sure we can come to an accommodation together; whether that will be love, it's too early to say. I'm willing to give our father/daughter relationship a chance, what about you?'

Eleanor was speechless. It was frightening to think she was this cold bastard's daughter. She hoped there was something of her mother in her, though of course that might not prove to be much of a bonus either.

Brandishing the gun, Eleanor attempted to match her father's indifferent tone, 'I'll give you a better deal than you gave my mother. At least, you'll see the bullet coming.'

Her father considered her in a studied, calculating manner, 'My dear, you don't have it in you to kill, certainly not in cold blood. You've only killed twice before - once was an accident and the second time to save Paul.'

Eleanor ignored him continuing as if she hadn't been interrupted, 'You probably even had your own grandson murdered. My baby.... my son....... and I never got a chance to hold him.'

Her father was about to say, 'But I ....'when the bullet hit. For a second he blanched, his blue grey eyes widening in disbelief, and then he was collapsing, a neat hole in his high patrician forehead.

Eleanor felt nothing, her emotions crushed into oblivion. She was an onlooker observing herself, wondering with curiosity whether it was she who'd pulled the trigger.

END GAME

55

Hours later, a shocked and dazed Eleanor was still sitting in the flat staring at two dead bodies, waiting for the police or neighbours to come. But there were no sirens, no noise of any kind, just unadorned silence. Eleanor knew she couldn't keep sitting there. Now was not the moment to fall apart, she had to be resilient. There was nothing for it but to ring Sentry astonished that she still knew the number. An anonymous person on the switchboard answered, and Eleanor said flatly, 'Connect me with Mr Caruthers or someone like him urgently.'

Half an hour went by before she heard Mr C's voice. She said, 'This is Eleanor, I expect you remember me. I've shot my father, your Chief, Sir Alan Duridge Smith. He was a double agent working for the Russians. Of course, you may have known all along and been working for them too. But I don't care anymore who did what or with whom; I've had enough of the games and double dealing. I need a team from your office to clean up here, isn't that the technical term you use to dispense of dead bodies? There's two of them by the way.'

There was a sharp intake of breath from the other end. Eleanor continued, 'Paul Kerris is the other one. He was working for my father.'

Mr C could hardly speak, 'Eleanor, what happened? Tell me everything.'

'No, I don't intend to ever explain or be debriefed by anyone. This is a total mess that your office will have to clear up. I want to get out of here. If you try to stop me or arrest me, I'll go to the newspapers. I've had years of ducking, diving and fearing for my life. All I want is peace, and to get on with my life, what's left of it.'

Mr C mumbled something like an apology, 'Eleanor, I'm sorry. We'll do all we can to help you. I'm as shocked as you are, I had absolutely no idea your father was working for the Russians, you must take my word for that. No one in this office had either.

Years ago your father, a well respected senior officer, asked us to keep you safe and make sure your life ran smoothly. Everything that happened to you was not of our doing. Claire has been beside herself since you disappeared. We searched high and low and couldn't find you. My dear, please believe we mean you no harm. Come back, and we'll help you get back on track.'

Eleanor was adamant, 'I want nothing more to do with Sentry. What I do want is a one way ticket to Vancouver in the name of Eleanor Barton and £100,000 in used notes. You and the government owe me that much at least, for all I've been through.'

Giving him the address of the flat in Cheltenham, she added,

'I want the airline ticket and the money delivered to me at Heathrow Information Desk, twelve noon tomorrow. Don't attempt to stop me or imprison me, as I've made a record of everything and lodged it in a safe place.'

Mr C tried to speak but Eleanor cut him off, saying firmly, 'I'm beginning a new life as from tomorrow. I don't want to hear anything more from you or yours ever,' and she slammed down the phone.

…

Boarding the plane the next day, Eleanor tried to feel relaxed and optimistic about her future, but it was hard to shake off everything that had happened. Finally she'd taken charge of her own life but at what cost? Would she ever get over Paul, and what about killing her own father? She had to believe that she wasn't a chip off the old block, or what hope was there for her?

Sentry had fulfilled their part of the bargain, and now she had money and a new name. But was that enough? Would she ever feel happy and secure again. Where was that ingenuous, loyal, loving girl she used to be? Sure, she was still young. Maybe she could marry, have a family. Perhaps there was a something or someone out there for her.

The stewardess greeted her pointing out her seat, and Eleanor did her best to smile back but it was an effort.

As she checked her seat number an elderly gentleman got

411

up, bowed and asked, 'Can I help you, Madame? What seat are you looking for?' Eleanor showed him her boarding card.

'Oh that's lucky, isn't it Alex,' the old man said smiling down at a small boy of about nine or ten, who was sitting quietly by the window, 'this nice lady is going to sit next to us. Please let me introduce myself,' Vasily said, 'I'm Ivan Orlov and this is my grandson, Alex. We're going to start a new life in Vancouver, aren't we, Alex? Would you prefer the window or the aisle seat, my dear?'

ABOUT THE AUTHOR

Rosemary Hamer is retired and lives on the Wirral. 'The Shadow Shaper' is her second novel. Her first novel 'The Christmas House' was a dramatised version of her mother's early life.

Printed in Great Britain
by Amazon